THE GHOST
of the
MOUNTAIN KINGS

A NOVEL

This book is a work of fiction. Names, characters, places, and incidents are either the product of the author's imagination or are used fictitiously, except where otherwise noted. Any resemblance to actual events, locales, or persons, living or dead, beyond these references is entirely coincidental. (v3)

THE GHOST
of the
MOUNTAIN KINGS

A NOVEL

DANIEL S. HOLT

SHAKER SONGS & MUSIC

Music and song are central to the spirit and community of the Shakers. Original Shaker hymns and dances appear throughout this novel, reflecting the importance of music in their worship, labor, and daily life.

The lyrics included in the story are drawn from historical Shaker sources and are presented in keeping with the traditions from which they originated.

Readers interested in hearing recordings of the Shaker songs referenced in this book may visit:

danielsholtauthor.com/shakersongs

(Or scan the QR code below.)

For Dad, as promised.

Part 1

PROLOGUE

Jarek Dorrell did not believe in ghosts. Or killing people. At least he didn't used to.

But as he looked up at the angry face of the man of God whose grip was tightening around his neck—a man who had been dead for over a hundred years but was now very much alive and very determined to end Jarek's life—he knew he had changed his mind.

His wide eyes darted around the room as he started to panic, searching for anything he might use to save himself, but he saw only what was left of the office around them: capsized chairs, bookshelf contents strewn about, and field tools fallen from their pegs, far out of reach. The floor sparkled with the remnants of small bottles of medicinal tonics. Quills from a crushed blue box— "Superior Office Pens"—lay scattered across it.

A flurry of paper receipts cast into the air during the struggle drifted downward behind a straw hat resting in place above the furious eyes just inches from his own. Eyes of a man he had come to know and fear.

Labored breaths rushed towards Jarek's face, cool against the blood running from his forehead, compliments of a steel riding crop—that menacing lump of metal—that had been applied there moments before. His weakening hands, slippery with his own blood, held limply to those wrapped tight around his neck as his heart beat hard within his chest. He looked to the windows, his mind going distant as he realized that in exactly 125 years, he would be walking into this very room as a new student at a school that did not yet exist. *His* school.

Words of warning he'd received just days before flashed through his mind: "Leave here, Jarek Dorrell. Get out and run, and don't look back, or someday it may be your body we're puttin' in this common grave."

He should have listened.

Jarek pressed both hands upward against the gritted teeth leering over him—one final attempt to save himself as his wide-open mouth fought for air. It was hopeless. He needed a miracle.

Paralyzing fear twisted inward, his mind spinning towards the inevitable reality waiting at the bottom: *This is what it's like. Death. This is it.*

He closed his eyes, regret giving way to acceptance, and in his final thoughts asked himself, "How did I get here?"

But he knew the answer.

He entered a room he should have stayed out of.

He opened a book he should have left closed.

Then, he saw a ghost.

CHAPTER 1

September 4, 1991

"Almost there, pal." Jarek's dad smiled at him in the rearview mirror. "Big day."

Jarek watched the New York turnpike slice cleanly through rocky jags in the growing foothills. As they headed east on Route 20 towards the Massachusetts state line, everything he saw reminded him that this place would be very unlike home. Small openings in the dense woods revealed run-down historic homes and bigger woodpiles than he had ever seen, most protected by a large barking dog. Aside from the rare moments when the winding road peaked over a hill so he could peer above the treetops for a moment, the only way he could see any distance was by looking straight up at the sky.

He could tell his parents were nervous; he was, too. His dad tried to make small talk to set them all at ease.

"Remember, our family is from up here somewhere, way back anyway. Your great-grandpa. In March of 1883…"

Jarek interrupted, "'In March of 1883, Elijah Dorrell came to be.' I know, Dad. Anything else?"

"Sorry, pal." His dad's eyes found his in the rearview mirror. "That's all I know about him. Good thing it rhymes, I guess, or we might not even know that! Point is, you shouldn't feel like too much of a stranger here in the mountains, right?"

No answer.

"You know..." his dad said quietly. "You know...you can always pray about it if you ever want to."

"No thanks. It's been a while." Jarek said flatly, "I'm not gonna start now."

"Yeah," his dad said with a nod, turning his eyes back towards the road.

They drove through the tiny town just before campus. A gas station, video rental shop, and convenience store—three different sections of the same cinderblock structure—passed by, then a diner, an antique shop, and little else. The family was silent as the car began up the mountainside Jarek would soon call home. He would be getting out not to visit but to live. His parents would pull away, and this second chance—this thing they were sacrificing so much to give him—would be his to win or lose. He *had* to succeed here. His stomach was in knots as they climbed the hill.

They turned onto the main road, and as the car entered campus from beneath a canopy of trees, Jarek felt like he had crossed through a portal into another time. Old buildings came into view and passed one by one, sagging lines of the time-weary structures suggesting they would prefer to retire from supporting the weight of human endeavors—some commendable, some not, most somewhere in between—after so many years of loyal service. Old windowpanes were speckled at the edges from repainting over the decades.

Jarek was glad for the sense of permanence the place had. Everything fell apart months ago—including him—and he had been adrift ever since. He hoped this new chapter would help him put himself back together.

A student in an orange vest directed Jarek's dad to a parking spot along the edge of the field as Jarek looked at the vast, open expanse before him. Acres of perfectly green grass stretched far into the distance, extending to the edge of the mountainside plateau on which campus sat, then dropped out of sight, offering an uninterrupted view of the distant valley below. Foothills marked the horizon many miles away. Another field spread out to the left and another beyond. White soccer nets appeared tiny upon their surface.

The confident stride of certain parents and kids alike made it clear who was returning and who was new. Jarek was a new kid, but not the only one. Other new arrivals walked along the footpaths in the sunshine, smiling apprehensively as they found their way to teacher meetings and orientations before locating their dorms and meeting their roommates. Most parents lingered longer than they had to, making beds, filling dressers, and hanging clothes before nervously departing, hoping for the best.

"Well, thought we'd have you at the house for a couple more years, pal," his dad said, ruffling Jarek's dark purple hair before thinking better of it and dropping his hand. "But 16 isn't so early when you think about it. Some of these kids are freshmen!"

To Jarek's right, about a quarter mile away, was the Tannery; a large, maroon barn structure with a small pond beside it. It felt more significant now that he saw it up close, but everything is significant in the anxiety of a new place. They were now walking to that same maroon barn for a meeting of new students and parents.

Was he really going to stay here? No more childhood bed and sentimental trinkets on his bookshelf? No more parents down the hall? No more Andrew?

No more Andrew. The distraction of this new beginning gave way to the familiar panic he felt whenever his brother came to mind. Like someone had snuck up and leveled a punch into his chest. No more Andrew. Home would never be the same. And this would never be home.

His mom stopped to face him as they walked. Jarek was wearing a black ascot around his neck, which she reached forward and adjusted for him.

"He would love to know you were wearing this. I'm glad you have it," she said with glassy eyes, placing her hands on Jarek's cheeks. "What a nice memory of him. We were all so proud," she smiled as they resumed walking. "His coat is in your trunk. That should keep you warm up here."

Jarek's palms dampened in his clenched fists as he walked beside his parents. His mind focused on the crunch of gravel underfoot, and he found himself imagining he was a tiny insect on the hard-packed dirt. The pressure from footsteps of giants above scratched and broke the gravel stones around him as he looked up, helpless and unseen, waiting for the final fatal footfall. Another ant waiting to be crushed.

RETURNING STUDENTS LED SMALL TOUR GROUPS, TELLING CURIOUS parents about the school, the history of the Village it resided in, and the lives of those who constructed the old buildings around them. They were called Shakers.

"The Shakers," their student guide said, "were a pretty unusual bunch. The first Shakers gathered here, cleared the woods, and cut the roads to start their own utopia in this very spot starting in 1785. There were as many as 600 at their peak 40-50 years later. Most of these buildings were built in the mid-1800's. You can imagine how busy these little roads must have been, all those people hard at work. There's a mass grave up there on the hill." He pointed towards the nearby woods.

A mass grave? Jarek wondered how many people were buried there as their guide continued "And plenty of dusty books on campus with pictures of the Village and Shakers, too. They fizzled out, but their legacy is everywhere. Shaker names, Shaker music, Shaker buildings, Shaker chairs. And," he added with a smirk, "Shaker ghosts."

"Sorry, ghosts?" Jarek asked.

"Well, depends on who you ask," the student smiled. "There are lots of stories. People hearing things, seeing things, walking faster when they're alone because they feel like somebody's watching them. Never happened to me, but I'm hopeful." He shrugged. "Maybe it's just rumors. Who knows?"

Jarek nodded in agreement. He didn't believe in ghosts. Not at all.

CHAPTER 2

"New kids! New kids! New kids!"

After a long and teary-eyed goodbye, during which his mom kissed his cheeks a dozen times and his dad affectionately whispered some last-minute advice, Jarek walked alone toward the first students-only commitment: lunch.

Jarek and a few other students—just as new and uncomfortable as he was—shuffled warily into the Dairy Barn. A multi-purpose building named for the Shaker structure which originally stood in its place, the Dairy Barn housed the gymnasium, student center, theater, infirmary, and cafeteria. As luck would have it, the only available table was right next to the table with an incredibly loud student whose "New kids!" chant drew stares from across the cafeteria. After several attempts to speak with each other over the noise, the new kids eventually gave up, which meant they could hear the loud guy's jokes about them doing his laundry that much more clearly.

Jarek's mind spun as he overthought every interaction, every sight, and every sound, trying to decide how difficult this new chapter might be. Failure wasn't an option. His parents sacrificed a lot so he could "start over."

"Charisma," his dad once said, "is positive energy that makes people want to be around you because your enthusiasm for your task, for life, or for them individually makes them feel good and feel validated." Jarek knew he didn't have charisma. Here he was with new schoolmates, and all he was doing was silently staring at his turkey sandwich.

Jarek picked through what was left of his lunch and walked up to the tray window—as he'd seen others do—without saying goodbye to his tablemates and headed for the exit. But as he passed through the door, something hit him in the back. Surprised, he stopped and turned around to see a lump of brownie squeezed in a ball on the floor before his feet. He looked toward the noisy table. The girls looked disapprovingly at their plates and didn't say a word, but the loud guy—silent for the first time—sat staring, expressionless, right at Jarek. No smile, apology, joke, or anything else. Just staring. Confused, Jarek looked at him for a minute in a vain attempt to figure out the deal before turning around and walking out. The idea that there would already be a problem here created a feeling of familiar discouragement in Jarek's chest and made him miss home.

"Well, great," he whispered to himself. Maybe this new start was a bad idea after all.

He tried to forget about it, thinking instead about the Tannery and heading out for another look.

JAREK HEADED DOWN THE GRAVEL PATH TOWARDS THE IMPOSING OLD barn, past the vast plateau of the soccer field, looking down over the valley to his left.

Seeing the sun set into the valley and watching barn swallows twitter overhead calmed his mind after the cafeteria incident. Other than the crunch of gravel beneath his feet and crickets chirping in the distance, it was silent. Lightning bugs flickered at the shaded edges of the field, and dragonflies circled over the pond in the warm breeze as he passed.

To his surprise, Jarek heard beautiful piano music floating through the still evening air from a distance away. Drawing closer to the Tannery, he realized it was coming from within. He walked quietly into the open door of the structure so as not to disturb whatever was taking place inside.

The sweet and musty leather-smell of structural timber that has served its purpose for generations hung heavily in the humid air, and he wondered what stories the old barn would tell if it could. The music grew louder as he stepped through the threshold into the main room.

A well-worn wooden floor ran the length of the ample space, back to front, and piles of supplies covered in plastic occupied much of it. A grand piano, impeccably clean compared to the other surfaces, sat atop a small permanent wooden stage at the far end. Rumpled on a nearby bench was a dusty old tarp that he could tell had just been removed.

The notes from the keyboard rose and fell, and he caught his breath as his eyes brought into focus both the piano and the person playing it. It was not a teacher, as he expected, but definitely a student, most likely his year, and undoubtedly beautiful.

Jarek was absorbed in watching her play. Her eyes were closed in concentration, her head nodded, and her hands moved slowly across the keys. He didn't know what she was playing, but it was quiet, sad, and felt like the perfect soundtrack for its time and place. For him, anyway.

The girl had thick, chestnut-brown hair that fell in waves around her shoulders and hung lightly over an untucked long-sleeved shirt. He wanted nothing more than to walk over to the bench, sit down like they were friends, and listen. He told himself that if he didn't know he'd be interrupting, he'd do that. For a moment, he almost believed it. Instead, he moved along the back wall, took one last look at her in the fading sunlight, and slowly walked out, frustrated with himself for not saying hello, and frustrated that he cared.

He walked the short leg around the pond, past the headmaster's house, and found himself thinking about his parents. They needed him more than ever, but here he was, hundreds of miles away from them, feeling guilty, alone, and already unsure if this was the right decision. He thought about Andrew and wished he was at his side like he used to be.

Campus was quiet as Jarek walked along the main road with the old Shaker Meetinghouse—repurposed as the school library—passing on his right, the large dark windows looming over him.

A chill swept through Jarek, and with it came the unmistakable sense that someone was watching him. He started, quickly turning to the right, and swore he saw a figure disappearing from the middle window as a cool evening breeze blew down the mountain. The gust rustled the leaves overhead, and in the wind, he heard a voice whisper his name.

Jarek.

His mind was already playing tricks on him. This discouraging thought slowed his steps as he continued on, speaking aloud to no one: "...and I'm imagining things."

CHAPTER 3

"But do you? Do you believe in, I don't know, the undead? Spirits…ghosts?"

Seeing that her question had stumped the young man sprawled across a nearby armchair, a short, blonde girl turned to Jarek as he took a seat on the sofa and rifled through his backpack.

"Hi. It's Jarek, right? We met at orientation. I'm Emily. Em."

"Yeah, we did. Hi, Em," Jarek said.

A long driveway led from the main classroom building to a building called Brethren's—Jarek's dormitory. He had walked beneath the 60-foot evergreens that flanked the gravel path and entered the Common Room, which served as a social hub for students in their little free time. Common Rooms were the only places in the dorms where members of the opposite sex were allowed, and all were similarly provisioned: there were a few sturdy and beat-up dorm-style couches, a pay phone on the wall, which residents fought over each evening, and if they were lucky—a television set with more than three channels.

Em turned her eyes back to the other student, her persistent gaze making it clear she was waiting for a response.

"I don't know," the boy answered. "I never thought about it much before I came here."

"A bunch of people talk about it," another girl added.

"Talk about what?" Jarek asked.

"Ghosts," Em said, opening her eyes wide and adding "Spoooooky" with a smile.

"Some of the teachers say for sure they've heard things," the boy added, "but it beats me. The radiator pipes clang so loud when the heat comes on that, yeah, if I didn't know better, I'd probably think the devil himself was tryna beat my door down."

"Jarek, what do you think?" Em asked.

"Ghosts? Like…dead people sneaking around, trying to creep us out?" Jarek asked. "I think it's a bit… I don't know… dippy."

"Dippy?" An English teacher and dorm parent named Mr. Drummy had just walked through the door and saw them sitting together. "What's dippy?" he asked. "Hi, Em."

"Ghosts," Em said, turning to Mr. Drummy. "Or Shaker ghosts, to be specific."

She turned her head back and responded to Jarek. "But completely? This building. It was built in what…like 1830? It's been here for over 160 years, right? It used to be buzzing with people coming and going every day—hundreds over the years. All dead. You think no one is…left behind?"

"Lots of people think otherwise," Drummy interjected, adding with a shrug towards the steps. "Guys, come on upstairs."

Students always jumped at the chance to hang out in a faculty apartment. It was where the best conversations occurred with the teachers they admired, and invitations were rarely extended, mainly because such visits were generally frowned upon as something that would diminish authority. But Mr. Drummy didn't seem to stand on ceremony.

A little winded after climbing four flights of stairs, they entered a sparsely furnished space: half living room, half kitchen. The only furniture was a faded, navy-blue couch, a bean bag that took up much of the floor, a brimming bookshelf, and two Shaker chairs beside a wooden table. It looked like the apartment of someone who had just moved in, didn't give much thought to presentation, and was obsessed with books, which were stacked on every surface.

Jarek figured the dozen or more that were open and face down were the ones Drummy was in the middle of. Tiny pins held dozens of notes to a bulletin board by the sink, forming a haphazard wreath of reminders around a chart that read "Class Schedule" across the top.

Two posters of Bob Dylan were the only wall decorations: a concert bill for a show in Manchester in 1966, framed; the other, a profile shot of a young Dylan through a windowpane. Below were the words, "I accept chaos; I'm not sure whether it accepts me."

"You guys have to hear this—I got it last week. Dylan at Town Hall, April 12, 1963." Drummy swung the arm of a beat-up record player over the spinning disc and, after a few rhythmic clicks, adjusted the volume. He held a book out to Jarek with off-handed familiarity that surprised him. The cover read "Bob Dylan, Lyrics, 1962-85."

"Oh, cool, thanks," Jarek said. He knew nothing about Bob Dylan but started respectfully thumbing through the book as the sound of a guitar being tuned against the grainy crackle of bootlegged applause filled the room. He wasn't sure what to make of the moment, but Mr. Drummy was willing to talk about things that mattered to them, and they were grateful for the gesture.

Jarek and several classmates had met Drummy the day before, on the first full day of classes. They had walked into Wickersham—the grand old brick building at the center of campus—found their way to the right room for their English class and curiously noted the person at the teacher's desk with his head down. Jarek wasn't sure if it was the teacher or if someone had come in to take a nap, but a couple returning students muttered "uh-oh" and smiled as they filed in to take their seats, so he figured this must be somehow normal. When the bell rang, the slumped figure sat bolt upright, quickly getting the attention of the startled students. Then he looked around the room through the thick lenses of his black-rimmed wayfarer glasses and said "Hello" in a deadpan tone.

"I'm Mr. Drummy," he went on, after a moment, in a more animated tone. He gave the collar of his wrinkled, short-sleeved shirt a tug as if it were proof-positive that he was the teacher, adding, "Let us all make fun of my name now and get it out of the way: Drummy. Dummy. Scummy. Big fat tummy." He then leaped up from his chair and energetically proclaimed, "Okay! Let's begin."

Jarek smiled now, sitting in the cramped living room of this sarcastic and often cranky teacher who seemed to be universally beloved by the students. Mr. Drummy grabbed another book from the tall stack atop his bookshelf and handed it to Em as Jarek tilted his head to read the other titles: *The Sun Also Rises, The Catcher in the Rye, Catch 22.* Faulkner, Dostoevsky, Flaubert—dozens of classics flanked by poetry compilations of Ginsburg, Kerouac, and DiPrima. His bookshelf was a study in contrasts.

"These are the lions," Drummy said, gesturing towards his bookshelf. "Civilization would not be as we currently know it if it wasn't for them." He stared into the distance as he finished his thought with the words, "Talk about a legacy."

There was a pause as the students considered his words.

"So," Drummy finally said, looking at each of them. "When I walked in, you guys were talking about ghosts?"

"Yeah," Em said.

"And Jarek thinks they're... what was it... 'dippy'?" Drummy asked.

Em gave Jarek a playful smile, knowing he was on the spot.

"It seems a little silly," Jarek said.

"Does *it* seem silly, or the people who believe it seem silly? There's a difference."

"Uh, both?" Jarek muttered.

"Do you know what *ad hominem* means?" Drummy asked.

Jarek shook his head but was comforted that no one else knew either.

"Aristotle. Arguing the person instead of the argument. Humans have long believed we go somewhere after death. A belief in the afterlife has been a part of every major civilization in human history. For centuries, this belief has been accompanied by curiosity about how we get there. Of all the people who have died throughout history, isn't it possible that there are a couple…" Drummy leaned in for emphasis "…who may have fallen through the cracks?"

"What do you mean?" Em asked.

"Even if we're just talking statistics," Drummy continued. "All those people dying, moving on. Millions. Tens of millions. And not even a few for whom the process wasn't perfect?"

Jarek was deep in thought, so Drummy threw him a rope. "But hey, the most brilliant minds in human history have wrestled with the question of what comes after death. Don't worry about not knowing the answer. They never figured it out, and we won't either." He winked.

"Yeah, but ghosts? I mean… there's no real proof, right?" Jarek said, "Most people who say they've had some kind of 'ghost' experience are a little… weird."

Drummy gave Jarek a serious look as he replied. "Jarek, it's a question that brings us to the greatest irony of human existence, which is this: Every single person that came before us—all over the world at every point in history—has died. Every single one. Yet none of the living have any idea what happens. Crazy, right?"

"Yeah," Jarek said, his eyes distant. "No one knows what it's like. Death." He wished Andrew was there so he could ask him. He hoped he'd say it wasn't so bad.

Drummy continued, "But as long as human understanding has held with the notion of a soul and an afterlife, some have believed that certain souls, especially those who suffered unnatural deaths, might hang around. What we now call 'ghosts.' It's not some new-age invention. So, let's be careful," he said, looking at Jarek, "that we don't discount the notion based on who we think believes it. Maybe the weird ones are the only ones not afraid to share their experiences. Sometimes people who are different have more courage than the rest of us." Drummy looked at Jarek, "You know?"

Jarek, with his combat boots and purple hair, appreciated that Drummy was paying him a compliment while delicately making his point.

"Yeah, for sure, that makes sense," Jarek said.

Drummy raised an eyebrow at him, adding, "Plenty of very smart and reliable people have had experiences here on campus that you might find pretty interesting."

Jarek nodded to show he'd keep an open mind.

"Something to think about. You may have a different opinion before too long." Drummy gave him a knowing smile, adding, "Now that you're here…"

Jarek remembered the figure in the library window as a chill ran down his spine.

CHAPTER 4

"Okay, everybody—good morning, good morning!"

After the first few days of classes, students were asked to gather in the field for "icebreakers." The athletic director blew his whistle to get the attention of the 100 half-asleep teenagers who milled about the field.

Morning fog from the treetops on the mountainside flowed slowly down through campus to the immense plateau of the soccer field, then down to the valley below, settling in a white pool around the few structures that peeked above. It reminded Jarek of the sheets of cotton snow he and Andrew would lay beneath the Christmas tree each year so his dad could begin setting up the Christmas village they all loved.

"Good morning, good morning!" Jarek turned to see Em smiling sarcastically as she approached. "Holy crap, it's early for this," she added, taking a swig of coffee out of a thermos she carried around in the mornings.

"Yeah," Jarek said, "no kidding." He watched two groups of six students trying to outrun each other while holding hands, then he turned and gave Em a deadpan look, which she responded to with a sympathetic smile.

Jarek tried to focus. Faculty were having students participate in trust-building games. After warm-ups, students were split into groups of six. The first activity had five students lying in the grass like sardines in a can as the sixth lay lengthwise across them, and they all rolled forward in unison to see how far they could go before they either ended up too far apart or the person on top rolled off or in between them. It was goofy, but return students took it in stride; new ones quietly sought each other's company so they could navigate their discomfort together.

He looked towards the edge of the field and said, "It's creepy out here." Between the fog and the old buildings he now called home, he couldn't help thinking the Headless Horseman might come charging out of the mist at any moment.

"What? It's nice!" Em smiled and gave him a nudge with her shoulder, nodding towards the valley. "In a few weeks, all this beautiful, 'creepy' nature will be bright red and orange as far as the eye can see." He couldn't help but admire her positivity, even if it was too early for more than a small dose.

Jarek heard a spirited laugh above the din of chattering students. He turned his head, immediately recognizing the girl from the piano the day before. She was doubled over in laughter at something a classmate was telling her. He couldn't look away, now for the second time. She wore a wrinkly, untucked button-down shirt and ripped jeans with paint on them. He wondered why. Her hair was held back by a blue band emblazoned with the school's crest that he recognized from the welcome packets they had received. He watched her notice a new female student who looked uncomfortable, introducing herself and telling her what she was looking forward to later in the day.

Jarek found himself staring at her cheekbones. He shook it off and tried to pay attention.

"Okay, guys, one more shuffle!" the athletic director shouted with a smile as the students milled about grabbing classmates until groups of eight were reformed for the final exercise.

Jarek squirmed when he saw the loud kid on the other side of the group he ended up with. He had learned his name was Dave, but everyone called him by his last name, Morak. Morak maintained his volume at all times, cranking it up when his lack of coordination became obvious. Once a few moments passed with the two of them nearby and no apology from Morak about the brownie incident in the cafeteria the day before, Jarek determined none was coming.

"Okay!" the athletic director continued, "Now comes the best part."

A dozen classroom desks sitting at the edge of the field without explanation were quickly moved out onto the lawn by several students recruited for the task. As students turned their heads, wondering what the desks could be for, the athletic director gave another blow of the whistle to make sure he had everyone's attention and continued.

"The last thing we're going to do in groups this morning is the trust fall." He was used to raising his voice above student noise, and his instructions rang across the field. "Watch how we do it." Eight faculty stood in two rows facing each other with their arms held out, forming a tight row of hands with upturned palms. Another faculty member stood on a desk at the end of the two rows, turned his back to the group, crossed his arms over his chest, and closed his eyes. He then took a deep breath, called out "Falling," and fell blindly—and quickly—backward into the extended arms of his colleagues.

The athletic director stepped aside with a respectful nod to the Head of School, Headmaster Worthing, who moved forward, slowly looked across the entire student body, took a deep breath, paused for effect, and addressed the students.

"Trust," he said. "Trust and accountability." The headmaster paused again. "Trust and accountability are critical to the life of this community. All of us—students and faculty—must be able to rely upon each other. To trust each other, to be accountable to each other. Whether this is your fourth day," he put his hand on the shoulder of one of the new students who smiled uncomfortably, "or your fourth year" he did the same to a student on the other side of him, who raised his fists in the air and let out a howl. "Or maybe it's your FORTIETH year!" he said, wagging his finger at an imposing gent with white hair, a big white beard, and amber aviator sunglasses. Students let out a cheer, and the white-haired teacher lifted his hands in an "aw shucks" gesture, which was in stark contrast to his imposing look. The headmaster continued, "ANYONE who calls this place their home has a responsibility—we *all* do—to each other. The interpersonal and community bonds we build here will help us through the academic challenges ahead and those we will face after we have moved on from this place. The dangers and the adventures of life await. If we can do THIS together, we can do THAT together. The trust fall is a symbol of just that: Trust. We rely on everyone who calls this place home."

"Huh," Jarek whispered to Em. "That was pretty good."

"Worthing's fancy way of saying 'follow my many rules,'" she said flatly.

"Let's do it," the athletic director said with a clap of his hands as each group gathered around a desk. "Bigger guys go in the middle of the catchers. That's where most of the weight lands. No offense, ladies, just keeping it safe."

Each time the word "Falling" sounded above the din, students turned to watch. Jarek did his best to pay attention as the first couple of people in his group took their turn. He looked at Morak out of the corner of his eye, figured he was pushing 220 pounds and dreaded having to be part of catching him.

Soon, it was his turn. Jarek figured the trust fall was a lot like the stage diving he'd done plenty of times at the many punk shows he had been to, so he climbed onto the desk, eager to show his lack of hesitation, and turned his back to the catchers, crossing his arms over his chest and taking a deep breath. At that moment, looking out across the groups, he saw the face of the girl from the piano looking right at him. He froze momentarily; she was waiting to see the fall and catch. Jarek took one last look at the group behind him, making eye contact with Morak, who gave him a friendly smile.

"All right, here he goes," he said encouragingly. Maybe he wasn't so bad after all.

Jarek's hands tingled, and his heart beat faster as he called out "Falling" and let his body drop.

When the human brain senses danger, Jarek had learned, the hypothalamus, pituitary gland, and adrenal glands work together to release cortisol into the body, speeding up breathing, heart rate, and response time, and heightening perception. This heightened perception allowed Jarek's brain to process the moments of his fall in slow motion: looking up at the sky, falling backward, arriving at the hands, feeling there were too few, and quickly hitting the ground. His head struck the hard earth with a heavy thud.

The shock of the impact slowly dissipated through his skull, and he opened his eyes to see a few concerned faces looking down over him. "Oh my gosh, are you okay?" one of the girls asked.

"Jesus, Morak," one of the guys said as he helped Jarek up.

"Guess I lost my footing," Morak replied, looking at Jarek with a half-smirk before turning and walking away.

Jarek looked back towards the piano girl. She turned away just as he caught her eye, and he knew she had seen the whole thing. Most of his new classmates were still watching him, though, and trying to be discreet, as people do when someone else has been humiliated.

So much for good first impressions.

CHAPTER 5

"Jarek..."

As he brushed himself off, he turned to see Drummy sitting on a bench at the edge of the field, waving him over. Jarek was embarrassed but grateful for the sympathetic gesture. "Sorry about that," Drummy said as Jarek sat beside him.

They sat quietly, looking across the field towards the sunlit valley below. "The Berkshires aren't so bad, right?" Drummy said. "All those dead white poets, I can see why they liked it up here so much, whatever their faults." He kept his eyes forward, the furrowed brow behind thick-rimmed glasses showing he had something on his mind. His messy dark hair made him look like he had just rolled out of bed, too wrapped up in his thoughts to worry about appearances, or as if he was in a state of internal conflict—an anomaly, like his bookshelf. For some reason, Jarek was glad for it.

After a moment, he broke the silence. "So, Jarek, do you have siblings?"

"Yeah," Jarek said, "a brother." The familiar ache he'd escaped for a while returned.

"Older or younger?" Drummy asked. He waited a few seconds, then a few more, and said, "Hey, are you with me? Is he in college? At home?"

Jarek took a breath. "Um, neither," he said.

"Okay, where does he live?"

Jarek looked away for a moment, then out across the field.

A red-winged blackbird descended into sight and settled in a nearby tree. Its red corporal shoulders shone in the sun, a silent officiant presiding over the gravity of the moment.

"He…um. He doesn't."

Drummy turned and looked at Jarek, waiting an extra moment to ensure he had heard correctly. Jarek stayed still.

"God," Drummy whispered. He took a deep breath, lifted his squinted eyes across the field, and settled on the blackbird. "Jarek, I'm so sorry," he said.

They sat silently as the bird raised its wings for a moment, took one final look around, and disappeared.

JAREK WALKED INTO THE CAFETERIA, ANNOYED WITH HIMSELF WHEN HE realized he was looking around for Morak. His head was still pounding, and he wasn't hungry, but dinner was the one meal they weren't allowed to skip each day. Jarek was already learning the rhythm of the cafeteria: fish on Monday, chicken on Tuesday, casserole on Wednesday—each night with a side of vegetables out of five or ten-pound cans.

Students and faculty shuffled into lines to receive whatever the large steaming steel containers held in store. Friday was always the same: shepherd's pie, the chopped-up remainder of everything served earlier in the week with a smear of mashed potatoes on top.

He sidled up to a table with those he knew, by this point, were likely to become his meal-time companions: the quirky kids. A couple had parts of their heads shaved, one wore combat boots like his, and all were obsessed with music. One of them spent the previous summer following Phish around the country. In a big school, each of these kids would be sitting with a group much more like each of them, but here they were collectively the "other" category. Not the athletes, not the better-dressed grade-getters, not the foreign students…just the "others." Fledgling social awareness, disdain for authority, and cutting sarcasm— that's what they had in common. He fit right in.

Drummy gave Jarek a "hello" head nod from his table among the teachers, where they sat making small talk, interrupted only when one of them got up to tame an unruly student. Jarek went up to grab a piece of lemon meringue pie, devouring it quickly before heading out to get his books. Morak watched him leave from across the room.

CHAPTER 6

"What is 'complex PTSD'? Well, it's a trauma response."

Jarek began meeting with Ms. Stondell, the school guidance counselor—at his parent's insistence—twice a week, right after he got to campus. At his old school, he met with his guidance counselor once a week, about four times as much as the average student. When Andrew got sick, it doubled.

She pulled a slightly oversized, yellow piece of paper out of the only folder on her desk, which Jarek recognized immediately, feeling a little sick. He squirmed in the comfortable armchair and focused momentarily on the battery-operated "Zen fountain" which sat on a small table beside her desk. Both needed to be dusted.

"It can manifest itself in many ways," she continued. "One is structural changes to a part of the brain called the amygdala, which can cause heightened behaviors, like aggression, particularly when we experience stress. Sometimes, it causes people to relive the trauma in their minds over and over again, but it varies depending on the person. If someone has certain predispositions," she looked at him to indicate he was the "someone" she was talking about, "the impact can be more significant. But it can be managed with the proper interventions."

The paper in her hand was the standard form the guidance counselor at his old school would send to parents after an "incident." It shared the school's observations alongside the disciplinary summary from the principal's office. It was the form that meant you were in trouble. A knot formed in Jarek's stomach as it always did when he saw those yellow forms in the past.

Ms. Stondell looked over the top of her glasses. "You know what this is, right? I figured you already read it. There's some cool stuff in here. I'm going to read it aloud, okay?"

"Yeah, I guess, sure," he said, not wanting to be difficult.

"'*Jarek's intellectual curiosity is complimented by his remarkable memory. Everything he reads, he absorbs—clinging to his memory word for word even weeks later, especially when he's quite interested in the subject matter. In all my years in education, I've never seen anything like it.*'"

He knew this one—his parents had read it to him months before. She looked up from the paper and said, "My, my," with a nod to show she was impressed and then continued reading.

"'*It is clear that the lessons regularly assigned in his classes are considerably below his ability level, which is why I'm having a hard time understanding why he rarely completes his homework. I'm also afraid the situation with his brother is impacting his classroom performance and his ability to engage socially with his peers as well. His mind is constantly wandering.*'"

She looked up from the paper at Jarek and said, "It ends with '*Let's discuss.*'"

He pictured his old guidance counselor, Ms. Max, and her past "yellow form" talks. Her tiny frame and mouse-mannered disposition gave her the appearance of someone who would either burst into tears or fall right over if anyone yelled "boo," so Jarek found it hard to be frustrated with her. But he had had less patience for Ms. Max's simple-minded questions once Andrew got sick.

"*When you say you think it's 'unfair,' what do you mean?*'" she had asked. He hadn't bothered answering. Hearing her again refer to the gut-wrenching reality of Andrew's sickness as "the situation with his brother" made him just as angry now as it had when she first filled out that form.

"Jarek, why are you here?" Ms. Stondell asked, putting the paper down and leaning toward him.

"I'm here because my brother died, I flipped out, and I attacked a teacher," he responded dryly.

"No, Jarek. You got expelled because you attacked your teacher. You're *here* because 'we'—the school—believe you show more promise than almost any other student on campus. Your IQ is off the charts—you're brilliant—yet your grades were terrible because your previous school was not the right place for you. You've been through a lot. I know. But your future is much brighter than it might seem from where you are sitting right now," she said. When he didn't reply, she pressed on. "Have you ever heard the expression 'grow where you are planted'? Think of yourself as a tree in need of the right soil."

"I was planted back home with my brother," Jarek said dryly. "When he died, my tree died."

He looked again towards the yellow paper.

"Does this bother you?" she asked, holding it up before putting it back in its folder.

"No. Or, I don't know, maybe." He nodded to the folder, "All my worst stuff floats from shrink to shrink and back in a little folder that follows me around forever?"

"Well, not exactly. It's for continuity of care," she said with a sincere tilt of her head.

"'The situation with his brother,' is a bit of an understatement, no? She couldn't just say Andrew was sick? Are we lab rats?" he said with disgust, adding, "and my mind doesn't wander 'constantly.' It's just that… I can't get it back when it does."

"How so?" Ms. Stondell asked.

Jarek took a moment. "Well," he said, "everything will be going along just fine, and then it's like somebody flips a switch and, I don't know, I just go somewhere else."

"What's a 'switch'?" She asked.

He let out a long breath. He wasn't yet ready to acknowledge the near-constant struggle he'd been dealing with long before everything happened with Andrew, but she meant well, and her stare wouldn't let up.

"That's what my parents and I call it. 'The switch.' It's like..." he paused for a moment. "it's like my brain is the lead car on a subway train, and I'm a passenger. All the cars behind are the things that happen the way they're supposed to if I'm going the right way. You know?" he said. "As it goes through the stations, I look at the signs on the pillars to make sure I'm in the right place, and I see it and I'm glad. But other times, it's different."

"How is it different? What happens that makes it different?" she asked.

"Well, something will happen that speeds up the train a little—an idea, a memory, I don't know. And suddenly, it's like someone else is in charge of where it goes. Or at least, I imagine someone is because, in my mind, I like to pretend someone has more control of it than I do. So I imagine a small, hunched-over man in a dirty wool coat standing on the side of the tracks. He's wearing an old fedora hat that covers the top of his face, and he's chomping on a cigar and smirking at me as he pulls the switch, and the train suddenly rocks and shifts as he sends me down the other track. I know it's in my own mind, and I can't control it. But if it's him, it's like I have someone to blame."

"And then what?" she asked.

"Then I head down the other track. And then, I don't know—nothing: no pillars, no signs, no checkpoints. At first, it's cool because I don't know what happens next, you know? Could be going anywhere, someplace amazing—a daydream, some cool city—I don't know. Sometimes, I think it will leave the tunnel out into a green valley with huge mountains, and, like, sheep on the hills, little fences, stuff like that. Other times, it gets faster and louder; cracked tiles are racing past, out of focus, and the train starts to rattle and sway."

He closed his eyes. "On the outside, in real life, I stare into space. Or sometimes I get angry, it depends. But on the inside, it's just… no conductor, no brakes, and I hold on tighter until it's so fast my feet are off the floor, I'm floating, the lights blink until they go out, and it's just loud and fast and dark and me there alone and no way to stop it. Nightmares, dreams, panic. I don't know. That's the switch."

BEEP, BEEP, BEEP, BEEP

"Hey, switch back to me, Jarek. We need you here."

Nine months earlier, Jarek and his dad had walked under the buzzing neon lights of a busy hospital corridor toward the room where his younger brother Andrew had again spent the night. They kept a deliberate pace, eyes forward, but still caught glimpses of other kids in various stages of their "journey" through open doors. All were as bald as Andrew, some skinnier, and for the first time in about six years—since Jarek was ten—his dad took his hand. He smiled when he did it and looked down at him. "Love you, pal." But Jarek could tell that his dad, a relentless optimist, was uneasy. The realization brought to Jarek's mind such a rush of panic for his brother that he stopped. His dad must have seen the look on his face—the blank expression, the distant gaze—because he spoke again, but Jarek didn't hear him, looking instead at the scrub hats on the nurses standing behind the front desk on Andrew's hall. As soon as he saw them, his mind went to happier times with his brother.

When Jarek and Andrew were little, their mom would take them to a German bakery on Saturday afternoons to pick up a cake for "coffee hour" at church the following morning. The women behind the counter wore little paper hats. If the boys were good, they would each get to pick one piece of fruit-shaped marzipan. Later those nights, Jarek and Andrew would sneak into the kitchen well after bedtime, leaning their washed, brushed, and pajamaed little figures into the soft glow of the refrigerator to stare at the mesmerizing creation. Eventually, their mother would appear out of the dark, shuffling them off to bed with a warning and reminder of the one Sunday when she and fellow congregants removed the cake from its box to notice dozens of tiny fingerprints where the frosting used to be. They had "learned the hard way" (not that their mother was ever particularly strict) never to touch the cake again, even if their curiosity brought them back three or four times for another look.

"Jarek…" his dad had said again, standing before him in the hospital hallway. "Hey, pal. Where'd you go?"

Jarek started. "Hey. Yeah, I'm here. Sorry, Dad."

The beep of Andrew's heart monitor welcomed Jarek into the doorway of his brother's room. Every time it was the same; the last couple of steps to the door made him a little sick to his stomach, as he anticipated what new signs of deterioration he would see on his brother's face, or what was left of his fading spirit. He would hear the beep just as he entered, look at Andrew, and then Andrew would look back—more tired every time—and Jarek would stifle his shock as best he could and lean down to hug him. Dread, *beep*, shock, *beep*, hug. Same thing every visit. Jarek had been having nightmares since his brother got sick, but they were more frequent now. In the worst of them—the one he had the most often—when he entered the room, there was no beep, and Andrew didn't look back. The last couple of visits, he started letting his father go in first.

"Hey, buddy. How'd you sleep?" Jarek's dad smiled as he walked through the door and held up a handful of comic books, "I thought you'd like these." Andrew looked at them briefly, then his eyes went back to his father's face, watching him as he made a little show of fanning the comics out on the side table where Andrew could reach them through the steel rails of his bed.

Jarek leaned over to hug his brother, his heart sinking a bit more when he saw how pointed one of Andrew's hip bones looked despite the sheet resting over it. On the wall opposite Andrew's bed, Jarek had hung two pieces of drawing paper the boys had filled out and colored in Sunday School years before. "What is your name?" the worksheets asked, and "Who is your hero?" The first read, "My Name is: Andrew. My hero is: My Brother." and the second read, "My Name is: Jarek. My hero is: My Brother."

"Hi, Mr. Dorrell. How are we doing today?" A portly nurse with very long brown hair had stepped into the room and was speaking a bit too enthusiastically for Jarek's liking. She continued, "My name is—" Jarek interrupted. "Hope Tollefson, R.N., Pittsburgh School of Nursing."

"Oh," she said, with a smile, cocking her head to the side out of curiosity.

He continued, "You've been working here for three years. People compliment you most often on your smile. You spend your free time with your husband at your son's baseball games and love cookouts, as long as your dog Bosco doesn't sneak too many hot dogs. Your goal each day is to give 'hope,' like your name, to your patients, and your favorite thing about coming to work is the people." The last couple of words had a hint of sarcasm.

His dad smiled at the nurse in case she noticed as well. "I guess he saw your profile behind the desk on the way in."

She turned to Jarek: "How did you know I was your brother's nurse today?"

"I didn't," he said. He prattled off the same information from two of the other profiles.

"Wow!" she said, eyes wide with stunned surprise, "That's crazy."

"He's having fun; don't let it alarm you," his dad said. "He has a photographic memory—just remembers things forever sometimes."

Andrew had been quietly watching the three of them, too weak to engage. Jarek looked at his taught cheekbones, stared at the floor momentarily, and then looked impatiently back to the nurse.

"What do you want?" he said, unsure how she didn't see she was intruding.

"Easy, buddy," his dad responded.

Most times, when his dad called him "buddy," it was an attempt to lighten the mood, especially since Andrew got sick.

"The scrubs are to help keep things clean, buddy," he had said when they first walked into the hospital. "Fewer germs means people get better quicker, and their medicine can work better, like Andrew."

Jarek looked up at his dad. "Does his medicine work?"

His dad put his hand on Jarek's shoulder. "We are here to find out from the doctors how well the medicine is working and make sure he has what he needs to get better and come home." He gave his shoulder an affectionate squeeze that lasted a few seconds longer than usual. Jarek could tell he was barely hanging on.

"Your brother is so strong, buddy. I know the medicine is working great," his dad added. Jarek believed him but saw the shadow that passed over his face when he said it.

Before too long, he'd know he was lying.

BY THE END OF THEIR SESSION, JAREK WAS SPENT.

"Well, that's enough for today," Ms. Stondell said. "See you in three days. Hang in there, okay? No switches. Deal?" She smiled.

"Sure." He nodded, knowing it was an impossible promise to keep.

When Jarek climbed into bed that night, Andrew was all he could think about. One of his two roommates, Taki, clicked away on a just-released Gameboy he brought home from last weekend's trip to the mall—along with brand-new skis, boots, and every piece of ski clothing he might ever need. He had a habit of playing Tetris after lights out, and the *beep, beep, beep* of turning blocks sounded across the room as Jarek fell asleep.

Moments later, he was dreaming.

He saw blue skies overhead and water all around him. The noise of Taki's game sounded somewhere in the distance.

Jarek was out in the middle of the ocean, and Andrew—the earlier version, before he got sick—was beside him. There were no boats, no planes, no people, and no sign of land in any direction, just the two of them holding on tight to a section of floating wood—all that remained of a shipwreck hundreds of miles from shore. They each had one arm around the other's shoulder, the same way they did when they were kids and a scary movie made it hard for them to sleep. They drifted alone, doing their best to hang on, whispering words of encouragement to each other despite their loosening grip.

A white beacon flashed above the water's surface from a deflated lifeboat drifting nearby. It was beeping the rhythmic chime that had been the soundtrack of their family's most heartbreaking and terrible moments. The one that had haunted most of Jarek's waking and sleeping hours since. The *beep beep beep* of Andrew's heart monitor sounded in one-second intervals, counting the final moments until their strength was gone and the brothers, still embracing each other, sank into the deep.

CHAPTER 7

"Guys, just grab these last two boxes and pull the door shut behind you, and we're done." The teacher had his arms full as he looked back, sweat soaking the collar of his shirt.

With the first month of school behind him, Jarek was getting used to the Wednesday morning routine. "Hands to Work, Hearts to God" was the Shaker motto, and the school put the "Hands to Work" part into action for three hours every Wednesday morning. Sunshine, rain, sleet, hail, monsoon; no exceptions. After shoveling in the last few bites of French toast, it was time for everyone to head into the crisp Fall air to start their work. The leaves coloring the mountainside had spread down into the valley, their color peeking just above the line of fog and mist that still obscured it from the night before.

Today, Jarek's work crew was assigned to the Shaker Museum. He had heard about it and knew which of the old brick buildings up the road it occupied, but he had never been inside.

Jarek and five other students were led through the museum's main room all the way to the back, where there was a private door so small he thought it must have led to a broom closet. They ascended a flight of creaky stairs into the attic, which smelled of old wood and was packed full of items of all shapes and sizes covered in sheets that sent clouds of dust into the air when disturbed. They squeezed past each other up and down the stairs again and again, carrying boxes full of dusty books that were now being donated to the county library.

Before long, they were finished. Each one grabbed a final box and headed out. Jarek did as well, but as he made his way to the steps, a long object under a sheet caught his eye. He lifted the corner and saw something that must have been completed with great pride by whatever hands constructed it many years before: a wide wooden bench with hundreds of small holes spelling the words "Mount Lebanon" in the beautifully curved back.

But as quickly as he took in the artisanship of this discovery, he was drawn to something behind it—another sheet over what appeared to be a pedestal. Jarek looked over his shoulder, sure that these things were off-limits—that he shouldn't be in this inner sanctum of Village history by himself. He heard the pick-up truck out front—the old engine burdened by its load of books—fading quietly into the distance. His crew-mates must have called for him, but he didn't hear. When he didn't respond to his name, they probably figured he could walk. It wasn't far back to the center of campus.

He was alone.

He grabbed the edge of the sheet and pulled, watching it slide to the floor as an ornate, hand-carved pedestal emerged from beneath. On top, there was a book. Leather-bound with twine that had been glued until solid, it was thick and discolored at the edges. He put his hand over his mouth to stifle a cough as the dust settled, and he stepped closer. The cover was deeply imprinted with an old typeface. While the edges of the letters had faded with time, they were large, and the words were clear: *An Account of the Events of the Village.*

He carefully took the frayed bottom right edge of the cover between two fingers. The effects of time had split the leather; stains on the bottom left showed evidence of water damage at some point in the book's long history. He felt a sudden chill run through his body and heard his name in the air, *Jarek*, as he jumped and looked back over his shoulder. Sure he was alone, he looked down at the book, and his eyes scanned the cover. It read: *The United Society of Believers in Christ's Second Appearance: Community at Mount Lebanon. An Account of the Events of the Village. 1860–1870.*

Streaks of sunlight peeked through crumbling insulation in the walls, making it possible to read a hand-written subtitle that appeared to have been added as an afterthought. He moved towards it and looked closely at the faded cursive text, squinting as he muttered the words he saw before him: "The Book of the Mountain Kings."

He held his breath, slowly opening the cover as the ligaments of the binding creaked with age. It was an ongoing ledger of daily activities within the Village. He turned the brittle pages slowly, his eyes scanning each one as it passed.

"Still praying the Lord God will have mercy on our parched vegetables and right soon" was the first. Several entries later, he read: "Sisters' House rain damage still awaiting repair despite the dry weather," scribbled by the same hand.

Some days had entries; others didn't. One thing this snapshot into the days and minds of the former villagers made clear: They kept themselves quite busy.

Jarek focused on one entry in which the author, or one of them, spoke in first person for the first time. "Discussion of ledger has created more questions than answers. I grow more concerned but will allow time for resolution. We are all most grateful to Brother Thaddeus for his diligence in solving this mystery." He wondered what that was about.

The book was hundreds of pages long. As he flipped forward more quickly, it opened naturally to a middle section where old photos were affixed to the pages—photos of buildings, documenting changes that had been made to structures, and of the land, showing progress excavating new expanses of the outer fields for additional crops. Others were posed and somewhat formal photos of Shakers themselves; some were standing or working in the fields, others seated and posing together for what was (Jarek realized) a much more extensive process than he was used to for one individual photo. An individual with a big device—the likes of which many had not seen before—had to set up and slowly gather his subjects, ensuring they sat perfectly still while this alien contraption studied them to capture what was probably the first—and for many, the only—photograph they would ever be in.

He was sneaking into things he had no business sneaking into, and he knew it. When Jarek was a kid, on those rare occasions when he was the only one at home, he would rifle through his dad's sock drawer to see what exciting things were there: unique coins, two-dollar bills, his grandfather's antique pocket watch. He would take each item in his hand and turn it over carefully in his fingers, wondering where it came from and how much it was worth. Inevitably, he would linger too long, and his dad would walk in. "Jarek, mind your business," he would say, like he always did, and Jarek would jump. A guilty intruder caught in the act.

He was sure at any moment someone would jump out at him now—maybe whoever he'd heard whispering his name in the dark, or maybe one of the solemn faces in the photos before him—telling him he'd been caught. Telling him to mind his business. That these secrets were not for him to intrude upon. His heart beat quickly as the minutes ticked on. When he was sure he had stayed too long and his absence likely noticed, he gently put the book back on the pedestal, replaced the sheet, and walked out, his head filled with thoughts of the mysterious lives he had just intruded upon.

"I DON'T MEAN TO BE RUDE, BUT THAT'S ONE OF THE DUMBEST THINGS I've heard since this conversation started."

"Wait...what? Which part?" Jarek was startled at the tone of her comment.

Her name was Elizabeth Frances Lamb, but she went by Beth. She had made a great first impression, playing the piano so beautifully as he watched unseen. But that impression was quickly tempered by the ones that followed.

"The idea that we somehow need to take an artist's work—or any creation—at face value and not view it through the context in the time it was produced or the society which they were part of when producing it. It's ridiculous."

"Well, that's not exactly what I said," Jarek countered.

Drummy heard the escalating tone and intervened, "I think Jarek meant the art speaks for itself, didn't you, Jarek?"

Beth was on a tear. "No, art isn't art because it makes us feel swell or looks pretty; it's a matter of context—with anything—art, music, architecture. The pyramids are amazing because they were built before hydraulics, power tools, cranes, and concrete. We could build them in a week now, with little effort. Our highway system makes the pyramids look like a set of children's building blocks if we're not taking both in context. Heck, building blocks themselves are a huge achievement," she smirked at Jarek, adding, ". . . if you're a caveman."

He couldn't tell if she was challenging him for fun, given her flare for ridiculing his infrequent contributions (now for the third time in as many classes this week), or if she was just annoying. Either way, the only time they'd ever spoken was during these classroom arguments, and she was starting to get on his nerves.

"Building blocks. Whatever," Jarek scoffed.

The depth of disappointment at realizing what the beautiful girl who had first captivated him at the piano was really like sank into his stomach. He let his focus drift until he heard Drummy land on a topic that interested him—and might give him an opportunity to win a sparring match with Beth.

"And what is it that makes us believe we *can't* be seen by those that have died? Or that they might actually attempt to communicate with us?"

Mr. Drummy had a habit of letting conversations run wildly off-topic to keep students engaged, so when the discussion moved from art to royal families of Europe to inter-family murders to ghosts haunting their descendants, he let it slide. Moments later, they were once again deep in a debate about the existence of Shaker ghosts, wondering aloud if those who lived and worked and died in the old creaky buildings might still be among them. It seemed to be a popular topic of conversation at the school. Some students were genuinely freaked out by it, but all paid close attention.

"It's just never happened before. There's no proof," said Jarek.

Drummy raised his eyebrows. "Proof? There are probably hundreds of documented cases of people seeing—or feeling—what we would call 'ghosts.' The presence of the dead. Many of these documentations are from a time when very little in the world was written down, which means it was real enough, or scary enough, for them to grab a quill and take hours to write about the experience. Do you have any idea what a pain in the ass it is to take a quill pen in your hand and dip it into a gloppy pot of ink hundreds of times to write pages of information? Have you ever done that?"

"No," Jarek said flatly, "I've never done that."

"How often do any of us document experiences of any kind even now, with backpacks full of notebooks and half a dozen ballpoint pens at our disposal at all hours of the day?" Drummy asked the class. "If they bothered to go through the trouble of writing about something, it must have been extraordinary."

"If we saw a ghost, then, yeah, I think we would write about it. It's a big deal. Why wouldn't we?" Jarek said.

"That's my point! Dozens of incidents have happened on this very campus, many in this very building: objects being placed in one spot and moments later being somewhere else, footsteps in an empty room, silhouettes in the hall, faces in the windows. People have sat alone, completely still and quiet, and felt something brush past them. They've heard whispers in the dark." Goosebumps ran down Jarek's arms as he remembered hearing a voice whisper his name twice since he'd set foot on campus. "These things have happened all over the world. And they've happened right here," Drummy gestured around him. "And they still do."

"But Jarek Dorrell doesn't believe in ghosts. Not yet, anyway," Drummy said with a smile to wrap things up upon seeing the clock.

The rest of the class took his cue, and the noise of closing books, backpack zippers, and shuffling chairs took over as everyone moved quickly to the exit to head for lunch.

Jarek admired Drummy—the way he thought and spoke, his slight disdain for authority. If he ever found himself in a tough situation, in need of a confidante, Jarek figured he could count on him.

As students gathered their books, Mr. Drummy added loudly above the din: "Oh, and you'll all be asleep, but the Alpha Aurigids meteor shower will be happening late tonight. I plan to see a few before bed if I can—cold, but should be a clear night. There's a world outside. See you tomorrow."

He always said that at the end of class, "There's a world outside." Jarek liked it.

CHAPTER 8

Jarek's alarm went off at 12:30 a.m.; he kept it next to his head so he could turn it off before it woke his roommates. He loved the night sky on campus and was determined to see these shooting stars.

Getting out of bed—still dressed—he put his boots and jacket on, grabbed a blanket, and snuck out of his room, down the old creaky steps, and out the door. He looked over his shoulder more than once to make sure he wasn't seen, ducking away from the light cast by the few lampposts into the shadows between the old brick buildings and the vertical pines as he made his way across campus and out into the dark, vast expanse of the soccer field

Campus being on the side of a mountain, the sky looked huge from just about any location. On a clear night, the result was an incredible canopy of stars. He looked for those he could recognize as he slowly stepped into the dark field. Amid the thousands of white specks, he found Arcturus off the handle of the Big Dipper and Spica below; his dad taught him and Andrew those. And all the way straight backward, way up in the sky was Vega. It was silent, solitary, and perfect.

"Jupiter is about to enter Scorpio," he thought. He'd throw his blanket down and get comfortable… Just a few more steps, and…

"GOD! You scared the *hell* out of me!" someone shouted as Jarek jumped. The immediate howl of whoever he had just tripped over jarred him entirely out of his calmness back into reality.

"What? Gosh, I didn't see you!" Jarek stammered, "I mean, I *can't* see you. Crap, I'm sorry. Are you okay? Are you all right?"

"Yeah, who is it?" an irritated voice asked.

He recognized it at once: Beth. His whole body tightened.

"It's Jarek. Jarek Dorrell" he said. "We're in writing and lit together."

"Oh, right. Hi. I was half-asleep. What are you doing here?"

He was so surprised that he almost forgot to answer her question. He wanted to tell her the truth, but he had the distinct sensation it would make him feel like an idiot. He did it anyway.

"I, um… I wanted to see the meteor shower," he said.

"Ha, right," she said.

He felt like an idiot.

"Really?" she added.

"What are *you* doing here?" Jarek asked.

"Same thing," she said. "Have a seat."

He paused for a moment. He had been expecting complete solitude for hours and tried to adjust his mindset and behavior from that of solitary stargazer to that of a friendly, funny, easygoing guy. Who was he kidding? He was never that guy, and he knew it. But he'd give it a shot, and, truth be told, he was very interested to see how this would turn out.

"Do you…do this a lot?" he asked.

"Do I 'come here often' you mean?" He could almost hear her rolling her eyes. The funny, easygoing guy clearly had yet to make an appearance. The moment drew out for an eternity as he tried to figure out what to say next.

She lifted her chin and looked at the sky.

"What's your favorite star?" he asked.

She stared at the stars overhead for some time before responding quietly, "Do I need one?" He could just make out her face in the moonlight, smiling at him in the dark.

"*Need* one? No, but you might want one, just so you have a better answer than that," Jarek said.

Okay, that was better. Good recovery. He smiled back.

Having been at the receiving end of her quick wit and cutting sense of humor more than once, Jarek knew Beth didn't suffer fools lightly; this was a pass/fail moment. He'd have to stay on his toes to avoid getting dismissed out of hand for being unintelligent, unsophisticated, or—the kiss of death—uninteresting. He pictured himself tiptoeing through a minefield, wondering when a leg would get blown off. But they were here and alone; there was no turning back.

Jarek hadn't asked anyone to join him. Who would want to lay in the field in the pitch-black cold, staring at the stars? Just him, he thought, but maybe her too. As much as she made him want to pull his hair out, he couldn't help but be fascinated by her. She seemed different from the others. He realized—whatever her chiding—they had something in common. They were alike in their difference—the same in their otherness, and he was intrigued.

"So, do *you* do this a lot?" she was messing with him again.

"Maybe as much as you trip strangers in the dark."

He breathed deeply to calm his racing thoughts as she scooted closer, leaning against him for warmth as they both lay on her blanket. He stayed perfectly still so she wouldn't move away. He heard her take a deep breath more than once and knew she was nervous, too. Here they were, after all, alone together in the middle of the field at midnight while the whole world was asleep. He could see the outline of her face and knew she was watching him in the cold and silence, her dark eyes looking right into his thoughts in a way that would make him turn away if he could see her clearly. Her first impression at the piano had recovered. He decided that was the real her when no one was watching. She was even more beautiful than before.

They watched the sky together for the next hour, the silence only occasionally interrupted by a gasp and a point in the direction of a flash of light. When it was nearing 2 a.m. Beth yawned; Jarek did immediately afterward. It was their cue to pack it up.

"You never told me your favorite star," he said in an attempt to draw out the moment for as long as possible..

"Not sure I have one; I think I like them all. Maybe I'll tell you my favorite goddess instead," she said.

"Who is that?"

She ignored him. "But wait, are we still strangers?"

He paused, trying to think of something witty, but was at a loss. In the quiet seconds that followed, he surprised even himself. He lifted his hand towards her face, touching her cheek with his fingertips. She stayed perfectly still as he drew the tip of his index finger slowly along her jawline, feeling the softness of her skin and hearing her shallow breath move closer to his. He hesitated for a moment but then felt the assurance of her hand on the chest of his coat as she moved closer, and he did as well, until his lips found the warmth of hers in the dark.

CHAPTER 9

Jarek knew if he got caught on the way back, it would earn him the dreaded "Restriction" status. Reserved for students who did something particularly dumb, restriction removed the few activities and already limited social time students could enjoy amidst their busy weekly schedules. Jarek was not interested in restriction, so as deftly as he snuck across campus to see the stars hours before he now had to sneak back.

They reached the gravel path beside the field and Beth gave his hand a squeeze before walking away toward the girls' dorms; he watched her silhouette appear for a moment in the dim light of a lamppost before disappearing again into the dark. He smiled, still surprised by the moment they had shared, and charted his course through the shadows, back into Brethren's dorm, and quietly up the steps to his room.

He tiptoed up the steps in the dark and into the bathroom. The tiny bulb of a smoke detector overhead cast just enough light to show the shape of the sinks and counter before him as he quietly brushed his teeth and turned to leave.

But at the same moment Jarek turned towards the door, he saw—out of the corner of his eye—movement in the mirror. He stopped and held his breath, slowly turning his head. Beyond his own reflected form, areas of dim light appeared where only darkness had been a moment before.

He strained his eyes to see more clearly, then he gasped, his entire body stiffening with fear. Slowly fading into view before him was the image of an old man—not a wisp in the distance, but right there, staring into his face. The man had white hair, a long white beard, and wore a black hat. He looked right at Jarek and mumbled something that sounded very far away. Too scared to move, Jarek stood perfectly still as the figure spoke again and again, three syllables that grew louder each time as Jarek stood, terrified, transfixed, straining his ears and making out the words: "*...consensus... consensus...consensus.*"

The image faded away just as quickly as it had appeared, and he was left frozen in place, wondering if his eyes, his mind, or his classmates were playing tricks on him. His heart beat hard in his chest. He wanted to run out of the room and tell his roommates what he saw. He wondered what they would think—probably that he was nuts. He was seeing things. That's all it was. He took a deep breath, turned, and walked out.

As he climbed into bed, Jarek could hear his roommates' slow breathing. He forgot entirely about the field for a moment, staring wide-eyed at the ceiling. That day, in history class, they talked about the many people who built and lived in these same buildings back to the 1780s. He had imagined their serious faces, wondering what they were thinking as they stared at the photographer for the photos he had seen at the museum. Theirs looked like a lifeless world: black and white photographs, black and white clothes, black and white buildings, black and white lives. Did they ever smile? Experience joy? Living the way they did; men and women always separate, celibate, not having a real family—parents like his or a brother like Andrew. Never being able to visit with a girl you like. Did any of them regret it? Was the work too much? Were they happy? They didn't look it. They looked bloodless and miserable.

He faded off to sleep, thinking of their faces and—above all, despite his best efforts to forget it—the one he imagined in the mirror.

But moments later, Jarek was awake again.

His eyes were still closed, but something was different. He swore he heard singing in the distance, many voices together growing louder, each note followed by the unmistakable slide of a sharp blade repeatedly cutting down into rocky soil. His body was heavy. He knew this feeling; he was dreaming. He heard the sound of a whip, followed by the sound of a horse-drawn wagon: the creaking of the frame seat, the heavy breath of the horse, and the sustained crunch of the hard wheels moving along gravel.

He opened his eyes.

Jarek was outside, sitting on a stone wall he didn't remember. Before him was the open expanse he knew as the athletic field, but it looked very different. The well-kept grass, white lines, and soccer nets were gone, and in their place was an immense and neatly tended garden, row upon row, section after section—impeccably tidy—each one brimming with vegetable greenery of all shapes and sizes stretching into the distance. A group of neatly-dressed men in collared white shirts and broad-brimmed hats worked the field in every direction. Jarek watched as they carefully scratched the soft earth with their tools, pulling giant vegetables out of the ground and placing them into a wheelbarrow brimming with produce, the greenery sticking up and out in all directions. He breathed in deeply and smelled the tilled earth. To his right, he saw the wagon he had heard; a horse leaned into its yoke, pulling the heavy load along the gravel path towards the Tannery.

Jarek turned his head, and his eyes widened as he saw his classroom buildings, now impeccably maintained and spotlessly clean, surrounded by at least a dozen other structures he had never seen before. The activity of individuals in and around them made it clear that these were not classroom buildings—at least not yet. And this was not campus. Not yet. But he knew where he was. His dream had brought him to the Village, the Shaker Village, and the people around him certainly weren't students but were the Shakers themselves. Before him and around him, speaking and laughing and working. Very unlike the black and white versions he had seen in photographs, they were alive and in full color.

He turned to look again at the field just in time to see a woman walking past with an aggravated sense of purpose. She turned towards him and stopped dead in her tracks, studying him momentarily as the surprise in her eyes turned to anger. She pointed a finger at him and exclaimed: "You!"

"HUH!" JAREK STARTLED HIMSELF AWAKE FROM HIS DREAM AND QUICKLY looked around to see his room and the sun coming up through the curtains hanging from improvised dowels cut for the purpose. Shadows of the tall fir trees outside swayed back and forth on the thin cloth.

"What the heck..." he whispered, irritated and confused as he rubbed his burning red eyes. He had slept terribly.

His roommates were still sound asleep as he sat up and looked around the room. Settlement cracks marked the plain white plaster walls. His room was a triple: Jarek and two others. One was a kid from New Orleans with feathered hair, a classic rock obsession, and a pair of aviator sunglasses that were rarely off his face. The other was Taki—short for Takahiro—a friendly and respectful Japanese kid with unlimited funds. His latest purchase was a talking alarm clock. As Taki was a very deep sleeper, the enthusiastic voice became monotonously painful pretty fast: "Good morning! The time is 6:30 AM. Good morning! The time is 6:35 AM. Good morning! The time is 6:40 AM." Jarek's internal clock had begun to have mercy on him by waking him up about five minutes before this routine of banter, snooze, banter began.

It was past time for Jarek to step out from under his warm comforter onto the cold floor so, begrudgingly, he got up.

CHAPTER 10

"Hey, there!" Jarek quickly turned around at the greeting.

"Oh, hi, Em," he said.

He was hoping to see Beth that morning, continually looking around to see if she was nearby. She hadn't been at breakfast, and he felt a sudden dread at the thought that maybe she didn't want to see him.

"*Oh. Hi.*" Em mocked his deadpan tone, "Don't sound so excited."

She was wearing a faded jean jacket over a yellow cotton shirt with a tiny flower pattern, her slightly fuzzy blonde hair pulled back into a little wet bun, as usual.

"Hoping for someone else?" she smiled.

Jarek ignored her question. "Why is your hair always wet?"

"Because it's impossible for me to wake up on time," she said. "I take a shower to wake up but I'm not a morning person. I never have time to dry it before breakfast."

"Oh," Jarek said.

He looked at her brown hiking boots, top holes unlaced wide enough to catch the pantlegs of her faded jeans. Em had bright blue eyes and shoulder-length sandy blonde hair which framed a perfectly symmetric face, the expressiveness of which did justice to her persistently empathetic nature. While Jarek had been on campus for about five weeks, this was her third year. After Morak had let him fall to the ground, she asked him a couple of times in the ensuing days how he was doing. They chatted a bit each time and, before long, became good friends. She had a distinct and relaxed stride that was her way of telling others that not much in life was too worth worrying about.

Jarek smiled at her as they walked beside each other past the granite hitching posts towards the tall and imposing brick building where most classes were held. Other students approached the rear of the building along the gravel path from the dining hall. He held the front door open for her, and she gave a sarcastically deep nod, "Thank you, sir," and smiled as he rolled his eyes.

"Hey," Jarek said. "What's your first class?"

"You're *in* my first class. Algebra, duh."

"Right. Algebra. 8 a.m.," Jarek stammered. "Gosh, I'm tired. I thought I was going to…"

"Hurry up," she said with a smile, walking through the door, nodding him in her direction, and leading the way to the third-story classroom which—thankfully for how little sleep he'd managed—had morning sunlight streaming through the windows and onto the desks as they settled in and opened their books.

A few minutes into class, Jarek found himself absent-mindedly gazing at the sun on the swaying green branches of the tall fir tree just outside the window. He looked at Em briefly, her eyes fixed on the teacher, chin up as always, endeavoring not to miss a single word. Her sincerity stood in stark contrast to his sarcastic cynicism. His eyes went down to her plain and heavily used backpack, which lay partially opened. He had asked her why she always lugged that heavy bag around with six or seven books in it. "So I can use free moments to do the reading, duh," she said. He now noticed they all had a "used" label on them.

As the teacher began writing the first equation on the dry-erase board, Jarek remembered Em saying she wasn't a morning person, yet she was consistently the most cheerful person in the dining hall at breakfast. It occurred to him that she had found her place among the many other types of kids within the student body while remaining uniquely herself, and that she probably had some real strength of personality when she needed it.

". . . because *that*, ladies and gentlemen, is how we evaluate expressions with two variables."

Algebra was not Jarek's strong suit, especially on little sleep, but this particular morning, he was in such a fog that he sat in class wondering if he was awake or dreaming and trying to figure out what things helped him know the difference.

He gazed towards the window.

"...the associative rule of addition. And *next*, ladies and gentlemen..."

The drone of the teacher's voice faded into the background as his mind left the room entirely.

"Ladies and gentlemen..."

". . . Ladies and gentlemen. LADIES AND GENTLEMEN, we bring you the Dorrell Brothers' Family Circus, greater than the greatest show on earth!" Andrew was standing on the cushion of the armchair in the living room, his voice echoing through a cardboard tube his mother had given them after using the last of the paper towels.

Saturday morning was always the highlight of the week. It was the one day they were allowed to watch TV, other than special occasions—like *Rudolf the Red-Nosed Reindeer* or *A Charlie Brown Christmas* at the holidays—when they would sit excitedly on the couch on either side of their mother as a graphic "SPECIAL" would spin across the screen, knowing children all over America were squirming into place all at that exact moment in anticipation of their one opportunity to see a broadcast they looked forward to each holiday season.

Saturday meant no shoveling breakfast in and no being wrestled into coats and backpacks with difficult zippers as the words "miss the bus" were repeated amidst the chaos. It meant "family breakfast" of pancakes and bacon, cartoons in their pajamas, and their dad peeking over the paper to provide a stern "No," "Not too rough," or "Is that a good idea?" when the situation required.

One Saturday, their dad took them to Madison Square Garden for the Ringling Brothers, Barnum & Bailey Circus, "The Greatest Show on Earth." The car descended into the Lincoln Tunnel after they paid the $2.25 toll, and the boys whispered to each other as the dirty white tiles passed quickly beside the window. They imagined a crazy person with a crowbar standing on the side of the road surface, staring aggressively at the stopped vehicles and the imploring faces of their passengers as he whacked away at the tiles, which chipped and shattered, as water began spraying through until the entire tunnel flooded and everybody drowned.

Before walking into the circus, the boys noticed on the concourse the fiber optic handles with a white switch, circus logo, and ten-inch plastic strands that waved back and forth off the end when you twirled them. "Just $6! Available in blue or red," the sign said.

"Here you go," their dad said cheerfully, handing one to each of them. As their eyes widened in surprise, they whispered to each other, "Twelve dollars!"

No matter the moment of the performance—clown car, grizzly bears, lions delicately placing their open mouths around the head of their 90-pound female trainer, or motorcycles spinning in a circular cage—anyone who looked to section 416, seats 44 and 46, would have seen a constant whir of increasingly dim circular blue light as Jarek and Andrew, in their excitement, spun and spun and spun their lights, entirely certain that (as far as anyone else in the audience was concerned) they were part of the show.

Every moment of the ensuing days was spent planning their circus performance or discussing how they were going to pack the toys they needed and get the bus into the city to offer their services to the man with the big mustache in the long red and blue sequined coat who was clearly the boss of the operation. They would parade around the living room—Andrew barefoot in fire truck pajamas and Jarek in his Incredible Hulk onesie with vinyl feet—raising their knees high to replicate the pomp of the performers' entrance as Andrew jumped up on the armchair to announce the next part of the show.

"Man-eating elephants from the jungles of India!" he would shout as Jarek looked up with admiration, smiling gleefully and eager to perform. Andrew would jump down and lead the way, bending his head over and walking in slow circles on the carpet with one arm hung down—his elephant trunk—bellowing loudly *womp, womp, womp, womp* as Jarek followed directly behind in imitation, his still undeveloped, four-year-old speech making the words *momp, momp, momp, momp*.

Jarek would laugh and follow his big brother until Andrew turned around and held his hands up like claws, shouting, "Greater than the greatest show on earth! Tickle tiger!" and poking his fingers into Jarek's ribs. Seconds later, they would laugh hysterically, both grappling for advantage as their dad called them to the table and their mom, as they took their seats, reminded them that it was time to say grace.

"Mr. Dorrell. Jarek? Jarek!" his teacher's voice brought him back, and he guessed from the annoyed look in her eye that she had been saying his name for some time.

"Um, what?" Jarek muttered, "Sorry..."

CHAPTER 11

"Hey, night owl," Beth whispered as she approached Jarek from behind.

He had relived every moment from the night before: Beth, lying beside him in the dark, their jousting banter and comfortable silences keeping his undivided attention for hours. The stars overhead and the smell of her hair as they lay close were all he could think about. But as the day passed without sign of her, he grew more discouraged. Now, walking to the science building for the day's last class, he heard her voice and showed much more enthusiasm than he would have liked.

"Oh, hey." He tried to sound nonchalant to counterbalance the excited look he knew he had on his face.

"How was your night? What was left of it, I mean," she asked.

Immediately, his mind jumped to his strange dream about the Shaker Village. God, with her on his mind, he had almost forgotten. And the face in the mirror. A ghost? No. No way.

He pushed those thoughts away. Finally, here she was, and he found himself stammering in her presence and even staring at his shoes as she made small talk about her day.

The first time Jarek ever kissed a girl was behind the youth group building at his church late on a cold fall night. They looked up at the sky as he grabbed her hand and pulled her close, both absorbed in what seemed like a moment of life-changing significance as he brought her lips to his, initiating what may have been the clumsiest kiss in the history of clumsy first kisses.. Eventually they headed back inside to their friends, glad of knowing they had crossed a threshold together, even if, deep down, they were unbearably embarrassed in front of themselves and each other.

The feeling Jarek had at this moment was almost as awkward.

"Um… it was good, I guess," Jarek said.

"You guess? Good sleep? Bad sleep? Too-short sleep?" she smiled.

Could he tell her about the ghost and the dream? Of course not. It was just more evidence that moving here had finally been too much. What he saw in the mirror was a figment of his imagination. That's why he had the dream. And that was that.

"Good sleep, just fine," he was back on track. "And a good day, too. How was yours?"

"My dad has some finance co-worker who is on the Board at a college he wants me to go to—he's really into it, I don't know—so he 'put in a good word,'" she said, making air quotes with her fingers, "and as a result of that good word I had to spend hours on the phone with an admissions officer and an academic advisor, and now I have to catch up on a whole day of classes."

"Ugh, I'm sorry," he tried to sound interested, but the only thing he could think about as he watched her lips move and heard her confident and easy-going tones was the very satisfying fact that he had kissed those very same lips just last night. Then he looked at his watch.

"Yikes, I'm late for class, I have to go!" The last thing he wanted to do was go to class at the moment, but he could feel himself growing uneasy trying to carry on a normal conversation with her in broad daylight—not arguing in class or alone together in the field. So he walked off waving goodbye as she stood still, a bit perplexed at his brevity before turning away.

"Well, look who it is!"

Jarek had the pleasure of not seeing Morak for several days, but here he was, looking right at him and standing right in the middle of the small hallway that led to the business office, where Jarek was headed to collect the $20 of weekend spending money his parents could budget for him, in addition to the wild tuition they were somehow paying. He was pretty sure they had taken out a loan against their house, but they didn't tell him because they didn't want him to feel guilty. They said, "Just do your best in your studies." God, how disappointed they were going to be.

Jarek ignored Morak and started past him.

"What? Where are you going?" Morak added.

"This way," Jarek said.

Morak blocked his path. Jarek tried to push through as Morak leaned against him.

"Move, you prick," Jarek said under his breath, pushing forward as they planted their feet against each other. It was the invitation Morak had been hoping for.

"What?" Morak pushed Jarek against the wall with one hand. "What did you say? Hey, nice ascot or whatever this is," he said as he grabbed the black cloth knotted around Jarek's neck, "It's Edgar Allen Poe!" Morak's friend Billy—usually nearby and always troublesome—looked on snickering.

Jarek pushed Morak's hand off, trying again to get by and bring the confrontation to an end, but Morak wouldn't have it. He put his hand on Jarek's left shoulder and shoved him to the wall. "What? What, Edgar?" he repeated.

He stared into Jarek's face and, getting no response, brought one hand down with a smack onto the large stack of books under Jarek's arm, sending them tumbling to the floor in a series of thumps. Papers slid out of their folders and spread across the carpet. Several students were watching from down the hall.

Anger rose within Jarek like he hadn't felt in a long time. His heart beat faster, and his hands started to shake. He knew this feeling, and it never led to anything good. He imagined himself sinking his fist into Morak's face. *No, no, not now, not now*, he said to himself.

He remembered one of the times his dad picked him up from his old school after he lost his temper, leaving a classmate with a bloody lip. He could hear his voice: "A proportional response, Jarek. Things come up, but you have to have a proportional response."

Jarek took a deep breath, eager to control himself, choking his bottled-up rage as he leaned down to push his books and papers together in a pile. The only thing holding him back was the idea of screwing this whole thing up. He couldn't have his parents get a phone call about a fight. No way.

Morak walked away, laughing. Em appeared at Jarek's elbow and bent down to help him pick up his things. "David!" She called out, reprimanding Morak as he walked away. She then turned to Jarek. "God, I'm sorry," she said with sincerity.

"Seriously, what the hell is with that guy?" Jarek snapped.

Em looked around to see that the other students had walked away. "Well...," she began. "It's complicated."

"I think, deep down, David is afraid of things he doesn't understand. Like your boots, your hair, whatever."

"Yeah, whatever," Jarek said.

"It's not just that though. Your parents dropped you off, both of them. They got out and gave you the biggest hugs and said nice things. They seem so awesome, your parents."

"Thanks. Yeah, they are."

"He could tell. We all could. You guys had a long goodbye when they dropped you off. You know how David got here? He took a bus. So...umm, that's why he hates you. You all love each other—his family isn't like that, and he hates you for it. His dad is a jerk—the kind of person who crushes the spirit of those close to him. That's exactly what he did to Dave and his mother, but Dave still worships him. His mom gave up on being happy with him and then gave up in general a long time ago. Their divorce was just finalized. It was a whole big thing."

Jarek listened, somewhat sympathetically, despite himself. He actually felt bad for the guy.

"And here's the other thing," she added.

"That wasn't enough?" Jarek asked.

"Well…when Beth got here last year, David really liked her. They were friends a bit, but not for long—they didn't have much to talk about. When it was obvious that he liked her, she started talking to him less. She's too nice to say it to him or anyone else, but she thinks he's an idiot."

Jarek's delighted smirk gave him away, and Em gave him a look.

"Ok," Jarek said. "What does this have to do with me?"

She laughed. "You're such a guy. Your cluelessness is cute."

Em knew nothing of Jarek and Beth's time in the field.

"You mean the way she picks fights with me in English class? Super charming, sure," he said.

"Morak hates you because he's in love with Beth, dummy," Em said. "And as anyone around here can see from a mile away; she's totally into you. You're lucky—she's amazing."

He could feel his face about to break into a ridiculous grin and was afraid he would ask her to say it again, so he quickly changed the subject.

"You know, I didn't like you much at first. Before I knew you, I mean." Jarek said. "You were sitting next to him when he threw that brownie at me in the cafeteria, and you just sat there, so I figured… guilt by association. But after icebreakers, when you checked on me at lunch, later in the day, and then at dinner, I knew I wasn't being fair. So really, if he wasn't a prick, we wouldn't have become friends. Or at least not so soon. So I owe him that, I guess."

Em' took a deep breath and gave him a heartfelt smile, but there was more.

"David actually grew up one town over from me. Our moms are close. Anyway, you know how it is here: 130 people. You can like someone, love them, or hate them, but you can't *not* know them. But the thing is, when he first showed up, he was different. The same curly hair sticking out under his hat, and he'd always been pretty loud, but he was different."

"Clumsy like a clown but without the fun?" Jarek quipped.

"Well, he was a lot happier then, and glad to be here. He knows he's not particularly smart or insightful, so he made up for it with loud jokes and occasionally pitching in when anything required heavy lifting. He was always a loudmouth, but he was fun and funny."

"So, what happened?" Jarek asked.

"The summer after freshman year, word got around that he had gotten into trouble of some sort. His parents didn't get along. It was his mom's idea to send him away to school, mostly to get him away from his dad's mean temperament. Whenever he wanted David to get his cigarettes, he'd shout 'Lucky Strike'—the brand of cigarettes he smoked—and before long, that became his nickname for David. It was his way of telling him he resented him, like he had a lucky strike for living there and being supported by his parents."

"Nice guy, just like his son," Jarek quipped.

Em continued, "Anyway, once they split, his mom started dating a philosophy professor from the community college named Will. He was sort of a bookworm in a blazer type, the polar opposite of Dave's dad, but a good person and kind to her, which she wasn't used to. He tried being nice to David, bringing him gifts, game tickets, things like that—but David hated him. So when his mom asked if he would watch Will's dog while the two of them went away for a long weekend, he had an idea."

Jarek raised his eyebrows, afraid of what was coming.

"Yeah," Em said, "it's bad. The dog had epilepsy and would have seizures if he didn't get his medicine. David was supposed to take the dog out in the morning and evening, change its water, and give it food with the medicine mixed in. That was the deal. Well, they were gone for four days. Dave didn't go."

"Not at all?" Jarek asked.

"Not even once. The dog died there along on the kitchen floor. Will absolutely loved that dog. He loved Dave's mom, too. But the animosity from her ex and now her son had just gone to another level, and he was understandably freaked out. So he called it quits. Dave didn't feel any remorse for the dog—he was already so messed up—and neither did his dad. When he told his dad they'd chased Will away, his dad gave him a beer to celebrate. Such a creep. His mom got pretty depressed. Still is. She lives alone in a beat-up old apartment. His mom told my mom that his last advisor evaluation talked about him going downhill. 'Wasted potential,' it said. Now he's just angry at the world and acting out."

Jarek was taken aback by what he was hearing. "Wasted potential." "Angry at the world and everyone in it." He hated to admit it, but he and Morak seemed to have a lot in common.

CHAPTER 12

With a lousy night's sleep and another long day weighing on his eyelids, Jarek got in bed and passed right out. Moments later, he felt a breeze against his cheek.

He kept his eyes closed for a moment to listen. Wagon wheels crunching along the gravel road, a whip's small snap, and a horse's heavy breath at work. A light breeze across the field carried the smell of dark soil, fresh-cut vegetables, and the iron-heavy water that rolled down from the mountain's mineral-rich heart to fortify both. The lilting tones of voices in the near distance were unfamiliar, as were the words themselves.

"Thank ye, Brother," in one man's voice.

"Hello, Sister Mary," in a woman's.

Jarek opened his eyes to a squint in the sunlight. He was on the same stone wall he had been before, and as he looked around, he found that his ears and nose had not deceived him. Men in white dress shirts worked a group of garden rows in the distance; the larger among them extracting the beets below with brute force, while the smaller demonstrated that proper spade strategy could yield the same results with little grunting and less sweat.

Two Shaker men carried sacks of grain and buckets of fresh water towards a trough at the edge of the field to refresh the horses of town folk reviewing the crops. They were customers, and their presence and satisfaction were critical to the Village's survival. The mechanical groan of the mill made it clear that the Tannery was fully engaged. From everything Jarek saw around, the place ran like a well-oiled machine.

The chime of a familiar bell sounded across the Village, and all work suddenly stopped.

"Whaddya know," Jarek said to himself, surprised that—from the sound of it—it was the same bell he heard regularly at school.

Workers in the field rolled up their sleeves and wiped their brows, heaving billowing stalks into waiting wagons. Visitors concluded nearby discussions and began to depart, as brothers and sisters streamed from nearby structures towards the heart of the Village as the bell rang.

A final gentleman reviewed the long-tilled rows as he came in more slowly than the rest; Jarek figured he was in charge of the group. He had a long grey beard and wore a black hat with a wide round brim that stuck straight out unceremoniously, perfectly encircling his grey head. Jarek realized he'd been staring, that the old man had been staring back, and that he was now coming towards him.

"Get moving," he said, matter-of-factly.

He then grabbed Jarek by the collar and pulled him along beside him.

Jarek had no choice but to follow along, so as the man let go of his collar, he continued in the same direction. He looked down at his clothes to find he was wearing the same long straight slacks, white button-down shirt, and three-button wool vest as the rest of the men—all as dirty as if he had worked the field himself—as he followed them into the ground-level washroom of a nearby building and got cleaned up.

Lost and with no idea what he had gotten into, he did his best to mimic the activity around him. When others grabbed clothes off pegs in an adjacent room, he put on the only set that looked like it might fit him. It was tight, and he knew he looked ridiculous—the sleeves were halfway up his arms—but he squirmed into them and followed the others up the main road and into what Jarek knew as the library.

At school, in his own time, this space had rows and rows of books, computers, display cases, and stairs to an entire upstairs cubicle work area. Now, it was empty, and the vastness of the space struck him. The large windows allowed light to stream through, now unobstructed, as Jarek looked towards the wide arch of the ceiling high overhead.

Several men peeled off for other conversations upon entering the building, and Jarek followed the remainder of the group, quietly moving towards the opposite wall and standing still, unsure of his purpose.

He then saw a thin woman walking deliberately toward him. Jarek recognized her as the woman who snapped "You!" at him in his first dream just before he woke up. She wore the same long, dark dress as the other women in the room, fitted on the top with long sleeves and flaring out at the pleated bottom, but otherwise totally unornamented. A simple, triangular shawl hung around her shoulders with the point facing down in the middle of her chest, and on her head was a small and straightforward white bonnet, with the untied strings hanging next to her ears. Unlike the other women, she wore gloves. She had a plain but expressive face, with circles under her eyes suggesting she was no stranger to responsibility. Her small stature was perfectly counterbalanced by her determined stride as she walked up to him, clasped her hands in front of herself, leaned her face toward Jarek's and asked emphatically, "Who are you?"

Since she was only the second person who spoke to him, and things didn't go so well with the gentleman who pulled him from the field—he kept quiet. After a moment, she moved in and grabbed his arm, led him away from the group and leaned in closer, Jarek presumed, to give him a piece of her mind.

He wanted to run but didn't know where he'd go once he was outside. After a final look towards the door, he braced himself as she looked him right in the eye and said quietly but with firm resolve: "It would serve you best to stay right here." He got a feeling she meant it.

She gestured towards a row of benches against the wall and kept one eye on him as she walked away. He took a seat, becoming more uncomfortable with each uncertain moment.

Jarek now understood why he had seen a collection of carriages outside as he watched a swarm of visitors enter through a separate door. The gathering seemed to be a social opportunity for some, and the extravagant dresses worn by many women stood in stark contrast to the humble attire of community members. The former focused on the opportunity to be seen, while the latter looked like a somber procession of Puritan nuns who had lost their way. The women were accompanied by their gentleman-farmer husbands, all of whom were engaged in an intense discussion about grain prices. They were uniformly attired in polished shoes, neatly trimmed beards, and identical chains across their vests towards small pockets where their timepieces were stowed.

Jarek turned his attention to the far opposite end of the building where there were three doors, with men continuing to enter through the far left and women the far right. All were cleaned up for the gathering, and Jarek noticed with interest that the middle door was seldom utilized. Occasionally, it would open, and someone would enter, usually alone. Those on either side of these individuals would give a curtsy or a nod as they passed by. Jarek realized the men and women who used the middle door were of particular esteem within the Village. One of them regularly received the most eager and reverential greetings, "Hello, Brother Thaddeus," they said, one after another, as he entered. He greeted each one with kind words and a friendly smile.

Jarek was sitting on the back-most bench in a row of three, with three others similarly positioned to his left and his right, forming a seating area of nine benches for those few members of the Village who were unable to participate. To his right were three older men sitting quietly; to his left, two older women whispered as they looked around the room. In the row in front of them, there sat a boy, partially turned away from Jarek. He looked about 11 and had his light-brown hair tidily combed to the side. When the boy turned his face forward towards the center of the room, Jarek's eyes widened in surprise and he froze. The boy was, without a doubt, the spitting image of his brother Andrew. Back when he was younger. Before he got bigger. Before he got sick. Before he was gone.

The woman who had just scolded Jarek walked up to the boy, leaned over with the same determined glare, pointed her finger in his face, and spoke a few sharp words as he stared at the floor. His hair was wet. He had cleaned up when everyone else did—but his clothes were filthy.

"Oh, no," Jarek whispered aloud. He looked down at the visible socks under his far-too-short pantlegs and was overcome with guilt as it dawned on him. The boy sat alone staring dejectedly at the floor as the others milled about with energy, in trouble because he was the only person in the entire room who was not neatly dressed for the gathering like the others.

Because Jarek had taken his clothes.

After a moment, an elder stepped in front of the gathering of several dozen guests and made a brief announcement. Jarek watched as several dozen villagers lined up in the middle of the room, divided equally between men and women. They faced each other in parallel lines, ready to begin.

Silent anticipation built within the room as one of the women held her hands outwards from her hips, palms up, and all in the room fell silent. Her timid but angelic voice filled the space above and around them to the attentive stares of her fellow villagers.

(Song: "In Yonder Valley")

In yonder valley, there flows sweet union;
Let us arise and drink our fill.

The winter's passed, and the spring appears;
The turtle dove is in our land.
In yonder valley, there flows sweet union;
Let us arise and drink our fill.

The women joined her in repeating the verse, and the men joined shortly after. Jarek jumped as the group punctuated the verses with a stomp, then drifted in lines towards each other and apart, towards and apart again, arms bent with hands upturned to the ceiling. They paced faster, shaking their palms to the floor as if they were casting water off newly washed hands. The energy was electric. More songs followed, and they shuffled, danced, and chanted until all the villagers moved together in lines, in circles, in numerous forms across the floor, huffing, sweating, and smiling at the joyous and enthusiastic spectacle they were creating for themselves and their guests.

Jarek sat with his mouth open, staring at the dancers' wide eyes and sweating faces and those of the onlookers, transfixed by a ritual like nothing they had seen before. The final notes rang through the air, punctuated by the last emphatic claps and stomps that shook the floor and windows.

After several seconds of silence, the entire assembly clapped twice in unison and began anew.

(Song: "Joyful Praises")

God has brought (CLAP) the restoration (CLAP)
We are fixed (STOMP) in the rock (STOMP)
Strength and glory (CLAP) of the nation (CLAP)
Praise and sing (CLAP) ye little flock (STOMP)

When the song was over, all those who had danced stood upright—gasping for breath from their exertion—as men and women moved apart, adjusting vests and dresses, wiping brows, and nodding at each other in understanding that the invigorating display had satisfied their need to exercise both their spirits and their bodies. They were eager to get into the cool evening air, so—just as quickly as they assembled at the beginning—they proceeded to the exit.

The young man whose clothes Jarek had stolen hung back, unsure if he should get up or await instruction after the finger-wagging he had received earlier. Jarek kept pace with him as he had no idea where to go. Still not certain where he was—or why—Jarek decided to say hello and see what would happen.

He walked beside him amidst the crowd of fatigued worshippers slowly working towards the door.

"Hey," Jarek said.

The boy was surprised. "Beg your pardon?"

His dirty clothes looked almost identical to the clean set Jarek had taken: dark wool slacks, a button-down shirt, and simple leather shoes caked in mud. As he walked, the boy's bowed head bobbed lightly, deferential to everything and everyone around him.

"Hello. I'm Jarek."

"Pleasure to meet you, Jarek." the boy said timidly, and nothing more. He looked at Jarek politely, though skeptically—an understandable response, Jarek realized. None of these people had ever seen him here before and, as far as this young boy was concerned, Jarek just got him in trouble.

Jarek walked beside the boy and couldn't stop looking at his face. His resemblance to Andrew made him feel even more guilty. The boy looked ahead at the woman who had scolded him, clearly discouraged. Jarek could feel his distress and wished he could help somehow. "It's okay," he said quietly, "don't worry. I'm…I'm sorry about the clothes. I'll explain it wasn't your fault." The boy nodded his head, perking up a bit. Jarek was glad.

The young man lifted his chin and now gave a grateful smile to anyone who offered a courteous "Hello, Brother Lucas" as they passed, responding to each with a "Thank you, sir" or "Thank you, ma'am." He was young, withdrawn, and his interactions seemed to take effort. But he wasn't lacking in that effort, and this large family seemed to admire him for it. After each smile and hello, his hazel eyes, beneath his youthful tufts of hair, would resume their distant stare.

Jarek knew nothing of the wave of people he was surrounded by or of this boy. But as he was no stranger to the effects of heartache and loss himself, Jarek could easily see the outward signs of a struggle within the boy. He had no idea what brought Lucas to the Village, but he clearly carried the burden—despite his youth—of a life lesson or two. Jarek could tell those lessons were learned the hard way.

What Jarek couldn't tell was that the path before Lucas would get much harder still, that they would travel that path together, and that it would change both of their lives forever.

CHAPTER 13

Jarek cringed as Lynyrd Skynyrd came blaring from his roommate's radio, jerking him back to reality and letting him know that he had overslept.

He kept his eyes closed for a moment and thought about his dream. Most times, when he dreamed, he was little more than an outside observer of events he had no control over, jumping from one moment to another and leaving out the moments in between. Dreams were sort of an abstract highlight reel in which his legs couldn't move, he was unable to speak, or else he was surrounded by people from unconnected chapters of his life. Other times, they were a senseless garble from his subconscious. He once dreamt that Joseph Conrad was cutting the turkey at his family's Thanksgiving dinner, reciting creepy quotes from *Heart of Darkness* as his aunts and uncles looked on. "We live as we dream—alone. While the dream disappears, the life continues painfully," Conrad had announced with a flourish as he presented the carved meat to the table and everyone applauded.

But these dreams were different. Jarek knew where he was and had control of his actions. Time seemed as linear and well-ordered as it was during his waking hours. They were so vividly real that it freaked him out.

He sat up in bed as his roommate threw on his boots, flannel, and aviators before brushing his feathered hair and shouting "You're gonna be late, man," as he hurried out.

Jarek looked around the room: the wood floor, the cracked walls, the sloppily painted windowpanes that looked towards the trees and buildings beyond. Some things were profoundly different from what he had just seen in his dreams; some were the same.

The colors, the smells, and the sensory texture of everything he had just experienced were striking. While before he had only seen these villagers in photos, he had now seen them in real life; their faded clothes now colorful and put in motion by the bodies, thoughts, and day-to-day activities of those who wore them. The contrast was stunning: the women's coats a brilliant royal blue, their caps not age-stained ivory but a proud and perfectly bright white. These were not black and white mannequins struggling unsmilingly from a bloodless past; they were living, breathing men and women in a world not so very unlike ours. They may have resigned themselves to their lifestyle's limited clothing options, but they kept them neat and clean and wore them with pride.

Jarek smiled sympathetically at how suddenly real, vulnerable, and human they had become. "Just like the rest of us," he said aloud.

But it then occurred to him that—despite all their humanity, or because of it—they had all been gone for a very long time. Death had assigned to each and every one of them the hour and minute it would arrive to claim them, and that's precisely what it did.

Jarek's smile faded at the thought as he repeated quietly, "Just like the rest of us."

CHAPTER 14

"Really? You were watching me in the Tannery? Creepy." Beth smiled.

They were in the library sitting in side-by-side cubicles where they had arranged to study together, though neither had looked at their books for more than a moment or two since they sat down. Opportunities to talk alone were so few and far between. They could catch up on their studies later.

"Well, I mean, I walked in because I heard music, then I stopped and stood in the doorway for a minute, and then I left. It's not like I was peering in through a crack in the walls."

"I'm messing with you," she said. "How long did you stand there?"

"I don't know. Just a couple seconds," he shrugged.

"Or…" she teased, looking him in the eye.

"Or, I don't know, a minute."

"Really?"

"Yeah, or a few. Okay, maybe a bunch of minutes. A small bunch, though, not a big bunch," he smiled.

He was embarrassed but could tell she liked knowing how much he enjoyed watching her play. "I watched until you folded your music. I would have stayed longer if you didn't."

"You know, if I saw you there, I would have been totally creeped out."

"I know. And thanks." Jarek laughed.

"No, no, but I actually think it's charming." She put her hand on his shoulder, leaning her head against the edge of the white-painted wood that served as a divider between their cubicles.

"So, I have to say, *this* I still don't understand," she said, taking the end of the black cloth tied around his neck between her two fingers and feeling the soft texture. "What is this, like an…ascot?"

"Well," he said, slightly defensive, "It was meant to be temporary, but then I got used to it."

"Is this like a Mozart thing? The 'Poe' thing?" she asked, referring to Morak's derisive nickname.

"No, I don't think so," he said quietly.

"They only come in black?" she gave the cloth a double tug, adding a tugboat *mert, mert* for effect.

"Ha," he smiled. "No, they don't only come in black; I only have one. I'll tell you about it sometime."

"Well, it sure goes with your dress coat, but maybe not these big, what are they, combat boots?" she smiled.

"Hey…" He pretended to take offense.

"No, I like it all together. It makes you look like punk gentility or something."

"Thanks, I think." he said.

"I'm still trying to get you. You know more about classical music than I do—bordering on obsession—and I've been playing since I was eight. You listen to all this other noise, which instantly gives me a headache." He had been skimming a pile of books while they spoke; she gestured towards the stack. "You read this obscure stuff here but barely do your homework." She lifted her hands to emphasize her point. "I think you're the smartest space cadet I've ever met."

"It's not noise. It's ground-breaking stuff—it changed music forever. But hey, I can't blame you for having bad taste. I blame your parents."

"Hey," she said. All expression left her face, and he realized he had made a mistake but wasn't sure what.

"Gosh, what would they think of you?" she said, fiddling with the leather strap bracelet on his wrist.

The thought had never crossed his mind, and now that it had, it made him nervous.

"Geez, thanks for making me squirm," he said.

"What? No, they'd like you. They'd just have to get to know you."

"That's helpful as well, thanks."

"No, my dad is just…kind of old fashioned. He would ask me if you get all A's, first question. Headmaster Worthing loves him because they're cut from the same cloth. That, and my dad gives a lot of money. My dad thought roommates would be bad for my grades, so Worthing gave me a single. Just like that." Beth played with her pen and avoided meeting his eyes.

"Okay, maybe I'll make sure I'm not here on parents' weekend. What about your mom?" Jarek asked.

"It's not as bad as it sounds. He's okay, just not so good at affection. My mom, well, she pretty much follows his lead, always, in everything. It's sad."

"What does she do?" he asked.

Beth looked up. "About what?"

"About work?"

"Oh, well, she's always wanted to open a shop, and I think she'd be good at it. She's really smart." Beth said.

Jarek knew there was more. "But…"

"But my dad isn't into it." she gave a discouraged shrug. "He works too much and doesn't know who'd keep everything else together if she did."

"What kind of shop?"

"I don't know, antiques or decorative things with a cool history. Something like that. She thought about just doing it and springing it on him once it was set up, but of course, that wouldn't work. He controls the money and wouldn't give her what she needed to start. He's much more into the house being in order, and they like to entertain, so he thinks she doesn't have the time. And then he'd be up to his own devices a lot more, as in having to take care of himself when she can't get away from work, which he doesn't want. He's in finance, long hours. My grandparents were super broke when he was little. That's why he's always pushing and pushing me about school." Beth looked tired at the recollection.

"Wow. I wouldn't have guessed any of this." Jarek said. "You don't sound like either of them…or even a combination of them." As soon as he uttered these words, and for no apparent reason, his mind took him away from the pleasure of her company and quickly went down a rabbit hole of quickening panic: he liked her too much, they were too different, this couldn't end well. A familiar feeling rose within his chest—pain, loss, grief—and he wanted to hold her tight to delay the inevitable. He tried to cover it up, but it didn't work.

"So your parents are a neurotic banker and traditional housewife, and here you are with the punk kid with combat boots. Oh wait, I know this story: 'Debutante banker's daughter hangs out with bad boy for fun then comes to her senses'?"

"Hey…" she said flatly, quickly seeing through his pretense of making a joke.

"No, really. Happy to entertain you," Jarek said, doubling down. "Thanks for the heads up."

His sarcasm—and his questioning of her sincerity—hit a nerve.

"I'm NOT my parents, Jarek!" she snapped, and he immediately regretted making her feel like she had to say it.

"Hey, whoa…" he put his hand on her arm, "Beth, gosh, I'm sorry. I didn't mean anything by it."

"Right. Sure you didn't." She looked at her books.

"Seriously, I'm sorry," he said.

"You're not the only one under pressure, you know. My family is nothing like yours, Jarek. They don't call. We almost never talk unless my dad's asking about grades or giving me a hard time about something."

"Really?" He asked.

"Yes, really." Beth said and paused. "Here's kind of what it's like: When I was little, my dad insisted that I learn how to ride.

Jarek looked confused. "Ride?"

"Horses."

"Of course."

She gave him a look but continued.

"I happened into Dressage—this super formulaic thing where you have to get the horse to trot, walk sideways, stuff like that. I didn't want to do it. I hated it. Where I grew up, it was popular—with a certain crowd, anyway. And he was excited about it. I thought it would make him happy, so I went every day and practiced and practiced in the heat and cold and taught the big, sweet, clumsy animal they got me how not to trip over its own feet all the time. Each time I competed, I climbed in our division, full of girls my age working just as hard as me. I started at 23rd and didn't expect him to be impressed. After a few competitions, I was in 12th, then 8th, then 3rd."

"Wow, that's amazing," Jarek said.

"Well, each time I looked at him in the stands, he was sitting there watching. Silent. I just thought, 'I'm not good enough, I'm not good enough,' and knew if I worked a little harder, he'd finally tell me he was proud of me, that it had meant something. I was up against around 60 girls in the division every single time. Anyway, so the next event, I did it—I beat everyone. I was number one."

"Really?" Jarek said with raised eyebrows. "Geez—that's incredible."

"Number one. All that work for months and months. When he could get away from work, I'd see him looking from the stand and think, 'This will be it. This time, he'll stand up and cheer, and everyone will know that's my dad and he's proud of me.' But I'd see him just sitting there watching silently. Finally, I did it—no higher to climb. I thought he'd be ecstatic and counted every instant waiting for him to give the celebration I knew was coming. Hollering from afar wasn't his style, so maybe he was waiting 'til he was right in front of me. But we got to the car, and he was still so quiet. Then he grabbed his door handle, and I couldn't hold it in anymore.

"I said, 'Dad! Hello? I just won—first place! Number one. I beat everybody, didn't you see?

"And he turned his head to me, smiled, and said 'Yes. Yes, you sure did. *Now* the key is to see how long you can stay there.' He unlocked the car, got inside, and shut the door. As usual, we rode home in silence, and he never said another word about it again."

She stared into the distance. He heard her breathe heavily from the hurt brought to the surface, and her eyes filled with tears.

Jarek ran his hand along her arm. "Jesus, Beth, I'm sorry," he said.

"Well. It is what it is," she shrugged, sadly.

"Hey." He looked at her. "I know you're your own person, and—whatever your parents say or do—I think you're perfect."

"Well, that's a bit dramatic," she smiled, "but thank you."

"Is your mom more… I don't know… affectionate?" he asked.

"My mom is so used to playing second fiddle. She's like a shell of forgotten dreams. She loves me. I know she does, and I love her. But I'll never be like her. Ever." He saw her chin tilt slightly upward as she spoke, "That's why I don't let anyone mess with me."

"Like I said," he responded, leaning over to kiss her slightly parted lips. "Perfect."

CHAPTER 15

"Have you ever seen the stars, Jarek? Truly seen them?"

The seed store was a busy place with a variety of customers, both in purpose and regularity. Farmers would travel many miles to find it stocked with whatever they required based on the season, tossing ropes over their wagons for the journey home, their beds overloaded with seed sacks, fertilizer, tools, fresh produce, brooms, and occasionally a well-made garment for a wife. Creaking wheels, clapping hooves, snapping whips, and horses chuffing into their heavy load filled the dusty air in busier times. Those who lived locally would stop by more often, enjoying the camaraderie of those Brothers and Sisters with whom they had become friendly, leaning over from time to time to tell an accompanying child about the Village and its unusual inhabitants. Soon after, they would leave with jellies or some of the many pies the Village turned out every week to keep them coming back, placing them carefully beside them to ensure they were delivered to their families unspoiled.

The devout and determined woman who ran the seed store was Sister Abigail. As he was now a regular and familiar presence in the Village, Jarek had been assigned to her to assist with the bustling operation as the days grew cooler. Abigail was, in fact, the sister who had spoken to him during his first dream, calling out, "You!" as surprised by his presence as he was. She had also scolded him—a stranger in their midst—during his second dream, moments before he witnessed the first dance. She was slight of frame but had a strong upright posture—bordering on proud, despite her deep and sincere humility.

"Yes," Jarek replied, "Yes. I think I've truly seen the stars."

"Good," she replied with a nod. "When you see little bright lights, like stars, be thankful to God, for they are specks of angel's wings." She often quoted the words of their founder, Mother Ann, who lived and died over a century earlier and for whom she—like all Shakers—had great reverence.

As the weeks passed, Jarek and Abigail had the opportunity for many conversations in the slow mid-day or early evening moments and became—as far as he could tell—good friends. He took great care not to say anything that wouldn't make sense in this time long before his own, and listened eagerly to her insights about Shaker history, the Village itself, and "The Way," which the villagers called the lifestyle they had chosen. One afternoon, she explained the unusual relationship between the store and its visitors.

"Jarek, our many customers are a blessing to us. They give us the income we need, especially before the winter, but there's a reason our newer arrivals do not usually work here in the store. It is one of the areas of the Village providing interaction with those who are not of The Way. Everyone is different; their own life experiences bringing to us their own strengths, but also their vulnerabilities. One does not know when the corrupting influence of the outside world might find its way into the minds of the more impressionable."

"But *I'm* a new arrival," he said.

"Yes, you are, dear. I have taken you under my wing because I believe there is 'more to you than meets the eye,' as they say, and I'd like to keep *my* eye upon you." She smiled.

Abigail was not educated traditionally, but she didn't miss a thing. Jarek had made up a story about being an orphan, which he knew was unconvincing, but she didn't pry. He knew she would insist on more information at some point—like how he had come to them in the first place—and had no idea what he would tell her.

Still, for now, she seemed to accept his story at face value and was a great teacher and companion, making sure he didn't run afoul of the numerous Village rules and answering his many questions about "The Way" and those who followed it.

Her long dark hair was pulled back under a bonnet every day like that of so many other sisters, but Jarek noticed she wore it differently; always entirely covering both her ears. Also, unlike other sisters, she always had gloves on her hands, either a white pair or one of darker material. No matter how dirty or precise a task they were performing, she always had the gloves on.

Jarek knew there was more to Abigail than meets the eye, as well.

"So why 'Shakers?'" he asked. "And…can you tell me again about Mother Ann?"

"Jarek, Mother was our founder. The return of Christ on earth in our times. She came here in 1774 with several followers, and here we are, 100 years later, in 18 villages across eight states, villages just like this one, saving the souls of those in need and sharing the blessings of Mother with the world. Mother is the female manifestation of God's dual nature, just as Jesus was the male. If you know your scripture: Genesis 1:27, 'So God created them, male and female he created them.' And so we know that God's intent for us is one of true equality between male and female. This is what we believe, and this is what we practice. This puts us at great odds with the world of the fallen, where men have both relished in and abused a boorish state of dominance over half of God's creatures since the beginning of time."

Jarek listened attentively. He'd heard most of this in Shaker history class, but hearing it from Sister Abigal made it feel less like a historical footnote and more like the collective social and spiritual transformation of real-life, passionate people.

She continued, "As to the term 'Shakers,' we are of Quaker origin historically, and our manner of dance and praise earned us the term 'Shaking Quakers.' The outside world started calling us simply 'Shakers.' Our ownership is communal, we believe in confession to our elders as they are ordained by God, and we believe the human impulse to engage in warfare is a vehicle of the devil, which is why our brothers did not partake in the bloody conflict that recently spilled the blood of thousands, despite our ardent opposition to the evils of slavery.

"And as you know, we are celibate; we do not marry or have children," Sister Abigal went on. "Men and women board and work almost entirely apart from each other. The act of physical relations is a source of pain and suffering the world over—Original Sin—so we cast aside matters of the flesh, focusing instead on perfecting our relationship with the almighty, whom we offer praise through both our song and our toil."

"'Hands to work, hearts to God,'" Jarek said with a smile, grateful that a concept so important to her had resonance in his own time.

"Yes, dear, exactly. Hands to work, hearts to God."

Jarek was struck by the sheer strength of their conviction regarding equality of the sexes. He remembered an essay he had to read for social studies class called "The Continued Struggle for Equal Pay," and it was all he could do to not jump up in front of Abigail and tell her that 100 years from now, the outside world still wouldn't have it right. His admiration for the Shakers was beginning to grow. They were way ahead of their time.

Abigail shared much more about the Village and its inhabitants. She was hopeful about their future and sure that, despite recent setbacks, they would continue their growth and thrive for centuries to come. Jarek listened with a sorrow that grew stronger with each passing moment. He knew the future that awaited them was not the righteous march to expansion and societal awakening of their dreams but a slow diminishing shuffle down the long road to obscurity and extinction.

CHAPTER 16

"Good morning, the time is 7:15 am!"

It was getting much harder to get out of bed in the morning. The dreams now came to him every night, and he awoke just as tired as if he hadn't slept at all.

Taki has seen him struggling in the mornings but was far too polite to wake him up, so he let his talking alarm clock do it instead. As the repetitive chatter was unbearable, Jarek started setting his own alarm clock to wake him with the news at 7:10.

His red eyes gazed up at the ceiling as he counted how many times Taki's clock had sung its song. "23," he said aloud, slowly pushing the sheets down and reaching for the small white wire basket that he carried back and forth from his room to the bathroom morning and night.

He got to class late, ignoring a sidelong glance from his teacher and avoiding eye contact with everyone else—especially Em, who had grown increasingly worried about his appearance and evasive behavior the past few weeks. He slid into his desk chair at 8:03 and assumed he didn't miss much.. Waking hours were now wholly consumed by distress and confusion about his all-consuming dreams.

The most perplexing thing about the double life he was leading was Lucas. Jarek was starting to think of him as a friend, which was strange enough. But there was a shadow in Jarek's mind whenever he thought of him, and he couldn't quite put his finger on it. Lucas had begun to seem less cheerful and much quieter, as if he were somehow diminishing. Jarek wondered if he was in some kind of trouble.

"LUCAS, COME ON!"

On especially hot days, when work in the fields had concluded, some of the villagers would participate in a swim. Men and women would never swim at the same time, of course, but those who wished would gather, appropriately attired, and proceed to the stream largely hidden by the woods at the very back of the Village. Now, it was the men's turn.

Several brothers were ahead, some walking fast and some running, taking their vests off as they went, running in a line along the grassy edge of the cornfield and immediately out of sight of the rest of the Village. Jarek was nearer the back of the group and encouraging Lucas, walking more slowly behind, to hurry.

"Come on—so we don't run out of time!" Jarek hollered with a smile, gesturing him forward.

The friendly and appreciative demeanor that made Lucas endearing to those in the Village had continued to fade; he was distracted and without energy. Jarek wondered if he was homesick, although he hadn't yet asked what "home" was, or used to be.

They approached the water together amidst the laughs and shouts of others in various stages of wading or getting into their underwear; long johns that covered them from their necks to their wrists and ankles.

"I would prefer not to," Lucas said.

"What? Come on, we've been burning alive in the field for hours—get in!" Jarek gave Lucas's vest a yank, his shirt coming up with it, and froze at what he saw.

There was a large purple bruise on the left side of Lucas's back, extending up and over his shoulder.

"Lucas, what the..." he tugged the other half of Lucas's shirt up in the back as the boy tried to squirm away. He saw four long red marks across the middle of Lucas's back. "What's this? What the hell happened?"

"Jarek, you shouldn't use such words."

"Lucas! WHAT happened?" Lucas cringed a bit and turned his head away at Jarek raising his voice to him. Jarek slowed down. "Hey, I'm sorry. How did you get this?"

"I fell," Lucas said meekly.

"Fell?" Jarek was skeptical. "Fell what, down a mineshaft?"

"No, no. I was in the family tree," he stammered. "I was in the family tree...and I fell."

The family tree was a large oak in the middle of the Village. Legend said that it was planted from an acorn brought across the ocean by Ann Lee herself and that acorns from the family tree were used to grow other trees in the middle of all the other Shaker communities. It tied them all together in a manner that the Shakers found very symbolic. Cutting the trees, climbing them, and doing anything except admiring them from afar was strictly forbidden.

"You were in the family tree. *Why* were you in the family tree?" Jarek was skeptical.

"I wanted to climb it...but I'm afraid I lost my footing and fell backward. My shoulder struck a limb on the way down, and a few branches scratched me good before I hit the ground. I didn't tell anyone because I don't want to put anyone through trouble for me."

Lucas's averted eyes made it clear that he wasn't telling the real story, or at least not all of it.

"Well," Jarek said, pretending to accept the explanation, "let's just swim and cool off. Then we can get you to the infirmary; we'll just tell them you...fell out of a different tree. Come on, let's get in."

"Okay," Lucas said. And they joined the others.

Lucas seemed more like himself again as the boys shook of their clothes, caught their breath, and sat on a log beside the water.

"Lucas," Jarek said, "when did you get here?"

Lucas looked at him, a bit confused.

"To the Village," Jarek added, "How did you come?"

"My parents," Lucas said.

"Your parents what…?" Jarek didn't want to pry but had to know.

Lucas said flatly, "They dropped me off."

"Oh, yeah," Jarek said, pretending it sounded familiar. "But," he added, "when or…why?"

"My father," Lucas paused momentarily at mentioning him and continued, "Well, we moved a lot. My father had a temper. Or *has* a temper."

Jarek thought of the bruises he saw, but they were new. "What kind of temper?" he asked.

"He and my mother were both steel mill workers. Well, sometimes."

Jarek waited quietly as Lucas took a deep breath and continued.

"He would get very upset—'very upset,' my mother would say—with his bosses. My mother would call them his 'episodes.' After each one, he'd get fired or worse. Sometimes, we'd have to leave town."

"Leave-leave? Like, move?" Jarek asked.

"Yes," Lucas said, "Move. People would talk, and then he couldn't get hired anywhere, so we would move. But then his episodes got worse, and we had to just leave so he wouldn't get arrested."

"You had to…run?" Jarek asked.

"Yes. He hit his boss. We left late at night. That time, it was farm work, but my mom thought people would talk everywhere, so wanted to do something different. He promised and promised he wouldn't do it again. It was ruining everything. She was so happy when he got a better-paying job. He was working the blast furnace at Bethlehem Iron Works, down in Pennsylvania. Sparks would fly around there; that's why it paid better, and they would always burn his coat and sometimes burn him, and my mom would do her best to fix him up, cleaning the black holes burned into his arms. It got so bad that he couldn't work the chute, so he was switched to a lower-paying job at the rolling mill."

"Sorry," Jarek said, "but what's a rolling mill?"

"They make rails, as for the railroad, and they do it fast because the railroad companies are competing to see who can make it across the country first. The boss was loud with him, even yelling to get him to go more quickly, so he had—as my mother would call them—one of his 'episodes.'"

Jarek had been looking at the ground listening but looked up at Lucas. "Was it a bad one?" he asked, quietly.

"Yes, I'm afraid so. He hit him with something, and the man didn't get up. I don't know if he ever did or what happened, but my father saw it was bad and ran out. He got the wagon and my mother and our things and came to school, walked right in and into my class, grabbed my hand and pulled me out just like that. I didn't have many friends in school; I came in the middle of the year. My mother did what she could, but my clothes were old and dirty, so they made fun of me." He paused for a moment, then looked at Jarek and added, "Imagine that: too dirty for a mill town."

"Gosh, Lucas, I'm sorry," Jarek said.

"Too dirty for a mill town," Lucas mumbled to himself again before continuing.

"I had some friends there, though. Two. One good one. I couldn't even say goodbye. A couple minutes later, we were back on the road again, and my mother was crying and telling me she was sorry, but I wouldn't see them again, and she knew I would miss them. We were going north. We didn't have anywhere to sleep, so we made do and kept going for a week. She would say she was sorry so many times each day, especially when she gave me a few crackers for dinner each night. I don't know what happened to the guy in the mill, but my mother thought we wouldn't be settled anytime soon.

"Pretty soon, my mother said something about a village in the Berkshires. 'It would be best' and the like. I didn't know what they were talking about. My father insisted he would change and said he wanted me around because we were a family, but she knew he just wanted to make me work somewhere to make money. When we came here, they said it was about getting him a job, but before I knew what was happening, they got back in the wagon without me, and my father whipped the horses..." His voice trailed off.

"Wait, you didn't know?" Jarek was wide-eyed with surprise, looking at Lucas's glassy eyes as he stared into the distance.

"No," he said, wiping one eye. "I didn't know. But then I realized. I screamed out for my mother, just cried and screamed, and ran after them as fast as I could, but they kept going. My mother looked back at me with one hand on her mouth and the other on her chest, then holding it out like she was reaching for me, crying so hard. My father had his mill coat on, with the black burn marks on it, and he didn't turn around. That's the last I saw of them. That's how I remember them. His back and her crying, and I kept running until my legs slowed down, and they got farther out the road and disappeared."

Jarek could think of nothing to say, as Lucas pressed on.

"I just sat there," he shrugged. "I didn't know what to do, so I just sat down right in the middle of the road. It felt like forever. I think I was waiting for them to come back. Seeing them coming up the road and realizing it was a big mistake. My mother would hug me, and I'd get back in the wagon, and that would be it. But they didn't come. One brother and a couple of sisters saw me there, or saw them leave maybe, and came to me. One of the sisters put her hand on my shoulder. I remember that sometimes, just that hand on my shoulder."

"What did they do?"

"I'm sorry, son' the brother said. He called me 'son.' Then he looked at me and said, 'You'll be fine. You're home now.' Then he reached down with a handkerchief and wiped my eyes. It wasn't much, but at that moment, it was something."

He paused for a moment, wiping his eyes, and staring into the distance.

"He smiled at me." Lucas laughed. Jarek couldn't imagine what he thought was funny.

"'We'll take good care of you, my boy,' he said. 'My name is Thaddeus.'" Lucas's eyes were distant.

"Wow, Lucas." Jarek's head spun as he tried to digest everything Lucas had just told him. He didn't know what else to say. "I'm sorry."

"Yes," Lucas said. "That's what everyone says. 'I'm sorry.'"

"What was it like here at first?" Jarek knew it was a dumb question, but he figured Lucas was picturing his parents disappearing down the road after abandoning him and was trying to take his mind off of it.

"Just fine, I suppose. I ate a lot more food than I'd ever had, and it was good," he smiled. "The brothers and sisters would check on me, try to keep me busy meeting everyone, learning the fields and the store, the songs."

Jarek nodded.

"Thaddeus brought me things I'd need—plenty of clothes. I'd never had new shoes. After I got here, I had two pairs. Two pairs! He said the heat of the fields wasn't good for me, so he had me help him in his office. He always gave me things, especially if he saw me 'going distant,' as he called it, staring out the window or at the floor when I was thinking about my parents. I'd see him around the Village, and he was big—his person, I mean, but his personality, too. He was confident and strong, and people respected him. I'd see him do things for people, nice things. The opposite of my father. I looked up to him."

Jarek was listening to his story but wasn't sure why the observations he included were in the past tense. He wanted to remember to ask at another time.

CHAPTER 17

Campus was at its best in the fall and became more beautiful with each passing day. A wave of changing leaves from Canada had crept down into the Adirondack Mountains, straddled the Vermont state line, and progressed into the Berkshires, transforming red oaks, sugar maples, birches, and alders into a blanket of colors that slowly spread from the top of the mountainside down into the valley below.

Visitors from near and far bundled up to drive the scenic byways. Farm stands fully stocked with every possible assortment of apple butter, flavored honey, and decorative corn husks stood ready to receive sightseers, impulse buyers, and well-wishers in one final commercial push before they shut down for the winter. The crunch of tires rolling into their gravel parking lots assured them that the fresh coats of red paint and fire pits by which customers sipped their mulled cider were more than worth the effort.

Campus life pressed on day by day, largely unaware of the outside world and mostly unnoticed by it. Soccer practice brought most of the student body to the edge of the field each evening to cheer on their classmates and watch the sunset over the valley below. All were eager to make the best of the crisp weather before frigid temperatures had them stuck inside for months, and there were worse things to do with their time than count the veins of smoke trailing up into the sky from the burn piles of farmers doing a final clean up before the coming snows.

It was nearing the end of one such practice that Jarek found himself sitting beside Drummy. As he always did when something was on his mind, Drummy took a deep breath.

"So, Jarek." He turned away from the setting sun and looked right at him. Drummy spoke quietly so teachers and students sitting on the benches and standing nearby, their eyes turned towards the field, couldn't hear him over the frequent whistles echoing in the distance. Jarek liked knowing they shared such confidence.

"I've meant to ask you but couldn't find the right time. Is everything okay? And if you say 'yes,' I'll know you're lying."

"Hah. Um. Yes?" Jarek gave a half-hearted smile.

"Well," Drummy paused, "We're friends, right? I consider us friends. As much as a teacher and student can be."

"Yeah, sure. I mean, of course. Of course, we are," Jarek said.

"Okay, so here's what I know about my friend Jarek."

Jarek didn't know what was coming next, but he appreciated that someone of Drummy's caliber was concerned.

"What I know about my friend Jarek is that when he got here, he was curious. He was glad to be here. He would ask insightful questions in class. He saw connections. He was...I dunno...advanced." He paused, then continued. "I never used to see you with a thousand-yard stare, but I do now—often—and even in my class, which I'm flattered to know is your favorite, but it makes it more obvious. So, something's going on."

He looked at Jarek and waited.

The benches were beside the gravel road that led from the Tannery back to the central part of campus. Drummy's class was indeed Jarek's favorite, but he hadn't heard a word of it today. Even at this moment, he was thinking about how he had walked this same gravel path a dozen times over 100 years ago, at least in his dreams.

"Anything you want to tell me?" Drummy added.

"Nothing, really. I'm tired, I guess. I feel out of it." Jarek responded after a moment.

Drummy said, "I'm gonna keep asking, so you might as well get on with it." Jarek could tell he didn't have a choice. He thought for a long time about not telling him. But if he didn't tell Drummy, he wouldn't tell anyone, meaning he'd have to continue spiraling towards whatever inevitable crummy outcome waited for him if he couldn't figure it out.

"I've been, um, having these weird dreams," Jarek said.

Drummy shrugged. "Okay, and…"

"And…uh…I think I saw a ghost." Jarek made a skeptical face when he said it. He knew it sounded crazy.

"What, like an actual ghost? Come on." Drummy laughed at the irony of Jarek's change of heart. "You don't believe in ghosts, right?"

Jarek was silent.

"Hang on. You're serious?"

Drummy looked at Jarek and saw the hint of regret in his eyes for speaking up. For the first time since their conversation began, Drummy also noticed how deeply exhausted Jarek looked. Almost hopelessly so.

"Oh, hey, hang on a minute. I'm sorry." Drummy said. "This is really bothering you. Jarek, really. Please accept my apologies."

Jarek took a deep breath and proceeded to tell him everything. The dreams, the old man in the mirror, Lucas, and the Shakers. And Beth. Definitely about Beth.

Drummy asked dozens of questions: the day-to-day life of the Village, the clothing, how they all interacted, how they spoke, what the Village looked like with so many more buildings, and even how the food tasted. At first, he was asking to figure out what kind of fantasy Jarek was having, ready to tell him to get more sleep. But as Jarek continued, he grew more wide-eyed, and as his questions—and Jarek's answers—became more specific, his expression went from skeptical to stunned and relentlessly curious. When Jarek was done, Drummy was staring into the distance, his eyes darting back and forth as his mind raced through all he had just heard.

"Jarek, this is wild. The first thing is I…uh. I'm not, like, a shrink or anything," Drummy said.

"Jesus, thanks," Jarek mumbled.

"No, but what I am is your teacher, so your brain is one of the things I'm responsible for. I'm also your dorm parent, so I'm concerned about your life outside class, and—as far as this spooky place goes—I happen to know a lot of stuff. My obsession with Shakers has always seemed like a waste of time, to me anyway. But the things I've learned about them, what they thought and how they lived—not just collectively but as individuals, well, some of the things you are saying are…"

Drummy paused, deep in thought.

"Are what?" Jarek asked.

"Are things that no one else here knows or would ever bother to find out. Things that *you* could never make up. I mean, half the questions I just asked you—about the far side of the original Dairy Barn, for example—is stuff I've wondered about and haven't been able to figure out at all, and you just knew. It's almost like…"

"Like I was there," Jarek said.

"Yeah, exactly like that." He paused for a moment. And then another. "This is… crazy. I don't get it." He looked into the distance, adding, "It's really cool, though. Hey, does your purple hair go with you, or…" he smiled.

"Yeah, well…I think I'm losing my mind. Glad it sounds cool, and no it's brown when I'm there." Jarek added glibly.

"I'm sorry. I was just trying to lighten the mood. That was dumb," Drummy said with a look of regret on his face. "You're not losing your mind. I mean, at least I don't think so. I'm a little stunned, frankly. But hey, so you think this is gonna happen again? Another dream?"

"Yeah," Jarek said, "probably tonight. It happens every night now."

Drummy looked at his watch.

"Shoot. I've got a faculty meeting. Hey, tomorrow after second period, I'm free. Remember every detail you can. Write it all down if you have to. I want to know everything."

"Okay," Jarek said.

"And hey… hey." Drummy leaned down to look Jarek in the eye. "Hang in there, right? These dreams and… all of this is super bizarre, just mind-blowing. I don't know. But pace yourself, I guess. If it's any comfort, I always feel like I'm losing my mind, and this may finally finish the job. So, if you're losing yours, we'll lose them together."

"Right." Jarek nodded.

"Seriously, keep me posted. But more importantly, take care of yourself, okay?" Drummy said, adding another "Okay" in conclusion.

"Okay." Jarek agreed. He watched Drummy walk off into the distance with a sense of great relief that somebody knew, and that somebody was Drummy. He understood it—or at least some of it—and as Drummy disappeared into the small door of a distant building, Jarek was relieved for his presence and very, very grateful for him.

He was glad to have something else to think about a moment later.

"Hey, you."

Beth's voice was a welcome sound after the intense discussion he'd just had. The sun had set during his chat with Drummy, and the grey sky now cast a bluish tint on the field as lamplights along the gravel path flickered on. He hadn't seen her coming and did his best not to sound as excited as he felt as she approached.

"Oh, hey," he said clumsily. She smiled.

"You didn't see me comin'?" She smiled. "Walking up this whooooole way?" She wiggled her hips. Jarek smiled.

"No," he said. "I would have noticed."

"Charmer," Beth said.

She smiled at him, and he forgot everything else.

"Any reason you're sitting here in the almost-dark staring into space instead of watching soccer practice? Well, if it were space, I'd get it," she smiled, "but it was more like…the grass. Or the dirt. Any reason you're sitting here in the almost-dark, staring at the dirt? Something going on?"

She was still and raised her eyebrows a bit as she asked. Her sincerity grabbed him by the ribs, as always.

"No, no, not really," Jarek said. "It's kind of a long story."

"Well, if there's one thing we have a lot of around here, I mean, I don't mean right this moment, but in general, it's time."

She did an exaggerated flop onto the bench beside him, putting her hands on her knees to show she was ready to listen. He wanted to kiss her right then and there. They heard the banter of distant voices, and both turned their heads to notice a few stragglers heading up the main road to dinner. Among them was Morak, glaring at Jarek as he walked. Jarek looked back, pissed that another nice moment had been screwed up by the ever-present nuisance Morak had become.

Beth looked back to the field. "Well, like I said, maybe not now. Everything's okay, though?"

Jarek was still looking back at Morak, just long enough to notice his middle finger. He turned his eyes back to Beth.

"Yeah, of course, everything's okay," he said.

She looked at him long enough to tell he didn't mean it.

"We haven't been able to talk for a bit, and you seem—I dunno—distracted or…upset."

He wondered why girls always had to use the word "upset." Some words were good for anything, like "shit." A thousand uses. "Upset" though he had no use for—he didn't know if he had ever been "upset."

"No, I'm not upset," he said.

"Oh," she hesitated, adding, "okay, well…*ugh.*" She threw back her head in frustration as a group of freshmen walked past, giggling.

"I just hate feeling like we can't have a real conversation ever—at least not without half the campus watching."

"You mean want me to meet you in the field again?" he asked.

"What? God, no. I want to hang out with you, not freeze to death. Look don't get the wrong idea, but…"

He was perplexed. "Okay…uhh…"

"Feeling daring?" Beth said.

"I guess so?"

"You have a lot to tell me, I think. So…come by later?"

"Like…after study hall?" he asked.

"No," she said, "I mean much later."

"Oh?" His face showed his surprise at the suggestion, and he stammered a bit, "Ohhh, wow, okay. Um, yeah. Yes, sure, of course."

"Hey!" She gave him an exaggerated stern look, adding, "Like I said: don't get the wrong idea."

"No, no…or I mean, yes, but no, I wasn't…or I didn't mean…I mean, I didn't think *you* meant…"

"Good." She nodded, acknowledging they were on the same page, and then smiled. "Great. Think you can pull off 11? Will you be awake?"

"Um, yeah, that's cool," he tried to sound calm as a counterpoint to the stammering he just did, knowing full well he'd be jumping out of his skin in the dark, fully dressed under his covers, staring at the clock and the ceiling.

He had never been so eager for lights out, but a couple hours later he was in bed, silent in the dark, unable to do anything other than review the timing in his mind a dozen times. "The walk takes seven minutes during the day on the road. Off the road, maybe 10. What if somebody comes? How long does it take for someone to walk by if I need to duck away? Should I give myself 15 minutes? What if I can't even leave the dorm?"

As he lay in bed, every creak and footstep he heard on the floors above or below, sounded like a devastating assurance that the plan was off; he couldn't leave, she'd wait up, and he'd never get there, and she'd think he was a jerk.

"If you wanna be on time, you gotta be early," his dad used to say. The large letters of the digital clock didn't want to change, but slowly they ticked by: 10:28, 10:30, 10:32.

"Gah, screw it." He quietly pushed the covers off, looking towards both beds across the room to make sure his roommates were asleep before gently putting one boot on the floor. He moved slowly, the sound of his breath so loud in his ears he thought sure it would wake the entire dorm. He hit one creaky spot on the floor. Taki rolled over but stayed asleep.

The door to their room was heavy. He pressed a sock around the catch to stifle the loud *clunk* it made any time anyone came or went, then snuck silently into the hall and descended, ghostlike, down two flights of steps before quietly exiting into the cool night.

CHAPTER 18

"Hi," Beth whispered, peeking into the dark hall before letting him in. She looked him in the eye as he moved past her through the doorway. When she smiled, her lower lip tended to go just the tiniest bit crooked. She hated it, but he loved it, and it held his stare for an extra moment as he quietly said, "Hey."

He could tell she had spent some time getting ready, and he smiled as she pretended she hadn't fallen asleep shortly after. Her hair tumbled loosely to her shoulder, resting on the black and red checked button-down flannel she wore. He imagined her tidying up this warm and comfortable space, ready for his arrival through the cold and dark, and just as nervous as he was about the moment he showed up at her door. Now that she was here before him and they were finally alone, he was observing and appreciating every small detail around them so he could remember them later.

At first, she was too perfect. Too talented, too smart, too beautiful, and too uncomplicated—for him, anyway. But the little things he'd discovered in recent weeks—her complicated family, fiery temper, heartbreaks, and disappointment—made her that much more fascinating to him. Now, her beautifully imperfect smile, the pillow line on her cheek, and the tiny freckle on the edge of her upper lip were right there before him. She moved past him into the room, dimly lit by the lamp on her tidy desk, as he breathed in the smell of ocean-scented perfume, clean laundry, and vanilla Chapstick.

"You don't have to just stand there," she said, folding her legs comfortably under herself in her desk chair, "unless you want to."

"No, no, sorry," he snapped out of it, taking a seat where she had gestured on her bed. He tried to find just the right spot, not so far back on the mattress to seem presumptuous and not too close to the edge to seem uncomfortable. It didn't work. His nervous, upright posture made him look like a kid posing for a class picture. She looked at him and laughed. He did, too, and with that acknowledgment out of the way, he could relax a bit.

After some small talk, Beth asked about Jarek's parents.

"Seems like you're close to them. That's amazing," she said. "I could tell when they dropped you off. They both gave you the biggest hugs. I saw you watch their car disappear down the road. That was cute."

"Well, yeah, I was trying to be cute, so," Jarek said, though beneath his sarcasm he was a little self-conscious that he had been watched so closely in a moment that he remembered as one of heartache and panic—despite how calm he appeared on the outside—as he prepared to brave the unknown alone. He was always close to his parents, but they were all inseparable since Andrew died. Sometimes they would cry together. Then they would stand up, his dad would call out "Group hug!" and as the three of them embraced, his mom would say "All we have is each other, but that's enough," as they wiped their eyes. Jarek remembered watching their car disappear up the road and wished, more than anything else, that Andrew was there to start this new adventure with him. "Now it's just me," he said to himself.

He knew he sounded defensive just now with Beth and regretted it, adding, "I knew they were gonna miss me, and I was gonna miss them, and I was right."

"I didn't mean anything by it. I'm sorry," she said.

"I know, it's ok, me either," he said, squeezing her arm.

"Your dad whispered something in your ear right before he let go. I saw you sort of stop for a moment and look at each other. What did he say?"

"I, um…I can't say," Jarek said.

"No?" she asked and paused. He didn't answer.

"Well. In that case," she said, "tell me the rest. I'm jealous of you for having parents who are so *present*. I'm sure you all have had some wonderful times."

"Yeah, some," Jarek said, "and some bad ones too."

"Well, tell me one of the wonderful ones," she said, sitting up to show she was eager to listen. "Tell me a story about your parents—when you were growing up—something that's, you know, really *them*."

Her enthusiasm to learn more was cute, and the fact that she wanted to focus on the positive for his sake meant more to him than she could know.

"Wow, okay," he said. "Let me think for a minute. Something that's…"

"Really *them*," she said again, taking a piece of his long bangs and twirling it in her fingers while she looked at him patiently in the dark.

"So my dad is an accountant," he said.

"Really? No way."

He looked at her with raised eyebrows and asked, "Why not?"

"I mean… no reason," she said. "It's just that accountants tend to be a little uptight, and—" she gestured at his hair. "Sorry, I interrupted."

"He's not, and *shh*!" he said and gave her a nudge.

"Hey!" She pretended it hurt.

"So, my dad is an accountant…" he paused extra long to see if she'd interrupt. She made the motion of zipping her lips, and he continued.

"He's wicked smart and interested in everything: books, science, music, history. He loves making me remember things, especially about family—even the ones we know almost zilch about. 'In March of 1883, Elijah Dorrell came to be.' That's the one fact anybody knows about my great-grandpa, whoever he was. That and the fact that he was from somewhere around here. Upstate, anyway. Remembering who came before us is huge for my dad. Anyway, when I was little, we didn't have much money, not that we do now, and our house is simple, but it's ours. They are proud of it, and we love it."

She let out a little *aww* and squeezed his arm.

"It's an old cobblestone house on a little winding suburban street. Pavers to the front door and shrubs at the edge of the front yard, which my dad hates but puts up with because they've always been there."

"He's sentimental, like you," she smiled.

"Ha, well, my dad works a lot, especially at certain times of the year. 'Work hard and prosper, do a good job,' all that. He takes on these charity cases—people who need help but can't pay—and honestly, I think he works hardest for them. One day, my mom says, 'Sweetheart, you seem to do the most work for those who are most broke.' We had just finished eating without him, and I looked a little sad during dinner because we were supposed to put up a tent in the yard that they gave me for my birthday.

"So he kissed my mom, and she told him that I asked why he has to work so much for people that don't pay because that means he's not with us, but also he's not even making money, which is how they buy toys and things for us."

"That's adorable," she said.

"Adorable? I'm glad you think so. I think it sounds awful. Anyway, there was this little old lady my dad was helping; her name was Mrs. Grissing, and when my dad tucked me in that night, he said, 'Buddy, do you know why I help Mrs. Grissing?' And I grumbled, 'No.' And he rubbed my head and said, 'Mrs. Grissing is old, and things are a little harder for her because her husband is in heaven now.' I was starting to learn what that meant and said, 'In heaven for real?' trying to get my head around her being like my mom and dad and then being alone. He said quietly, 'Yeah, for real buddy. So it's good for me to spend some time helping her so she can be okay on her own. There's a lot of stuff she used to do for him when he got sick, but there's a lot of things he used to do for both of them, and some of those things are the things that Daddy knows how to do. We're always supposed to help each other, you know? But sometimes, when someone needs our help, and something about us lets us help in a way *no one* else can, that's when we are 'called by name.' That's when God says, 'Jarek, you're the only one here. Go help that boy that somebody's not nice to,' or 'Jarek, help that nice old lady cross the street.' That's when we are called by name, and those are the most important times. We have to help when we can, Jarek, because there are lots of times when we can't.'"

Jarek paused as Beth looked at him. "Wow, that's kind of amazing. I'm stealing that," she breathed.

"Yeah, I'll never forget it," Jarek said. "He said, 'So that's why I help her. I'm sorry we couldn't put your new tent in the yard. We'll get it to tomorrow, promise.' And, of course, we did.

"When I went to sleep that night, I pictured my dad going to see Mrs. Grissing with the worn-out leather briefcase he had. It had a squiggle of permanent green marker on the side from when I was tiny. My mom howled when she saw it because my dad loved that bag, but he looked at it, then looked at me, and just said, 'It's okay, Buddy. We'll fix it.' Of course, it couldn't be fixed, so he said, 'I like it this way because it reminds me of you.' My mom told me about a time a big client he worked hard for wasn't going to pay him—it was devastating—but he looked over at his bag and saw the squiggle, and it made him smile."

"Gosh, I love that," she said, draping her arm across him. He rested his hand on it.

"So I pictured him walking into her front door, a run-down old Victorian house with a leaky roof. Inside, a sad old widow is sitting in the dark, staring at a pile of papers that she doesn't understand until my dad walks in. Then she jumps to her feet and says, 'My knight of numbers!' with tears in her eyes as he prepares to provide advice, consolation and—to her great relief—some company. If my dad got discouraged, my green squiggle would be there to help. I thought he was a superhero after all that. I never saw Mrs. Grissing's house, but I didn't mind my dad missing dinner to rescue her."

Beth was quiet for a moment. And then another one.

"Did you fall asleep?" he said quietly in case she had.

"No," she said, sniffling as she rolled off the bed to go to a tissue box in the dark and blow her nose. "I'm sorry," she said.

"My gosh, no," Jarek said, "Don't apologize. Did I upset you? Did I remind you of something?"

"Yeah," she said, "A lot of somethings. But they're all disappointing." He wished he knew what she meant. She added, "That's so beautiful, that story. I love everything about it."

She rested her head on his chest and stayed quiet. He didn't want to interrupt her thoughts, so he stayed quiet, too. They stayed still for a long time, his hand resting on her lower back as she lay beside him with her chest against his. He loved feeling her breathe.

He had heard her take a deep breath like she was about to say something and then stop. After she did it two more times, he looked down at her face in the dark.

"What is it?" Jarek asked.

"Well, I just. I wanted to ask… how are they now? They're there alone?" she paused, looking up at him.

"Oh," he said with a sigh, taking a moment to think. "Yeah, they're okay, I guess."

"Is it hard for them, you being here?" she asked.

"Yeah. Yes, it's hard for them. It's much harder than they'll ever say, but I can tell. It's hard for all of us, but no one wants to talk about it. It's like I don't want to tell them it's hard because I don't want them to be worried or discouraged, and they don't want to tell me it's hard because they don't want me to feel bad about being away when they need me. The one thing we want to discuss, the one thing that is endlessly on our minds, is the one thing we never can because it almost hurts too much to put into words, and talking about it won't change anything anyway."

She let the gravity of this sink in for a moment, then carefully said, "The first time you told me about your brother, I had so many questions, but… I didn't want to ask anything you weren't ready to tell me."

"Like what?" Jarek said. "You can ask me anything."

"I just wondered," she paused. "I wondered what it was like, you know, after. What were things like before you left to come here?"

He looked towards the window out into the dark. "It's kind of a blur, really," he said.

"Yeah," she said, trying to sound like she could understand. They both knew she didn't, but he appreciated the gesture.

"We all cried a lot," he said, "My mom cried to my dad. My dad was trying to be strong for us. He had been for months, but he just couldn't anymore. Suddenly, he was really into baths, which he never was before. He'd go in there and leave the faucet running the whole time. One night, I put my ear to the door and figured it out. I heard him crying. That's why he was going in there. To cry. He didn't want anyone to hear him."

She didn't say anything, just held onto him more tightly.

"A lot of days, my mom didn't even get out of bed," he said. "She'd be upstairs—my dad would say she didn't feel well—while I mostly sat on the couch staring at the television, not watching, avoiding anything with families, anybody dying, and anything about music. That was one of the things we talked about most—me and Andrew—we both loved music."

Beth's hand rubbed his arm as he continued.

"I just sat there day after day, and time just passed. Weeks," he said, pausing for a moment as he remembered. "I would sit in his room for hours just looking at his things, reliving the story of every item and where it came from, especially if we got it together. He was proud of his signed baseball and told me every time he held it, 'This ball was signed by Mickey Mantle himself!'

"All his stuff—CDs, sneakers, a little collection of wood and model elephants from our grandma, model airplanes hanging from the ceiling that we made together, they're all exactly where we left them—they still are. It's like a tiny museum about his life with only three visitors. Each of us would come in secret, cry alone, and leave before anyone knew. I'd sit there with this ache in my chest and try to will him back—like if I concentrated hard enough, he'd just come walking in like before. I knew it wasn't doing me any good to just sit there, to dwell on it, but I felt like I was dishonoring his memory if I didn't. I don't know. At first, I'd push my face into his clothes or pillow. They still smelled like him. It made me cry every time, but it was him—really him. Now, it all smells like dust. Nothing smells like him anymore. It's gone."

He lifted the ends of his ascot to his nose and breathed in.

"Was this his?" she asked, touching the smooth cloth. "You said you'd tell me about it sometime."

"Yeah, it was his, and you're right—I did," he said with a nod. "Well…about this time last year, Andrew decided he wanted to try acting. Our school announced that the Spring play would be a Sherlock Holmes story called 'The Speckled Band,' about a guy who murders for money. He uses a poisonous snake with spots on it—hence the title—but really The Speckled Band represents evil. It's exactly the kind of story Andrew loved. He tried out for the lead role, of course he got it, and he was incredible. The whole town talked about it for weeks. He was a star. It was one of his proudest moments. He wore this in the play," Jarek said, putting his hand to his neck, "and this, it's a British Naval officer's coat. He loved it." he put his hand on the folded black cloth beside him. "My parents were beaming," he smiled and let out a quiet sigh. "He was diagnosed a few weeks later."

He felt a shudder in Beth's chest as she listened. She ran her hands down the cloth of the ascot as if she were admiring it.

"Anyway, so yeah, summer passed one sad moment after another. Then, one day, my mom came into the room. I sat up, but she saw me wiping my eyes. 'Sweetie,' she said, 'It's time to start packing.'"

He stopped there.

"Jarek, it's all…" She paused to wipe a tear. "It's just so heartbreaking—that you have to… How terrible for all of you. Your poor brother. Your parents sound just so lovely," she sniffled.

"We're really close—they're amazing. I just want to make them proud. I don't care about much of the rest."

"I love that," she said. "And I love that you just said that."

"Well," he said, "it's true, but guess what?"

"What?" she said, genuinely curious.

"Your parents love you, too," Jarek said, "They just don't know how to show it."

She responded by lifting her face to his and kissing his cheek as she wiped a tear from her own.

"Thank you," she said. "You know, you must be the kindest guy I've ever met."

"Thanks, I guess." he shrugged and smiled.

"But this is not about me," she added, "not at all."

She sat up a bit. "Let's not talk about our sad stories anymore, okay?" she said.

"Yeah," he nodded, "yeah, that sounds really good."

She put one hand gently on his opposite cheek and drew his face closer, slowly moving her lips to his. He responded by wrapping his arms around her waist as she moved onto his lap, taking his face in her hands. Before long, they were both lost in the moment, in each other, and in one long, passionate kiss.

Suddenly, Jarek stopped.

Beth drew her head back in surprise and started to say, "What's…"

"I, um, are you sure?" Jarek interrupted. "Like…sure, sure?"

She looked confused.

"Sorry," he added, "Is that kind of…old-fashioned?"

"Okay," she said, giving him an exaggerated side-eye. "First, who's in whose lap?" she asked with a smirk, tapping her temple with one finger to show she was thinking and giving her hips a slight wiggle.

"Okay, what's second?" he asked.

"Second is: thank you." She drew her fingertips down his cheek and added, with a sincerity that surprised him, "And it's not old fashioned." She looked down into his eyes, added, "Not at all," and affectionately pressed her lips to his for several seconds.

His hands moved slowly from the legs of her jeans under the back of her shirt to feel the smooth skin of her waist.

"These radiators—it's always so hot in here," she said.

She unbuttoned the soft flannel shirt she was wearing, pulling it off the v-neck t-shirt underneath and tossing it to the side as he breathed in the smell of her perfume and coconut shampoo. She moved her hair around to one side, and he looked closely at the bare skin of her neck before placing his lips there, slowly kissing, then moving slowly lower to the base of her deep-cut collar.

She responded by reaching for his shirt until he leaned forward, and she pulled it off of him. She looked down admiringly at his chest, reaching down to the bottom of her shirt, and tugging upwards over her head. He took a deep breath as he saw her smooth skin in the dim light, the curve of her waist, her bare arms, and the tiny straps of her navy-blue bra over her perfect shoulders, inhaling deeply at the sight of her and the intensity of the moment.

She sat up a bit, holding his face again in her hands for one more kiss before saying, "Hang on, I'll be right back."

He watched her closely, transfixed, as she took three steps across the room toward the small lamp on her desk. Before flipping the switch off, she turned her head to see him again in the dim light, her hair brushing across her shoulder as they gazed at each other across the small open space between them.

"Wow," he said.

"Yes?" she lifted her chin.

"Just, wow. You look like a model on one of those blue jean billboard ads over Times Square," he said.

"That's unique," she said, smirking at his clumsy compliment.

"And me?" he smiled and raised an eyebrow.

"Hmmmm." She made a show of thinking hard. "You look just like you, but with your shirt off."

"You sweet talker, you," he said. Then, he got quiet for a moment.

"I, um..." His tone became more serious. "I don't know..." he paused. "I mean. Just being here with you."

"What?" she asked.

"Well... I'm pretty sure this is another dream," he said, "so let me kiss you again before I wake up."

"Just once?" she smiled, and her face made it clear she felt the same nervous anticipation that had his heart pounding.

She looked at him, ready to find her way to his waiting arms in the dark and turned off the light with a click.

THE FEELING OF HER HEAD RESTING PEACEFULLY ON HIS CHEST MADE it very hard to decide to exit into the cold night, but when the clock at her bedside read 3:00 AM, he knew it was past time. He listened to her slow breathing for a moment to make sure she was sound asleep before gently moving her head to her pillow, kissing her forehead, and getting up.

When he approached the door, he turned around for one more glimpse of her and the moment they had just shared. He exited her room, made his way silently down the hall, and went out the side door of her dormitory into the night to walk the edges of campus unseen.

The only moving figure for miles around, he quickly made his way through the dark, smiling ear to ear at a feeling within himself that he had thought was gone forever.

He felt content. For the first time in a very long while, he was happy.

CHAPTER 19

Exhaustion. Distraction. Reprimand. Guilt. Every day was the same. Jarek's sleep was never restful, and his dreams were taking over.

Every room he entered confused his mind as he endlessly compared each one to the 1860s version of itself, which he had been in hours or even minutes before. He could barely tell the two worlds apart as waking hours faded into a blur. He was failing miserably in all his classes, and his mind and body were paying the price. But he dragged himself through to the end of each day, eager to return to the new life he knew awaited him after he closed his eyes.

Most nights, he heard the voice of the old man in the mirror whispering to him as he fell asleep, "Consensus…Consensus…" Seconds later, he woke up back among the Shakers.

A row of pegs mounted on long boards ran the length of each wall a couple of feet below the ceiling. From one of the pegs hung the clothes he had been given, exactly where he had left them at the end of his previous dream. It was continuity amidst the chaos. No matter how little he slept or how concerned he was about his diminishing grip on reality, the dreams plodded on uninterrupted. He would fall asleep at school and wake up in the Village. He would go to bed in the Village and wake up on campus: same room, same spot, different world.

His previous dreams—ever since Andrew had first gotten sick—were, according to his psychologist, "PTSD dreams about panic and loss." In them, he was surrounded by sharks but unable to swim, chased by wolves yet unable to run, or just at Andrew's bedside watching him die again and again, completely unable to stop it. Every night had brought a new nightmare. But in this dream—for it really was one long, continuous dream interrupted only by his need to get out of bed and go to class each day—he woke up in the same place. He picked up exactly where he had left off, and there was nothing surreal or dream-like about it. It was just as real as his time on campus. Maybe even more so.

CONSENSUS, CONSENSUS...

Jarek had stared for an hour at a crack that ran across the length of the ceiling, knowing it would be gone when he awoke in the Village, when the building was new and pristine. A tall fir tree swayed in the dark outside his window. He heard whispers as its branches brushed the glass. Ms. Stondell would say it was his mind "manifesting another negative iteration of trauma response." Whatever it was, he'd had enough.

He forgot he'd agreed to meet with Drummy and instead spent hours in the library secretly poring over books about bipolarity, schizophrenia, grief disorders, and other things that were even worse. Page after page about delusions, visions, the psychology of dreams and their meanings, and—when all else failed—ghosts. But he found no answers. He thought again of the one place he might find some.

The Shaker Museum was full of antiques and irreplaceable pieces of history. Aside from a history class going in once or twice a year, it was off-limits to students. Always. Period. The collection he'd caught a glimpse of in the museum's storage room that hot fall afternoon many weeks ago was under the care of a very small number of museum curators and historians. It was all he or any other student had seen of that space or ever would. Jarek knew very well that finding a way in was precisely the kind of offense that would get you kicked out of school immediately—no questions asked—never to return.

He would have to go at night, but the idea of sneaking all the way across campus into that eerie place in the dark alone—with the eyes of Village elders on four-foot poster board staring at him in the dark—was terrifying. If he got caught, he'd be expelled. He had no idea where he'd go if that happened, and in truth, he had come to love the school. This journey, frightening and fascinating as it was, would come to an abrupt end.

He kicked off his sheets in frustration and sat up in the dark. He couldn't continue like this. He had to go back.

He kept one eye on his roommates as he quietly put on his jeans, sweatshirt, and his brother's coat, which he wore constantly once it got cold. Classmates and teachers could recognize him from far away by the dark silhouette it formed from the back, fitted with a slightly flared bottom that flapped open in the slightest breeze. He gave his shoulders a shrug to settle it into place, laced up his boots, and snuck out the door, down the steps, and into the night—looking carefully over his shoulder every moment, moving among the dark spaces where he couldn't be seen. He heard nothing but his footsteps and the leaves rustling in the trees overhead as he escaped the lights at the center of campus, heading to the distant three-story brick structure waiting for him in the dark.

The building was the most secure on campus, so the doors were always locked. The value of the items inside was immeasurable—historically and monetarily. The famous but exceedingly simple "Shaker Chair," for which the Shakers were so well known, sold for about $4,000; on his last visit to the museum, Jarek had seen no fewer than 15 of them in one corner, covered with dusty sheets and cobwebs.

He stepped cautiously to the front door, looking over his shoulder to make sure no one was watching. One bare yellow bulb by the door cast a little light. He thought about unscrewing it but didn't want its absence to raise suspicions. He grabbed the handle and gently applied pressure to the thumb press so the ensuing click wouldn't be too loud.

It was locked.

"Dangit," he said. He left the tiny porch, walking as quietly as possible along the dark side of the building. In the moonlight, he saw the dark squares of the windows come into view and looked around for options.

Jarek had been so focused on getting to the museum without getting caught that he hadn't thought about how he'd get in. It was reckless, all of it, but here he now was, pacing the back of the building in the middle of the night in a manner that—even during the day—would have aroused suspicion.

He looked at the sheer back wall of the building and realized his only chance was finding a ladder. He hoped that—due to the height of the windows—no one would bother locking them. He paced around a few structures nearby until he came to the campus work shed. It was used to store machinery, tools, and firewood. As luck would have it, the ladder he'd used many times during Hands to Work rested on the ground beside it.

He winced each time the extension rope rang against the metal in the dark, making his way to the back of the building, looking around carefully, and climbing up to the rear window of the main floor which—because the building was tucked into a slight hill—was one story up. He then held his breath—one moment away from knowing whether he'd get any answers or if this was just a waste of time.

He put his hand on the underside of the top of the window and pushed. Nothing. He pushed harder; it creaked slightly. It was locked, which meant the other window about ten feet away at the same height would be locked, too. "Dammit," he whispered. He pushed as hard as he could one last time, and suddenly it gave way. One loud crunch and whoosh of transferring air, and the window was open.

Jarek moved through it and slowly into the front room, remembering the layout from the last time he was here as he reached his hand alongside the wall that divided the floor into two large rooms. He found the light switch in the dark, touching it for reference but leaving it off as he pulled out of his pocket a tiny camping flashlight Andrew gave him for Christmas two years before, but when he clicked the button, nothing happened. He cursed his roommate for constantly using it and never changing the batteries.

He reached for the knob that controlled a small track of lights in the room and, not taking any risks in case the administrator on duty happened to be doing rounds, turned it down, pushed until he heard a click, and very slowly turned it back up just enough to see the serious and knowing stares from eight black-and-white faces of Village leaders. All long dead, but very real, and right before him.

Among them, he saw the face of one gentleman, sharply dressed and wearing a broad-brimmed black hat and jacket, his chin slightly lifted as he peered at Jarek. Crossing his vest from one pocket to another was a gold chain. Jarek thought he looked familiar; none of the other faces did. He wanted to turn off the light before anyone saw even the faintest glow in the window from outside, so he turned amidst the circle of somber faces to reach for the switch.

"Whoa!" He started backward at the image immediately before him, staring wide-eyed at the much larger-than-life face, so real it looked as if it was ready to speak. As far as Jarek was concerned, it already had.

It was him. The ghost.

Jarek waited for the furrowed white brow to expand, the eyelids to raise imploringly, the old but rugged chin obscured by the long white beard to move again to slowly speak one mysterious word over and over: "consensus…consensus…" He had heard it in his head and seen this face in his memory every night for weeks. But this time, the face didn't move. Its eyes fixed on Jarek as he stared a little bit longer, looking to the bottom of the photo for any inscription or date, but it was blank. No date, no name, no nothing.

The idea of being in the dark with the face of the ghost before him gave him the same familiar chill he felt each time he knew he was being watched. Each time he heard his name whispered in the air. He was sure the eyes were following his every move. He turned his head in the other direction, making sure he knew where the doorway to the steps was so he could get up into the attic. He then flipped the switch off and crossed through the void in the dark. His heart beat quickly as his foot found the first step, and he gripped the railing with a sweaty palm.

He almost hoped the voice of a teacher would pierce the dark to let him know he was in big trouble, telling him to stop what he was doing. But he was compelled forward. He couldn't stop himself even if he wanted to, even if he wasn't terrified. The hair on the back of his neck stood up as he continued up, eager for the secrets he was about to discover. He had counted the steps when he was here with his classmates—thirteen—and did so again to confirm since he knew he wouldn't be able to see a thing on the way back down.

Six more unbearably loud steps. His breathing resonated in his ears as he stopped for a moment. His photographic memory was often an annoyance, but it came in handy in this type of situation. He closed his eyes to revisit his first time in the room, drawing a map in his mind to guide his steps.

"Small path here," he put one foot forward. "Six steps, this way..." He began slowly, taking care not to veer off course, remembering the clutter of items on either side. A tiny red light from the exit sign behind him helped him see the barely discernible outlines of sheet-covered objects around him, like so many ghosts in the dark. He was sure the sheets were about to fall in unison, revealing the faces from the room downstairs. They would come to life, ask him what on earth he thought he was doing, grab him in the dark as penance for his intrusion, and see to it that he was never heard from again.

He took three more steps and extended his right hand to find the cool glass of the window, slowly moving toward the back of the room. Under a small hole in a recessed section of the aged wood-frame ceiling was old and twisted bare wire. From it hung a paint-specked and dusty 40-watt light bulb, which he reached for in the dark.

Jarek then stumbled across the base of a four-hook coat rack, which vibrated across the wooden floor. "Dammit," he whispered, catching it just before the top tilted back to smack him in the face. He imagined invisible eyes upon him, every item in the room crying out in voices he couldn't hear, conspiring to keep him from the thing that every ounce of his being was drawing him closer and closer to. The one thing that would help him understand what was happening to him. The book.

He moved his hand forward, searching for the pedestal upon which the book rested. "What if it's not here?" he thought with panic. "What if it's been taken away and…"

His hand found something in the dark, and he sighed in relief. A smooth sheet atop the rectangular outline of the leather cover. He slowly reached his hand straight overhead, finding the cool glass of the light bulb, gritty with settlement dust that had been drifting down from the ceiling for decades. He gave it a tug.

With a quiet click, the blub came on and, to Jarek's relief, his own nervous breathing and the creek of the electric wire swaying in the narrow-drilled hole overhead were all he heard.

His hands shook as he grabbed either side of the white sheet. He pulled it back with a flap, releasing a cloud of dust into the air that startled him. Bolting upright as he held his breath and shut his eyes, his head hit the light bulb overhead, sending it swinging on its cord. When he slowly opened them, he saw the book rhythmically appearing in and out of view by the light of the swinging bulb.

He stared wide-eyed at the cover and paced his breathing. Here it was. Finally: *An Account of the Events of the Village.*

He picked it up, felt its weight, and turned it over. Looking at the back cover for the first time, he saw something that caught his attention. A symbol. He leaned closer in the dim light to get a better look. It was a cross within a circle. Behind the cross hid two triangles, point to point, one up and one down. The circle itself was a serpent swallowing its tail—an ouroboros—forming a medallion resting upon two outstretched wings of fire. He didn't know what it meant, but he felt a shiver run through his body as he looked at it.

Flipping the book back over, he saw the smaller hand-written inscription on the cover again, whispering aloud, "The Book of the Mountain Kings."

He then held his breath and slowly opened the cover.

He turned each page and was struck by every flourish of the handwriting before him. The book appeared to be a catalog of diary entries about the life of the Village, written by people who had been dead for a very long time.

Many days were blank. Entries skipped forward to days or events that were of particular significance. On some pages were photos of land, buildings, diagrams of proposed structural changes, and, occasionally, people. Some of them he recognized from history books or old photos around campus. These were the originals of what had become some of the most well-known historical images from the Village.

He quickly flipped through the pages. There were three distinctly different handwriting styles. While this book covered about ten years of the Village's history, at least three people appeared to bear responsibility for the writings in different periods of the book's composition.

He was overwhelmed with guilt as he slowly read the entries. Some were very personal thoughts and recollections from lives long forgotten. His violation of their secrets became more pronounced with the turn of each delicate page. But he knew time was short. He flipped again to the pictures to take one final look.

More fields, buildings, and dour faces glaring at him for intruding. He flipped one more page, looking closely at several figures working in the field. His eyes opened wide in an instant and he caught his breath.

There, staring directly at him, was a small boy with a shy smile. A bundle of grain was in his hands, bound by a role of twine held beneath his arm.

Jarek was stunned. He stared in disbelief. It was, unmistakably, Lucas.

CHAPTER 20

"Can I ask what's rolling around your teeming brain?" Beth said with a smile.

They were sitting close together on a bench at the edge of the soccer field just after first period, looking through what was left of the morning mist hanging over the valley below.

Jarek had been thinking about Lucas and trying, once again, to come to terms with the fact that the double life he had been living may not be just a figment of his imagination. But he couldn't tell her that.

"I feel like I'm, I don't know, losing track of reality or something."

She raised her eyebrows. "What do you mean?"

"Well…like…sometimes, when I think about Andrew…" Jarek paused. "It's like there are two chapters of my life. The chapter with Andrew—which was every day, my entire life—and then the chapter without him, which is now—just a matter of months. The earlier part seems so much more real, like this is all just a dream. I picture him coming here, just showing up to surprise me, walking around one of these buildings and just giving me a big hug. And that's when I realize that all of this…" he nodded towards campus "I mean... my being here and why and him being…gone was all just a dream. But then I remember it isn't. He's not coming. And it hits me like a ton of bricks every single time."

Beth looked up at him, but both of their thoughts were interrupted by the bellow of a familiar voice over the quiet. Morak was holding court in the "smoking pit," a little roof on four posts at the edge of the field which was the only designated smoking location on campus. He hadn't noticed them yet, but their conversation was clearly over.

"Come on," Jarek said, getting up and extending a hand to Beth.

Sure enough, as they stood to leave, Morak's voice called out: "HEY POE!"

Jarek let out a frustrated sigh.

"Please just ignore him," Beth said, pulling his hand forward a little bit.

"POE! EDGAR! CAN YOU HEAR ME? NEVERMORE!"

"God, he's an idiot," Jarek said.

"He's sad. Sad and lost," Beth responded.

"Oh, is that what it is?" Jarek said sarcastically.

"POE! HELLOOOOOOOO!" Morak hollered again as Jarek, still holding Beth's hand, turned around and looked at him.

"Oh, you can hear me? What's up?" Morak said, raising his arms in the air with a challenging smirk. "IS THAT A RAVEN OR A CHICKEN?? NEVERMORE! BUK BUK BUK!"

"Jarek, please don't," Beth said.

He turned around, and they started to walk again. Beth sighed in relief that the situation didn't get worse and was glad the moment was over.

But seconds later, Jarek felt a heavy thud against his back. He turned around to see a lump of wet sod at his feet. He stared at it, knowing the muddy underside had left a large brown stain on the back of Andrew's coat.

He clenched his teeth as his breathing quickened and his heart beat faster—everything faded from view other than Morak, standing there smiling, eager for the altercation he was trying to create.

Jarek was fed up with being humiliated. He felt a "switch" coming on as he tried to let go of Beth's hand, but she held on tight.

"No, no, no, Jarek," she said imploringly.

"Forget it. I've had enough," Jarek said, turning away from her, wanting nothing more than to get to where Morak stood.

"Jarek, no, please, please don't. Just think about it: Headmaster Worthing, restriction, your parents, please come on." She pulled at his hand, moving closer to put her other hand on his cheek. "Please don't, for me, please."

"HELLOOOOO!" Morak yelled once more.

Jarek tried to shut it out so as not to upset her. "The only reason I haven't beat the hell out of that guy is I don't want to get in trouble," he said.

"No, no, please don't," Beth said. "Jarek, he's bigger than you."

"Boy, you always say the right thing," he said sarcastically with a shake of his head. He looked at her eyes and was surprised to see how anxious—almost panicked—the moment had made her.

Slowly, he felt his mind return to normal, like the train was back on its tracks. "Forget it," he said, more to himself than to her. "It's fine. It's fine."

She nervously scanned his face to make sure he meant it.

"Seriously," he added, "don't worry. It's fine. For now."

She smiled and squeezed his hand. "Okay," she said, putting one hand on his cheek and letting out a sigh of relief that the moment had passed.

"Whoa, I gotta run," she said, looking at her watch as she turned to go. "But wait… I don't think I'll see you again today. So, um, see you at 11?"

"Yeah," Jarek breathed, not entirely over the Morak exchange.

"Great," she smiled a little extra to encourage him to move on from the previous moment, "See you later."

"See you later," Jarek said.

"But sometime soon," he added as he turned away, "your friend and I are going to have a very serious disagreement."

"FIRST, THANK YOU FOR NOT TAKING THE BAIT EARLIER."

Jarek had again snuck across campus unnoticed, showing up at Beth's door a few minutes after 11.

"Yeah," he said as he got comfortable. "no worries."

"No, really. It meant a lot to me. I know that *you* know you don't want to get in trouble here, so I was trying to help. And, selfishly, I can't have you getting kicked out," she said, playfully scratching his chin with her fingertips.

"Thanks," he said, "I just… I'm not good at those moments. Or walking away from them anyway. And that 'hellooooo, hellooooo,' it just set me off. I haven't been able to get it out of my head for, like," he looked at his watch, "13 hours."

"Really? Don't worry, he was being a jerk." Beth said.

"No, it's not really that. It just… it reminds me of something. Sort of…a mistake I made, and how I got here. Or how I ended up leaving my old school, at least."

"I'm not following, I don't think," she said.

"Well," Jarek said, "I don't think you'll like it." He took a deep breath, resigning himself to sharing something that might very well change her opinion of him. "When Andrew got sick, he had a lot of visitors. My mom kept everyone updated and cards poured in. But then he got even sicker, and things changed. I went to school every day, but we all kept to ourselves. My mom stopped answering the phone, and my dad didn't go to work—so nobody knew how sick he was. And he was really sick—I felt like my chest would crack open every time I saw him. It was the most painful thing I could ever imagine. Still, I wanted to be there—just shoving my face in my worst nightmare—something worse than I could ever imagine, watching him deteriorate—because that meant I was by his side, and that was the only place I wanted to be, every possible second, because he was still here… and I knew before long that, um…" he paused to compose himself, "that he wouldn't be. Anyway," he said, "that's where my head was. And then, one day, I was in class, and my teacher, Mr. Stover, who was always half-jerk at best, asked me if I did my homework. I'd never been so good about it before, but then I didn't do it at all, ever. I mean—it was the last thing on my mind. But he just started sounding off, making fun of me, in front of everybody."

"Oh my gosh," Beth said, "I can't imagine a teacher doing that."

"Yeah, maybe he had something going on, I don't know, but he goes, 'I don't get it. Was I not clear? Why is there always some complication with you?' I heard a couple of snickers from the class, but he kept going, 'It's at home, it's lost, you didn't get to it, you got to half of it. What's next, your dog ate it? Anyone else in here whose dog ate their homework?' And everybody goes, 'No.'

"I never liked him," Jarek said, "but still I was surprised. When Andrew got sick, I had no control, you know? I'd have jumped off a bridge if I thought it would have helped him even a little, but there was nothing I could say or do to stop him from getting sicker. The more I prayed, the sicker he got, and I was tired of feeling helpless. But that day in class, I felt not only helpless but helpless and getting mocked for it. And I just… I have these moments…"

He paused.

"Sometimes—if something big happens or, I don't know, stressful or something—It's like my brain gets tunnel vision. Whatever sets me off is the only thing I can see, hear, or focus on. My heart beats faster, my hands kind of shake, adrenaline maybe. It just takes over. Usually, I can't even remember it after. Like, I remember most of what I'm telling you about, but some of it I don't remember at all. I know because people told me after.

"Anyway, as he says this, he's walking around my desk. I can feel it happening inside me, so I try these little tricks I learned for 'self-management' from the school shrink: 'find a focal point'—my pencil, 'count slowly'—1, 2, 3, tap my foot, clench my hands—

nothing helped, so I'm sitting there silent staring down, and he's behind me: 'Hellooooo, Jarek. Helloooo!'

"Well, I heard one more snicker from the back of the class, and I just snapped. When the next 'Hellooooooo' started, that was it."

"That was what?" she asked.

"Well, I just… I turned as I stood up, and I just…" he paused momentarily, interrupting his story. "I mean…this thing…this unbelievably terrible thing had just happened. Why Andrew? Why *my* brother? It wasn't right, it didn't make sense, it wasn't fair, and I was angry. But who could I be angry at? No one. Obviously, he didn't know yet, but that was it, and he was the closest target. I grabbed his neck, put my foot behind his leg, and pulled him back off balance and down to the floor. I just… I had no control.

"He fell back and looked stunned, then his face turned bright red—just irate. I didn't know what he would do, so when he put his hand on the floor to get himself up, I stomped down on it as hard as I could. He just let out this howl; it was awful. Maybe if I had told him to shut up earlier, I wouldn't have gotten so mad—I'd have had better 'self-management'—I don't know. Everything that built up in me was pouring out. When he tried to get up, I leaned down and punched him right in the face."

Beth looked quietly at him as he spoke—her eyes wide in disbelief.

He continued, "A bunch of the girls were screaming. I didn't even hear it... it took three of the biggest guys in class to pull me away. I don't know why he acted like that, but I felt terrible—just really guilty. I still do.

"We had talked about my going to another school, even before Andrew got sick. My parents had said, 'We think another place might be a better fit. But we don't want you to feel forced into anything, okay?' But when I saw Mr. Stover sitting on the floor of his classroom, staring at the vinyl tile, and wiping the blood running from his nose, forced or not, I knew I was leaving.

"Anyway, they pulled me off of him, and suddenly, you could hear a pin drop. Everyone was silent—just in shock, and I was standing in the middle of the room, just staring out the window with a blank look on my face. I remember looking out across a field that climbed a hill and seeing the clouds above. Just this big blue sky with beautiful clouds going past like any other day. My brain was in a swirling panic of grief and anger, but it was like I had tunnel vision. Everything around me fell away; at that moment, it was just me, the field, the hill, and the sky. I felt this urgent need to tell them something—something too big for the prying ears and small minds and fickle hearts of humans. They needed to know that something terrible had occurred. So awful that the world, and everything in it, would never be the same.

"'My brother died.' I mumbled. Maybe I thought it would start to rain. Maybe the trees would bow their heads, or the hills would crack open. Anything would do. Any sign that whatever heart might be out there in creation had broken, even if only a little bit, so I knew his life mattered."

Jarek kept his eyes forward.

"After I said it, I heard a couple of gasps in the room. Somebody started crying. That brought me back. I remembered I wasn't alone. I looked down at the floor and said again: 'My brother died.' Then I walked out."

Beth was quiet for a long time.

"So," Jarek said, "do you think I'm a psycho?"

It took her a minute. "No," she said flatly. "I mean, that's, I don't know. That's a psycho thing, for sure."

"Yeah," he said to her and himself, as he knew it changed her opinion of him. How could it not?

"But I've never known anyone who has been through what you've been through. And then to have a teacher mock you. I mean, the worst moment of your life was just…?" She looked at him and squeezed his arm.

"The night before," Jarek said. "but he didn't know that. My parents were beside themselves, and I didn't' know what to do, so I went to school. I wasn't thinking straight."

"Yeah, but..." she started to say but didn't finish her thought. "Gosh, your brother," she said with a sigh, putting her hand to her mouth.

"He was my soul, you know?" Jarek responded.

"God, I'm just so sorry." She leaned against him with her arms around his waist.

"Thanks," he said.

"For what?" Beth asked.

"I don't know. For getting it, or for understanding, for not running, I don't know. I mean now but, in general, too," he said. "It's hard to explain, but it's like...when I'm with you, you're already who you are—your wonderful self—but also..." he continued, "the time we're together is the only time that's sort of...enough. "

"Enough what?" she asked.

"Enough for me to not think about him every second, about seeing him suffer. Enough for me to feel a little more normal. I mean, not that I've ever felt normal, but you're the only thing that makes me happy enough to forget about it all for a bit."

She squeezed him tighter. "Well," she said, "that's probably the biggest compliment I've ever received in my life."

"Good." Jarek smiled, the weight of the subject matter showing on his face.

He would wait, but he had one more thing to tell her. If beating up his teacher didn't send her running, surely the fact that he was seeing ghosts and hanging out every night with those who were long-dead certainly would.

CHAPTER 21

"Have a seat."

Jarek had been "invited to a discussion" in Headmaster Worthing's office later that week. He arrived to find Worthing standing by the window of his well-appointed office, clearly awaiting Jarek's appearance. In his left hand were several papers with notes of various penmanship, which Jarek correctly assumed were written by his teachers.

Jarek took two steps into the room, his faded jeans, flannel, and boots making him feel even more like a fish out of water in this, the shiniest and most intimidating location in the entirety of the otherwise weathered campus. He turned and sat in the dark leather armchair that Worthing had motioned to with a tilt of the papers. The squeak of the leather put him more on edge, and he was careful to sit with his feet flat on the floor so as not to draw attention to his mud-caked boots. He adjusted himself in the seat. It squeaked again, so he sat still, his back uncomfortably straight, and waited.

In his right hand, Worthing held a small watering can. He took his time slowly and attentively distributing water into the soil of a Ficus plant, which sat on a piece of marble precisely cut to serve as a shelf atop the old radiator beneath the window. The plant was perfect: no browning tips, no trimmings, no stems, or other distraction marred the tidily attended soil beneath or the shine of the leaves, which looked as if they had been recently dusted.

Jarek was small in the depth of the chair, and the size and height of Worthing's desk made him feel more so. As Worthing settled into his high-back seat behind his desk, he was only visible from the shoulders up, with the glare from the window behind him causing Jarek to squint to see his face.

"Look, Jarek," he tried to act casual. His classmates told him after that Worthing was always a hard-ass, especially on male students. Rumor had it that his son was brilliant, did well at Williams, and later dropped out of a master's program in engineering to pursue his real passion: theater. As a result, they hadn't spoken in nearly two years. "I'll cut to the chase. It's important for you to do well here," he said. "Do you see this plant?"

Jarek wanted to say, "Yeah, I get it," to shut down the childish example he knew was coming but instead nodded as Worthing continued.

"This plant needs water." He momentarily held up his copper watering can and gestured the brass tip towards Jarek. "It needs sunlight," he said, nodding towards the window, "and it needs healthy soil," he added, gesturing ceremoniously to the flowerpot.

"Whatever happened before I can forget about," Worthing said.

Jarek figured this referred to "the incident" that got him kicked out of his old school, and he didn't appreciate it.

"But what we are giving you here," he added, "is water, sunlight, and soil. That being the case, there is no excuse for *this*." He held up the paper he had been reviewing as his tone changed. "You're consistently late. Your work is sloppy. You've fallen asleep at least twice in class in the past week, according to what I've got here, and I'm sure there's plenty I haven't been told about."

He looked again at the papers. "Here," he said, pointing. "'Jarek seems listless, aloof,' and here, 'not committed to the subject matter,' and this is a good one: 'Jarek is in a fog which I cannot extract him from no matter how hard I try.'"

Jarek was starting to sweat. He had nothing to say.

"'No matter how hard I try'?" Worthing stood up. "These people have other students to teach, Jarek! So, tell me, what fog? What's the story?" Worthing looked at him sternly, but Jarek saw behind his stare that he was genuinely perplexed and maybe a bit concerned. Maybe he really did have a heart in there somewhere, even if his circumstances had driven him to become—without a doubt—a relentless prick.

"I know having you come here is not financially easy for your parents," the headmaster went on. "And they will be very disappointed to see these." He again held up the papers. That one hurt.

"Look, I don't say much about the silly things you do with your clothes and hair, as much as I don't see the point. You're a smart guy. That's why you're here, but smart isn't good enough. Effort, Jarek. Persistence!" he tossed the papers onto the desk and looked Jarek in the eye. Jarek sat silently with his hands on the knees of his faded jeans.

"In any case, I at least know you're smarter than this," he said, firmly planting his finger on the papers one last time. "And it's best you start proving me right."

He stared at Jarek for three endless seconds.

"Thank you," he said in conclusion, and Jarek understood this meant *get out*, which is exactly what he did.

Jarek walked to the Tannery, feeling uneasy. When Beth wasn't in class, she would sit inside and play for hours. If he ever couldn't find her, he knew she was there, where he first saw her. He would walk in, sit quietly next to her on the piano bench, and she would put her head on his shoulder as her hands moved gently around the keys. Sometimes, he would sit behind her on the bench, his legs around hers, his hands on her waist, and lean his head over her shoulder to watch her play. Or he would push her hair to the side and gently kiss the back of her neck, doing his best to distract her as she smiled and tried to focus. The bench was small but more than big enough to accommodate the two of them in a sitting position and, as they had learned on at least two late-night occasions so far, other positions as well.

This time, though, she wasn't there. Afternoon sunlight streamed across the lush green fields just outside, through the windowpanes, and across the old wooden benches. The piano was covered, and the room was silent.

WHEN JAREK SNUCK ACROSS CAMPUS LATE THAT NIGHT, HE TOLD BETH about the Worthing meeting.

"Wow, that sounds awful," Beth said. "I'm sorry." She leaned up and put a small kiss on his chin.

"Are your parents coming up for parents' weekend?" she asked.

"When's that?"

"Seriously? It's next weekend," Beth replied.

"Ah. I dunno," Jarek sighed. "I guess it depends on if my dad has to work; he gets busier this time of year. I kind of hope not."

"What? Why? I thought you'd want them to come."

"I'm okay with them not seeing Worthing for as long as possible, or calling him, or thinking about him. Or checking their mail. When you're avoiding the headmaster at all costs, the last thing you want is for him to have a nice long chat with your parents."

"I can tell something's really been bothering you. Whatever it is, it's that big of a deal?"

"Big enough for my grades to suck and Worthing to be up my ass? Yes."

She sighed. He cringed. He hated the threshold that they had just crossed. The one where she joined the ranks, however briefly, of all the other people who were disappointed, concerned, unsure of what the problem was, ready to tell him at every turn that they wish he would apply himself.

"Look." She took his chin in her hand and moved his face back towards hers, so he had no choice but to meet her gaze. He wasn't sure what was coming next, but he wished they could go back to three minutes ago before the subject ever came up. "Can I provide some context here?"

"Sure," Jarek said.

She moved in closer, looked up at his face as he looked down at hers, and placed her soft lips against his for an affectionately firm five seconds, each one of which he appreciated fully.

"I like that context," he said.

She drew back, still holding his chin and his gaze.

"Well, here's the rest. I care about you. A lot." She moved her hand from his chin and lightly drew one finger across his cheek. "I can't have you imploding, and I can't have you getting kicked out," she joked, unaware that this potential outcome was already present in his mind.

"Don't worry," he said.

"Yeah, but...what's the end game? Whatever this mystery issue is that's messing everything up, is the end in sight? The past few weeks, you've been different. What happens next week? Next month? I want to hang out with *you*, not your ghost." The irony struck him.

He could see it in her presence, persistent gaze, and body language. This was the moment he had dreaded.

He had two options: tell her everything...or tell her nothing. Tell her why he seemed like the walking dead. Tell her a ghost talked to him, and he has since been traveling through time and living with some crazy people who have been dead for over a century. Sure. Tell her that. Perfectly normal. He was sure it would go swimmingly. She'd say, "Oh, is that all?" then kiss him and grab a CD she'd meant to tell him about. Right.

The reality was, she would either think he was nuts—legit clinically crazy—or, more likely, that he was completely full of crap. And if she thought he was completely full of crap, she would question his honesty about anything and everything else, and that would be the end of this delightful thing, whatever it was.

The other option was he could tell her nothing. *Everything's fine*, he would say. But she would know he was lying and slowly drift away from him. He had no idea how things were going to turn out, whether he was losing it or if he'd even be here in a few months, but at the very least, it would be nice to have her by his side through it; head on his chest, his hand on her shoulder, fading in and out of sleep.

"I'm afraid to tell you about it because I like this," he said, pushing her hair behind her ear, "the way it is. And I don't want to mess it up."

"Well," she said, "two things. The first is you already told me about punching your teacher in the face, which, let's be honest, is something else. And I'm still here. And the second," she looked up with a smirk, "I'm not giving you a choice." She gave him a playful pat on the shoulder. "Oh, and the third," she added.

"There's a third?" he asked, feigning excitement.

"The third is that whatever it is, or whatever is going on with you, clearly isn't working if you're gonna stay in school here, which is where I want you."

"Yeah, I know," he said, grateful for the sentiment.

"So…come on. Out with it. I can't help if I don't know."

He sighed. Beth looked at him eagerly, concerned, and waiting. "So…here's the thing," he began. "I've sort of been…having these…crazy dreams," he said. "I don't even know how to explain it."

"What do you mean 'crazy dreams?'" she asked.

"Well, I guess, about the Shakers. Lots of dreams. And I, um, I'm pretty sure I saw a ghost. Not *in* the dreams but before the dreams. But I think it's all sort of the same thing. It's hard to explain."

"Wait, a ghost?" Beth asked. "What do you mean? When… where?"

"In my dorm—in the bathroom mirror. It was an old man."

Beth paused. "You saw an actual ghost…"

"At least I think so. An old man with a beard. He looked at me and said something—I don't know what it was. 'Consensus' or something like that. And right after that, I started having these dreams. Like real dreams. With the Shakers."

"Ooookay," Beth said, half smiling, but looking confused.

"Yeah, but it's not like I'm dreaming about them. In these dreams, I'm, like, *with* them. They started right after I saw the... the ghost. Then they were maybe once a week. Now I have them all the time. And they're, I don't know, very real. The people know my name, and I know theirs. I'm on a work crew, and we eat together, and I go to their dances, and every day proceeds from the day before. And then I go to sleep in the room they gave me—my Shaker room—and guess what? It's the same room I live in now in Brethrens! Then I wake up, I feel like I haven't slept at all, and it's the beginning of another day and time to go to class. I try to concentrate but I can't, and my friends in my dreams are all real people with real names and faces. And one of them is a boy named Lucas, and he's in trouble, but I don't know why, and I'm trying to help him, but I don't know how."

Her dark eyes stared at him, stunned and expressionless in the dark.

"These are some dreams," she said.

"That's the weird thing," Jarek said. "I don't know if they're really dreams. It's starting to feel like they're not dreams at all."

"Okay. You've got Shakers on the brain; every night you dream about them and...you're making friends." She hesitated, confused. "But you think they're not dreams. So, if they're not dreams... what are they?"

"I don't know. If you were my old guidance counselor, this is when you'd start telling me about my brother, PTSD, white matter, and the pre-frontal cortex."

"Huh?" she said, and he realized his last remark didn't help.

"It's like I'm one of them. Every time I go to sleep here, I wake up there and go about my day, and it's not like a dream. It's like I'm really there. Does that make sense?"

Beth wasn't following. "I don't get the difference."

"This kid Lucas, I know his whole story, everything about him. And I feel like if I don't help him, something terrible is going to happen."

She paused. "Yeah, this is all a little crazy. Maybe you need a long weekend or something?"

"No, No," he said, sitting up. "Every time I go to bed, I'm here in the same place—same buildings, same roads, same fields—but it's the 1800s! I'm telling you, I'm—like—in this double life, and it's eating me alive because I don't get it at all."

She waited.

"But I'm *there.*" Jarek was emphatic. "I'm physically *there*, living my life with them, every day. I've seen pictures—the old ones from the Village—and the people in the pictures? I've seen them. I *know* them. Their names, their faces, how they act, and what they think."

He stopped talking and looked at her. She gazed at him in silence, her eyebrows slightly raised in concern.

"Forget it," he said and looked away. "I shouldn't have said anything."

She exhaled and, from the look on her face, he could tell she was carefully considering what she would say next. "Um, this is pretty crazy."

"Well. You always know just what to say. I shouldn't have told you," Jarek said. He meant it.

"No, no, I'm glad you did." Beth touched his arm. "I want you to be able to, you know, tell me things."

"Yeah, but..." Jarek shook his head.

"Come on," she interrupted as delicately as she could. "Not only are you having these crazy dreams that apparently are ruining everything you're here for, but you think you're traveling through time where you have a little buddy, too? What would *you* think if someone told you that?"

"I'll prove it to you," Jarek said. "I have an idea. Come with me."

CHAPTER 22

"Wait, I don't think we're supposed to go in there."

They had snuck out of her dorm, looking around to make sure the coast was clear. Jarek held Beth's hand and pulled her towards the side of the museum. "Don't move," he said, walking around the back of the adjacent building while she stood in the dark, her hands nervously gripping each other, until he emerged with the 20-foot ladder he'd be using.

Beth paused. "You're not serious."

"Serious as a heart attack. This thing is a little unwieldy," he said, moving towards the base of the building. "So…"

"So, stay out of your way?" she asked.

Jarek's mind was focused on the ladder. "Yeah, kinda," he said.

He grunted under the weight as he placed the feet in the dirt and looked up to make sure it rested below the right window before he pulled the rope, wincing a bit at the noise of the brackets hitting each step as it extended.

He gestured to the lower steps, "Ladies first."

"What?" Beth said with surprise. "No way."

"Your call." He put one foot on the base of the ladder and started up the steps slowly. "The ladder is a little wobbly, so wait until I'm through the window before you start up."

"The window? God, you're crazy," she said.

"Ooh, that stings," he said with a smile as he started up.

Once he had climbed to the top and through the window, she took a deep breath and followed. He took her hand to help her through, watching her head against the base of the open window as he guided her inside. The floor creaked in the dark as he heard her nervous breathing.

"I don't like this. This place gives me the creeps," she whispered, "I can't see a thing."

"Follow me," he said, taking her hand in the dark. "Don't let go."

"Trust me, I won't," she said as he gripped her sweaty palm.

They crept across the floor and up the small, uneven steps to the attic. She saw the tall, shrouded furniture—ghostlike shapes in the dark before them—and stopped.

"Jarek…" she said.

"Shh, it's okay," he said, tugging her hand forward.

"Do you feel like you're being watched?" she asked.

He turned his head back to hers in the dark, smiled, and said, "All the time."

His hand fumbled overhead for the chain under the small bulb he knew was there. With a click, its column of light pierced the dark as she turned her stunned eyes away, then slowly back, staring wide-eyed as she read the words on the cover before her: *An Account of the Events of the Village: 1860-1870.*

"Yeah," he said. The look of anticipation on his face made her nervous.

She read the handwritten inscription below in a whisper.

"'The Book of the Mountain Kings.' Jarek, this is creepy. I want to leave," she said.

"No, no. This is why we're here. Look…"

She leaned close as he flipped forward. "But what…" her fingers interrupted his turning of the pages as she pointed to a blurred image in black ink at the bottom of one page, asking, "What's this?"

He peered down. Someone had long ago inked the cross symbol from the back cover onto a page. The cross itself was encircled by a serpent swallowing its tail. Two wings of fire were below.

He stared at it for a moment before catching himself and responding. "I don't know," he paused, "but I think it's important. Don't worry about that now. What's today's date?" he said.

"October 30th," she said quickly.

"Every time I dream, it's the next day. I mean, yesterday, in my dream, it was October 29th. Tonight, it will be October 30th. This book—whoever wrote it—is like a journal of things that happened in the Village. Some days have entries, most don't."

He flipped a few pages forward and brushed some dust off the top right corner to show the date more clearly.

"What's the most recent entry? Look here," he pointed.

"October 24th," she paused momentarily and whispered, "1866."

"What does it say?"

"Something about soil," she said, still in a whisper, the moment weighing on her chest.

"And what's today's date?" he flipped forward for her. "What do you see?" he said, pointing to blank lines below.

"Nothing. It's blank."

"Right," he said. "Remember that. October 30th is blank."

He turned off the light, took her hand, and retraced their steps across the crowded room in the dark.

"I don't understand," she said.

"You will."

He helped her slowly down the stairs, her nervous breathing echoing in the silence around them, interrupted only by the occasional creak of the stairs and old floorboards. He turned on the small light in the front room, and the tall and dour faces of the elders stared right through her from their black and white posterboards. She gasped.

"This," he said, pointing to a woman with high cheekbones in a white bonnet, and speaking as casually as he would of an old friend, "is Sister Abigail."

"Jarek, you're scaring me."

He moved to the next face. "This," he said, pointing to a man with a wide-brim hat and piercing gaze. "This is Brother Thaddeus."

She stared in disbelief.

"And this…" he took several small steps and raised his hand before the visage of an old man with a long white beard. He stared into the wise old eyes and paused.

"Who's that?" she asked.

"I…I don't know," he said. "I don't know his name."

They looked at the time-weary and deeply wrinkled face, certain it was studying them as well.

"But I think he is why we're here. I think…this is his idea… somehow. And I get the feeling he has more to tell me."

Jarek stared at the dark eyes as she pressed nervously against him from behind. He looked at the face for another moment, then spoke quietly.

"This is the ghost."

Her eyes were wide open in the dim light as one shaky hand covered her mouth.

"I want to leave, Jarek, please," her voice quivered. "Please."

"Don't be scared; trust me." He flipped the switch off to make their exit. Moments later, he had put the ladder back, and they were making their way carefully through the dark.

She couldn't wait. "Jarek I'm so freaked out I want to hide in my bed. Please walk faster."

They approached the back door of her dorm, and he gently put his hands on her shoulders and turned her around.

"Don't worry," Jarek said. He could tell it didn't help. "I don't know what's happening, and it scares the hell out of me, but I think it may be important."

He kissed her lips briefly before continuing, "First, I will prove that I'm not crazy, and that whatever this is, it's real. I have something I have to do, then you'll believe me. Good night."

"What do you mean you have something you have to do? What does that mean? When?"

He smiled over his shoulder as he walked away.

"Right now," he said.

Then he disappeared into the dark.

CHAPTER 23

"Jarek, slow down!" Lucas said with a laugh as the boys moved through the towering stalks of wheat.

"Jarek, too fast!" Lucas called out again, the distance between them growing.

Numerous workgroups went out into the Village each morning to conduct every manner of labor: tending livestock, preparing meals, structural repair, tanning, and many others. Jarek and Lucas had been regularly assigned to the same team and, after several days, began spending the better part of their time together on and off the field, sitting together at meals, climbing the orchard trees, and exploring the many acres of the Village. Jarek was five years older, but they were good company for each other, so neither cared.

"You're supposed to keep up!" Jarek teased, looking back over his shoulder.

They were working among the many brothers spread far and wide in the expansive grain field that looked down over the valley, assigned to help bring in the harvest.

The brothers regularly sang Shaker songs as they worked, swinging their tools in unison as their voices rose across the field.

(Song: "I'll Spend and be Spent")

I'll spend and be spent in the cause of my God, my all I freely resign.
I'll take up my cross and travel from loss and be faithful while here in time.
I'll spend and be spent in the cause of my God, my all I freely resign.

I'll take up my cross and travel from loss and be faithful while here in time.
Though billows may beat and waves o'er me ROLL, yet true to my trust I will be.
For God he is able the winds to control, and bear me over the sea.

Jarek joined after hearing the words once through, enjoying the crescendo at the word "roll" as it echoed off the mountain.

By far the most energetic of the bunch, Jarek and Lucas decided to create a competition. Jarek swung a heavy cradle scythe at a blistering pace, smiling as Lucas followed behind, attempting to gather and tie the stalks quickly; a bundle of grain was in his hands, bound by a role of twine held beneath his arm.

Looking up, Jarek felt the moment was somehow familiar to him. Then he saw it: At the edge of the field, a visitor ducked under the hood of a four-lens bellows-style camera atop a tripod. He and Lucas looked in the man's direction as he called out to them. A moment later, a bulb popped atop the device. Jarek paused momentarily, realizing the photograph that had just been taken was the same one he would see of Lucas in the museum more than a century in the future.

He was brought back to his surroundings as an elderly brother on horseback slowed as he passed by. "You lads make quite a team. Very good, brothers," he said with gratitude. They both smiled at the recognition, though Jarek's quickly faded at the word "brothers."

A short time later, their task behind them, the two boys stood by the Tannery pond as Jarek instructed Lucas in the art of skipping stones.

"Make sure your pointer finger goes along the flat edge like this," Jarek said, showing Lucas the stone in his hand and adding, "Keep it flat," before slinging it forward to skim across the water as they counted the skips.

"Seven! Wow." Lucas said, trying again with his rock and dejectedly noting, "Two."

As they looked for flat stones, Lucas suddenly remarked, "Thank you, Jarek."

"What, this?" Jarek nodded towards the pond. "Sure," he said with a smile.

"I mean, not just this," Lucas added. "Just…"

"Just what?" Jarek asked curiously, turning to face him.

"I, well," Lucas paused. "I'm… I'm grateful. Since you got here, I mean."

"Oh wow," Jarek said, touched and taken aback. "Lucas, of course."

After a moment, he smiled at Lucas. "Are you hungry?"

"Yeah." Lucas winced to show he meant it.

"Let's go eat," Jarek said. "I'm starving, and the smell of that pie is calling my name."

And the two unlikely companions walked with purposeful strides toward the smell of baked ham and apple pie.

CHAPTER 24

"So, these dreams. They're still happening a lot?" Drummy asked.

"Yeah," Jarek said, "pretty much every night."

He was in Drummy's apartment, where he'd been invited to listen to a live recording of a Dylan concert Drummy had recently scored a rare bootleg of. Jarek figured he wanted to talk. Aside from the Dylan posters, there was now a full-page picture of Richie Havens, clearly ripped from a magazine, a poster titled "Irish Poets" with a picture and quote from all the famous ones, and a green-tweed easy chair , comfortable enough to keep around even though it had clearly seen better days.

"You decorated," Jarek said.

Drummy was in his usual attire: a slightly faded white V-neck t-shirt, which drew a little more attention to his affection for baked goods than he would like, a pair of dated blue jeans, and plain running sneakers. His habit of running his hand through his thick dark hair during moments of intense academic debate, of which he had many, kept his coiffeur at high alert above the thick dark rims of his glasses. He looked, as always, like some existential question had gotten him out of bed earlier than he would have liked.

"So, more often now. Okay, that's what I figured from looking at you." He gave Jarek a concerned look. Jarek appreciated it.

"Anything new to tell me?" Drummy added.

"Yeah, I guess so," Jarek said. "I, um, I've been to the museum."

"Here? Alone?" Drummy asked.

"Yeah, a couple of times at night."

"Well, that's risky. How did you get in?" Drummy was perplexed.

"A ladder to the back window," Jarek replied.

He raised his eyebrows. "Wow. Okay. And…?"

"Well, the people in my dreams are in the museum. I mean… their pictures are there," Jarek said.

"The people in your dreams are in the museum? Let me get this straight: you started having the dreams, you managed to get in the museum, and in the museum, you saw pictures of the people you've been dreaming about?" Drummy said.

Jarek nodded. "You've been in there, right?" he asked.

"A dozen times, at least," Drummy said.

"The ones in the front room. The people in the photos. I know them. In my dreams, I mean."

"In the front room. The Elders?!" he leaned forward. "You're sure the dreams didn't come *after* you went to the museum?"

"I'm sure. I have them every night now, and the people I know—in my dreams, I saw them in the museum after the dreams started," Jarek said.

"How many dreams did you have before you went to the museum?" Drummy asked.

"I don't know, ten dreams? Twenty?" Jarek said.

"And you're sure? It's the same faces?"

"Yes, yes, yes," Jarek said impatiently. "I know them as well as I know some of the teachers here. One, her name is Abigail; I know her as well as I know you."

"Holy hell. Sister Abigail? Abigail Dorrance?" Drummy asked.

"I don't know her last name," Jarek said.

"Well, that's her last name," Drummy said. "She's one of the most important leaders the Village ever had."

"Really? Not yet, I guess, or at least not when I know her. Look, I want to figure out what's happening. I'm starting to feel like I'm losing it," Jarek said.

Drummy looked at him. "You're not losing it, and it makes a ton of sense. Well, at least part of it does. I mean, clearly, it's happening, but I have no idea why. When we talked last time, I told you I believed you because I know you're honest. But...I had more reason to believe you than you knew."

"What reason is that?" Jarek asked.

"As you know I'm a bit of a history buff when it comes to this stuff, the Shakers, the Village. So, I have something to show you. Here, take a look at this."

Drummy reached for a large and heavily worn volume that rested on its side on the top corner of his bookshelf. He brushed the dust off the faded leather cover with his hand.

"This book is..." he thought for a moment. "They were careful about their public image. There's a lot they didn't talk about, especially with outsiders. Some of it takes a little getting used to, frankly. I've read this book twice, mostly out of morbid curiosity. At first, I thought it was a bunch of hocus pocus, but there are a couple of interesting things here and there, and maybe it's making a little more sense these days."

"What is it about?"

"Well, it's about ghosts. The ones you don't believe in," Drummy smirked. "Or have you changed your mind?"

"I guess I haven't had much of a choice, unfortunately," Jarek replied.

Drummy parted the cover, and the book opened to an etching of a skeleton wearing a hat—the same ones worn by most Shaker men—and crawling out of a carefully cut rectangular hole in the ground. A grave. Below the image was a chapter heading etched in large Gothic font. It read: "Gifts from the Restless Dead."

"It took me months to read all of this," Drummy said. "I'll make it easy on you."

He stopped and looked at the floor to think for a moment. What he was about to explain was serious and unusual, and he wanted to make sure he got it right, for Jarek's sake.

He took a deep breath. "Jarek, there are some things that those who were here before us, the Shakers, were capable of. Or thought they were anyway. That's what this book talks about."

"What kind of things?" Jarek asked, nervously waiting for the answer.

"You ever get the feeling you're being watched? Here, I mean, on campus. Like there's something unseen somewhere in one of these old buildings—in the basements, the closets, the corners, the top floors? Maybe you pass under a dark window on a walk across campus later at night, and you feel it watching you, sure something is peeking over your shoulder. But the second you turn around, it's gone?"

"Yes," Jarek said. "Yes. All the time."

"Well, Jarek, those of The Way," he paused, "Those of The Way believed, or learned, or maybe just stumbled into, something the rest of us would find…incredible."

"Okay." Jarek held his breath.

"Well," Drummy said. He seemed unsure of how to proceed. "It's about…time."

"Time?" Jarek asked, "What do you mean?"

"They believed that time was… how do I say this…" Drummy paused and ran his hand through his already tousled hair. "They believed that time, for them anyway, was not a linear reality and that they—or at least some of them—were not bound by the present. They believed they could revisit the past. They believed they could interact with the future in a way the rest of us aren't able to."

He looked at Jarek, asking, "Does that make sense?"

"No," Jarek said flatly. "I don't have a clue what you're talking about. Sorry."

"Okay, okay." Drummy started over. "We believe there is the past, the present, and the future, and never the twain shall meet, right? So, aside from a particular moment that joins one with the other, these two dimensions are totally unrelated. So, this moment when I snap my fingers"—he snapped his fingers with a flourish—"is only connected to the past and future by the moments that came immediately before and after. Aside from that, they never have anything to do with each other. The past, whether it's ten seconds, ten years, or ten centuries, is the past. Inaccessible to us in every possible way. Flip the script, and the same applies to the future."

He looked at Jarek to see if the first concept towards making his point had sunk in.

"Okay," Jarek said, "I'm following."

Drummy continued. "Well, the Shakers believed something similar: past, present, and future. But they also believed that they were not constrained as the rest of us are regarding the… inaccessibility of dimensions other than the present. They believed that, through their worship, they could minister to the dead. To share The Way with those who, for whatever reason, were not exposed to it during life. Salvation, post-mortem."

"Wow," Jarek said, "that's wild."

"It gets better," Drummy smiled. "They also believed that some among them were able to not only minister to the dead, but it seems," he paused, "that some among them had taken the extraordinary next step."

"What step was that?" Jarek hung on every word.

Drummy lowered his voice a bit. "That they were able to find the dead at that point in time when they were living and minister to them there. In the past. Maybe in the future, too."

Jarek was speechless.

"They believed this was possible, but that very few of them could actually pull it off. Not all of them. There's no written explanation or proof of where such an ability came from or if it was real. Maybe they made it up, or maybe they figured it out themselves—something to do with their strange and fervent relationship with God. I don't pretend to know the answer, and nobody else does either. Maybe fanaticism comes with some perks from the man upstairs." His sarcastic grin punctuated the final few words.

"I thought you didn't believe in the man upstairs?" Jarek quipped.

"Well. Mostly, I don't. Or sometimes I do and I'm just pissed at him, or her, because we're all so screwed up. Anyway..." he said, pivoting back to the issue at hand, "I think it's possible, entirely possible, that the feeling we've all had that there's a presence here, something we can't quite see, can't quite put our finger on...maybe they were real. I dunno."

"They? Who are 'they'?" Jarek asked.

Drummy nodded. "Well, Jarek, not 'who' but 'what.' 'They' are something the Shakers called 'Spirit Gifts.' They believed in them very strongly. Not only could the living minister to the dead, but the dead could give a 'gift' to the living. Imparting wisdom or guidance to those who came after. To tell them things." Drummy paused. "From beyond the grave."

Jarek's lack of response encouraged him to continue.

"The dead talking to the living..."

"Yeah, I get it," Jarek said impatiently, "and..."

Drummy interrupted, "And how do we know this?"

Jarek nodded.

"In some of the journals they kept, and in letters, there are numerous incidents of villagers writing things like 'I received a gift from brother so and so. He told me that younger members of our community suffer because they are not embracing The Way,' but then we find that the brother they have mentioned died several years before. 'Spirit Gifts' were messages from God about how the Village should proceed. These were delivered by 'instruments,' that's what they called those who claimed to have received such gifts from the dead. Needless to say, there were times when some members made these visions up as a way to get attention or settle old scores."

"Wow, like the Salem witch trials."

"Pretty much," Drummy said, "Except no one was executed, thank goodness. But *if* any of the gifts were real, and *if* imparting gifts to the living is something they really figured out, well, then maybe they are reaching out—so far into the future, for whatever reason—to share wisdom with you." Drummy smiled. "Or maybe they just like you."

Jarek didn't smile back.

Drummy was quick to respond. "I'm not trying to be glib; you've been through a lot. But if I'm right, maybe something about you makes you the right person for him to reach out to. Which is the next thing…"

"Oh, there's more," Jarek said impatiently. "Great."

"If the gifts are real, maybe they can be imparted not just in visions but in dreams, as you have experienced. This book," Drummy put his hand on the open pages; Jarek took one look at the skeleton crawling out of the grave and shuddered as his teacher continued, "talks about the restless dead 'reaching forward,' not only imparting wisdom to the living, but appearing to them and, somehow or other, even bringing them back to them."

"Back to them," Jarek raised his eyebrows, "like…back in time?"

"Yes," Drummy said. "And, unlike the gifts that imparted wisdom, 'reaching forward' would be done by those who may have died prematurely, or unfairly… unnaturally. Why they would reach forward, for what purpose, or if it actually occurred outside the imaginations of the overzealous…no one knows."

Jarek interrupted, "So there's reason to believe I'm not crazy."

"No. No, you're definitely not crazy. But, from where we now sit, it looks like this brother might be among what they would call 'the restless dead,' not just sharing a gift with you but 'reaching forward,' in which case you, Jarek, for whatever reason, are the instrument."

Jarek stared at him, unable to process what this all meant as Drummy continued.

"But that's about all I know. Though there is one other thing…" he said

Jarek was eager, "Yeah?"

"Well, you may not be the first student this has happened to. There are some accounts of another student here, in 1952, who had an experience similar to yours. Dreams. Vivid, all-consuming dreams. And in them, according to this book, he was living with the Shakers in the 1820s. He, too, thought he'd seen a ghost, though it was a woman. He said he was trying to save her, but from what nobody knows. They thought he was delusional."

"Oh my gosh," Jarek said. "What happened?"

"No one knows for sure. He started sort of…fading away, just struggling. People thought he was having episodes. Then, early one morning, he didn't show up for class. A teacher went to find him, and he was in his room. It looked like he was resting peacefully, but he was…in bad shape."

Jarek's jaw dropped. The gravity of the last few words sank into his mind and chest. There was a question he was afraid to ask, but he had to.

"Um… so… what room?"

Drummy hesitated, took a deep breath, and looked him in the eye.

"Yours, Jarek. He lived in your room."

"Christ, Mr. Drummy!" Jarek stood up. "I thought this conversation was supposed to make me feel better…"

"Well, no. I mean, yes, but listen—sit down—this is important. They thought he had taken something—overdosed on purpose. But this was a young, happy kid—the same age as you—and, in hindsight, all the signs of the same struggle. He was out of sorts, talking all the time about dreams. About a girl who was in trouble of some sort. He spoke about it so often that his isolation got worse; people thought he was nuts and thought he tried to hurt himself on purpose. But if it was true, even if he just *thought* it was true, why would he poison himself when he was involved in something so profound? When he believed with every ounce of his being that he was being called to something so important? Something he was committed to doing?"

Jarek suddenly felt he understood this kid very well.

"He wouldn't," Jarek said. "Never."

"Right. His blood tests were negative. He didn't take anything. But they showed certain markers for immense physical strain—like he was a weightlifter or a triathlete after a race. Like he had just come through some immense physical struggle."

"I don't get it," Jarek said.

"Listen, yours is only the second experience like this I've ever heard of, and I've looked everywhere. So we don't have much to go on, but I think…how do I say this?" He paused as Jarek waited nervously. "We need to consider the possibility that whatever struggle he was involved in to save this girl had ramifications. Mental and, maybe, physical."

Jarek stared at him and asked, "What are you saying?"

"I'm saying I think maybe he was in some immense physical conflict in his dreams…and he lost."

"Lost as in…" Jarek asked.

Drummy hesitated momentarily, adding, "Lost as in he… well…"

Drummy spoke slowly as if he was trying to unlock a mystery.

"Maybe through the strain of all of it…maybe his mind was so thoroughly convinced that it was real and—to some extent, as you know, maybe it was, that I think that was…that was it."

"That was *what*? Jesus!"

"He…well," Drummy said quietly. "He died, Jarek."

Jarek stared at Drummy in shock. His mind raced. He shook his head a bit and took a deep breath.

"Okay. Okay, let me get this straight. This and everything else, I mean. In these dreams, if that's what they are, if I die in them…

then I actually die for real!? Die. Dead. Like funeral, cemetery, crying parents, 'He was such a nice guy,' the ever-after and all that. Actual death?"

Drummy sighed and looked down, wishing he had another answer. "I don't know. Maybe. It's possible." They sat silently for a moment.

Drummy continued. "Look, I'm sure you've got a hundred questions, and I wish I had the answers, but I don't. Here's the thing, though. There's someone else here who knows much, much more than me. And I think he's someone you need to talk to. I've shared with him what you've told me."

"What?" Jarek said with surprise. "We had a deal! Between you and me, that was the deal. I don't want anyone else to know."

"Yes, Jarek, but this is important, and if what I think is happening is actually happening, we need to get it right. You don't have to tell him. I already have. So, let's go. He's expecting us and is pretty old-fashioned, so let's not be late."

CHAPTER 25

They walked silently across campus under a heavy grey sky, heads hung low in thought and Drummy's hands deep in his jacket pockets away from the damp cold.

Jarek was surprised to find they were heading for the library, the same building he had been in a dozen times in his dreams, each time struck by how large, empty, and vibrant the space was. He could practically hear the rhythmic stomps and see the faces of the sisters and brothers dancing emphatically, their faces flushed pink in a swarm of movement and song and life that was so much more colorful and animated than anyone seeing its likeness looking back on it now from the present would ever believe was possible.

But now the space was carpeted and full of bookshelves. The top floor of the balcony—a recent addition—looked down from above and was filled with cubicles, trash cans, and outdated magazines. Back in the Village, it was a place of frequent celebration and frenetic worship. But now it was back to its hum-drum self: study space doing its very best despite its somewhat neglected status.

They entered through the middle of the three doors. Jarek hesitated; he wouldn't dare go through the middle door in his dreams—it was for elders only. The door latch was the same, and he loved the familiar "chunk-click" sound as Drummy's thumb pushed the button down and the lever in the back released.

"Why are we going here?" he asked.

"We're going to his office."

Jared assumed he meant the librarian. There was only one office in the library, and it was his. He was a kind, upright old fellow in his sixties who kept to himself. He graduated from the school in the '50s, went to a tweedy New England university, and then came back to teach—so he had been on campus, in some capacity or other, for most of his life.

They walked to a small, windowed office far in the back of the main floor, and as Drummy placed a two-rap knock on the heavily repainted old white door, a stern voice from inside replied, "Come in."

"Hi, Matt," the librarian said as Drummy entered, gesturing to a couple of faded leather chairs before his desk. "Have a seat."

"Thanks, Earl. Jarek, this is Mr. McCracken."

Jarek had only seen him from a distance before, and he was a much more imposing presence than he expected. His buzzed white hair had probably been cut the same since he was in high school. He had weathered cheeks and wise, piercing eyes.

"Hello, sir," Jarek said. He tried not to wince as McCracken's friendly but powerful handshake folded his knuckles in on themselves.

"Hello, Jarek," he said, much less sternly. McCracken pushed a stack of books and yellow documents to the side of his desk as Drummy took a seat, smiling with a familiarity that made it clear this introduction had been discussed in advance.

Kind but serious, McCracken was a God-fearing man who led chapel services on campus and spent many years as a greatly admired school hockey coach. Quick skates, a ready stick, and a heavy shoulder made him a force to reckon with every winter when the pond next to the old sheep barn on campus froze over, and students gathered at 3 p.m. each day for tough lessons about hockey and life, always delivered with a smile.

"On point," he would say to his players, "means 'find, focus, finish.' Find the play, focus—don't let your emotions take over, and finish—do what you're there for—make the hit. Get it done. Find, focus, finish. On point."

During pivotal plays, they would hear him yelling, "On point! On point!" From the edge of the ice. They listened. He knew hockey inside and out, and his ability to drive a flattening check on an opponent at just the right moment was legendary.

These days, McCracken mostly pored over old documents in his office or slowly walked across campus with stacks of books under his arm. He interacted with students during Hands to Work as head of the wood-chopping crew. When he got to work, his woodpile grew at three times the rate of even the fittest student. If an axe handle broke, McCracken would grab a draw blade and a length of hickory; students would watch in awe as he expertly planed the wood, sending chips flying as his hands moved in a blur for mere moments. He'd stop as quickly as he'd begun, presenting the brand-new handle to a wide-eyed student with a couple of spins and a flourish that showed he still had abilities with a stick.

"I understand," he said, as he slowly moved back to his chair, "you've been having a difficult time here as of late."

"Yes, sir. You could say that."

"Well, Jarek, I am particularly interested in these types of things," McCracken said. "Mostly academic, of course, but somewhat more than that, which I'll explain. I've heard a bit about your experience, thanks to Mr. Drummy keeping me informed, but now I want to hear it from you. Start at the beginning. What's been going on?"

McCracken's chair creaked under his tall frame as he leaned back. He noticed Jarek's hands were firmly affixed to his knees, and one was shaking a bit.

"It's okay, son," he said. "Deep breaths. First, tell us what you saw, and we can go from there."

Jarek was somewhat comforted by these words and the easy-going manner in which they were delivered, but he didn't know if he should think of this as a support group or an inquisition. He began anyway.

"Well...I was looking in the mirror in my dorm. It was late. And I think I saw a ghost. That's when the dreams started. One that night, then one maybe a week later. Now I have them every night."

"I see. Well, first, let me say I understand you're going through a harrowing experience. You've also shown quite a bit of resilience in a circumstance in which most others would have entirely imploded by now. You owe a great debt of gratitude to Mr. Drummy," he nodded in Drummy's direction, and Drummy nodded back, "for understanding what was happening and mentioning it to me. He and I share an intense interest in such matters." He paused.

"He did tell me, Jarek, about the ghost. And the dreams. And he told *you* some things that very few people know about. So let me pick up where he left off, with the understanding that these conversations are to be kept in the absolute strictest of confidence. As we have not shared your travails with anyone outside this room, we expect—require, really—that in exchange for helping you navigate the road ahead, and behind as well, you'll share nothing of our discussions with anyone. Sound good?"

"Yes, sir," Jarek replied, squirming a bit.

"Well, my apologies for making it even more uncomfortable, but should we discover you've gone against your word, these conversations will have to end immediately. This difficult experience you are caught up in will have to run its course with whatever energy you have left to preserve yourself and your presence here in this school. We'll, of course, wish you the best. Does that make sense?"

Jarek bristled a bit at the browbeating, as well as the tone. He looked back at McCracken and, with some tone of his own, replied, "Yes, sir."

"Good!" McCracken's demeanor lightened up immediately, and he was again friendly and curious. He continued.

"We will do our very best to help you through this, Jarek. You have my word. So, Matt tells me he showed you a book of particular importance to the Village that he has in his possession."

"Yes, he did," Jarek replied.

"Well, as Matt explained, Shakers believed in what they called 'gifts from the dead.' That the dead somehow spoke to those who were living. We have evidence of this. Journals where the authors write about receiving a 'gift' from brother or sister so-and-so with advice or wisdom of some sort, but we find the individual had died long before the entry was written. Do you understand?"

"Yeah, he told me." Jarek nodded.

"I know," McCracken said, "and I'm telling you again."

He continued. "What we don't know is how their ability to share gifts from the grave may have grown into something much more advanced: an ability to do something we call 'reaching forward.' Reaching forward and pulling someone back in time. The living no longer receiving wisdom from beyond the grave, but experiencing *actual* time travel, which is extraordinary. Jarek, the logical conclusion we must draw is that whatever wisdom needed to be conveyed was so important it had to be imparted firsthand. Of course, we don't know how they did either of these things. We don't have any written accounts of reaching forward actually occurring, and (as far as anyone is concerned) there has never—in the entire history of the Village—been an occasion in which it has."

"As far as anyone is concerned..." Jarek repeated.

"Yes, that's right." McCracken smiled at Jarek's perception. "But there are a couple of individuals who know of one occasion when it may have happened. Only one."

"Some kid in the '50s," Jarek said.

"Right. Well, he wasn't just 'some kid.' His name was Keith Hinrichs. He was a classmate of mine, and he was my friend. The mystery of his death is one of the reasons I've been here for so many years. No one knows with any certainty what happened to him. He may have just been overwhelmed." McCracken paused, adding, "But probably not." He paused again and looked out the window. "We were the very best of friends."

Jarek waited nervously for whatever hopeful statement he thought might come next.

McCracken forced a smile. "Your journey will have a better ending, I promise you." Jarek was comforted by this assurance, but not much.

"Jarek, they referred to the individuals who received these gifts, these gifts from the dead, as the 'instrument.' There are many examples of so-called instruments receiving gifts, and we've found no evidence—spoken or written—that these gifts brought any distress or hardship to the individual who was the instrument."

McCracken looked to Jarek to make sure he was following.

"Reaching forward," McCracken continued, "Now that's much different. We have little to draw from as far as how the Shakers themselves categorized the idea of reaching forward, so let's say it's like a gift on steroids. For the dead to grant a gift to the instrument, they somehow convey a vision into their minds, usually through their dreams. Dreams just like yours, Jarek."

Jarek nodded.

"But," McCracken continued, "reaching forward, crossing into another point in time, or pulling someone from the past or future into yours? That's a much larger undertaking. More advanced, more complicated, and, it seems, much harder on the instrument. Your experience seems to be a combination of both. So, we are now aware of only two instances of reaching forward, and from all we can tell, they are extremely taxing on the physical and mental state of the instrument. In this case, you. We therefore might presume that such an undertaking is equally exhausting for the spirit making the effort to reach forward. It may take a herculean amount of effort on the part of the deceased. So, Jarek, if I might interrupt myself to ask you a question: why would they bother?"

He waited.

"Because something is wrong? To fix something?" Jarek asked.

"Yes," McCracken nodded, "Exactly. Not only is something wrong, but something is *so* wrong that a spirit has re-engaged with this mediocre mess of humanity they've left behind to fix it. Something has happened that is so terrible in its outcome, such a deviation from the natural order of things, that a spirit has temporarily turned its back on the ever-after, on the presence of the almighty himself, just to set it right. Do you understand?"

"Yes, yes, I do." Jarek nodded. "So how does it happen?"

"Well, we don't know. It's possible only a select few of the Village elders even knew about it, much less were able to do it. For those that were—who knows? Maybe God has shown them favor for their good works." He shrugged at how outlandish the suggestion sounded but paused momentarily because he meant it. "Or maybe it's a particular skill, the secrets of which were only shared with a small group of individuals. What does seem to be the case is that a chosen few could reach forward to an instrument among the living, and when they did, the kind of experience you are having was possible."

Jarek was on the edge of his seat, his sweaty palms resting on his knees. McCracken continued.

"So Jarek, to sum it up: they believed that through their worship, they could minister to the living in their own time and the dead from their own time as well: brothers and sisters who had passed. They believed they received visions *from* the dead through gifts given to the living, and, to a lesser extent, they believed some among them could move through dimensions to do the Lord's work. Are you seeing a theme?" he asked.

"Yeah," Jarek said, "like the rules didn't apply to them."

"Which rules?" McCracken prompted.

Jarek thought for a moment before responding: "Time."

"Yes, Jarek, exactly," McCracken responded with enthusiasm. "God granted them the ability to transcend the parameters that confine the rest of us. They could step out of them, moving freely between two different dimensions, and maybe bring others along for the ride as well. In my unfortunate friend Keith's experience—very similar to yours—he existed in two different chapters in time—one among the Shakers and one here on campus—each proceeding day by day and hour by hour in conjunction with the other. More like the activities of two different towns occurring in a given week, rather than a century or more apart.

"Jarek," he continued, "Their ability to reach forward was, or is, entirely dependent upon the Village we now call home. The frenetic dancing and singing and praying that the zealots we all here celebrate participated in was the tool that allowed them to channel the spirit of God through time to those who died 'unsaved,' exposing their souls to salvation, even after death. But reaching forward—transcending the constraints of time and death in a physical sense—well, it can't be a coincidence that the two instances we know of happened in the same location."

Jarek raised his eyebrows in surprise. "I don't get it."

"One thing we know for sure is that your room, Jarek, was once occupied by a Village Elder. Certain rooms on campus were of particular spiritual significance due to their occupants; through the entire history of the Village, they were occupied by the most pious and highly regarded of the elders. But they also had a physical attribute: a curved ceiling that spoke to their spiritual significance. In the case of a non-linear time manifestation like the one you are having—the instrument is not only the individual…but the room itself. The place where the manifestation occurs."

"So my room is a… time machine?" Jarek asked.

"Well, perhaps your room is one factor among several that must align for you to have the kind of experience we are here to discuss. As you know from Matt, we believe the feeling of 'being watched' that many here have spoken of for years is proof that spirits can, indeed, appear among us and—though we only have two examples—even bring us back to them, even as much as (in your case) 125 years into the past. The Shakers certainly believed it was possible, and perhaps your room is a key piece of the puzzle."

McCracken smiled to lighten the mood. "At least it would explain years of spooky happenings and ghost stories that have become the stuff of legend."

Jarek sat silently, trying to process all he was being told. It was exhausting.

McCracken then held open the same book Drummy had shown Jarek earlier. The skeleton's menacing grin mocked Jarek's predicament as his outstretched arms lifted his body from the grave.

"Okay," Jarek said. His heart beat heavily as he tried to further digest everything he was being told. He could feel the sweat in his clenched palms.

"Look, I'm not really up for this. I mean, can they…or he…or whoever…find somebody else?" he asked.

Drummy responded with surprise, "Jarek, but this is incredible. Aren't you curious?" He looked Jarek in the eye, adding, "We *will* figure this out with you. I promise."

"Yeah," Jarek said. "Sure, but… I feel, I don't know. I can't sit still. I sleep, but I'm always tired. I wake up and don't know what *year* it is. The first thought I have every morning is, 'Where am I? Have my parents been born yet? Or my Grandparents, for that matter?' Or am I here, on campus—real life—where brand new Shaker friends who have been dead for a hundred years come to say hello in my mirror?"

Drummy occasionally nodded but was otherwise unflappably focused, giving deference to McCracken, the greater authority at the moment.

Jarek added, "I still don't get how you know all of this. I mean… you're…the librarian?"

"Jarek," Drummy interjected to correct Jarek's disrespectful tone.

"That's all right, Matt." McCracken said, "He's under a lot of stress. Aren't you Jarek?"

"Yes," he said apologetically. "Yes, sir, I am."

"I am what you see here and around me" McCracken explained. "I'm the librarian. I mind my business and do my job; people leave me in peace. But as far as the mountain is concerned," Jarek noticed he spoke of the mountain like it was a living being, "and for the sake of those who came before us and those who will come after, I'm the only living member of what is, at its core, a very old and very secret order of caretakers, going back for as long as these buildings have been here. We serve our purpose for as long as we can and then pass our responsibility to whomever we believe will be most capable of performing the duties next. It is an immense responsibility and a heavy burden to bear. Most, even among the Shakers, did not even know that we existed. Nonetheless, we make sure things don't get too…out of hand. We have been called the mountain's conscience, we have been called its memory, we have been called its soul. Some have said we are the 'Mountain Keepers.'"

"Some say the 'Mountain Kings,'" Drummy interjected with grave admiration.

"The Mountain Kings." The words rang in Jarek's ears as he pictured them scribbled on the cover of the old book in the museum attic: *The Book of the Mountain Kings.*

Jarek let this new knowledge sink in. The serious responsibility McCracken bore, what he knew, and what he might be capable of, caused Jarek to see him in an entirely different light.

"Jarek," McCracken took a more serious tone. "I want you to tell me if you recognize this man."

McCracken held up an old, faded black and white photograph in a tattered, dusty wooden frame. In the photo was the face of a stern old man with a long white beard. Jarek snapped to attention, stunned and staring at the familiar face.

"Yes," Jarek whispered. "Yes, I do."

"Who is he?" McCracken asked.

"He's…" he stammered, unable to find the words, "He's the ghost…in the mirror. He spoke to me."

"He spoke to you, did he?" McCracken raised his eyebrows in surprise and continued.

"Jarek, this is Brother Elijah Armstrong. He was…well…he is one of us. From 1851 to 1866, he was one of the guardians I spoke of, and among the most revered elders the Village ever had.

"Did he die?"

"Son, this photo was taken in 1862. Of course he died," McCracken replied.

"I mean…*how* did he die?" Jarek asked.

"Well, we're not sure. Some of his writings lead us to believe there were…complications during his tenure. Things amiss in the Village. He died of natural causes by all accounts, but suspicions remained and still do. His death is the most enduring mystery of the Village and something I, and many others, have spent countless hours trying to solve. Years. We had fully given up on getting to the bottom of it, so the fact that he is reaching out to you, Jarek, is nothing short of astounding. We've read every page, chased down every clue, and turned over every stone. It was so long ago that we had fully given up on the idea of ever getting to the bottom of it. This is a stunning development."

Jarek looked to Drummy in disbelief.

McCracken looked towards Jarek once again, his voice dropping as the dire seriousness of his question came into focus: "What did he say to you, Jarek?"

He leaned forward, waiting anxiously as Jarek brought the words that had haunted him for so long to the tip of his tongue.

"He said…well…it sounded like 'Consensus… consensus… consensus.'"

A floorboard creaked overhead. They all looked up with a start before fixing their eyes back on each other.

McCracken paced his breathing as if the gravity of the information he was receiving was overwhelming even such a seasoned intellect as his. He leaned towards Jarek and spoke in a whisper. "Our order, Jarek…" he held the picture closer so Jarek could see the word in pencil below the photo, "it seems they wanted you to find me. Because he was one of us. Many, many years ago. Not consensus, but…"

Jarek looked closely at the inscription under the photo, reading the faded cursive word in a whisper…

"Conscientia."

CHAPTER 26

Jarek's head was spinning when he and Drummy left the library.

"Let's take a seat," Drummy said, gesturing towards the benches on the side of the adjacent path overlooking the field. "I don't know about you, but I need some fresh air after all that."

Jarek's head hung low. "Yeah," he said.

Their feet crunched upon the gravel as they walked silently below gray late-day clouds and sat on the same bench they sat on the last time they were in this spot. When Jarek first told Drummy about the dreams. They stared out across the field into the valley, and neither spoke. The gravity of all they had just heard was entirely consuming their thoughts.

"How do you feel?" Drummy asked.

Jarek turned his head to Drummy. "Are you kidding?"

"No," Drummy said.

"Oh boy, where do I start?" Jarek gave a sarcastic smirk, his fatigue getting the best of him.

"My grades suck, so my parents are gonna be crushed even if I don't get kicked out. I've made a new friend who hasn't been alive for over a century. The ghost of a guy who died suspiciously is hanging out in my mirror and he was, by the way, part of some crazy order of long-dead secret farmer guardians whose most recent member just stared straight through me for two hours. And they have, by the way, given me a non-optional invitation for a repeat visit to a bunch of religious kooks who work like dogs, dress like monks, dance like loons, and don't get laid, but it doesn't matter—because they're all dead anyway!

"I'm in the middle of all this crazy hell. It's only happened to one other person, ever, and—guess what—he's dead too! So, the world is collapsing around me. I feel fantastic, thanks for asking."

"Whoa. Okay, man, let's slow down," Drummy said. "You had a lot on your mind already—some pretty confusing stuff—and that last conversation, I think, didn't help."

"*No?*" Jarek feigned surprise

"It did, though," Drummy continued, "give us some context to help us better understand what you're experiencing and why. Would you agree?"

"Yeah, sure, I would. Lot of good it does me," Jarek said.

"Jarek, what pulls us apart in difficulty—anyone faced with a challenge—is fear. Fear of the unknown. But you understand you're not lost, and you're not alone. You have a guide," Drummy said, nodding back toward the library. He then put his hand on Jarek's shoulder and added, "and a friend."

"Yeah, I know," Jarek said, "I…I'm grateful." He meant it.

Drummy paused before continuing. "This is crazy stuff, just mind-bending. The more you think about it, the more confusing it gets," he forced a laugh. "But we must think it's happening for a reason, even if we're not sure what. But we have two options, okay?"

"Sure, shoot," Jarek said.

"It's happening as a result of the 'unexpected' death of Brother Armstrong."

"Yes," said Jarek.

"Or," Drummy continued, "it is happening due to whatever it is that's making you feel concerned about your friend Lucas, a largely unknown member of the community about whom there are few records. Maybe it's about him."

"I get the feeling it is. I just don't know why, not yet anyway. But he's in trouble; I can feel it," Jarek said.

"Jarek, I know you're exhausted, and I know that all you want is for this to end. But correct me if I'm wrong, it seems maybe like—after today—somewhere within you, you've changed your mind. Do you… do you want to learn more? Keep going and see what happens?"

Jarek thought for a long moment before responding. "I thought I was going crazy and wanted it to stop." He gave a tired smile, "but this seems like a big deal, whatever it is. Bigger than sleep, grades, all that. I mean, I'm even more exhausted now than I was then, but this makes it easier. You, and McCracken," he nodded towards the library.

Drummy interjected, "And Beth?"

"Yes, definitely yes."

"You told her?" Drummy asked.

"I had to. I'm sorry. Telling her was the only thing that helped. I'm sorry."

"It's okay." Drummy gave him a consoling nudge with his elbow. "I understand. So now you know what's happening—if not why—and that we are here for you. But this is a real decision, Jarek," he said. "Your studies will continue to suffer, you realize, and that…well…it probably won't end well, at least academically. So that's a big deal, too."

"I know." Jarek nodded. "It's weird. I've always been kind of…I don't know, an outlier, a misfit. But what's weird is now, I'm spending all this time in a place where I'm more of a misfit than ever, but when I'm there I don't feel like one. Maybe I fit right in, a misfit among misfits."

"I don't think you're a misfit," Drummy said.

"Um. That's because you're a misfit, Mr. Drummy," Jarek replied.

"Ha! Yeah, I guess that's right," Drummy replied, adding a sarcastic sigh to show how little he cared. "But Jarek," he said thoughtfully, "you're still resolved to see this through?"

"For Lucas, yes. But I don't know how yet."

"So, let me put on my teacher and dorm parent hat and ask you something: Why are you so committed to helping Lucas?"

"I…I feel like I understand him," Jarek said.

"Huh. Okay." Drummy looked perplexed, adding, "Look, Jarek, this is all exciting for both of us, but it's important that I remind myself—and you—that my number one concern is making sure your time here at school goes well. That it helps you find your stride and sets you up for college or wherever you want to put your obvious gifts to use. That's my job as your dorm parent, as your teacher, and as your friend. I want to see you succeed. So, it's cool that you 'get' him, but there's a real possibility that you'll be asked to leave if your grades don't improve. Worthing has you in his sights already; you know it, and I do as well. Why all this for a kid you just met? He may not be in any trouble at all."

"He is, I know it."

Drummy looked straight into Jarek's eyes. "But why, Jarek?"

"Well, he," Jarek straightened his back and took a deep breath. "He reminds me of my brother."

Drummy flinched a little, as if Jarek's words hurt to hear. He looked at Jarek for a moment, then out across the field, speaking quietly as if to himself. "I get it," he said, nodding slowly. "I get it now."

"And since I couldn't…umm…" the rest of Jarek's words got stuck in his throat as his eyes filled with tears.

"You couldn't help him, so you want to help Lucas," Drummy said, putting his hand on Jarek's shoulder.

Jarek was quiet for a moment. He remembered his dad telling him why he helped Mrs. Grissing: *When something about us allows us to help in a way no one else can, Jarek, that's when we're called by name.*

Jarek said quietly, "I'm called by name."

"You're what?" Drummy asked.

"I'm the only one that can help," Jarek whispered. "Nobody else can do it. I'm called by name."

"It's okay," Drummy said, holding Jarek's shoulder. He said "Okay," again to show the matter had been concluded. They would proceed together down the path before them, whatever it was and wherever it might lead.

CHAPTER 27

"Jarek, honey, are you doing all right?"

Jarek had waited patiently in the common room for the pay phone to become available. A South Korean kid had been in line before him, giving him apologetic looks as his parents—feeling especially chatty at the start of their day—refused to let him off the phone despite his cues.

"Yeah, mom, I'm good. Lights out in a few minutes, but I wanted to say hi," Jarek said.

"Jarek," she said, "I know when you just say 'I'm fine' or 'I'm good' and don't say anything else that something is wrong. Is everything okay there? Things are going well in your classes? You sound down."

"No Mom, seriously, I'm just tired. Been studying hard this week and, um...there's a branch outside my window that kind of scrapes in the wind and has been keeping me up," he lied.

"Oh, well can someone cut it?" she asked. He heard the concern in her voice over such a little thing, and guilt welled up within him.

"Yeah, I told them about it, and they're going to cut it, so it's fine. Everything else is great," he said.

"Sweetheart, I'm glad. If anything is wrong, you tell me, okay? We want this to be…" she paused, as she always did when she got choked up, "we want this to be a really good experience for you, okay?"

Jarek paused as well, thinking first about what a kind heart she had and then how terrible it was going to be when this good experience finally fell apart and he broke it. His own heart sank at the thought of it.

"I love you, Mom," he said.

"I love you a ton, sweetie."

He hung up.

"SERIOUSLY, IS EVERYTHING—YOU KNOW—OK?"

Jarek was wondering if he looked worse than he realized, as everyone seemed to be worried about him at the same time.

Em leaned towards him across the worn wooden table as the chatter of students departing the cafeteria faded into the background.

"Yeah," Jarek said, "I'm fine."

She wiped her hands on a course cafeteria napkin like she was preparing for a speech, looked up, and gave him the persistent, wide-eyed gaze she always deployed when she expected an answer. "Nah," Em said, keeping her eyes on him and seeing him squirm, "you're not."

"Seriously," he said, mocking her by opening his eyes wide and looking into hers. "I'm fine."

"First, don't be a jerk. Second—seriously, you're not, and it's obvious. It has been for weeks. You look exhausted—beyond exhausted. What's going down? You're just…not yourself."

"Yeah," he said, knowing she wouldn't let it go.

"Look, everybody has a hard time with SOMEthing." She wagged her head playfully, and he smiled.

"It's not… I mean. I don't know. Sometimes I just… have a hard time with some things…" He paused. "Memories."

"So, let me try," she said. Em held the fingertips of both hands together before her, furrowed her brow like a psychiatrist performing an evaluation, and spoke with a satirical German accent: "Venn you first arrived, every-ting vuz new and distraction vuz easy…" She then stopped joking as her composure changed, and she said sincerely, "But now that it's not, you really miss your brother."

Jarek was stunned by how accurate she was.

"Yeah, I guess that's it. I mean, sort of. The thing is, it was like…everything I knew blew up all at once. Your whole life, things are a certain way, and then suddenly it changes so fast, and that was just a bunch of months ago. So… I don't know." He looked down for a moment. "Sometimes it's just hard to get used to."

"Well, I bet that's the understatement of the year," Em said sympathetically.

"Part of me feels like I'm going to hear Andrew calling out to me," he said, "and I'm going to open my eyes and find that I'm back in my bedroom at home; he's down the hall waiting for me to go outside with him, and his sickness and all of this here and everything else that came after was just one long, terrible dream.

"And," he continued, "I've always, I don't know. A lot of things aren't as easy for me anyway—I mean, going way back, years. Sitting in class and just regurgitating information to get good grades and all that. It's like… I'm just not, I don't know, I'm not good at it."

"Yeah," she nodded.

"I've got this ADD brain," he poked the side of his head aggressively with one finger to show his frustration, "which is always in the way. I've always been… I mean, I know I'm smart. I've always been really smart, I just…" he tried to find the words. "It just sucks to be—this won't sound right, but… it sucks to know you're the smartest person in the room, but no matter how hard you try, you can't seem to consistently do the things that everybody else finds so easy."

"I know," she said. "I totally know."

"It's like there's a smart part of my brain, but it's held prisoner by the rest. The part that can't stay organized, be on time, study, or remember things five minutes later. I can tell you every word of conversations I had years ago. I can recite every single item that was on the bookshelf in my childhood bedroom. I remember blocks and blocks of text; it's like my brain takes a picture, and I look at the picture later, and it's all there."

"I know," she said, "It's crazy some of the stuff you remember. Everybody talks about it."

"Really?" he asked with surprise.

"Yes. You've got this intense, brilliant brain and when you're plugged in, it's wild the stuff you come up with," she said.

"Yeah 'when I'm plugged in.' But I can't tell you a single thing we talked about today in algebra. I mean…" he paused. "Big picture: I've always been one for getting distracted easily, but the thoughts that used to distract me were regular things, normal life stuff, just distractions. But now it's like, I sit in class, but my mind is in the hospital next to Andrew. The things I said to him, the things I didn't, watching him fade away. All this terrible stuff…" his voice cracked for a moment, "it all plays in my mind like a movie that I can't turn off, and then all this other unrelated bad stuff follows it."

"Bad stuff like what?" she asked, leaning towards him more.

He didn't want to pull her into everything—the other reason he looked so beat down—but talking about the rest was helping.

"Like… these sort of visions, hyper-focused, always bad, usually involving someone I care about dying."

"God, that sounds terrible," she said.

"Well, it's not just 'sounds' for me. I don't hear it, I see it, and I promise it looks worse than it sounds," he said.

"I wonder if…" she hesitated. "I think you've got some PTSD from what you've been through. Did you talk to the counselor about it?"

"Stondell? Yeah, it's all we talk about. All this talk forever—emotional trauma, neuro this, cognitive that. 'It's okay, Jarek, everybody's different' blah blah blah. A lot of good it does me." Jarek shrugged. "I just want to be normal."

Em gave his arm a nudge. "Jarek, I'll never be able to understand all you've been through, ever. I can't even imagine. I hate that you have to go through it. I'm so sorry."

"Yeah," he said. "everybody's sorry."

Em looked at him, "But what you were talking about before—I do get it. School is super hard for me, too. I actually suck at it."

Jarek drew his chin back and raised his eyebrows in surprise. "What do you mean? You're an amazing student."

"Yeah, everybody's amazed." she said, adding with a whiny tone while drawing quotes in the air with her fingers, "'Oh, you do *so* well on all the tests—I *wish* I did so well. You're *so* smart!' I probably do triple the studying as everyone I've heard that from. Jarek, it takes me an incredible amount of work to get good grades. I'm not good at it. I just pretend to be and hope my grades follow suit."

"Really?" He was stunned.

"Yeah, dummy," she said playfully, "really. Why do you think I carry every book around all the time? I hardly remember anything unless I do the reading, like, three times, and that's because I have CAPD."

"Aaaaand that means what?" he quipped.

"It means Central Auditory Processing Disorder. Basically, it's like my ears hear something…but they sometimes tell my brain only part of it or mix it up," she said.

"Really? Wow. So, what does that look like?" he asked.

"It looks like me carrying my books around with me all the time, studying way more than everybody else, and being unable to listen in class while taking notes because things get mixed up, and I'm so afraid of missing something. That's why I always have my tape recorder in class. But the bigger thing is," she took a deep breath, "I kind of…I get depressed."

Jarek raised his eyebrows in surprise.

"Or, I'm supposed to say…" she sat up in mock formality and cleared her throat. "I have been struggling with major depressive disorder since I was a child, but with the proper interventions and management strategies, I've learned how to excel in my studies and thrive socially."

He tilted his head in a slight bow at her performance, then got serious. "Wow, Em, I had no idea."

"Really? None?" She seemed genuinely happy to hear it. "My wet hair, that you chide me about every morning, what do you think that's about?" she asked.

"Oh, I just figured you like to sleep in or take long showers, I don't know," he said.

"No, those are the days when I almost can't do it. I just lay there in bed, and my body feels like lead, and I can't move. But..." she said firmly, "I work around it. I have a special second alarm—my 'point of no return' alarm—and it's set for the absolute last moment when I can still get up and be where I'm supposed to be."

"The 'point of no return' alarm. I like that." Jarek smiled.

"So," she said, "when I hear everybody buzzing around, heading out, making it all sound so easy, I'm laying there thinking, 'What's my problem? Why can't I be like them? Why is this so hard for me? Why do I have to be so... different?'" She nodded at him to acknowledge his mention of how often he himself got the "everybody's different" trope, as she had heard it many times herself.

She continued, "Then the alarm goes off, and I do the one thing I promised myself—no matter how I feel—that I'll always do in that moment. I recite a quote. Do you want to know what it is?"

"Yes, of course," Jarek said eagerly.

"'The person who follows the crowd will go no further than the crowd. The person who walks alone is likely to find themself in places no one has ever seen before.' That's Einstein."

Jarek looked at her for a moment, her words resonating deeply as he thought about his challenges before Andrew got sick, his harder journey after, and the mystery unfolding each night in his dreams. He truly was finding himself in places no one had ever seen. No one living, at least.

"Wow," he said. "That's the best thing I've heard in a while."

"It always gets me up, although sometimes it's at the last minute. That's when my hair is wet." She smiled. "So yeah, it takes me a lot of extra work to do well. It takes even more for me to be cheerful—I give myself pep talks, like, five times a day, and the very littlest thing can derail me. If someone says or does something unkind, or I'm proud of working super hard on an assignment I know was easy for everyone else but I get something wrong, my brain goes down a destructive path, and there's no stopping it. It's like somebody flipped a switch, and I can't flip it back." she said.

"Wow," he was stunned. "It's crazy that you just said that. A 'switch.'"

"That's exactly what it's like," she said, adding, "Jarek, I guess what I'm trying to say is that you may be alone in *your* struggle, but you're not alone in struggling. None of us are. And don't worry about being 'normal.' Nobody normal has ever changed the world. Maybe you're different, maybe your life experience is different, but it's that difference that makes you brilliant, and you *are* brilliant, and I know it will take you to places no one has ever seen."

Jarek took a deep breath and looked at her with glassy eyes.

"Em," he said with deepest sincerity, "you're a wonder, and I'm lucky to have you as a friend."

"Nah. I'm just me," she said with a smile as they stood up to head to class.

CHAPTER 28

"Come on, hurry," Jarek said. He looked over his shoulder at Beth as he leapt up the museum steps.

It was Wednesday morning, which meant everyone on campus was diligently working on tidying up the grounds. During Hands to Work, groups of faculty and students cleared brush from the edge of the field, replanted the small gardens abutting the faded bricks at the base of the classroom buildings, and painted faded doorways around campus. Crews armed with tall rakes scratched at the blankets of red and orange fallen leaves, loading them onto waiting tarps, which they dragged to burn piles at the edge of the field. Billows of smoke rose into the crisp air against the background of fall foliage that rolled into the valley below.

A carefully timed and simultaneous "bathroom break" was all he needed to show Beth something he'd promised her.

He asked her to meet him near the front of the museum, now unlocked, and was happy to find her waiting for him nearby.

The latch clicked. "It's not half as scary during the day," he said, pushing the door open.

"For you, maybe," Beth said.

He held her hand and quickly moved through the front room. She tried not to look back at the faces she found so terrifying during her first visit but couldn't resist. The eyes of the mysterious bearded man seemed to be following her.

Moments later, they were upstairs.

"Jarek, I don't understand," she said.

"Look," he said, carefully opening the book.

"We were just—"

"*Look*!" he said again. "What day is it?"

Beth replied, "November 1st."

"What date was the last entry? The last written entry, do you remember?" Jarek asked.

"October 24th, something about soil. Then November 4th," she said.

"And what about October 30th?" Jarek asked.

"'October 30th is blank. Remember that.'" She quoted him and smiled, confused as to why it mattered.

"Here," Jarek said, pointing firmly at the page he had opened to.

"October 30th," she read. Her eyes widened and moved slowly down the yellowed page.

"Oh my God," she said. She looked at Jarek in surprise and quickly back down.

"Read it," he said.

She caught her breath and stared at the page.

Jarek gave her a nod. "Go ahead."

"'October 30th, 1866.' Jarek, oh my God," her eyes were wide with disbelief as her unsteady voice quietly read the deep black words scratched onto the page.

"And...?" Jarek said.

She inhaled slowly to steady herself.

"'October 30th, 1866. Barn pasture gate unfastened. Better part of morning gathering 14 cows from wandering in the fields. Personal or mechanical error unsure. Brethren installed a second latch.'

"I don't understand—it was blank," Beth said.

"Funny thing is, the latch works like a charm—tough as nails—I had to pry it open." He smiled.

"So...wait. You're saying...*you* did this?!" Beth said.

He looked back at the book and whispered, "Good idea, right? I told you it was real."

She stared at him in stunned silence, then said in a nervous whisper, "My God, Jarek, I don't get it. I thought you were… I don't know…imagining things."

He looked her in the eye and enjoyed the feeling of relief that welled up within him. She believed him. He couldn't lose her now, at least not because of this.

"Let me show you a picture of him," Jarek said.

"Of who?" she said.

"Of Lucas."

He flipped back to the photos in the middle of the book and found the picture of Lucas in the field.

The picture was different this time. He looked more closely, squinting as he leaned in. "Jesus!" Jarek jumped back in shock as Beth started from his reaction.

"What? What is it?" she said, quickly looking at him and back to the page.

Jarek's face slowly re-entered the glow from the overhead light cast off the text, his heart beating hard in his chest. Beth looked more closely. She held her breath.

"Oh my God," she whispered in shock.

Jarek stared in disbelief and whispered, "I told you it was real."

The old photo was frayed at the edges, black and white, looking out across a field. Shaker brothers worked in the distance. Directly before the camera was Lucas, the same as before, but now, standing next to Lucas, was another boy. His hands and clothes were likewise filthy from toil. There, among these faces captured in time well over a century ago, right next to Lucas, was a new face that looked remarkably familiar.

She held her breath, examining every grain of the old image with wide eyes.

"Hey, guys?" The crew leader shouted from the front door of the museum. "What the heck are you doing? You're not allowed in there. Not the place for sucking face. Let's go!"

"Oops!" Jarek said, grabbing her hand and rushing them both down the steps.

The book lay open to the photo, and in it was Lucas, standing in the field, facing the camera, just like before. A bundle of grain was in his hands, bound by a roll of twine held beneath his arm.

Unlike before, a young man stood right beside him.

It was, unmistakably, Jarek.

CHAPTER 29

They hurried back to their work crew and didn't have a chance to speak again until they saw each other in the hall in Wickersham for a moment before afternoon classes began.

"Jarek," Beth said. "The book. I can't believe it. It's all I can think about. Is it true? You're really…there?"

"Yeah, I guess I am. I didn't mean to scare you. I needed you to believe me."

"God, I believe you. I'm scared to death, but I believe you." Her eyes darted back and forth across his face with excitement as she leaned in and spoke in a hurried whisper. "Good Lord, you look so exhausted," she said, affectionately placing her hand on his cheek. "I want to go with you. Can I?"

"I would love that—just the thought of it. I would love that more than anything," he looked into her eyes. "The thing is…I don't know how I get there, or why, so I don't think I could take you if I tried, any more than you could choose to take me into your dreams at night."

"You're kind of there already," she said with a wink.

"Beth, this isn't a joke. McCracken says it's happened, like, twice in 150 years, as far as anybody knows."

"Wow," she said, disappointed at the idea of not joining him and surprised at this new information.

"But…it's not just that. I think it's, I don't know, I get the feeling it's dangerous. Or it's getting dangerous anyway. You know the ghost? The elder? He was part of this secret group, an 'order' or whatever, and he died somehow... suspiciously. I think maybe it wasn't, you know, natural."

"Oh my God, really? A secret order? And...killed?" she raised her eyebrows, a bit too thrilled for Jarek's liking.

"Yes, really. And I think that's why I'm being...called, or whatever."

"Like, what, you're supposed to see it or stop it? What?" she asked.

"No, I can't." Jarek said, "I only go back to when I left off last time, and he's already dead."

"So there's something else you're supposed to do?"

"Maybe, and I think I know what it is, or at least what it's about, but I'm afraid to admit it yet. I feel like whatever bad thing is going to happen is why. But it may be more than that."

"What do you mean?" He saw growing concern and confusion in her eyes.

"I think maybe," Jarek said, "maybe it's the reason why I'm *here*, too."

"Jarek, what? Don't say that. You're here for this," she gestured to the building and classrooms around them. "You're here for school, and your parents, and yourself, and maybe," she said, putting her hand on his shoulder, "for me."

"Beth, I wasn't going to tell you this, but I want you to know everything." He looked her in the eye. "There's one other thing..."

"What is it?" she asked nervously.

"The other time this had happened to someone?" he said, "It was another student. A long time ago, in the '50s, and Beth," Jarek paused. "He, um...he died."

"What?! Jarek, no... no, no. Don't go back."

He shook his head in response as if to say she didn't get it.

"Please. Please don't," she begged.

The bell rang, and students began hurrying down the hall. Jarek looked at her and spoke clearly as he walked backward away from her and into the crowd.

"Beth, I couldn't stop it even if I tried. I don't know how."

She stood still, watching him walk away with panic in her eyes. Above the swirl of people in the hall and student's footsteps rushing down the staircases he mouthed the words "I'm sorry," before turning out of sight.

That night, when Jarek went to bed, he didn't stare at the ceiling. He didn't wish he knew what was happening to him. He knew. He didn't wish—like he had every night for months—that he could tell someone so he could feel like he wasn't alone in this. He wasn't. He didn't worry that something he didn't understand was wreaking havoc on his performance in school, his number one priority—for himself, his parents, and his teachers. He didn't spend time daydreaming about someday being part of something bigger than himself. He already was.

With a smile on his face and a warm sensation in his stomach, driving him towards whatever lay ahead, he fell right to sleep.

He woke up moments later in the same room, 125 years in the past.

Part 2

CHAPTER 30

Before long, and with Abigail's help, Jarek soon knew the routine of the seed store well enough to run it himself. He knew who within the Village brought various products that were to be sold to visiting customers, what times of the week were busiest, and who the most regular customers were.

Two of these most regular customers were gentleman farmers who were as unalike in every possible way as they were alike in the regularity with which they visited the seed store.

One was Mr. Finch. Impeccably dressed, exhaustively talkative, and it appeared, from the amount of money he so willingly parted with in the store each week, quite successful. He had many contracts with the Village for the provision of produce, seeds, cattle, and other items. As a result, he was held in higher esteem than other customers who had much less substantive business with the Village.

Another of these most regular customers was a local farmer named Clarence Goodell. One afternoon, Jarek and Abigail sat in the store, having prepared a large variety of goods for Mr. Goodell, for whom she had saved the best of her pies.

Jarek had never seen him smile and said as much to Abigail.

"Your curious interest in the manner of people is something I don't quite understand, Jarek," she replied. "Mr. Goodell is as honest, hardworking, and trustworthy a man as any we see here, perhaps even more than all the rest. He is a very reasonable gentleman."

Jarek had learned that "very reasonable" was reserved for the people and things Sister Abigail admired the most.

Her tone surprised him, but he left it at that. After a moment, she continued.

"None of us, Jarek, are living the lives we expected to. Clarence Goodell included." She nodded her head as she spoke these last two words to convey that they were worth emphasis. Jarek's face made it clear that he didn't understand.

"This is very private, Jarek, but if satisfying your curiosity this once makes you less inclined to such free observation in the future, then I believe I will be doing you a favor."

His eye was drawn to one of her gloves. She kept her hands close to her body when in his company, but he thought on more than one occasion that the two outermost fingers of her left hand appeared to move with less dexterity than the others. Her hand was before him now, and despite his best efforts, he found himself staring at the two fingers, which pointed slightly downward as the other three held the top of a wooden crate she sorted items into with her right hand.

She noticed his gaze and put her hand to her side as he looked back up at her face to indicate he was listening, and he waited.

"All conveyed to me by Brother Armstrong, you understand," she said, asserting that whatever confidential information she was about to convey did not come to her directly from Mr. Goodell, a married man and not of The Way, at that.

"Mr. Goodell and his wife wanted nothing more in their earlier years than to have children. To see them playing on the farm, helping tend the animals and till the land. To see them someday begin families of their own, working the family farm as they enjoyed their old age on the porch, surrounded by loved ones."

"I see," Jarek said, though his tone conveyed that he didn't.

"In his many visits, have you ever seen a son—or a daughter—with Mr. Goodell, as the other farmers bring with them for help?" Abigail asked.

"No, ma'am, now that you mention it. He comes alone."

"So, yes, Jarek. You see where I am going. Years ago, they discovered that Mrs. Goodell could not have children, and it broke their hearts. But as you may someday learn, Jarek, some pain is so deep and abiding that it doesn't merely break your heart. It breaks it once on the way in, yes, but then it finds a home within its chambers. It awakens just when you begin to feel the cracks have mended and strikes the walls like the toll of a mighty bell, reminding you that the pain lies within you, that your heart will break not once but a thousand times, and that the tiny chips lost with each new fissure have made it impossible for the pieces to ever quite fit back together again."

"Yes, Sister Abigail," he said slowly. "I do believe I understand."

She continued, "The silence of their home reminds them every day, but Mr. Goodell makes the best of things how he can. He does the work of three younger men and tirelessly cares for his wife with such attention as most men are not capable of." She paused, then added, "That is their reality, so please let this satisfy your curiosity, and might you further respect the privacy of others whose own trials are far beyond your understanding."

She saw Jarek look down and added apologetically. "I'm sorry, dear boy. Yes, you are correct. He doesn't smile much and has been even more somber as of late, as we all have since Brother Armstrong passed."

Jarek came to attention at hearing Brother Armstrong's name. "Were they close?" he asked.

"Yes, quite, Jarek. They were indeed."

She gathered her dress forward in her gloved hands and let the weight of her thoughts compel her into a chair beside her. She then stared blankly at a distant place on the floorboards, and Jarek saw the face of his grieving mother in her empty gaze.

He thought he might risk asking more about Brother Armstrong and hoped she would be receptive.

"Sister Abigail," he paused. "Why did Brother Armstrong come here?"

She gave a nod of her head making it clear she had asked herself the same question many, many times.

"You're wondering if he'd still be alive if he hadn't. I wonder as well, dear. 'Was it worth it?' To come here and do his best and die for it. Would he say it was worth it? Well. Yes, I believe *he* would, anyway." Jarek saw the tears well in her eyes and knew even if Brother Armstrong thought it was worth it, Abigail would disagree with him.

Constantly on Jarek's mind was the question of why *he* was there. He thought about details of the Village and its older and younger inhabitants. He thought about Thaddeus's friendship with Lucas, how Thaddeus paid much more attention to him than he did to other young arrivals, and Jarek was thankful Thaddeus had taken Lucas under his wing. Jarek had seen him engaged in many other acts of kindness in the Village.

On one occasion, he saw Thaddeus witness the emotional distress of a younger sister. He picked up a handful of flowers from a garden bed beside the road, handing them to her as she passed to lift her spirits.

On another, he had seen Thaddeus offer assistance to an elderly sister. She was halfway back to the heart of the Village when she realized she had left a personal item in the store upon locking up at the end of her shift. Thaddeus saw her dilemma, borrowed the key, and headed quickly up the road, returning moments later with the item, for which she was deeply grateful.

Jarek's concern for Lucas had continued to grow as of late, but along with it, there was now a growing sense that something was deeply amiss not only with Lucas but throughout the Village. He couldn't put his finger on it, but Jarek was sure that—whatever it was—Thaddeus would be a steadfast ally in setting things right.

CHAPTER 31

"Good evening, dear. We are happy to see you."

An elderly sister gestured towards a chair that had been saved for Abigail, as usual, among the six placed in a wide circle in the grass beside a hilltop building named for their founder, Ann Lee. Sisters occupied each of the remaining chairs, each looking up to smile at Abigail as she arrived.

"Thank you, sister," she replied.

The group gathered weekly to talk, to stroll the apple orchard, to receive some of Abigail's expert knitting advice, and—though they would never admit it—to gossip about the goings-on in the Village as the sun set over the valley below and their needles twittered into existence a shawl or pair of gloves for an elderly sister or a hat for a newly arrived orphan to make them feel welcome. Abigail would address her sisters affectionately and gladly begin answering any and all questions before she had even removed her own needles from their hiding spot in her waistband.

Among the ladies of the Village was a tacit understanding that, while they would never be able to entertain the romantic desires of men, the idea was no less appealing to them than it was to any other woman of that (or any) time. It may have been more so, in fact, as in their hearts, they knew it was something they could never have. This shared understanding was acknowledged sometimes by a knowing nod or a raised eyebrow, one woman to another, when a handsome gentleman from outside appeared in the Village.

But they sometimes heard rumors about the trials of some local woman or newly minted Shaker sister who had been mistreated by a man—husband or no—and shook their heads in disbelief, solidarity, and appreciation that the same fate could not befall them.

But the appeal of romance, even if theoretical, and despite the shortcomings of men themselves, endured nonetheless. It was in this complicated paradigm that Abigail, to the imploring smiles of her sisters—and after no small amount of chiding—acquiesced to perform a comic routine of sorts which her sisters had seen before and greatly appreciated.

"Oh, fine, dear sisters. If I must," she said with a smile.

She went to the back of the structure, taking in her hand a pitchfork which leaned against it, and stepped back towards her seated spectators.

Abigail then turned the pitchfork over with a flourish, tongs up, holding it by the wooden neck, and provided a long and deep curtsy to the metal head of the fork, imagining it to be the face of a handsome bachelor who had asked for the pleasure of a dance.

One of the sisters smiled, "Sister Abigail, shall we be your band?"

"Yes, please, sister." Abigail gave her a courteous nod and composed herself into perfect posture as the sister started to sing a quick little song.

(Song: "Who Will Bow and Bend like the Willow?")

Who will bow and bend like the willow?
Who will turn and twist and reel?

The others joined in as soon as they recognized it:

In the gale of simple freedom
From the bar of union flowing

Abigail held her free hand out to her imaginary suitor to the satirical "oohs" and "ahhs" of her sisters, quickly kicking one foot out before her and beginning an energetic two-step around the lawn as if she was blissfully absorbed in the presence and dancing talents of the most charming gentlemen she had ever had the pleasure of being acquainted with, all along keeping pace with the sister's voices as they clapped along in unison:

Who will drink the wine of power
Dropping down like a shower?
Fright and bondage all forgetting
Mothers wine is freely working

Abigail smiled as she pranced repeatedly around the circle.

Oh, oh, I will have it
I will bow and bend to get it
I'll be reeling turning twisting
Shake out all the starch and stiffening
Oh, oh, I will have it
I will bow and bend to get it
I'll be reeling, turning, twisting
Shake out all the starch and stiffening

At the song's end, Abigail stopped abruptly, kicking the bottom of the pitchfork handle, which sent the wooden shaft rotating around the outside of her hand like a baton to the horizontal position. She then grabbed the middle of the shaft and, to the delighted gasps of the women around her, brought her arm back and unwound her form with the dexterity of a pitcher, launching the entire device forward and watching it sail quickly through the air before planting itself with a thud firmly into the trunk of a nearby tree. Reverberations hummed through the handle as it vibrated to a stop.

The ladies clapped at the dance and the outcome, smiling with delight that this handsome, strong, but ultimately disposable gentleman had graced them with his company for a short time.

"My dear," one elder sister chided affectionately, "remind me of your life before you joined us?"

Abigail bowed with a smile and blushed but stayed silent.

"Indeed, whatever you were before," she continued, "seamstress or gladiator—I'm glad you're on our side."

Abigail curtsied, bowed her head, and spoke with the most solemn and heartfelt sincerity.

"I will always be on your side, sister."

CHAPTER 32

One afternoon, shortly before locking up the seed store, Jarek and Sister Abigail stood on opposite sides of a tall table, opening some packages that had just been dropped off. He unpacked a box of sewing needles, a device for quickly peeling apples, and replacement parts for sewing machines, struck by how little difference there was between some of these items and their modern counterparts. The community was self-sufficient, but there were things that they did rely upon the outside world for.

He noticed a slight change in Sister Abigail's demeanor as she drew out of one package an exceedingly large pair of black men's work boots. Jarek was learning that several matters in the Village might be much more complicated than they initially seemed, and some appeared to be heavy on her mind. Though she didn't say so, Jarek had a hunch at least a couple involved Brother Thaddeus, which was to whom—coincidentally—the box with the boots was addressed. She turned the boots over and let out a sigh.

"What is it?" Jarek asked.

"'It,' Jarek, is vanity. As much a problem here as it is anywhere else. Especially for some."

Seeing the curiosity in Jarek's face, she held the boots with the soles facing him. He saw embedded in the heel of each sole a large letter "T." "Custom made," she said flatly, "for Brother Thaddeus."

He looked at the large 'T' and back at Sister Abigail, who gave him a look suggesting her indiscretion in speaking so freely was not something to be replicated. He thought this was a good time to ask her a question he'd had on his mind.

"Sister Abigail, can I ask you something, if you don't mind?" he asked.

"Of course, Jarek. I may choose not to answer if I wish," Abigail said.

"Where…" he paused, proceeding carefully. "Where are all these people from?"

She waited momentarily and took a long look at him, then down to various items surrounding the legs of the neatly hewn bench they were sitting on. Jarek thought she would speak immediately, but instead she stared—not at him but through him. Maybe she didn't trust him.

"Sister Abigail?" he said.

"People come here from all over, Jarek," she said simply.

"I know. But…" He paused to consider how he would ask again the question she didn't want to answer. He could practically hear his dad saying, "*Jarek, mind your business,*" but his curiosity got the best of him. "I'm sorry, what I mean is…who are they? Why are they here?"

She sighed.

"Jarek, we are—in most ways—a second-chance community. People come to us because God has brought them here, in most cases, to try again. Geographically, they come from all over and from all manner of previous lives. But as to who they are as people, those of The Way can mostly be explained—as to their past—in one of four ways."

Jarek listened intently.

"There are those who maybe the Lord has not gifted with vast intelligence or industrial ability. Those who the world would—or has—taken advantage of. They come here to belong, to live in a place where people treat them kindly and don't abuse them. Our doctrine is, at its core, intended to keep us from the most basic inclinations that the rest of the world so readily pursues. In that regard, those who are a little too simple are less likely to be mistreated here. You could ask them to undergo any transformation you want—clothing, beliefs, lifestyle—they would do it because they feel safe here. They'll adhere to what we teach and believe it as devoutly as anyone else. But the truth is they are not philosophical or doctrine-driven people—they know that, and so do we—but their appreciation renders them among our most loyal brothers and sisters, and they work hard. They're here because we take them in and treat them kindly.

"The second group are those who come here with their demons chasing them, joining The Way to begin anew, to live a life of faith, and to leave their sinful past behind. Typical to many who come to faith through such transformations, they become somewhat fanatical, adhering to the rules much more ardently than those who taught them and eager to punish even the slightest shortcoming. This frequently severs their relations within the community, and they, ironically, return to the world and the very same demons that haunted them before."

"Yes," Jarek said, "I can see that."

She continued. "Most of us are in the third group. We are here because of the love we have for our brothers and sisters, and for Mother, and our belief in The Way. We understand that our little Valhalla here is not perfect and never will be, but it is ours, and we will preserve and protect it. Sometimes, we must adjust our lifestyle to the realities of the modern age, but we do so willingly so that we might survive and continue to do the Lord's work in the world. We are most interested in love, compassion, equality as we are all made by God, and protecting and nurturing one another into the version of ourselves closest to God's righteous intent for us."

She paused again.

"What's the last group?" Jarek asked.

"Well," she continued, "that group is the smallest, but also the one that presents the biggest challenge. There are people in the world who, their entire lives, want to be powerful or influential—or both—and can't do it. Perhaps God didn't give them the faculties that lend themselves to building wealth or the character necessary to be trusted and taken into the receiving graces of others. So they come here for that."

"They come for power or money? Or do they come because they want to change their ways and be faithful?"

"Well, it is not to be faithful, Jarek, that's group number two. Pay attention." She gave him a bit of a glare in jest. It was so out of character he couldn't help but smile. Maybe she trusted him after all.

"For power, maybe for money, too—however much there may be found of it here," she said. "And you can understand how some of our community— those who have been hurt by the world and are here for safety and honesty or who don't live by the sword or the dollar and are here because they trust us—you can understand how those individuals are easily preyed upon.

"Well," Abigail continued, "this small and unsuspecting and forgiving little enclave—flawed thought it may be—is a place where those in the fourth group can take advantage. Our challenge is knowing who these individuals are before they have caused too much damage to our community and our way of life. It is a very difficult thing to do, being a place that accepts anyone who cares to join and contribute, knowing who has a pure heart and who does not. Sometimes we discover things early enough, sometimes we do not," she said.

A look of sadness haunted her eyes. He imagined some past hurt done to the Village might be on her mind and that she—given her humility and her respected role in the community—might bear the weight for that hurt quite personally. He wanted to ask but didn't and found himself angry at the thought of her carrying the burden of whomever the offender was.

"In any case," she continued, "such people have always come and gone. Some have left with the contents of the till. One convinced one of our young sisters, 14 years old, that marrying him was God's will for her life. He was 62. Some steal away in the night with as much of our materials as they can pile into the wagon of a waiting friend. Maybe they were once sincere, maybe not, but their type has come and gone for as long as the Village has been here."

"But," Jarek said, worried his next question might be too bold, "What do you all, I mean, what does the Village… what do you do about things like that?"

Abigail spoke more quietly, looking around to ensure no one was nearby. "Well, there's another group I didn't mention because it is much smaller than the rest."

Jarek sat on the edge of his seat as she began.

"A few short years after the Village began, the elders noticed a problem."

"What kind of problem?" Jarek asked.

"Well, people were different here," she continued. "Different from the outside world and different from each other. Every year, every month, practically, new people would come, and old people would go. This could cause some unrest if not handled properly, and we've had plenty of occasions when people were here who never should have been and, well, their time in the Village—before we understood their character, you see—could be unsettling.

"The elders, many, many years ago, began designating one trusted individual to be a sort of caretaker of the Village. Their job was to watch over the buildings and ensure things were in good order, day—and especially—night. This latter part lent itself to minding more than just the buildings. The coming and going of people so often was too disruptive. Someone would come into a position of influence after only a couple of years, and the things they would change or advocate with all good intentions—usually—could impact the whole Village, sometimes in a way that was different from what some felt Mother would have wanted. It was too easy to let our restless brothers and sisters steer us off the path she intended for us.

"The caretakers, our watchmen, were always those who had the best interest of the Village, of all of us, at heart. They performed their role day and night, and the amount of complicated situations they discovered—and found others in—you wouldn't believe it."

Jarek thought of what students got up to when they snuck out of their rooms in the middle of the night. "I bet I actually would," he said.

She gave him a stern look and continued.

"Well, the third caretaker was a pious and very hard-working man named Francesco SanGiorgi. He was Italian, so no stranger to discrimination here in America, and—as his ancestors before—was a Waldensian. The Waldensians took vows of poverty, believed in abstinence, and—their greatest offense—opposed the corruption of the Catholic church. As a result, centuries ago, they were exiled from their homes in northern Italy. Those who stayed behind were tortured and murdered by the Catholic church, Brother SanGiorgi's ancestors among them. He was the only Italian in our community, and likely the only one many of our brothers and sisters had ever met."

Jarek listened attentively.

"This was not a matter of concern to the Village, where our form of equality, deeply rooted in our belief that we are all God's children, puts us very much at odds with the prejudices of the outside world. You've noticed, of course, that women hold just as many positions of authority in our Village as men and just as much discretion as to its exercise."

"Yes, ma'am," Jarek said, pausing momentarily before asking, "Abigail, is that why you're here?"

She raised her eyebrows at the boldness of his question before giving it some thought.

"Jarek, I'm here because I love The Way. I love Mother and her teachings. My own path has not been without troubles, and my brothers and sisters here brought me in without judgment as one of their own. They are more family to me than any I have ever had, and until the end of my days, I will expend as much of myself as is necessary to preserve what they have built here. It is my God-given obligation as an expression of my eternal gratitude, and to ensure that this place remains a refuge—many years after we have all gone into the company of the everlasting—for those who come after." Abigail paused to make sure Jarek understood.

"Sister, but," he said with some hesitation, "when you first came, I mean. When this was all new to you..."

"Yes, Jarek." She gave him a knowing nod for realizing she had left that part out to avoid answering his question. Very observant.

"Jarek, similar to what we discussed about Mrs. Goodell," she paused, "at one point in my life, I, too, hoped to bear children. I am, however, also unable to do so."

Her eyes looked beyond him for a moment, and he wondered what difficult memory she was revisiting as she continued.

"I long ago accepted that God did not bless me with that ability. While it is challenging enough for a woman to cast aside her maternal instincts when she has spent her young life desirous of having a family one day, some implications greatly exceed those of sentimental disappointment. Women in the outside world are unable to vote. We cannot own property. We have no role in industry or governance. Our intellect and abilities are almost entirely disregarded in any and all matters, save that of having and raising children. What this means is that a woman who can't have children or chooses not to is not doing with her body what society demands of her. She is therefore unable to achieve even the status of second-class citizen which society is willing to afford."

Jarek listened quietly as her words laid bare some of the stark realities of the world.

"Here," she added, "I am an Elder, I am a leader, I live and work and contribute and determine the form and shape of the future of this Village as much as any man. Maybe even more so."

She smiled briefly and continued. "You've also noticed that some in our Village are of African descent and that they, too, live as equals in our midst."

"Yes, I have," Jarek said with a nod.

"We have, on many occasions, purchased the freedom of those who would have otherwise spent their lives in servitude, even if we are loathe to provide capital to those engaged in the dehumanizing evils of buying and selling God's children. Jonah Crutcher was one, living among the Pleasant Hill, Kentucky, Shakers until the end of his days. Henry Jackson was an enslaved person, finding refuge as an esteemed blacksmith at Hancock before departing to recruit others of African descent to join the Massachusetts 54th regiment in the war to end slavery. Some came to us as free citizens: Sisters Harriet Jones, Betty and Phoebe Lane, Rebecca Jackson—a true prophet in Watervliet. Brothers Ransom Smith and Nelson Banks are some of the most spirited members of our community here on the mountain. They live among us as equals, away from the deeply racist and often murderous behavior that has spread like a cancer through society since the war's end and is, by any definition, unkind, unchristian, and barbaric. The more condemnation we receive from the outside world for these practices, the more pride we take in furthering our efforts."

Jarek sat in stunned admiration as she continued.

"Well, to what I was saying, God brought Brother SanGiorgi into our midst at the moment we needed him most, giving him the wisdom to see that he was called to preserve our cause and the sanctity of our traditions despite the many things that threatened them. Back then, elders tried to mitigate against the undue influence of newcomers by separating us into families. The Church Family housed the more senior of our order, those with the most significant influence over matters of the Village. At the same time, other families were designated for the novitiate so they could not have undue influence before their learning was complete and their commitment established.

"Sorry, the—the…novitiate?" Jarek asked.

"Yes, the novitiate are the newcomers. Their dedication to The Way is yet untested, and they remain most vulnerable to the influences of the world they recently left behind. So Brother SanGiorgi used his heart, his wisdom, and his knowledge of history to protect the soul of who we are—our long trajectory—in opposition to the temporary fits and starts that threaten to tear us asunder. He was equal parts watchman, advisor, counselor, friend, and disciplinarian. Heart of gold, nerves of steel, and an unwavering focus on our survival and protection, motivated in no small part by his knowing that the prejudice we experience at the whims of the outside world is the same he and his family had been subjected to. Our most senior elders held him in the highest possible esteem. They had seen him willingly and selflessly dedicated to the betterment of the Village and all those within it. His heart was pure. They therefore decided to grant him significant authority over Village matters. It was a great honor, a great burden, and entirely secret. Rank and file members had no idea such a position of responsibility existed. They still don't. He had become, in a sense, the conscience of the Village, and that was the title they bestowed upon him. He preferred his title be in his native tongue, so they termed him the 'Conscientia.'" She paused at the gravity of what she shared, then added, "He was the first. The very first. He is buried here," she said, nodding in the direction of the cemetery.

Mention of the Conscientia had Jarek hanging upon her every word.

"When Brother Francesco passed, another took the role and then another. Many years later, the honor fell to Brother Armstrong." She paused at his memory and continued. "We all know something about the Village: our own experience, our own perspective, our own secrets. You see, Jarek, there's a type of evil that finds a place like this attractive. A darkness. It comes and goes, but when it's here, we can feel it. Sometimes, it seems to arrive as an invisible vapor, creeping down the mountain at night and working its way into the fields, through the doorways, and into the hearts of our brothers and sisters, casting a pall over the Village itself and everyone in it. Other times, it comes in the form of a stranger arriving upon our road."

"A darkness?" Jarek asked.

She paused for a moment, staring into the distance, and continued.

"Some are here specifically to fight this evil. They are the Conscientia. Our guardians. They know things the rest of us don't know, or don't want to."

"What did Brother Armstrong know?" Jarek asked.

"He knew everything," Abigail said, looking him in the eye.

Jarek paused for a moment.

"Everything?"

CHAPTER 33

"Brother Armstrong and I worked very closely together for a long time, Jarek," Abigail said, her cracking voice at the end of the sentence making clear the extent of her affection for the man. "He saw me as a peer, not as an..." she paused "an underling. He respected me. He...he saw things in me that no one else has, and that I don't see in myself, and I held him in great regard and sound affection for it." Her hands were clasped together in her lap in a manner suggesting the kind of strained grief that is reserved only for our most beloved family or those whose esteem instills in us a sense of purpose which we may never have found on our own, and for which we owe them eternal gratitude.

"Jarek, you have been my near-constant companion since I first plucked you out of the field; how long ago?"

"Two months, ma'am."

"And you will mind me when I tell you that such camaraderie among brothers and sisters is roundly frowned upon here, as you know."

"Yes, ma'am."

"In our case, it is deemed acceptable because we are not peers within this community. You are a very new arrival. I am an Elder and am most certainly old enough to be your mother."

"I'm not so sure about that, ma'am," he flattered her.

"Thank you, Jarek," she nodded, "but it's true. And while I make no secret that I long desired children before my arrival, of course, I cannot now have them, having taken a vow of celibacy when I joined this devout and loving order of the brothers and sisters you see around me every day."

Jarek listened attentively.

"Everyone knows that brother Armstrong and I were…" she paused "friends. In our role as Elders, we spent much time together. Some know that I held him in as high affection as I have ever held any man and that his loss," she swallowed a small sob and continued "has deprived me of a very familiar presence. As a result of this grief I have experienced, Jarek, my peers are willing to look into their hearts and allow us to spend the time together that lets us maintain such confidence, which is somewhat counter to our custom here in the Village."

"Yes, I understand."

"So it will be without eliciting any judgment from you that I might explain that Brother Armstrong was as honest, devout, compassionate, and faithful a man as you might ever hope to meet. And I don't understand, I just don't…" Her voice trailed off as her hand covered her mouth and one solitary tear fell from her eye. "I don't understand his passing. But I can tell you that in the days before—in fact, that very morning, he was as much a pinnacle of stout health and energy and good cheer as ever. So I don't understand. It seems so unfair to take from this Village such a specimen of righteousness and goodness and leave others, others who are not one fraction of the humble servant that he was, to live on in the fruits of his labor and under the shadow of his absence. Many needed his beautiful soul in their challenged lives and still do now, more than ever."

"Why would God let that happen?" Jarek asked.

She responded with a stern look.

"My dear, the glib doubt of the non-believer is best entertained in the absence of the devout, for whom such questions are foundational, fundamental, and—distressingly—forever without answer."

He gave an apologetic nod. "I'm sorry," he said, then added, "And I'm not a non-believer."

He then kept quiet as she gave him an approving look and continued:

"There is no person other than me in whom Brother Armstrong shared such confidences as he had. Understand, my role here, even as an Elder, is somewhat routine. His, however, was one of great responsibility, and his role as Conscientia was one of great reverence, albeit a secret one. But through our confidences, I learned of the many things he was responsible for, burdened with, and aware of. There are many financial ledgers in this community. In our way, we are not only one small industry but many. While Brother Armstrong was, in many ways, the soul of the Elders of this Village, he was by no means the overseer of all our operations. He could make inquires, as needed, but as a matter of course, had little day-to-day knowledge of the ledgers."

"Ok," Jarek had a sense he knew where this was going.

"Brother Armstrong started noticing...inconsistencies in the monthly ledgers. Things he knew couldn't be right based on various bits of activity in the Village. Receipts were down for produce, yet the fields had a profound year. Seed store receipts surprisingly low at a time when by all accounts—including mine—they should be at historic highs. So, he began making inquiries. He asked to review the actual ledgers weekly and then daily. He was desirous of seeing the information that he was confident would assure him everything was fine. Upon his review, he became even more concerned, but shortly after, he stopped receiving them altogether, inquiries or not. Then things began to change."

"Receiving them from who?"

Abigail was quiet. Jarek pressed further.

"Who was Brother Armstrong asking for the ledgers?"

She looked towards the window from the chair where she had been carefully mending a sister's bonnet.

She looked back to Jarek with raised eyebrows to convey the gravity of what she was about to say and spoke in a whisper:

"Thaddeus."

Jarek's surprise must have been apparent on his face. "What I'm telling you, my dear boy, is this," Abigail added. "I'm afraid the darkness is back."

Jarek nodded, asking, "Abigail, how did he come here? Thaddeus."

She let out a sigh.

"No one knows, exactly. He told us he was from a German immigrant family in Bucks County, Pennsylvania. We discovered that that, at least, was true once we had made some inquiries. We also learned that he had been working the docks in New York, South Street Seaport, partaking of the habits of alcohol, gambling, and worse, all available in those parts. His boss discovered he had been trafficking in some goods that had been disappearing from arriving shipments. Thaddeus was confronted and struck him with a pick handle, causing serious injury, and then fled into the city. A group of men searched every bar and flophouse in the area for days, but he had already left. He used the money he had grifted to buy nice clothes, a black leather trunk, and one-way passage via carriage to a village in the Berkshires where he understood some religious types had some very profitable industries underway. They were called 'Shakers.'"

"Sister Abigail, but…those here in the Village seem to have such respect for Thaddeus. I see it every day." Jarek was puzzled.

Abigail gave him a stiff look. "Respect, dear? Are you sure? Or fear?"

Jarek nodded slowly, deep in thought, to show he understood.

"So this was not his first…enterprise?" Jarek noted.

"A hardened criminal, through and through," she responded.

"But how did he…get in? To where he is now, I mean."

"Jarek, some people have an air of bad intentions about them. Something wounded and sinister that puts a looming shadow in their presence. They know it and, for their own survival, spend much of their life's energy on developing enough charm, worldly knowledge, and charisma to put them into the good grace of others just long enough to bring their schemes to fruition. Thaddeus is one of those individuals: his exaggerated dignity, overtures of concern, and readiness to invoke God at every turn. Nonetheless, the more discerning among us see the man he really is. At least we do now. But his persistence and business knowledge had more of us accepting his presence and rapid ascent while he gravitated towards the money. He claimed to be a child of the church and could quote large amounts of text, knew a surprising number of hymns and even our songs, and generally spoke the language of the virtuous. There was no evidence of anything happening untoward, you understand?"

"Yes, of course," he nodded.

"Before long, though, his friendliness to some of the younger sisters in the Village began to draw attention. He would show much more interest in their happiness and well-being than he would in other members of the community. The sisters noticed first, then the elders; but all in their forgiving natures assumed it was one of his quirks and let the matter go unaddressed. By the time any real concerns were raised about his behavior, in that matter or others, he was solidly in control of the ledgers coming out of every facet of Village business."

"And people were much less inclined to get in his way once he managed all the provisions, yes?" Jarek asked.

"Yes, that's right. You'll find in life, Jarek, that groups of individuals often have the hardest time standing up against things they know are wrong. Each person excuses their inaction by feigning deference to the will of the whole. The whole itself then proceeds in a direction each individual knows to be wrong but does not have the courage to stop. This is a source of much evil in the outside world and here as well," she said.

"Where I'm from they call it 'shareholder value,'" he quipped.

She paused momentarily, then added, "Jarek, I forget myself; I am speaking far too freely for your young ears, and I should not do so. Understand my grief is the cause. I am sorry, dear boy."

"Wait, wait," Jarek protested, needing to know more. "But he was an elder by then, right? Thaddeus is an elder."

"By then, yes, which made it even harder. Anyone who opposed him saw a flash of anger that was nothing short of frightening. Aside from that, before long, he hired four gentlemen to assist with Village affairs. He said they were Shakers, or wanted to be, but we knew they were here to serve as his own hired hands. Soon after they arrived, they took to disappearing into town to partake of copious amounts of alcohol; and on at least two occasions, their return to the Village was marked by yelling and drunken singing in the quietest hours of the night. Brother Armstrong had suspicions about one of the men sneaking into the room of a younger sister against her will, though he didn't know which one and no one would speak to him of it. The men were all strong, as was Thaddeus, and neither they nor he were to be trifled with due to their position of physical and financial dominance in the Village. She kept quiet for fear of being vilified. The Village was the only home she had, and Thaddeus was a formidable presence within it.

"Brother Armstrong, as an elder, spiritual leader in the community and—most importantly—as Conscientia, kept up appearances in light of these circumstances as best he could, but he knew all too well that something was deeply amiss. He felt a shadow hanging over the Village and was the first to realize it."

"To realize what?" Jarek asked.

"The darkness was back," she nodded, "it had again worked its way from out in the world into our little utopia in the form of a figure of unknown origin. And ill intent.

"He told me that Thaddeus keeps his own ledger, that he had seen him with it once, and suspected that it accurately accounted both for how much money was truly coming into the Village and how much was ending up in Thaddeus's pocket. He knew if he could get his hands on it, he would have all the proof he needed to hand him to the authorities and have us rid of him forever. But he never saw it again and had no idea where Thaddeus kept it, so instead, he started to document inconsistencies. And he waited."

CHAPTER 34

"My goodness, Jarek, this is incredible stuff."

Drummy was on the edge of his seat as McCracken sat stone-still in his desk chair, deep in thought. At their request, Jarek had just explained what Abigail had conveyed in excruciating detail, and they were speechless.

If any of Thaddeus's contemporaries had ever taken a written account of his activities within the Village—if anyone dared—none had survived. The truth had been buried for over a century with those few who knew it.

"We cannot draw conclusions that are not available to us outside of the information you have provided, of course." Jarek nodded at these words from McCracken, who then turned his eyes towards Drummy, by far the more passionate of the pair, to convey this message was intended for him as well. Drummy nodded, too. "But this is incredibly illuminating. And to hear this nearly first-hand, Jarek! Well done, very well done."

Jarek wasn't sure he deserved the accolades. "I mean. I'm sort of…there anyway. It's not espionage." He wasn't trying to be funny but appreciated seeing McCracken laugh for the first time.

"So," Jarek said, bringing it back to the issue at hand, "I'm glad this is interesting and all, but it doesn't get to the crux of my own problem, I'm afraid."

"Which one?" Drummy asked, quickly rephrasing. "I'm sorry. What I meant was, what problem?"

"The problem of what I'm doing there!" Jarek stood up. "Why is this happening? Why me?"

McCracken thought for a moment about what he was going to say next.

"Jarek," he began, "You recall the three of us have spoken here about how they believed the dead could impart wisdom to the living through gifts. And how worship was a way to channel salvation from themselves to those who had already died, unsaved. Right?"

Sometimes McCracken was a bit too thorough. "Yep," Jarek said briefly.

"Well, your visit is occurring in 1866. That's many years after the death of Mother Ann. Much of what she said and some of what she believed has been passed down through oral tradition. Many of their members weren't educated. They couldn't read, so this made sense."

"Okay," Jarek was listening.

"About 20 years after your visit, in 1888, a book was shared throughout the communities. Before long, it came to be known as *The Book of Secrets.*"

"Lord," Jarek said. "How many creepy books did these people have?"

"Well," McCracken smiled, "technically, it was called *Testimonies of the Life, Character, Revelations, and Doctrines of Mother Ann Lee.* Before long, they recovered every copy, concerned about some of what was inside, and hoped they would never be seen again, especially by brothers and sisters of The Way. That's how it came to be called *The Book of Secrets*. One of the things this book made clear is the extent to which Mother Ann and those who were with her at the beginning believed in communication with the dead."

He quoted from memory: "'None could be deprived of the offer of salvation because they had left the world before Christ made his appearance; or because they had lived in some remote part of the earth, where the sound of the gospel had never reached their ears.'"

McCracken continued, "But what the book makes clear, Jarek, is that they believed not just in receiving gifts or sharing salvation with the dead, but actually seeing the dead. Has Abigail brought this up at all?"

"Actually seeing dead people? No. No, I guess she was saving the good stuff for later."

"Another Elder around her time, her brother William Lee, said, 'I know the condition of souls who have left the body. Where I see one soul in the body, I see a thousand in the world of spirits.' Quite a visual."

"Throngs of dead people everywhere? These folks were into some spooky stuff," Jarek said.

"There's another idea that presented itself through this text for the first time. We talked about 'reaching forward' as a possible explanation for what you've experienced. The dead reaching forward into the future to bring someone back. But with a careful eye, some discovered hints that something else was possible. The idea of the dead actually stepping into the future themselves. Traveling forward in time rather than beckoning others back. We don't have any evidence, documented, oral tradition or otherwise, suggesting this was real in any way, or that it was ever accomplished. But mysteries are unfolding in all of this day by day. It's important that we have a full scope of what they believed, no matter how outlandish it seems to us, just in case."

"Um, just in case what?" Jarek asked, perplexed.

"Oops!" Drummy looked at his watch. "Class in two minutes!"

He jumped up and headed out. Jarek followed closely behind, wondering why they so clearly avoided his question.

CHAPTER 35

"Oh, thank you, dear boy."

An elderly brother reached his hand out with gratitude to take from Lucas a smaller and lighter pitchfork he had brought him. Lucas, Jarek, and several other brothers were in the barn, moving hay bales to one of two wagons waiting just outside. "Did you go all the way to the shed to get this just for me?" the elderly brother asked.

"Yes, sir," said Lucas with a slight smile. "I thought it would be easier."

As the first cart departed with several of the brothers, the old man took a seat to rest outside, leaving Lucas and Jarek working the hay alone in the barn. Jarek was eager to chat with him, and as soon as he saw it was just them, he wasted no time.

"Lucas," Jarek said, "are you okay? I haven't seen you much—hardly at all."

"Yes, I am. Sorry about that," Lucas said.

"No, no, you don't have to be sorry," Jarek said, "but I've been wondering if you're all right. I haven't even seen you at meals. When I see you in the Village, you sort of mumble something and find a reason to go do something else."

"Understand, Jarek, I'm not avoiding you. I would never." Lucas said. He hung his head a bit, and Jarek regretted pressuring him.

"I know, Lucas," he said kindly, "you've just been really quiet. You move slowly, stare at the ground most of the time, and all that happy, friendly Lucas-energy that everybody loves—I don't know—where is it? What's wrong?"

"They moved me to a new room," Lucas said. "I used to have two roommates. Now it's just me."

"Is that it? Are you lonely because you're by yourself?" Jarek asked.

"The window faces the front, so at least I have a view," Lucas added.

"You don't like your room?" Jarek asked again.

"No, that's not it. I'm sorry, Jarek, everything is fine," Lucas said.

Lucas occupied himself as Jarek watched him, eager to gather anything more than the limited information he had been told. His mannerisms were so similar to Andrew's, especially in moments of discouragement, that Jarek couldn't help but stare.

"What?" Lucas said.

"Lucas, we're friends, right?" Jarek said.

"Of course we are," Lucas said with surprise.

"If anything's wrong, you know you can tell me, right? I'll help you, I'll fix it, whatever it is," Jarek said.

"Jarek," Lucas looked at him, "You're bigger than me and stronger. You're smarter than I'll ever be."

"That's not true," Jarek tried to object.

"Yes, yes, it's true," Lucas added, "but there are some things that are too big for you—even you, Jarek—to help me with."

Jarek knew then that something was genuinely wrong and was eager not only to rise to the challenge of helping his friend but to find out what—or who—was the source of his distress.

"Lucas," he said, "if that's all you want to say, that's fine. But nothing is too big."

Lucas shook his head in disagreement.

"Give me time," Jarek said. "I'll prove it to you."

CHAPTER 36

Sister Abigail was a bit shaken by the gravity of what she had conveyed during her conversation with Jarek. As the squeaking wheels of a carriage came to a halt outside, she collected herself and stepped out the door to greet the arrival.

"Mr. Goodell, how do you do?" she asked with a smile.

"Splendid, ma'am, thank you. How are you this fine day?"

"In good health, thank you."

Jarek could see that Abigail's mind was elsewhere.

"Sister Abigail, are you quite all right?" Mr. Goodell asked.

"Yes, thank you kindly, Mr. Goodell. Just a bit tired."

Jarek tried to help. "We have two bundles for you, plus your broom."

"My wife loves these, thank you. Wore the other one down to a tiny nub," he said, taking the broom handle from Jarek's outstretched hand.

Jarek noticed the weather-worn hands in which he placed the broom. He was, indeed, accustomed to hard work.

Mr. Goodell added, "I've also got two barrelhead of nails, a bushel of corn, and the floor planks in the wagon. Easy enough here. The brothers were kind enough to load me up." He smiled. "Not sure how I'll do all this at the other end though." He gave a self-deprecating shrug.

"Jarek, if you don't mind, can you ride with Mr. Goodell and help him unload?"

"That's kind, Ms. Dorrance, and I truly thank you, but he won't be back for a couple of hours."

"That's quite all right. I can manage without him for a bit." She gave Mr. Goodell a sympathetic nod. "Jarek, do you mind?"

"No, no, of course not," Jarek said. Mr. Goodell was one of the kindest of their customers and, from what Jarek had learned from Sister Abigail, certainly the most sincere.

"Brother Armstrong's horse is here for our use, so please tie her to Mr. Goodell's wagon as you ride with him. She is a very reasonable horse. Then you can ride her straight back when you're finished."

"Yes, ma'am," Jarek said, glad for the little time he and Andrew spent on horses at summer camp and hoping it would be enough.

"Brother Armstrong's?" Mr. Goodell asked.

Abigail gave a sad nod.

"In that case, lucky me," he said. "In addition to the help you are affording me, I'll enjoy this journey in the company of both Jarek and this honest companion of our dear departed friend, whom she served so well." The horse responded with a friendly chuff to his reaching out and rubbing her forehead.

Jarek loaded the few additional items into Mr. Goodell's already full wagon, hitched Brother Armstrong's horse to the rear, and sat beside him in front—as he had the reigns and was ready to go. The ride would take about 40 minutes, and as they began, Jarek was reminded that—in great contrast to the time he was from—people in the company of others generally did not feel uncomfortable with moments of silence. He and Brother Goodell sat silently, hearing the sounds of the wagon and the wind in the trees for many minutes before Mr. Goodell spoke:

"I am grateful for your assistance, Jarek. I trust I'm not taking from your responsibilities?"

"No sir, I would be minding the store with Abigail for two more hours, and it's quite slow, so this works out just fine," Jarek said.

"Well, thank her again for me when you return. And this pie," he nodded to the covered box between the two of them on the seat, "especially for the pie. I know it will be delicious. Name I hadn't heard before—Jingle Dolly?

"Jingle Berry. Sister Abigail is the only one who knows how to make it. We sell a lot of them."

"Well, my wife and I will enjoy it; it was very kind of her. Please do tell her," Goodell said.

Jarek smiled, "Of course."

"I know you haven't been here long, Jarek. I'm also not sure how well you know Sister Abigail as of yet, but she is the strongest and most dependable woman you'll ever meet. You, my boy, are lucky to be in her good graces." Jarek was intrigued by the similarity to Abigail's description of Mr. Goodell himself, which he had heard just a short time earlier. They were cut from the same cloth.

"Did she tell you how I met her…or how I met all of you?"

The "you" resonated in Jarek's ears, as he hadn't yet heard anyone from outside the Village refer to him as part of the community.

"No, sir, I'm afraid she didn't."

"Well, some things to know about Abigail—*Sister* Abigail, pardon me." He gave Jarek a stern look, assuring him that he should not attempt the same informality Mr. Goodell had allowed himself. "She's honest as the day is long and smart as a whip. I'm a God-fearing man, Jarek, so don't get the wrong idea when I tell you two things. The first is to say she takes 'do unto others' to heart more than anyone I've ever met. The second, well, like I said, I'm a God-fearing man. There's only one other thing I fear, and that is getting on the bad side of Sister Abigail Dorrance. She's got a heart of gold, but if you get in her way when she's set to a purpose, you'll soon wish you hadn't." He gave a knowing smile.

"I understand. But…" Jarek knew he was out of his depth as he continued, "Why is that?"

"Well, Jarek, because she may drive a fork through your chest! *Ha!*" The final exclamation was a voluminous bellow from the base of his chest, given as much out of admiration for Sister Abigail as in response to his own commentary. It reminded Jarek how large a man Mr. Goodell was.

The farmer slowed his manner for a moment, gave the harness a shake, and let out a sigh.

"Winters can be pretty cruel around here, as you know, or if you don't, you're about to find out." The thought of resilience led him to give one more snap on the reigns, with the sound of the horse's hooves picking up pace. "There's a doctor in town—only one for miles, and, well…this is a story, but…" he looked at the road ahead, "we have time.

"We had a storm here last winter. You weren't at the Village, but it covered the east coast, so I'm sure it hit you as hard as it hit us, wherever you were."

"Oh, yes," Jarek said, trying to sound like he knew what Goodell was talking about. "Of course. Terrible."

"It was the worst any of us had seen in a decade. After a few hours, the roads could not be passed by anyone. Let me tell you what happened just before it blew in."

Jarek was on the edge of his seat as the horses clopped along.

"Sister Abigail was in the store, as she is at odd hours occasionally. The store is a point of reference for visitors as it is what they are familiar with. People come with all manner of questions about anything from farming or pickling to cattle. Sometimes, they come to bring information about urgent matters in the outside world. It's how you all found out about the war, you know." Jarek knew he meant the Civil War and let his mind digest how near that bloody undertaking was to the minds of the people he now knew, including Mr. Goodell. Everyone lost someone. Jarek thought of two men in the Village who struggled with wooden legs.

"On February 3rd, Sister Abigail was closing down the store a bit late. She heard a big storm was coming and wanted to be there in case anyone needed final provisions. Before this storm came, there was such a wind as you'd think the skin of the world was about to be blown right into the sky. Howling, freezing wind. Lasted all day and through the night. In this wind and cold, she heard the loud rap of a metal cane head on the door. It was soon approaching dark, so she moved quickly to let whoever this late visitor was in out of the cold. When she opened the door, she saw nothing other than the long coat of a man on horseback at a gallop, moving down the road in the cold final light of day. Then she heard the cry of a small baby. She looked down to her feet and there, wrapped from head to foot with only its small pink face showing, was the face of a tiny baby boy—not more than one week old—wrapped in a bundle of greasy rags and lying in a wooden box in the cold. Just like the boxes you use at the store.

"She took the baby in that night and kept it warm. She went to the Dairy Barn and collected milk, hoping the baby would accept it, and he did. By morning, he was in better color, and Sister Abigail was much relieved."

"That's wonderful," Jarek said.

"Well. The storm was coming, and the wind was starting to howl. Abigail was giving the child motherly care. Jarek, you've noticed how much Abigail likes to sing, yes? I've learned many of your songs through her."

"Yes," Jarek smiled, "she's always singing."

"Well, you know she rocked that baby endlessly and sang to it the whole time. 'Oh, Give Me a Little Love.'"

Mr. Goodell, to Jarek's surprise, started to sing. As Jarek listened closely to the words, his imagination took him to Abigail's side, watching her sing to the small bundle in her arms as the wind blew outside. He could practically see her familiar smiling face leaning towards that of the tiny child and singing quietly.

(Song: "Oh, Give Me a Little Love")

Oh, give me a little love,
little love, little love
Give me a little love more

That love that will hold me
when trials assail me
oh give me a little love more

"You see, Jarek," Mr. Goodell continued, "Abigail, well, she and my wife share a disappointment that men—whatever *our* disappointments in life—can't truly understand, no matter how hard we try. Abigail, well, she's a Shaker. She loves the Village and everyone in it, but that means she will never have children.

"So, for Abigail, the baby was a gift from God, granted to her as thanks for her selfless devotion to everything and everyone other than herself. It was God saying 'Thank you.'

"But the baby had spent time in the bitter cold, likely hanging from the side of whoever rode him in on horseback, and he seemed to be ill. *Seemed* at first, and then—by the middle of the day—unmistakably was. He cried, screamed, and coughed, and it was clear that without help, he was in trouble. With the storm coming, it might be a week until he could get it. You people believe in medicine, but you have no doctor. Abigail was ready to take the baby to the doctor down in the valley, but the only closed wagon was controlled by…"

"Thaddeus," Jarek said.

"Very good, Jarek. Yes, Thaddeus. And Thaddeus doesn't believe in medicine or doctors. Or at least he says he doesn't. Frankly, I don't think he believes in much of anything at all, but I reckon he doesn't like anyone in the Village going to anyone outside who knows anything more than he does, no matter the subject."

"So, he said no?" Jarek asked.

"In a way. What he said was, 'I'll set this wagon on fire before I put it in the hands of a woman. Even if it's not her.'"

Jarek raised his eyebrows in surprise at the ferocity of the remark.

Goodell continued. "Mind you, the freezing wind is more than anyone can bear for more than a few minutes, and the doctor is

40 minutes by wagon. Those of us who are friends of the Village would have torn through Thaddeus to put that baby in the wagon with Abigail and get them on their way if we had known. Do you understand?"

"Yes, sir," Jarek said in earnest.

"I had my suspicions about him. Brother Armstrong was on to something, I think. But even he didn't think Thaddeus was capable of sending a woman and an infant into the frozen night uncovered and alone. Abigail believed this baby was God letting her be a mother, even in the Shaker sense, and she wasn't going to let it get sicker; she could never be so cruel. Thaddeus had his hands around the neck of the elders, though, at that point, so no one would help her. They were too scared. Except..."

"Except Brother Armstrong," Jarek guessed.

"That's right. But Brother Armstrong did not have a wagon. You understand everything is owned by the Village, but the elders decide how they are used. Thaddeus had taken the wagon as his own. He suspected Abigail would try to take it despite him, which she did, but she found he had removed the tongue and the queen bolt, so it was inoperable.

"Now, Brother Armstrong had two favorite horses, this beautiful animal here," he nodded to the horse tethered behind them, "and one other, which he gave to Abigail that night to take out into the wind and the snow, which had been falling for two hours before they left and was falling faster than I've ever seen. Brother Armstrong insisted on going with her, but another horse would have slowed her down, and Brother Armstrong was not a young man—it would have been far too hard on him—so she insisted he stay. She put one lantern over her shoulder and another on the horse, then wrapped the baby and herself as best she could, strapped it to her chest with some linens, mounted the horse, and began quickly down with her delicate passenger. Brother Armstrong and some of the sisters watched with grave concern as she disappeared into the snow and coming dark."

He paused for a moment and stared straight ahead, lost in the memory he was conjuring. Jarek did, too.

"I don't need to tell you what happens to this-here road when the temperature is so far below freezing, or what happens to a horse with frozen wind blowing in its face, or to a woman with the same—and both of them unable to see straight from the hard-driven snow."

"Did they make it to the doctor's?" Jarek interrupted out of eager concern.

"The doctor is four miles away. Even for a horse as strong as Brother Armstrong's, it was a slow journey in snow and bitter wind that could freeze your flesh in ten minutes if you let it. Before long, the poor mare's ears were iced solid, and her lungs reluctantly braced for each huff of frigid air. Every step on the frozen ground was a risk, but she knew her passengers were in peril, so she pressed on into the dark. That mare had a spirit of fire, like her rider. She was a loyal and noble animal. But the road is long for a night like that."

Mr. Goodell was quiet for a moment, looking at the same dirt road before him, and Jarek imagined the terrible scene he described.

"She sang to the child and the horse to offer comfort."

Mr. Goodell began to sing again, and as the words resonated in Jarek's ears, he heard them in Abigail's voice. He saw Abigail's face by the lantern's light, holding the baby close in the blowing snow and cold.

(Song: "Low, in this Pretty Path")

Low, Low,
Low, Low,
In this pretty path I will go
For here Mother leads me and I know it is right
I will sweep as I go, I will sweep as I go
For this Mother bids me and it is my delight

And the sword I will wield, and the sword I will wield
For Mother bids me so
And I will go, and I will go
For this is my work while here below.

Mr. Goodell paused momentarily, his thoughts succumbing to the dire circumstance he was conveying, and then continued.

"The cold took its toll, and, unable to see through the driving snow, the horse stepped into a hidden hole. Abigail had been focused on nothing other than the warmth of the child, but the stumble roused her quickly enough to hold the baby up towards the sky, making sure it would be uninjured as the horse went swiftly to the ground. The animal crushed her right leg. She still has a little limp, as you likely have noticed."

Jarek nodded.

"She held the baby close and got up, ignoring the pain in her leg, and looked to the animal, letting out a small cry when she saw that its front leg was broken. There was nothing she could do." Mr. Goodell paused. "This," he nodded toward the road beside them, "is where the horse would stay.

"Sister Abigail left one lantern on the ground before the horse, hoping the flame would provide the poor beast some company in its last moments. Then she stroked the animal's cheek, put the strap of the remaining lamp over her shoulder, held ever tighter to the child, and began limping down the road on foot as fast as she could. From time to time, she would look back across the growing distance between her and the lamp where the horse lay. That smart girl would know Abigail had turned to look towards her each time she saw her lamp swing in the distance and would whinny into the dark. When it was almost too far to be seen, she cried into the wind one final time. When Abigail turned around…she saw the flame no more." He paused again. "She was a good horse.

"Abigail was on foot in the howling wind, clutching that child as close to her chest as she could, determined that each step would not be her last. She walked the rest on foot, two more miles. It took another long and desperate hour. By coincidence, maybe fate, I don't know, I was at the doctor myself trying to see him before the storm set in. His farm is near mine. I had mishandled a spike right here," he showed Jarek a five-inch faded purple scar on the inside of his forearm, "and wanted him to take a look. He concluded with me, and in came a woman—thin as a rail, falling over and bright pink—her face swollen from the bitter cold, with a wrap of frozen cloths in her hands, whispering 'the baby, the baby.' She unwrapped the frozen rags and showed us a small baby that had been exposed to the terrible conditions that had so badly abused Abigail. We were shocked. Speechless. The doctor ran to the baby right away. I stayed, despite the snow, out of concern for this poor woman and her child."

He looked to the heavens for a moment and continued.

"You'll note you never see Sister Abigail without her bonnet, Jarek."

"Yes, other sisters sometimes go without, but never Sister Abigail," Jarek said.

"And, more uncommonly, never without her gloves," Goodell added.

"Yes. But why?"

"Jarek, the cold on the mountain can cut you like a knife. Well, that's all I have to say, out of respect, you understand."

Jarek wasn't sure what he meant, but it didn't sound good. "God," he said in shock, as the reality of all he heard settled upon him.

"Not sure God had much to do with it, son. Sister Abigail was beside herself with sorrow and with rage. After that night, she stayed in bed for days until some of her sisters convinced her that she needed real medical attention."

He continued. "She felt such sorrow, she didn't care. She was ready to give up, to the surprise of those who know her strength of spirit. She didn't care for her own sake, but some sisters kept at her, telling her how much they needed her, how much all the sisters did. They knew just what to say, which got her back on her feet. That's just her nature. But that night devastated her. She keeps to herself mostly—one of the most private women I've ever met—but she has had a fire inside her for Thaddeus ever since."

"But…what about the baby?" Jarek asked.

Mr. Goodell kept his eyes forward but paused for a moment. He gave the reigns a quick shake as he continued. "The baby had far too much cold. The doctor did all he could, but the baby kept quiet. Two days later, his heart slowed. And, so soon after entering this world, his little gasps for breath became slower, his eyes closed, and…"

Jarek held his breath and waited. Mr. Goodell was not inclined to show emotion, but the quiver in his voice gave him away as he spoke two final words.

"…he died."

"JAREK, I WANT TO SHOW YOU SOMETHING—COME WITH ME," SISTER Abigail said.

Jarek had returned from Mr. Goodell's farm a moment before and hitched his horse outside the store. It had taken more time than anticipated, as Mr. Goodell needed help relocating hay bales for the winter. Jarek enjoyed his company and was more than happy to help. He spent the solitary ride home thinking about all they had discussed. He had a greater understanding of, and more profound respect for, Sister Abigail.

When he arrived back at the store, she was sitting at the counter, looking down at her gloved hands as she mended with needle and thread one of the burlap bags they used to deliver feed throughout the Village and to customers at the store. The late daylight placed a shadow of the windowpanes on her shoulder and face as she sowed. She looked tired, somehow much more somber, even melancholy, now that he knew all he had heard. She hadn't seen Jarek enter, and he heard her quiet lilting voice sing softly as he approached.

(Song: "Love is Little, Love is Low")

Love is little, love is low
Love will make my spirit grow.
Grown in peace, grown in light
Love will do the thing that's right.

Her hands were still for a moment as she looked towards the window, deep in thought, before she realized he was beside her.

"Jarek dear, come along," she said, placing her work before her and walking past him into the orange of the sun over the valley below as she exited the main entrance. She didn't explain, slow her stride, or indicate where they were going. He realized by her demeanor that her brief exchange with Mr. Goodell about Brother Armstrong and his horse several hours earlier had brought difficult memories to the fore. Whatever errand she was now taking him on was decided upon during the hours she sat alone contemplating her grief and was of special significance. He was determined to pay close attention.

She spoke very little during their walk.

"Mr. Goodell was happy for your services?"

"Yes, ma'am," he replied, rubbing his sore backside, and doing his best to forget the uncomfortable ride back.

"This way." She stepped off the road up the hill to the right once they had walked at least half the length of the Village. While brothers and sisters were finishing their dinner together at this time, anyone in the seed store was given a reprieve, as hours were kept in such a way as to allow farmers finishing their late day tilling to make it to the store just before sundown.

They moved towards a small clearing, grass-covered and tidily maintained, at the edge of the Village. In the center stood a large white pillar. There were several small stones across the grass with initials upon them, carefully placed, but Jarek noticed with interest that the pillar was blank. Also carefully placed within the clearing were several cast iron spikes bearing small, half-moon iron pieces, in the center of which were names and dates. A chill ran through Jarek's body as he realized this was where they kept their dead.

Sister Abigail moved slowly and intentionally towards a marker in the far corner. She stopped before one of them, held her hands together, and stood perfectly still. Jarek heard her stifle a sob. He looked down and saw, etched on top of the small square white stone before her feet, the letters "E.A."

"Elijah Armstrong—Brother Armstrong," Jarek said. He looked quietly at Abigail's downturned face. While her eyes were wide open and determined as ever, he was sure he saw one solitary tear escape, which she quickly wiped away with her glove.

The next moments, at least in Jarek's memory, moved in slow motion. Perhaps it was the sincerity with which she spoke. Or the deep concern in her voice. Or hearing this woman—whom he held in such high regard—say something to him that he knew came from the very depths of her soul, even if he didn't understand it at the time.

Her head turned slowly to him, and her eyes looked at him sympathetically. There was more sadness in them than he had seen before. She leaned closer, took a deep breath, and chose her words carefully.

"Jarek," she whispered. "Leave here." His eyes darted beyond her to see who her whisper was intended to avoid—there was no one.

The next words she spoke sounded in his ears over and over again for days.

"Leave here, Jarek Dorrell. Leave here, and don't look back. Or someday it may be your body we're putting in this common grave."

Jarek stood, shocked and confused, watching the back of her head, her neatly tied bonnet and her blue dress, as she began to walk away. She then paused for a moment, looking back over her shoulder to speak one final word in a sharp whisper.

"Run."

CHAPTER 37

It was unseasonably hot for a late fall morning, as Jarek found himself among many brothers headed to work in the fields.

He had recently noticed something about Lucas's behavior which made him wonder. Thaddeus seemed more interested in Lucas than he had been before, but whenever he was near, Lucas became perfectly still and silent. During the course of any day, if Lucas was in the vicinity, Thaddeus would cast quick, angry glances in his direction. This interest made little sense to Jarek, given the different statures of Lucas and Thaddeus in the community and the fact that there was little reason for them to interact any more than Thaddeus would with any other child in the Village.

These matters weighed on Jarek's mind as he walked across the stubbled cornfield to an area where Lucas and some older brothers were sifting soil to remove rocks. Lucas moved slowly, collecting rocks from a standing sifter, and depositing them in a nearby cart. He was, again, uncharacteristically quiet.

"Lucas," Jarek called.

Lucas kept his head turned towards the soil and spoke quietly.

"Oh, hello, Jarek."

"Lucas, I've hardly seen you lately." Jarek reached for several rocks and tossed them in the cart.

"Jarek, I'm fine," Lucas said quietly.

A nearby older brother had been listening. "Not sure he's fine, I'd say," the old man quietly remarked, his warbling intonation suggesting he had come to the Village from somewhere deep in Appalachia.

"He was bleedin' this morning anyway," he added. "I get the towels from the bath house, and sure enough, his had blood."

Jarek looked towards Lucas. "Lucas, hey…" he said, leaning closer. When he did, he saw how pale and detached the boy looked. He also saw—now realizing Lucas had been keeping his head turned to hide it—a four-inch bruise along the edge of his jaw towards his ear.

"Hey, what's this? What happened?"

"Says he stumbled at the stairs," the old gent added. "Bad strokes of luck, this lad."

Jarek's questioning gaze looked straight into Lucas's eyes, and Lucas quickly looked away.

Something was wrong. Profoundly and terribly wrong.

A nearby shout pierced the air: "THIS is the same as you all sifted two days ago, and I asked YOU, Brother Jacob, to work in the right spot!"

No one had seen him coming as they focused on their work, but Jarek noticed the songs had ceased, and the brothers seemed to be moving more slowly in the fields. Just as this thought came to his mind, the angry bellow of Thaddeus sitting atop his horse stopped them all in their tracks. Jarek knew more about Thaddeus than anyone else, and he now hated him with a passion that clenched his jaw muscles. Jarek ignored his words and instead looked closely at Lucas as Brother Jacob stammered through his explanations.

Lucas was frozen in place—completely motionless, save for what looked like some quickened breathing. He stared at the ground with his fists clenched—not working, not moving, not saying a word.

"Lucas!" Thaddeus shouted, having turned his attention to the two of them. "Lucas, I hope you're doing your part."

Lucas didn't move. The old men had turned back to their work as Thaddeus's gaze remained fixed on Lucas. Jarek's was, too.

He saw Lucas's hands shaking. Then he saw, as Thaddeus turned away, a wet spot on the front of Lucas's pants. Lucas stared at the dirt motionless as the water quickly darkened the inside of his pant leg, trailing to the bottom, until it trickled down into his shoe and the soil beside it.

Jarek was stunned and motionless.

Someone had decided to move Lucas to a room where he would be alone. And now the hopelessness, the bruises, the blood, and—clearly—the terror. Jarek was numb with grief and shock.

He no longer wondered what was happening to Lucas.

It was Thaddeus.

CHAPTER 38

Jarek sat at the desk in his dorm room, skipping class again, his mind racing.

Gifts from the dead. Reaching forward. "Deviation from the natural order." Suddenly, it all made sense.

Brother Armstrong was not only sharing a gift with Jarek but also reaching forward. If what McCracken had told him was true, this meant Brother Armstrong was among what they called "the restless dead," which meant his death was likely as unnatural as the Conscientia had suspected through these many years, all the way down to McCracken's tenure. Jarek was the instrument. He was called by name. The one person selected to right a wrong that had occurred.

"But why me?" Jarek asked aloud.

Of the hundreds and hundreds of villagers and then students who had lived here over the past 125 years, why would the Conscientia choose him? He sat, staring blankly at the wall, wracking his brain for the answer.

Something fundamental had been missing in Jarek's life. Since Andrew, he was completely untethered. Nothing mattered. No sense of purpose moved him forward. His swirling thoughts merged in one place, and suddenly, everything was abundantly clear. What was missing was Andrew. Lucas was his spitting image in every way, and Jarek would stop at nothing to help him. Brother Armstrong knew it. He had chosen well. Tears welled up in Jarek's eyes as he realized that Brother Armstrong somehow understood him, solidifying his resolve to correct the wrong he had been called to fix.

The feeling of being watched, the voices he heard in the wind and in the dark, whispering his name. Now it made sense. The spirits of others were communicating with him, nudging him back on course when he flailed because they, too, wanted to see him succeed.

He wished he knew more. What they knew. He wished he could see what they saw. And then, as fast as he wished it, the same familiar chill ran up his spine, and he shuddered. He jumped slightly as a flood of visions came to him. Gifts. Gifts from the dead.

Though sitting at his desk, Jarek was taken entirely by the vision presenting to him. In it, he saw the reality of who Thaddeus was. Jarek witnessed again the moment when Thaddeus picked wildflowers beside the road and handed them to a young sister who was clearly upset. After Thaddeus turned his back, Jarek now saw the look of fear and disgust in the girl's tear-filled eyes as she dropped the flowers on the road, sure to step on them as she continued on her way.

He saw the moment Thaddeus offered to run back into the store for a forgetful elderly sister who had left an item when locking up. This time, he saw Thaddeus—during his brief moment in the store–removing half the contents of the till into his coat pocket.

He saw Thaddeus emerging from one of the women's residences, arms full of laundry, proclaiming with a smile to the puzzled sisters who came to collect it, "I've got these, dear sisters, hurry along to the Meetinghouse. They've begun! I'll drop them on my way."

The vision again shifted. Jarek didn't understand the final gift but knew he would, in time, and was afraid of what it might tell him.

He then found himself in a small room, the dark of night visible outside, as two figures—a man and a woman—sat beside each other at a small wooden table: Sister Abigail and Brother Armstrong. An oil lamp between them showed a look of deep concentration upon both of their faces, each staring intently at the bare underside of their left forearms, extended beside each other upon the table.

Brother Armstrong's fingers, a small bottle beside the lamp, and a small cloth on the table were all stained pitch black. He looked repeatedly from his arm to Sister Abigail's, meticulously moving his fingers over the surface of her skin as she winced in pain. "All right," he offered, "Almost there."

Jarek had no idea what he was witnessing. Before he could give it any more thought, Brother Armstrong's eyes snapped towards him, looking directly into his own.

"Jarek," he whispered.

The vision ended as abruptly as it began, and Jarek was again alone at his desk.

CHAPTER 39

Among his classmates at breakfast the following day, Jarek stared into space. He thought about what was happening to his friend and what, if anything, he could do.

He hadn't needed to ask Lucas many questions when they were in the field. Why put him through it? Jarek knew that within Thaddeus's heart, what was left of it, there was evil capable of anything. He hadn't suspected anything before now as—for the most part—there were so many pairs of eyes and ears around the Village. It would be very difficult to commit the kind of terrible acts Jarek suspected without being discovered.

Lucas was now alone in his room, however; and it was the final piece of information that brought everything together in a way almost too horrible to imagine. But he didn't have to imagine. He knew. He knew that the bruises he saw on Lucas by the stream were from Thaddeus. Thaddeus—with whatever reason he concocted—had instructed that Lucas be moved to his own room. He knew that Thaddeus had latched on to Lucas's unsuspecting trust, his joy at being in a place of love and support. He used it to curry favor before he began a barrage of regular cruelty that had altogether shattered Lucas's spirit, and physical abuse, which—it appeared—had almost shattered Lucas's jaw.

Jarek thought about his brother. What would Andrew have done if it had been Jarek? Anything. Everything.

But Lucas didn't have a brother. Or parents.

It was up to Jarek. He had to stop Thaddeus, and he would. Even if he died trying.

CHAPTER 40

The next few days were a blur. Jarek spent every moment thinking of what he could do to help Lucas. Dreaming up unrealistic scenarios, visualizing revenge, and trying—more practically—to consider Thaddeus's vulnerabilities and how Jarek could use them to his advantage.

Every idea hit a wall. Thaddeus was all-powerful in the Village. He controlled all the materials and money and had put the fear of God into anyone who would think of opposing him. He had expelled one sister from the Village just for speaking out against him. She was admired. She had been there for four years and was a positive and contributing community member. Thaddeus sent her on her way, alone out into the world, with some made-up justification, and let others know that if they tried to help her, they would be pushed out, too. Thaddeus was big, but more importantly, he had four men with him who served as his enforcers in the Village. No one liked them, no one trusted them, and no one dared get in their way.

Jarek was distraught at how hopeless he felt. There was no way to stop what was happening to his friend.

He spent a couple nights in the infirmary at the direction of Headmaster Worthing, who thought it might help him get some clearly needed rest, but his stress wouldn't allow it. In a fit of restlessness, he started exploring and, before long, discovered that the nurse's medicine cabinet in the adjacent room was unlocked. Looking over prescriptions administered to a number of classmates, he saw a Prozac bottle with Em's name on it and let out a sympathetic sigh. One bottle in particular caught his attention: "Restoril (Temazepam). Take one capsule at bedtime as needed for sleep." He paused for a moment but then, against his better judgement, put the entire bottle in his pocket.

He had taken to sneaking away to the museum as often as possible, to the Book of the Mountain Kings, looking for evidence of Thaddeus's activities. He had read Brother Armstrong's entry regarding suspicions of accounting; he hoped he might find more, but there were none.

He knew the book well by now and was aware of the significant events in the Village in the coming weeks and months. Aside from letting the cows out, his activities did not appear to have changed the book, or the future of the Village, the slightest bit.

But on his next visit, as he flipped forward to look for new entries, anything at all, he noticed one thing he hadn't seen before. The Conscientia were responsible for keeping the book. Entries for the previous years were written in a hand he had become very familiar with; it was that of Brother Armstrong.

As of late, Jarek had the opportunity to handle several accounting documents that Sister Abigail managed in the seed store.

Sitting quietly in the dark attic and listening for footsteps of anyone approaching, he stared at the open book, looking carefully at the penmanship. He inhaled sharply, his eyes opening wide at the discovery he made.

"Ah, how could I be so clueless!" he said, his eyes scanning the pages before him.

The long "L"'s. The extra flourish at the top of each "T." He immediately knew who they belonged to.

He flipped forward, scanning quickly for anything new, and noticed the following week looked much different from how it had before. Where there had been many brief entries about all manner of Village activity, there was now only one.

He read the heading at the top and froze, sure he had made some mistake. He blinked, shook his head, and looked again, slowly and deliberately reading each word from left to right as he whispered the words before him:

"An Account of the Death of Lucas Dorrance."

"What?" Jarek said aloud in shock. "What the…Lucas *who*?"

His eyes darted around the page. It couldn't be the same Lucas. Abigail's last name was Dorrance. Lucas's was not. But how many other Lucas's were in the Village? To Jarek's knowledge, none. It had to be him.

By the time he reached the end, he was in a state of shock. It sounded like…suicide? It couldn't be. The consistent burden dwelling within Jarek's chest became suddenly crushing. He took a deep breath. He had to think. He stared into the dark, his mind racing as he considered all he had read and what he had learned. Three things were now abundantly clear to him:

1. Thaddeus was the resident evil that brought the darkness back to the Village.
2. Abigail, since the death of Brother Armstrong, was the Conscientia. It was her words he had been reading.
3. Lucas, without a doubt, was about to kill himself. And nobody saw it coming.

CHAPTER 41

Jarek woke up in the Village the next morning and ran as fast as he could to find Abigail. He made one quick stop to get something he wanted to show her and shortly after found her at the back of the store organizing materials. It was early; she was the only person there. He had seen her very little since her pronouncement in the cemetery. The gravity of what she said and the conviction with which she said it—telling him he had to leave for his own good—had occupied his thoughts every moment since. Now that they were alone enough for him to ask for clarification, they had much more pressing matters to discuss.

"Hello, Jarek, you seem flushed."

"Sister Abigail, I have something I want to tell you."

She continued lining jars up on the shelf, not acknowledging the seriousness with which he spoke.

"Jarek," Abigail said. "I realize that I have been worried about Lucas lately—for many reasons. I think he feels disconnected. You know he feels little connection to those parents who treated him so cruelly and left him here with no kin and nothing but the shirt on his back."

"Yes, I know, but Sister Abig—" Jarek pleaded.

"Well," she said, with a ceremonial tilt of her head, "I've decided to let Lucas take my last name."

Jarek froze. He stared blankly at Abigail as the entry in the book flashed through his mind: "An Account of the Death of Lucas Dorrance."

"My God," Jarek thought, "it *is* Lucas!" The events he read about were now in motion. At the end of those events, Lucas would be dead.

Sister Abigail continued, "He is almost a son to me, at least in the Village sense, and I think it would make him feel like he has someone to depend on. After all, his situation can't be said to…"

"ABIGAIL!" Jarek interrupted.

She jumped. "Oh! Yes, yes, what? My goodness."

"I've got something to tell you," Jarek said. "Something important."

"Yes, dear," she said with concern, turning towards him.

"It's kind of complicated, it may be a bit confusing, and you're probably going to have a lot of questions…so I'm going to tell you the most important part first."

"Jarek, you're worrying me," Abigail said.

He ignored her comment; his message was urgent. "It's about something I read," he said.

"Read where?" she asked.

"That's the confusing part, so I'll get to it later," Jarek said. "For now, it's what it said."

Her nervousness was now showing on her face.

He hesitated momentarily before adding, "It's something…terrible."

"What is it? Something…written by who? What did it say?" Abigail grew more concerned.

"I'm not sure how to tell you this," Jarek said, "and it's going to sound crazy, but trust me that it's true, and it's real."

He took a deep breath and looked at her, determined to get the words out in a steady voice.

"Sister Abigail, Lucas is going to kill himself."

"Jarek. Jarek, what are you…?" she peered at him in confusion.

Jarek's expression did not change as she scanned his face to better understand. The look on her own quickly turned to shock and then panic. Her eyes darted around Jarek's face, more frantic with each moment as she searched for some immediate clarification.

"No," she said, shaking her head. "No, no. That can't be. I won't believe it. No.... No." Her voice trembled for a moment. "Who said that it was so?"

Jarek looked sister Abigail in the eye. She could tell by his face that he was entirely sure of what he was saying. Her jaw dropped as his next two words echoed in her ears:

"You did."

She looked at Jarek in stunned silence. After a long pause, she managed to whisper one solitary word: "What?"

He continued, "And you did because it's in the book."

Her eyes widened. "What book?"

"You know the book I mean, Abigail," he continued slowly, "because you are its current author: *An Account of the Events of the Village*." He pressed, "*The Book of the Mountain Kings.*"

She stared at him in disbelief as he continued.

"You are its author because you, Abigail, you are the Conscientia."

Her eyes looked directly into his as she stood stone-still and expressionless, gathering her thoughts for several long seconds. He wasn't sure how his revelation affected her, but as her hands rested on the counter before her, he heard the creak of her leather gloves gripping each other mercilessly tight.

After a long pause, she took a deep breath.

"How foolish—what do you know of such things?? Who is putting ideas into your head?"

"Do you deny it?" Jarek asked.

She lifted her chin in refusal. "I have no idea what you're talking about!"

Jarek spoke quickly. "Brother Armstrong knew something was wrong in the Village; you told me yourself, the darkness was back, and he knew it might get worse. Much worse. He didn't share the gravity of those concerns with anyone—not even you—but he needed to find a successor just in case. His death was a shock—to everyone other than him—but he had already asked you, hadn't he? If you would bear the responsibility? If you'd join the order of the watchmen? The Mountain Kings. The first woman, no less. Of course, you said yes because you love The Way, because you love your brothers and sisters, and because, Abigail, you were in love with Brother Armstrong."

Abigail inhaled sharply and looked at the floor.

"It's you, Abigail," Jarek said. You write the entries." He paused. "You're the Conscientia."

She looked like she had seen a ghost but said nothing.

Seeing how uneasy she was, he looked at her and spoke calmly.

"Abigail…here."

Jarek pulled a page of the book from his vest pocket, placing it on the counter beside a receipt she had written. The handwriting was identical. She looked at him blankly but said nothing. He then slowly lifted his hand from the bottom of the page, revealing an image hidden beneath as he took her left hand in his, gently pulling her arm towards him.

"Jarek!" She proclaimed. "Stop this at once!"

He ignored her, turning her arm over as he pushed her sleeve up with his opposite hand.

There was no need for further protest.

Her breathing was shallow as she stood quietly. Both of their eyes moved from the page to her forearm. The image upon each was identical. Tattooed into her bare skin were wings of fire and the symbol of a cross between them. The cross itself was within a circular serpent swallowing its tail.

CHAPTER 42

"Abigail, I know it's you."

She whispered a feeble final denial. "Jarek, how do you speak of such things?"

He wasn't sure if she was stunned or scared, but as she sat quietly for a few moments, Jarek noticed with surprise that the look on her face was shifting from denial to sadness.

"It's all right," he said calmly. "I can help."

"I'm sorry, dear boy," she said, her eyes reddening as her voice quivered. "It's just…" she paused and straightened her dress, attempting more composure. "It's a heavy burden to bear. And a lonely one."

"I know," he said, placing one hand on her shoulder.

"I must say, Jarek," she gave him a small smile while pulling her sleeve back down to recover her decency. "Very well observed, as usual."

He spoke slowly. "Abigail, Lucas is in trouble."

"What do you mean? What kind of trouble?"

"He is being abused," Jarek replied, "more terribly than you may suspect. He is…visited at night."

"Thaddeus…" she whispered.

"And Lucas is giving up." Jarek continued. "Abigail. Listen to me. There's an entry you're going to write in exactly eight days. 'An account of the death of Lucas Dorrance.'"

She let out a cry and placed one gloved hand over her mouth.

He now had her undivided attention and needed her to believe him. He slowed down. He told her everything he had learned about what was happening to Lucas. He wanted to tell her everything that would happen the day Lucas decided to take his own life. He knew it would be shocking, but he had to.

Moment by moment, step by step, as conveyed by her own hand—exactly one week in the future. He needed her to know because he needed her help to prevent it from happening. She was no longer just Sister Abigail. She was the Conscientia. She was powerful. If anyone could, or would, stand up to Thaddeus, it was her. They needed to do something, and quickly.

"An Account of the Death of Lucas Dorrance," he began. He drew from within his memory a snapshot of the page, reciting each word as if the book was still before him and feeling himself just as rattled by the news it conveyed:

> *Lucas Dorrance, being merely eleven years of age and a new and beloved member of the Village, did proceed to the very top of our community, to the belltower, which so many times had chimed in his ears a call to conclude the work he enjoyed and into the fellowship of those he loved. At which point, this poor boy—so elated to find this Village home yet ultimately treated so cruelly—placed a ladder below and climbed into the belltower, where he tied the rope around his small neck and hanged himself. For only the second time in the history of our Village, the bell rang twice mid-day. At noon, as is our custom, and again at 12:23 p.m. Sister Abigail Dorrance and others ran to see what was amiss, finding the small, unlaced shoes of young brother Lucas, gentle Lucas Dorrance, swaying at the end of the belltower rope as the bell itself chimed his untimely death."*

Jarek stopped. Abigail could hear no more, but there was no more to tell. He placed a hand on her shoulder and felt her body wracked with sobs.

CHAPTER 43

Jarek knew that Abigail's decision to give Lucas her name had been some small consolation she provided herself for the loss of the baby she felt was meant to be her own. The idea of Lucas's inevitable passing was more than even a woman as strong as she could handle. He sat silently for many minutes, hearing her sobs ebb over time as she composed herself.

"Jarek," she finally said, wiping her eyes and stiffening her posture. "Jarek I… I know you're from somewhere far away. The way you talk, the way you dress in our clothes, or attempt to, and some of the things you say. I have always known this. We are used to that here, and I accept it. But I'm starting to think the things I've observed are not a matter of simple geography." She paused for a moment and looked at him. "Am I…" she paused, "Jarek, am I incorrect?"

Jarek didn't know what to say. He looked at her silently. Then he looked at the floor.

She took a deep breath. "Jarek, dear boy, you are a lost young man. I know that you are. Maybe that's why you are among us. We are here for the lost, however they may arrive. You carry upon yourself the burden of a tragic grief. A grief that has changed you forever."

She looked into his eyes and continued, "I'm afraid you carry your guilt as well, dear. Still unable to accept that the terrible tragedy that came upon you and your family was something you were, in fact, helpless to prevent, no matter how hard you tried."

Jarek's stared into the distance as his eyes welled with tears.

"I believe, Jarek," she said, "these things may somehow explain why the Lord has brought you here. Tell me if you will, dear; when did he die?"

"He?" Jarek's voice shook with emotion as he turned to face her with surprise. "How did you know it was a he?"

"Because my dear boy," she spoke quietly, "I have seen him beside you many times."

"Sorry?" Jarek raised his eyebrows, turning to look at the space around them. He saw nothing.

"I don't pretend to understand the gifts that God has bestowed upon me, but the ability to see the spirits of the departed seems to manifest itself only to those who have greatly sacrificed of themselves for The Way."

"Is he…" he paused. "Is he here now?" Jarek nervously asked.

"Yes, dear. He is right beside you. He is nearer to you than I am."

Jarek stifled a small sob as Abigail asked, "Who is he?"

"He…" Jarek paused to wipe his eyes. "He was my brother…I mean, he *is* my brother… Andrew."

She gave him a sympathetic nod, adding, "Jarek, I believe I now understand you a bit better. You and your dear brother look very much alike," she smiled, "but he looks very much like someone we both hold dear, does he not?"

"Yes," he whispered with a nod, "Lucas."

"Can you…" his voiced quivered as he paused to compose himself, "talk to him? Can you tell him I love him?"

"You can tell him yourself, dear," she nodded slowly.

Jarek dried his cheeks with his sleeve, turning to face the air behind him. Abigail looked on with the pity of one not unfamiliar with matters of grief.

"Andr…" Jarek said, unable to continue. His face was contorted in grief as he stifled a sob and looked at the empty air.

"It's okay, dear," she said.

Jarek put both hands to his face, rested his elbows on his knees, and wept for the presence of the lost brother he could not see.

After a few moments, he did his best to compose himself. Abigail's concern for Lucas's life made her his best and only ally. He just didn't know where to start. "Sister Abigal, about Lucas…"

"Jarek, I need answers," she pleaded anxiously. "I think you have something more you want to tell me. Please."

"Yes. Yes, Abigail, I do. But it's going to sound…" he paused, "just let me explain, and after I do, I'll tell you anything you want to know. I'll start at the beginning, with Brother Armstrong. I knew about Brother Armstrong before you told me about him."

"Oh? How so…"

"Not from anyone here. I mean, not… currently," he said.

She looked puzzled. "Well, then from who?"

"I saw him once. I guess you could say he appeared to me."

Abigail raised her eyebrows and gasped. "A gift?"

"Yes, I suppose so—a gift. He spoke to me. And then I arrived here, or I dreamt I did, I don't know. But I'm here because of him. I think he called me here."

Her red and glassy eyes stared at him wide and frightened.

"Called you here? Jarek, I don't understand your meaning. Called you here from where?" she asked.

"From…" he looked at her sympathetically, took one deep breath, and, sorry for what he had to tell her, spoke slowly: "From the future."

CHAPTER 44

Abigail stared at Jarek in disbelief. He saw the blank look on her face and worried that the emotional roller coaster she was on might be too much for even as stout a heart as hers.

"Jarek, I…" She stopped.

"I'm sorry, Abigail. I don't know why, but I think Brother Armstrong brought me here somehow."

"But…the future? How can it be? Where? When?" she tried to collect her thoughts.

Jarek was concerned about saying too much, especially about the future of the Village and the people she loved, so he ignored her question.

"Tomorrow," Jarek paused, taking a deep breath, "Tomorrow you'll talk about running out of materials for seed packets: 'Having received assurance from Brother Thompson that the situation will be set aright, I will trust to his abilities and hope for the best.' In three days, you'll add: 'Materials for repair of the medicine shop foundation have arrived, and work will begin today.'

"After I leave here, after we are done with this conversation, you'll have a lot on your mind. You'll probably put an entry in the book, yes?"

"Well, perhaps…" she was puzzled.

"Think for a moment; what do you think you'll say? Don't tell me; think about it," Jarek said.

He paused for a moment as she looked at him, then he took a deep breath and spoke as if he was providing a recitation: "'I've had the most unsettling news from one of our more recent arrivals.'"

She started and looked at him in shock. He continued: "'I will leave matters in the Lord's hands and will serve as an instrument of his will in making sure the righteous prevail.'"

"Jarek," she pleaded. "Are you a conjurer to read minds? How is it possible?"

"Because before I woke up here this morning, I held in my hands a very old book. In that book was the very entry I just recited, quickly written late one evening many, many years before. But, Abigail, that evening is this evening; the unsettling news is what I've just told you, and those words are yours. You'll put them on paper shortly after I leave." He paused.

She was overwhelmed.

"I didn't read your mind, Abigail," he said slowly, trying to calm her. "I knew what you were going to say because, where I'm from—or when—you've already said it."

"Jarek," she said. He saw her hands shaking. "I give my trust to your good heart in understanding you mean well. But I cannot accept that the things you say are true."

"They are true. You *have* to believe me," he said.

"This is…" she slowed down, "in truth, this is not the first time I've heard of something such as this," she said. "We do, in some respect, believe such things are possible. But the only time I've heard of it before is rumors of a visitor we had years ago who befriended a young sister. This was long before my arrival."

"Yes," Jarek sat upright, "yes, he went to my schoo—" he stopped himself, reconsidering. "I know about him as well. I've heard that story. It's how I knew my time here was… was real. And now it's how you know I'm telling you the truth, Sister Abigail."

"But Jarek, dear, if that's the case—as I do believe it may be—and if Brother Armstrong called you here… well then that means what you've told me is a matter of the very most dire importance."

"Yes," he said, "very much so."

Jarek pointed towards the symbol which remained on the torn page beside them.

"Abigail—what is this? What does it mean?"

"This, Jarek," she said, looking down, "is the sign of the watchmen—the Segno Sentinelle—passed down from the very first Conscientia through our many long years. It now rests upon my arm, though I have serious doubts about my ability to live up to its expectation," she said glumly. "It is the seal of the Conscientia, each of us receiving it from our predecessor when they feel their tenure is nearing its end."

She lifted her sleeve again, pointing at each detail individually.

"The cross, Jarek, is a sign of faith and healing; our responsibility to those who have joined us to start anew. Behind is an hourglass, which you see is empty, signifying our ability to transcend the bifurcation of time—'before and after'—that constrains those not of The Way. The serpent—the ouroboros—comes to us from antiquity, signifying life, death, and rebirth, and the wings are those of the Heavenly Father, in flames for the purification of sins. Because 'Our God is an all-consuming fire.' Hebrews 12:29. The seal, all in all, signifies both what we believe and our responsibility to those of The Way in acting upon it."

Jarek was stunned, taking in every word while staring at her arm.

She then turned back to the matter at hand, speaking deliberately.

"If the things you have told me are true, my dear boy, then for the sake of our friend, we have much to do."

CHAPTER 45

Jarek's presence in the Village had grown significantly since his arrival. He was kind, hard-working, conscientious, and respected. There were only a few young men on campus; most of the other men were elderly or much younger and smaller than Jarek, so he was often called to help with heavier tasks, especially for some of the older sisters. He never said no, and they loved him for it. His clear alliance with Abigail had earned him additional favor, especially among those who (he now realized) saw her as their greatest hope to somehow, someday, escape the clutches of the criminal presence they had all fallen victim to.

He told her everything. How he came to the Village, how he found the book, and what else he knew about Lucas's passing, which wasn't much. She listened intently. He answered all of her questions but was careful of what he shared. The idea that this entire Village she loved and had dedicated her life to would someday be nothing other than a memory might be too much for her.

After much discussion, they turned to the matter of how they should proceed. Everyone within the Village was powerless against Thaddeus and his men. If they wanted to save not only Lucas but the Village itself, they needed help from outside.

They thought long and hard. Then, they came up with a plan.

Mr. Richard Finch was well known to many Brothers and Sisters on the mountain, particularly those involved with the numerous commercial undertakings that supported Village life. He was the most affluent of their customers, and the kindness and humility he demonstrated at all times made him a favored customer and predictable presence during his visits. None of the Shaker men and women who had made his acquaintance had ever heard him boasting of the success that made his fine dress, impressive horses, state-of-the-art wagons, and considerable spending on all manner of Shaker goods possible.

What was not predictable was the outcome of bringing Village matters to his attention. He had had no previous involvement in anything unrelated to his business with the community, but Abigail knew him to be trustworthy and possibly influential in the outside world as well.

It was Jarek's idea at the outset. He didn't want to put Abigail in harm's way should this not work out the way he hoped, so he decided he should be the one to reach out with a handwritten letter.

He had never written with a quill, and Drummy was right; it was a maddening way to write such an urgent message. The letter started with a plea for assistance. It then explained some of Thaddeus's misdeeds regarding Village finances, the unkind manner in which he conducted business internal to the Village, and how he was—clearly—taking great advantage of the hard work of fellow villagers to line his own pockets. What would have taken Jarek five minutes of typing at school took him nearly an hour and a half, one slow and gloppy scratch at a time. Having drawn her needles from the waist of her dress, Abigail twittered away nervously at her knitting until the letter neared completion.

Finally, it was done. Jarek hid it under some materials behind the seed store counter. When Mr. Finch came in the morning, Jarek would make sure the letter was securely wrapped within the receipts he would place in Mr. Finch's hand after his wagon was loaded for departure.

"Well, we have done what we can and what we should for now," Sister Abigail said. "I believe Mr. Finch will help us with some manner or other of intervention. Maybe he will go to the police, maybe someone even more influential."

Their hopes were high. This was, they concluded, their best and only option.

"Thank you, Jarek," Sister Abigail said sincerely, appreciative of his putting his name to the letter and his care for her in not allowing her to do the same.

Jarek, too, was confident that this would bring the matter to a conclusion. He was sure of it.

He had no way of knowing how much worse he was about to make it. For Lucas, for Abigail, and for himself.

CHAPTER 46

The following day, Jarek saw Lucas walking alone up the road. He moved slowly; head hung low, his young frame carrying him along with the posture of someone entirely defeated. A biting cold hung in the air. Snow-covered fields faded into the grey sky which hung over the valley beyond. Jarek followed him, unseen, up the road at a distance and watched him step slowly into the woods and snow and begin up the hill toward the graveyard. Lucas sat on the ground, staring at the small square stones that peered out from under a blanket of snow. Directly before him was one stone in particular. "E.A." The final resting place of Brother Armstrong.

Jarek approached quietly as Lucas gazed at the initials. The ghost. The Conscientia. The man who brought him here.

"Lucas are you okay?" he asked.

"Yes, Jarek," he whispered, seemingly indifferent to the intrusion. "Yes, I'm fine. Thank you."

Jarek saw another small stone nearby that had escaped his attention when he was with Sister Abigail. Brother Armstrong may not have been the only reason for her tears.

The marker did not bear initials like the others. One word and date were chiseled into the limestone: BABY. 1866.

"God," Jarek spoke under his breath. He didn't know the child Abigail lost to that dreadful storm was buried here.

Lucas noticed what Jarek had seen.

"God? No. No, I don't think so," Lucas said. "Everyone wants to leave this Village once the cold arrives. Maybe God did, too.

"The Bible says that the people of God are looked on with favor. Are we not looked on with favor, Jarek?" Lucas asked, turning towards Jarek as Jarek saw again the fading bruise on his chin. "Are we not people of God? I think we are." Jarek could hear the desperation in Lucas's young and defeated voice.

"I don't know, Lucas. I don't know."

"I was happy here," he sniffled and smiled up at Jarek, wiping one falling tear from his eye. "For the first time in my life. I thought I was… 'looked on with favor,' like the good book says. That this was a home for me, finally. My…obliging place."

"Your *what* place?" Jarek asked.

"Jarek." Lucas paused and swallowed deeply before continuing.

"Wouldn't it be a thing if we could…just pick out where we wanted to be, aught we wanted, and people around us were just… regular people? That's all. A house and loved ones, parents even…" He paused at the emotion that welled up within him. "And growing up 'til the house is my house, and the family is my family, and the farm is my farm. Folks coming around of a Sunday afternoon saying 'Hello, Lucas.' 'Good morning, Lucas.' I would get the milk and put the plates on the table, and we would sit there all together as long as we wanted. Everyone would be very obliging. 'You're a good man, Lucas.' 'Much obliged, Lucas.' 'We love you, Lucas.' I don't even care where it is, as long as it's just like that. My obliging place."

Jarek listened silently.

"Ah, well," Lucas said with finality.

"That sounds wonderful, Lucas," Jarek said.

"I see it in my dreams. My mother made it up. She would tell me stories about it before bedtime. It made me feel like we were in a better place, somehow. Not a cold shack in a company town, not freezing to sleep in the back of a wagon….someplace permanent.

"But even then, I knew it wasn't real. I don't even know those kinds of people."

Jarek tried to sound hopeful, even though he found little reason to: "I think you'll go there soon—we'll have a plan, and you'll leave here, and you'll go. Maybe I'll go with you."

"No. Maybe you'll get there on your own," Lucas said. "It's just a dream, Jarek."

Lucas sounded so much like Andrew had when he knew it was over, when he started giving up. Jarek couldn't stand it. He had knots in his stomach as sweat gathered on his forehead in the cold. He wanted to grab him and protect him with all his might so no one could harm him—anything to keep him from doing what Lucas himself probably didn't yet realize he was going to do.

Lucas stared at the stones and continued, "The day we left Pennsylvania, I was at school and my parents came to pick me up. My mother sat in that old farm wagon full of our stuff, and my father came into the classroom and took me by the arm. The teacher was talking about something that day. When you make a drawing or a painting—like an artist—there's a place where all the lines meet. If it looks right, if your picture is right, all the lines meet at this point far away on the horizon, too far for you or anyone else to ever get there. It's the place where everything comes together. It's called the vanishing point. My obliging place isn't real. It never will be. So that's where I want to go instead. Where everything comes together, and no one can find you. The vanishing point."

Lucas's eyes were red as he stared into the distance, his mind far away.

They sat in silence, but Jarek's heart was in a panic. He didn't know what to say. He didn't know how to stop the events that were now in motion—events that, 100 years from now, would be nothing other than a tiny, unnoticed footnote in the history of this bizarre and beautiful Village.

But there was one thing he did know. The presence of this dear young friend, this kind spirit, this giving heart, would not grace this place for much longer.

Jarek had two days.

In two days, the bell would ring in the Village, and Lucas's defeated young body would swing from the belltower rope.

CHAPTER 47

Damp and biting cold stiffened the joints of brothers and sisters as they moved across the field and down the road. Heavy grey clouds hanging over the mountain seemed ready to smother them at any moment.

They proceeded through the Meetinghouse doors, hardly speaking to each other as they entered and gathered in a wide circle around the floor. Every face betrayed the sense of hopelessness that had grown within them with each passing week, now almost unbearable, and there they stood. No one said a word; no one dared. The only things they had to say couldn't be said. There was nothing else.

After a long period of silence, one young Shaker sister stepped forward. She stared at the floor for some time before lifting her chin, extending her arms, closing her eyes, and turning her palms towards heaven. She began to sing for all of them, offering their collective grief to heaven with every tone of her rising voice.

(Song: "Low Down in the Valley")

Low down in the valley my lambs be found
secure from the tempests that now sweep around...

Several sisters closed their eyes in silent prayer.

tis low in the vale my blessings flow
but on the barren mountains
bleak and chilly winds do blow

Several buildings away, a young Shaker girl lay in bed, where she had been for days, having told her sisters she was too ill to go to the Meetinghouse. She implored one of them to stay with her, concern turning to panic within her as she was assured they would be right back, and she would hardly be alone for any time at all. But she was alone, she was not in fact ill, and she was now lying in bed, gasping in fear at every little sound she heard outside the building.

She spoke in a hushed whisper as her eyes darted around the room. "He's here…"

In the Meetinghouse, all listened silently:

Be strong though your tents are surrounded with foes
and vile persecutors rise up to oppose…

She heard the click of the latch on her door and jumped. The face of Thaddeus smiled at her as he walked through the doorway, and a wail of despair escaped her lips. She quickly pulled the sheet up to her chest in terror, kicking her feet against the bed though her back was now against the wall. "No, no, no," she cried as Thaddeus shut the door.

Be strong move as one and place your trust in me
remembering the righteous will ne'er forsaken be…

Thaddeus moved quickly, ripping the sheet down, and, with minimal effort, restrained her flailing hands. He climbed over the innocent girl now at his disposal and relished every moment of it.

Be strong though your tents are surrounded with foes
and vile persecutors rise up to oppose…

Thaddeus's hand pressed tight against her mouth, stifling her screams.

Be strong move as one and place your trust in me…

Her wails faded into sobs as he climbed off of her, assembled his clothes, ripped the sheets out from under her, and walked out.

...remembering the righteous will ne'er forsaken be.

Gathering sheets from the adjacent room, Thaddeus emerged on the porch and proclaimed with a smile to two sisters who were approaching with a laundry cart: "I've got these again, dear sisters. Hurry along to the Meetinghouse. They've begun! I'll drop them on my way."

WITHIN THE MEETINGHOUSE ITSELF, ALL STOOD SILENTLY IN THEIR circle. The growing sense of dread that had steadily crept across the mountain and into the heart of every villager now culminated in the same grim and inescapable reality: Thaddeus's grip on the Village was complete. The utopia they had dedicated their lives to was gone.

The darkness of despair hung heavily upon every one of them, burdening the very air they were breathing. In that moment, something felt immediately and terribly wrong, as if their collective heart was being pierced by an invisible evil. The sisters sensed it most acutely; several were in tears, covering their mouths with their hands as they comforted each other. One closed her eyes, tears rolling down her cheeks as she whispered with a shudder: "Someone just walked over my grave."

A singular sound broke the silence: the unmistakable creek of the Meetinghouse's center door. An imposing and familiar figure darkened the doorway.

CHAPTER 48

Thaddeus walked slowly through the center door and towards the assembly, pushing through the crowd into the middle of the open circle. He glared, expressionless, at the young sister who had just finished singing as she averted her eyes and stepped back to the group. There he stood, alone, turning to review those around him with a satisfied smirk as they stared at the floor.

Thaddeus's men were in the far back corners of the room, two on each side, but their menacing presence hung over the entire assembly. Their eyes were fixed on him, occasionally looking over the crowd, waiting to see what would happen next.

The silence dragged on for a full minute until, somewhere within the circle, a single alto voice rose tentatively above the silence.

(Song: "Voice of the Angels of Mercy")

Fear not fear not my beloved few
though the trump of war may sound…

Thaddeus tried in vain to determine the source. Numerous other women joined in from the back rows, growing louder in collective defiance as his eyes darted around the room.

and destruction may roar from the center to the core
and devastation lie around…

Several men took over, and their voices rose.

Fear not fear not my beloved few though the trump of war may sound…

The rising voices of all the men quickly joined.

And destruction may roar from the center of the core and devastation lie around…

The voices of the entire assembly rose together, several hundred singing as one, with all eyes now on Thaddeus.

For surely I, for surely I who have brought you from the depths of darkness
Will your souls protect while you do respect and follow my laws with exactness…

They sang again, punctuating each verse with stomps and claps echoing through the open space overhead.

For surely I, for surely I who have brought you from the depths of darkness
(CLAP) (STOMP) (CLAP) (STOMP)
Will your souls protect while you do respect and follow my laws with exactness.
(CLAP) (STOMP) (CLAP) (STOMP)
Fear not, fear not, my beloved few
(CLAP) (STOMP)
though the trump of war may sound
(CLAP) (STOMP)
and destruction roar from the center to the core and devastation lie around.
(CLAP) (STOMP) (CLAP) (STOMP)

Suddenly, as quickly as this moment of collective objection began, it stopped. The final note echoed in the space as brothers and sisters caught their breath. Hundreds of eyes stared straight at Thaddeus, and he stared straight back without a word.

One heavy stomp then united the group, followed quickly by another firm enough to rattle the windows in their frames as the whole assembly sang aloud in unison:

(Song: "I Bless the Day")

I bless the day that I could see
the glorious light of liberty
the day that I my sins confessed
(CLAP)
and in thy soul found peace and rest.
(CLAP)
Oh then I found a savior near,
(CLAP) (STOMP)
a tender mother kind and dear.
(CLAP) (STOMP)
Oh cleaned and healed, though bruised and sore
(CLAP) (STOMP)
said 'Go thy way and sin no more.'
(CLAP) (STOMP)
Sin no MORE, NOOOO!!!
(STOMP) (CLAP/STOMP, CLAP/STOMP)
Go thy way and sin no more.
(CLAP/STOMP, CLAP/STOMP)

Oh then I found a savior near
(CLAP) (STOMP)
a tender mother kind and dear
(CLAP) (STOMP)
Oh cleaned and healed, though bruised and sore
(CLAP) (STOMP)
said 'Go thy way and sin no more.'
(CLAP) (STOMP)
Sin no MORE, NOOOO!!!
(STOMP) (CLAP/STOMP, CLAP/STOMP)
Go thy way and sin no more.
(CLAP/STOMP, CLAP/STOMP)

With arms in the air, brothers and sisters began to spin in place, and the circle itself began to move in a clockwise direction with Thaddeus, ignored and despised, right in the middle. Voices rose louder as the entire assembly spun and twirled, clapped and stomped, their hands shaking at the heavens and then shaking at the floor, singing as they gyrated:

(Song: "On Zion's Holy Ground")

On Zion's holy ground are true believers found.
And there's no other one, and there's no other one.
And there's no other one can stand there 'round.
Low diddle-oh, diddle-oh diddle-oh-doh,
low diddle-oh, diddle-oh-doh-doh,
low diddle-oh, diddle-oh diddle-oh-doh,
low diddle-oh, diddle-oh-doh-doh.

Thaddeus stood in the middle, turning to watch the circle revolve around him. He smiled the same toothy grin he had used to charm so many present before they knew better, but he had put those efforts to rest long ago. No one could tell whether he smiled because he was impressed by the spectacle or because he enjoyed the continued challenge of the worthy adversary that stood collectively before him. The group continued to turn, singing louder still:

Low diddle-oh, diddle-oh diddle-oh-doh,
low diddle-oh, diddle-oh-doh-doh,
low diddle-oh, diddle-oh diddle-oh-doh,
low diddle-oh, diddle-oh-doh-doh.

A moment later, something happened that no one expected. To the surprise of all those gathered, Thaddeus raised his hands with the music, holding them towards the ceiling and lifting his eyes to heaven. He then joined the brothers and sisters in the dance, slowly putting one foot around the other as he spun around. The circle continued to move around him, again and again, with claps and stomps punctuating the motion. It then pulled apart, every brother and sister spinning and waving their arms individually, unified only in the claps and stomps that grew louder.

Thaddeus closed his eyes and began flailing his arms overhead. It went on and on as the warmth of the frenzied exertion fogged the windows, hollering voices filled the room, and thunderous stomps shook the very foundations of the building. They danced and sang, convinced the salvation they so desperately needed depended on it.

It was mesmerizing, unnerving, and by far the darkest dance Jarek had ever seen.

Thaddeus, in the middle of it all, howled and shook his chest at the ceiling like a man possessed while the rest, in their silent hearts, wondered how long it would be until he was cast into hell.

CHAPTER 49

Three days had passed since Jarek had placed the letter in Mr. Finch's receipts. Jarek wasn't sure how he would respond to a handwritten letter from a young brother he had barely met, but Jarek had placed it right in his hand so it couldn't be missed. Then, he and Sister Abigail nervously waited.

They imagined, in their minds and to each other, what was happening in the outside world in response to the letter and the various preparations underway to right the terrible wrongs that were occurring. Mr. Finch had likely informed the nearby village at Hancock, where the elders—infuriated by the damage Thaddeus had done to this otherwise peaceful and holy place—were notifying law enforcement and gathering a large group of brothers to accompany them to the mountainside. They would then collect Thaddeus and his men and take them away to pay for their crimes.

The days passed, and Jarek grew more concerned. What evidence did they actually have to bring charges against him?

"The justification that he is a man fully in the grasp of the devil," Abigail said.

While her simplicity was as endearing as her fortitude, Jarek realized he should have pushed harder to understand what Abigail felt were the possible outcomes of the letter. He had no idea how things worked in this time, in this Village, or between the Village and the authorities in the outside world. Her naivete might—Jarek thought—have put them in a dangerous situation given the circumstances. He couldn't fault her for that but was mad at himself for not thinking it through.

"Let's just wait and see," he said, hopefully.

On the fourth day, Mr. Finch showed up at the store to collect additional materials—feed bags, seeds, tools—which he had paid for but couldn't fit in his wagon on the previous visit.

"Hello, Jarek, Abigail." He spoke briefly, loaded his wagon, and climbed on to depart. Not a word about the letter.

Had he not read it? Were there things in motion that he didn't want to disclose to them? He couldn't have ignored it—Jarek had put it right in his hand. Maybe people were on their way to the Village that very day to make things right. They had to be.

Jarek handed Mr. Finch the reins. The farmer looked around, then leaned down.

"Jarek," he whispered, "I read your letter. I've consulted the authorities, as well as the elders at Hancock. They are gravely concerned and will bring the police to the Village tomorrow. You'll stand by what you've told me?"

Jarek's quick response made clear his excitement at what he was hearing and his appreciation for Mr. Finch's help. "Yes, yes, of course I will."

"Good. Now, keep things quiet. Have you discussed these matters with anyone else? Does anyone else know?" Jarek thought of Sister Abigail. Saying her name would add some validity to what he had told Mr. Finch, but Jarek didn't want to put her in any more danger than she was already in.

"No, no one else knows," he lied, adding, "I don't want to upset the Village."

"Good boy, son." Mr. Finch responded. "These are good people—they've been through enough. Let's keep it that way." He winked.

"Yes sir," Jarek responded, watching him straighten back up, snap the reigns, and turn back to give one more affirming nod as he began down the road.

"Oh, Jarek, my dear boy. Thank the good Lord," Sister Abigail said with a sigh of relief and tears in her eyes as Jarek told her everything.

Finally, the shadow that hung over them, the Village, and—most importantly—over Lucas would soon be lifted.

CHAPTER 50

The following morning, brothers and sisters gathered for the dance, and the bearing of those assembled was altogether different. Abigail had, perhaps unwisely, shared the joy of their coming liberation with the other elders, and they, too, were not as discreet as they may have been. It might not matter. After all, Jarek's letter to Mr. Finch put things in motion that Thaddeus would be incapable of stopping. While the reason for the elders' joy was not known by all the brothers and sisters, the rare glimmer of hope and optimism was infectious. The dance may have been slightly premature, but they had suffered long enough and had plenty to celebrate.

The energy was immense. Songs of joy and praise lifted their clapping hands towards the distant ceiling.

(Song: "Rights of Conscience")

Rights of conscience in these days,
Now demand our solemn praise;
Rights of freedom we'll maintain,
And our independence gain.

Arm yourselves, unsheathe the sword!
(CLAP)
Cries this servant of the Lord.
(CLAP)

Breaks the yoke at his own door,
(CLAP)
Clothes the naked, feed the poor,
(CLAP)

Let the eyes of priests and kings
(CLAP) (STOMP)
View the eagle's spreading wings;
(CLAP) (STOMP)
These are to the woman given,
(CLAP) (STOMP)
Guard the place where she is driven.
(CLAP) (STOMP)

Joyful smiles were upon every face in the room as voices rose to the rafters high above. Tears streamed down the cheeks of those who had been so profoundly wronged or suffered injury at the hands of Thaddeus or his men.

Thaddeus, for his part, did not bother to attend. He no longer had to feign an interest in spiritual matters now that his authority in the Village was complete. Two of his men sat in a distant corner now, stone-faced and observing, altogether clueless as to the reason for the heightened celebration they were witnessing.

The energy in the room continued to grow as every voice in the room joined in joyful unison:

(Song: "Angel Reapers")

Say brothers will you go with me
(CLAP)
Go to the land of promise?
(CLAP)
Say sisters will you meet me there
(CLAP)
In the land of the golden harvest?
(CLAP)

Say brothers will you go with me
(CLAP) (STOMP)
Go to the land of promise?
(CLAP) (STOMP)
Say sisters will you meet me there
(CLAP) (STOMP)
In the land of the golden harvest?
(CLAP) (STOMP)

Jarek was pulled into the circle as the worship intensified, and he danced among them as he had so many times before. Brothers and sisters clapped their hands in Jarek's direction. Sister Abigail, smiling and dancing nearby, refused—in her humility—to accept more than passing gratitude for her role in their victory. Instead, she directed well-wishers to Jarek and watched with fond admiration and a smile that brightened her eyes from the depths of her grateful soul. Hands were placed upon him, and the words "Thank you, Brother Jarek" were delivered to his ears repeatedly through the tears of worshippers whose adulation he was so grateful for, however undeserving he felt. He smiled as all those assembled, his brothers and sisters, thanked him for saving the Village.

It was only a matter of time, and brief time, until things were set right.

Claps and stomps rattled the windows and filled the air.

They had done it. Praise God.

CHAPTER 51

"Jarek, I'd like you to come in here so I can explain these accounts to you." Thaddeus tried to soften his usual authoritative tone. He added with a smile, "I'd like you to help me with the ledger from now on."

Thaddeus's office was in a three-story house next to the pond at the center of the Village. The windows afforded him a view of the hills and, more importantly, the road so he could observe who was coming and going. Two other offices in the same dwelling were dedicated mainly to overflow supplies and seasonal provisions. They contained small desks that were rarely used, with traffic in and out of the spaces primarily confined to a quick visit from a brother or sister retrieving a bag of seed, an ink well, a stack of blank receipts, or other miscellaneous material related to the business of the Village.

Thaddeus was dependably in his office most afternoons, at which times Jarek avoided the building entirely. On some occasions, however, when Abigail needed something from the supply rooms for the store, he would have no choice but to keep his head down, move quickly, and do his best to remain unseen.

It was on one of these occasions that Jarek found himself entering at the base of the building and ascending the stairs to collect some twine for sister Abigail. His conversation with Lucas in the cemetery consumed his every thought, and the idea of having to set eyes on Thaddeus, now that Jarek was fully aware of his true nature, filled him with anger and terror. The celebratory tone of the dance that morning had faded in the minds of the villagers, and Jarek's as well, as they again entered a period of anxious anticipation, wondering at every moment when their deliverers, whoever they may be, would arrive down the road and finally take Thaddeus away to receive justice.

These matters were heavy on Jarek's mind as he had quickly and quietly begun up the steps towards the material room for the twine. He hadn't seen or heard anyone else, so he breathed a sigh of relief as he concluded he was alone.

But as he had approached the top steps, he looked down towards his shoes and, directly next to his boot saw a footprint—recent as the mud was still wet—with an anvil-shaped "T" in the heel.

"Hello Jarek!"

Jarek jumped as Thaddeus's voice boomed down the staircase from the open door of his office, clearly relishing the opportunity to startle him. Thaddeus's men had seen the adoration given to Jarek at the dance that morning, but neither they nor Thaddeus himself had any way of knowing why. Or so Jarek hoped.

Thaddeus was in an uncharacteristically pleasant mood, which sent a shiver up Jarek's spine. Whatever was about to happen, he would be facing it alone.

Thaddeus stepped out of the way and put his hand out before him in mock formality, beckoning Jarek into his office. Jarek stepped into the room, realizing he had no choice in the matter, as his heart beat heavily in his chest. There was a plain desk before him with a simple wooden chair behind and a tall, time-worn cabinet leaning against the wall to the left, where books cataloging all orders for each of the previous six months stood vertically stacked against each other.

On the surface of Thaddeus's desk was a candle and wax seal stamp containing his initials, both sitting on a small, tattered piece of fabric cut from a large seed bag and stained with several drops of red wax. Beside them, a fountain pen stood upright in a small glass inkwell, the open mouth caked in pitch black, and a glass cup containing the iridium-tipped metal point pen he loved to show visitors, remarking "Best that money can buy." The grey light of winter dusk entered through the windows.

A seed advertisement on the wall read "Shakers' Best Garden Seeds." In the picture below the text, a little girl in a pink dress sat quietly on a bench. Her eyes were fixed on a young boy who carefully watched the contents of his watering can spill out onto a bed of delicate flowers below. Jarek noticed that this illustration of innocent and happy children was the only decoration in the office and cringed.

The very sight of Thaddeus gave Jarek a rotten feeling in his stomach. There were many things Jarek imagined doing to Thaddeus in the previous days. Helping him wasn't one of them. But Thaddeus was bigger than Jarek, much bigger. Jarek knew he had no choice but to comply, even if it meant they were alone for the first time. His attention was piqued at the mention of the ledger, so he walked in.

Jarek heard the door latch click behind him as he moved inside. "Come around over here, please," Thaddeus said, leaning over the desk and opening a book.

Something wasn't right. He couldn't see the look on Thaddeus's face as he walked around him, but his mind raced and his heart beat faster as he thought about the danger he was in. Adrenaline heightened his senses, as he heard the creak of a floorboard and a grunt. An instant later, he felt the full impact of Thaddeus uncoiling his large frame into a backhand that landed squarely on Jarek's cheekbone. A flash and explosion of pain sent a shock through his head, rattling his teeth and jolting his eyes within their sockets. The impact reverberated through his body as he fell back against the wall and slid down to the floor, stunned and unable to move.

"Welcome to The Way!" Thaddeus smiled. He leaned down and grabbed Jarek's shirt, lifting his limp body into the air before throwing him into a bookshelf standing against the opposite wall.

"I understand you've taken an interest in things that don't concern you, Jarek. And perhaps you've felt it proper to reach out to Mr. Finch?"

Jarek tried to regain his senses, silently shaking his head.

Thaddeus was impatient for a response. "Have you forgotten? Let me jog your memory." Thaddeus delivered one solid blow to Jarek's stomach, knocking the wind out of him entirely before grabbing Jarek's collar and shouting in his face, "Do you remember now?" A knee to the groin bent Jarek over, and Thaddeus quickly struck him in the lower back with the steel handle of his riding crop. Jarek grunted in pain.

"What did you expect? You're a fool," Thaddeus said, with malice in his voice.

"Mr. Finch, dear boy, is a friend of mine. We are partners, in a way, in the little business endeavor of which you are now aware."

Jarek's mind wandered into a fog of unfocused anger. He was starting to lose consciousness as Thaddeus's chiding faded into the distance.

Suddenly, he heard an urgent whisper, one word. It was the voice of Brother Armstrong.

"*Jarek!*"

It snapped him back to attention as he widened his eyes, shook his head, and focused. He knew he would take more if he didn't strike back. He had come too far. This would not be it. He wouldn't let it.

Through the fog and pain, he dug deep, imagining the faces of Lucas and Abigail in an instant. He pictured the headstone: "Baby." He pictured his parents. He pictured his brother.

With every ounce of strength he had, Jarek bent his knees, let out a guttural yell, and launched himself into Thaddeus's mid-section, putting him off balance as the two of them staggered against the opposite wall and the bookshelf emptied its contents on the floor. The beating Jarek had already taken had weakened him, even in his rage. His head pressed against Thaddeus's chest, applying pressure as he wound up to strike, but Thaddeus spun Jarek around, pulling the crop tight against Jarek's neck from behind as Jarek reached for it with his weakening hands. His face grew red with the struggle as he bent over, pulling Thaddeus onto his back and using all his might to flip Thaddeus forward over his head. Thaddeus landed on his back with a thud that shook the building.

Jarek looked down, ready to pounce, but Thaddeus was quick. He struck Jarek's knee with the steel handle—a crack of metal against bone that made Jarek howl—then sprang to his feet, quickly delivering another blow to the side of Jarek's jaw.

Jarek reeled off-balance and fell backward, his head hitting the three-foot wooden floorboards with a hollow thud. He was utterly overpowered. Thaddeus stepped over Jarek and sat down on his upper legs, making sure he couldn't move, as he smiled down at him like a helpless animal.

Within Thaddeus's troubled soul dwelled two unfortunate characteristics. The first was an explosive temper, and the second was the lack of any conscience to keep it at bay. He leaned forward, slowly wrapped his hands around Jarek's neck, and tightened his grip.

Labored breathing rushed towards Jarek's face, cool against the blood that ran down his cheeks from his eye and his forehead. His weakening hands, now slippery with his own blood, held limply to those of Thaddeus, wrapped tight around his neck. His heart beat hard within his chest as he looked to the windows, his mind going distant, and realized that in exactly 125 years, he would be walking into this very room as a new student at a school that did not yet exist. *His* school.

Jarek's hands pushed up against Thaddeus's sweaty cheek and gritted teeth, but he was completely overpowered. With terror in his eyes, his wide-open mouth tried desperately to swallow the air that would be his if he could only remove the vice grip from his neck. He needed a miracle.

"This is what it's like," he thought. "Death. This is it."

"I should kill you." Thaddeus lifted Jarek's chin with the steel end of his riding crop to look at him closely. "I would enjoy it," he said as Jarek looked up at him with one open eye. "That wouldn't look very good though, would it?" he added. "Not that anyone would care, if they even noticed. The woman though, she would notice, wouldn't she. Aren't you a lovely pair?"

He changed his tone momentarily, looking Jarek from head to toe. "Lucky her," he said. Jarek thought he might be sick as Thaddeus caressed the top of his head and pressed his lips against Jarek's cheek. "Such a specimen you are," he said. "You'll never see that witch again. But I promise I'll give her your regards when she's right at the end. Lucas, too—when I visit him tonight."

Grabbing Jarek's jaw, Thaddeus wrenched the boy's head upward. "Do you want to know about salvation? Let me tell you about 'The Way.'"

Thaddeus then put his face right before Jarek and hissed through his teeth: "This rabble of weak little victims. Whores, misfits, halfwits, and darkies. So holy and so pure…and so stupid. But…" He then brightened his tone, proclaiming like a traveling preacher, "Fruit on the vine and money in the till. Salvation! Jarek," he said, "welcome to 'The Way.'"

Thaddeus took a long look at Jarek before adding, "Now, my fellow vagabond, unless you want to find yourself in the presence of the heavenly father at the ripe and precious age of…whatever you are…leave this Village or I'll send you to him. I don't know who—or what—you are or where you're from, and I don't care. If I ever see you again, the last thing you will know in this world is my face, smiling down at you, as I squeeze the very last breath out of your tender throat." He slowly drew his fingertips across Jarek's neck.

Thaddeus then stood up, shook his hands in the air over his head and shouted "AMEN!" Then he straightened his shirt, spit the blood from his lips onto Jarek's pants, and walked out as routinely as if nothing had happened at all.

Jarek tried to stand up. He had to run to Abigail to warn her, but he was exhausted. Splayed out on the floor, his face running with blood; all he could do was lay still and pray someone would find him before it was too late.

CHAPTER 52

Jarek awoke to the sound of a mourning dove as sun streamed onto his face through a nearby window. His blurry eyes took in the scattered debris on the floor around him as he realized he was still in Thaddeus's office and, for the first time since his ordeal began, had woken up in the past. He knew there was a reason—something he was supposed to do—but he was too disoriented to figure out what it was.

"Ouch," he groaned. He ran his fingertips from a lump on his head to the dried blood on his cheek, then looked down at the red stains on his shirt and pants. Thaddeus's talent for delivering a beating had been thoroughly indulged at his expense.

Jarek walked across the Village with his head down, but once he heard singing from the Meeting House, he wasn't worried about being seen. He stumbled forward—a loose tooth garbled and clicked around inside his bleeding mouth. One of his eyes was swollen shut, so he led with his good one. He knew if he slowed down, he'd risk passing out again, and he wanted more than anything to get to the Tannery. Beth was always there first thing in the morning as it was the only time she was sure to have the piano to herself. A small voice in his head told him that this made no sense. He was in the Village and Beth existed in a distant future that had not yet begun. But something compelled him forward despite his pain and confusion.

The fields were a blur in the distance as he dragged his limp and beaten body forward step by step. He then heard something familiar. His pace quickened as the sound of her beautiful playing filled the air, growing louder as he approached.

He pushed the door open with one hand—the other was pressed against what he was sure was a broken collar bone. The music got louder as he entered. Rays of morning light streamed through the windows into the dusty space. The floor was pristine—as it was in the Village—but covered with the storage materials from the school. It was all blending together, his aching head and teeming brain confusing the two realities he had been living in.

Beth was there, her chestnut hair in the sunlight, her upper body slowly swaying in accompaniment as she looked down at the keys, unaware of his presence. "Jarek," he heard her say. The sound of her voice soothed his tired soul. "*Jarek,*" she said more insistently, but she didn't look up, and her lips weren't moving. He heard her voice again, much louder, shouting his name. Then she looked up at him, her eyes wide with panic, and shouted again, "JAREK! JAREK!"

CHAPTER 53

He woke with a start in his dorm room to see Beth leaning over him with a look of horror in her eyes.

"Jarek," she said with a gasp. "Oh, thank God.'

The local doctor stood nearby, carefully placing a cap on a syringe that had just been removed from Jarek's arm. Drummy stood nearby still as stone, hands clasped together as he nervously bit his lip.

"Thank God indeed," the doctor said. "That was close."

Worthing was nearby, arms crossed, looking at least as concerned as he was annoyed.

"I think you should hang on to these," the doctor said, handing Worthing the now nearly empty bottle containing what was left of the sleeping pills Jarek had stolen during his time in the infirmary. He had succeeded in convincing the school nurse that the only place he could sleep comfortably was in his room, where he began consuming them at an alarming rate and had been on a multi-day bender of sleep and little else.

"Son, listen to me," the doctor said, wrapping up. "You're in rough shape, frankly, and you look terrible. You need to eat more, and you need to sleep more. Much more."

Jarek blinked at the irony. "All I do is sleep," he thought.

The pills had been his only option. He knew it was only a matter of time until their absence was discovered, and he'd then be in a world of trouble, but there was no way his racing brain would have let him sleep without them, and if he didn't sleep, Lucas, Abigail, and the Village were lost. But he had taken too many, and it had nearly killed him.

In his resolve to save Lucas, Jarek had made matters worse—not only in his failed attempt to stop Thaddeus, which had put him into a rage, but on campus as well. He was in terrible shape, and people were paying very close attention with increasing concern. Would Drummy or McCracken themselves try to stop him from returning now that things had gone so far? Deep down, he knew going back was nearly impossible.

Before long, Thaddeus would know Abigail was involved in the letter. His retribution toward the entire Village would be quick and ruthless. Lucas would get the worst of it. Jarek wondered: had he changed the sequence of events at all? Maybe, when he read of Lucas's suicide, the book already accounted for Jarek's presence. Perhaps it was Jarek's presence that began the chain of events that would ultimately cause Lucas's death rather than preventing it.

There was no way around it. Jarek had put his friends in greater danger than ever. Jarek came up with the idea of the letter, and now Thaddeus was on a violent warpath to protect his criminal grip on the Village and keep himself out of prison. Jarek knew his intentions, as Thaddeus whispered them in his ear as he left Jarek, bloodied and bruised, on his office floor.

Thaddeus's words rang a dark echo through Jarek's mind. All he wanted to do was get back. He had been desperately focused on helping Lucas, but instead of preventing his death, from all he could tell, he had caused it. Lucas would be found hanging from the belltower rope in less than 24 hours. And it was Jarek's fault.

CHAPTER 54

The doctor wrapped up and quickly shuffled everyone out of Jarek's room. At Worthing's request, the nurse stayed behind to make sure he didn't have any more pills that they didn't know about. He desperately wanted to find Drummy and McCracken to tell them all that had happened and ask what he should do. But he couldn't leave. He also couldn't sleep. Going back was impossible.

Before long, the bell would ring and hundreds of rank-and-file members would awake to greet the new day. Among them the elders, Thaddeus and his men, Abigail and Lucas. The final moments of Lucas's life would begin to unfold, just as Abigail had written. The bell would ring, and he would be gone. And all Jarek could do was lay in bed under the nurse's watchful eye. He listened to the sound of his own panicked breathing and stared at the ceiling.

THE NURSE LEFT A DINNER TRAY ON JAREK'S DESK AND HEADED OUT into the dark as he feigned gratitude. Genuinely concerned, she arranged for his roommates to stay elsewhere on campus so he could get some much-needed sleep. They were on opposing couches in a faculty apartment with free reign of the TV and microwave, which, in campus terms, was a rare treat. For Jarek, it meant he could sneak out as soon as the coast was clear.

He crept along the back of the buildings—moving from shadow to shadow among the trees, avoiding the light from the windows of the other dorms that lit the frozen ground and careful to avoid the many sheets of frozen runoff along the way.

McCracken and Drummy were both in weekly faculty meetings, so he couldn't get to them. He desperately wanted to see Beth and tell her all that had happened. That she was right. That in living dual lives, he had failed in both. Hopefully, she'd put her head on his shoulder and tell him it wasn't his fault, that he did all he could, that maybe there was still time. Anything to assuage the aching weight that was crushing his chest and the panic that was tying him in knots.

By the time he got to the other end of campus, every bit of frigid wind was like a sub-zero blanket pressed against his face. He looked from the edge of the woods to make sure no one was around, hurried across an open expanse of snow to the back door of Beth's dorm and opened it without a sound. Moments later, he was sitting on the side of her bed, warming his hands with his breath as she looked at him. They had established a routine during his visits by now. Every time he came in, she would hug him, he would take his jacket off and sit on the edge of her bed, and moments later she would be by his side. They would stay close, always touching, and talk. This time was different. She sat several feet away in her desk chair and remained silent.

Finally, she moved her chair closer, with formality, careful not to make contact. He could tell she was concerned to see him in such distress, but when he looked into her eyes for more than a moment, she looked away.

He told her about his conversation with Lucas in the graveyard. How Lucas was defeated, how he was giving up. Jarek looked out the window for a long time, deep in thought. Affection and habit took her momentarily, and she reached forward and pushed a piece of his hair behind his ear as she looked at him. When he looked back, she turned away.

"I, um, I have something I was going to give you for your birthday." She took a small box out of her desk drawer. "There's a note in it because I didn't know if I'd see you now either. But…I guess it's better that you're here so we can talk instead," she said.

Jarek looked concerned. "Uh, talk about what?" He wasn't sure how much more he could handle.

"Jarek, this morning was the worst moment of my life. You know we thought you were actually dead for a minute? It was terrible. We were all in a panic. Doc gave you that shot, and suddenly you woke up. Seconds before, you were barely breathing."

"I'm sorry," he said, looking at the carpet. He thought with relief she just wanted to be mad at him a bit, and that was it.

He reached forward to put his hand on her leg.

"No," she said, pushing him away.

She shook her head, straightened her posture, and took a deep breath.

"Pills, Jarek?" she snapped, "and so many?" She raised her hands in disbelief. "Are you *crazy*?! You almost killed yourself! Is it worth it, Jarek—this fantasy of yours? Tell me because I want to know."

"It's not a fantasy, and you know it."

"It IS a fantasy because it's not REAL. It's not HERE! It's not THIS," she said, gesturing to the room around her. "It's not this," she repeated, pointing at the stack of books neatly piled on her desk. "It's not this," she held one of his hands in both of hers for a moment.

"I *can't* fail here, Jarek, I can't. My parents will kill me, and a second chance is something I won't get. I have an exam tomorrow, and I'm probably going to fail it because the jerk I love almost poisoned himself."

"Uh—the what that you *what*?" he wasn't sure which part of that last remark he wanted to focus on.

"Look, forget it. I can't. This is too much," she said.

"But..." he stammered, trying to figure out what—if anything—he could say in response. "But this is something that's..."

"I know, amazing, unusual, important, I know! But..." she slowed down from anger into sad resolve. "It's a dream, Jarek. They're just dreams."

He let out a pained sigh.

Andrew was surrounded by machines, wires running up him arms, down his neck, and into the folds of the hospital gown that betrayed his skeletal frame. Able to comprehend no other outcome for his brother, Jarek whispered, "You'll get better, Andrew. I know it."

Andrew lifted his tired eyes to him and said, "Jarek, it's a dream. It's just a dream."

"NO," Jarek burst out. Beth looked at him questioningly as he shook his head. Lucas was giving up, and now Beth wanted Jarek to give up, too.

He reached forward, put his hands on either side of her face, and moved in for a kiss. He knew it wouldn't change her mind, and he knew it would be the very last time he would kiss her.

She turned her head away. "No, Jarek. No, don't make this hard."

She placed one hand on his shoulder, moving it to his cheek as her eyes filled with tears. She looked into his and said quietly: "I'm so sorry, Jarek, I can't do this."

He stared at the floor for what felt like an eternity. The moment was torture, but he didn't want it to end because as soon as it did, everything would be different.

"Jarek?" she said. She waited for an answer, but he didn't provide one. Instead, he grabbed his coat and walked out.

CHAPTER 55

He buttoned the top lapel of his coat across his chest, pushed the knot of his scarf up until it just covered his chin, and braced himself for the cold, dark, and solitary walk back to the center of campus. He was angry. At Beth, at God, at Thaddeus, at the Conscientia for dragging him into this hopeless downward spiral. He walked quickly towards his dorm. They had taken his pills—so he doubted he could fall asleep, but he'd try. Tonight was his last chance. He was out of time.

His eyes were wet and stinging from the bitter wind hitting the tears that had welled in them but that he wouldn't let fall. This was not the time.

The task before him was too important.

He pushed his hands into his pockets away from the cold and felt again the gift box she had given him and the note he hadn't yet read. He fumbled the box open in the dim lamppost light and immediately stuffed into his coat pocket the smooth cloth it contained—a new "Poe scarf."

He looked back and saw her watching him from her window, her silhouette shrinking in the distance by the light of her desk lamp as he disappeared up the road He squinted to read her note, but it said what she had said already, too formally, too impartially.

It ended with the words: "I've been saving this gift for you and might as well give it to you now. You need a new one." He touched the familiar handwriting with his fingertips. The next sentence would echo in his head a thousand times. "They almost couldn't wake you up this morning, Jarek. It was terrifying. I can't do this. I wish things were different. I'm so sorry, Jarek. I'm so sorry."

It was too much. He needed to control himself. He counted, he tapped his temple, he took a few deep breaths. For once, it worked; his thoughts went in a different direction. There would be time to think about all of this later. For now, he had to focus on nothing other than saving Lucas. Thinking quickly, he realized he had to check the book one last time before returning to his dorm to see if anything had changed. He switched course and snuck into the museum. Flipping through the pages, he could see that all the entries were the same—because he had failed to change them. The dim red light of a small digital clock shone through the dark. Jarek looked down, slowly making his way to the window, but suddenly stopped dead in his tracks.

He stared closely at the floor, seeing something he couldn't believe.

"No, it's not possible." he whispered to himself. "Thaddeus?"

He moved more quickly to the window and noted the time: 11:21 pm. He then exited into the dark, his head hung low, for the frigid walk back to his dorm.

CHAPTER 56

No one else was in sight, just a few lit windows up the hill ahead and on the left. The streetlight in front of his dorm—right in the center of campus—was the farthest of all, blinking in and out of sight through the branches of a wind-blown evergreen between him and his nearing destination.

The frozen crunch of gravel under his feet sped up as his eyebrows stiffened in the cold. He knew his approach; he'd made it dozens of times. He'd avoid the lights in the center of campus and sneak out of the dark to approach his building through the back door, entering the warmth unnoticed. His footsteps on the gravel road and the creek of frozen branches overhead almost obscured the whispers he heard in the wind. He waited for familiar voices to call his name again.

But this voice was different, and then there was another. Two voices, in a hurry, and he wasn't imagining them. Anyone in their right mind was making their way indoors as quickly as possible. He slowed down as he approached, ducking behind a tree to investigate.

A repeated flick of light revealed at the base of a dorm—his dorm—the form of two students hunched over and facing the structure's base, struggling, it seemed, to light a cigarette. As he moved closer, the wind brought the acrid smell of gasoline to his nostrils. His eyes focused on two figures, one of whom fidgeted in their pocket before dipping a thick stick into a bucket and ducking against the building to avoid the wind. One more flick of light showed a bandana wrapped around the end of the stick to create a makeshift torch which was quickly engulfed in flames. The torch's light illuminated the large pile of wood stacked against the base of the structure and the face of its bearer: Morak.

Morak's sidekick Billy stood beside him. "Are you sure about this?" he asked. Jarek watched from a distance, seeing Billy anxiously look back and forth between the burning torch and the large pile of wood that Morak had intentionally left beside the dorm after Hands to Work that morning. *Maybe even Billy has his limits,* Jarek thought.

"Yeah, dumbass," Morak replied, giving Billy a slug in the arm for asking, "I'm sure. I hate this rotten place and everyone in it. My mom won't let me leave; my dad doesn't care either way. So... without a dorm, the school closes, and if the school closes, we get the hell out of here, right?"

Jarek was frozen in place. It couldn't be what it looked like. Could it? This was his dorm, and his room was right there inside, waiting for him so he could get back to Lucas. And it was late; everyone was inside.

Met with silence, Morak asked again, "*Right?*"

"Right." Billy nodded nervously.

Morak grabbed the edge of the nearby bucket, carefully tipping the rest of the fuel on the woodpile and holding the torch far away in his opposite arm instead of handing it to Billy. He wanted to do the honors himself. They looked around carefully to make sure no one was watching.

"This wood is soaked with gas," Morak said, "So I drop this," he waved the torch, "and we run. Got it?"

"Yeah," Billy replied, his eyes fixed forward.

Morak stepped back, looking up to the black sky overhead, the stars above, the bare tree branches blowing in the cold wind, some so frozen they creaked as they swayed. He looked at the wind in the trees and smiled, figuring it would help.

Jarek looked around nervously and tried to decide what to do. Everyone knew that these buildings, faced with an open fire, would be consumed in minutes. Fire escapes were everywhere, but would everyone make it out in time? What he really thought about, though, was one life in particular. If his room was destroyed, any hope of returning to Lucas was gone.

Watching Morak move closer to the fire, Jarek panicked. His heart beat faster as he looked around for anyone to call out to, but there was no one. His jaw still ached from Thaddeus, but it was just him—no one to ask for help—so he ignored it. He ran forward, unseen, just as Morak lifted his arm to throw the torch and watch the woodpile burst into flames.

Jarek drew closer and, in a commanding voice, yelled, "Don't!"

Billy, panicked at the possibility of being recognized, spun around and lunged at Jarek full-bore with a mid-section tackle. Jarek fell back and cracked his head against the frozen ground.

Morak stared indifferently, watching Billy get over Jarek, fists poised to shower him with punches, just as Jarek delivered a few solid upward kicks, getting Billy in the waist with a combat boot. Billy reeled and fell over as Jarek leaped up, giving him a hard kick in the ribs. Morak turned towards the gas-soaked wood as Jarek lunged at him, grabbing at the torch.

Jarek had slowed Morak down for a moment but instantly felt Morak's opposite fist catch him hard in his right side. He buckled forward and pushed his upper body at Morak, knocking him back against the building as he dropped the torch. Jarek grabbed it quickly, but as he lifted his arm to throw it into the distance, Billy landed a massive blow to his cheek. Jarek stumbled, falling backward onto the pile. It was two against one, and he was losing.

Jarek quickly hurried to his feet with his eyes on Billy but heard a grunt from Morak, "Over here, pussy." He turned to the right just in time to glimpse a heavy branch swinging towards him in the dark. It smashed him square in the nose, as he saw a flash and felt the crack of splitting cartilage resonate through his skull.

Billy laughed; Jarek barely heard it. He reeled, saw Morak, saw trees, and then saw the sky as he fell onto his back. The crunch of the brush was soft under his beaten frame, but the torch—still in his hand—fell onto the woodpile. He heard a rushing "thump" as it burst into flames below him.

Jarek sprung to his feet, the wet gasoline on the back of his jacket barely escaping the fire. He stumbled dizzily, the flaming torch still in his hand, as Morak's whispered shouts of "GO, GO, GO!" to Billy faded into the distance with their footsteps.

Jarek turned around. A column of fire quickly climbed the side of the building. He blinked twice to focus, unable to believe what he saw. The woodpile was consumed in flames, which now licked up the side of the building, five feet high, then ten, in seconds.

"Oh God, no, no, no," he said loudly to no one. He stared; he looked around frantically—no water, no nothing.

Panic-stricken faces began to appear in the windows, orange in the reflected light of the growing flames. They fixed their eyes on Jarek as he stood there, torch in hand, clear as day beside the fire. He looked around, saw there was nothing he could do, and started to run. His heart pounded in his ears, and blood ran down his face as he looked back at the burning building in the distance, his feet punching through the frozen surface of the snow as he ran. Suddenly, he slammed into something—a massive body in a black jacket. With a badge.

A local cop on his rounds happened to be driving through the campus interior a few minutes earlier. He exited his squad car when he saw a kid swinging a flame in the distance. He then saw the fire quickly engulf the side of the building as the shadow of a student ran directly toward him. Years of experience had taught him that when someone runs away, they're guilty, but Jarek saved the officer the trouble of a chase. The policeman simply took a couple steps into Jarek's path, and Jarek ran straight into him. Two enormous hands effortlessly lifted Jarek's feet off the ground and threw him down into the snow like a rag doll.

The cop looked up at the fire, then back down to Jarek, bleeding in the snow in pain and confusion.

Jarek had no struggle left in him as he was flipped over, the icy cold of steel handcuffs snapping tight around his wrists.

"Boy," the cop said. "You are in a world of shit."

CHAPTER 57

Jarek had a few interactions with police officers in the past. Living in New Jersey but always in Manhattan for a better band scene, Jarek and his friends would wander out of CBGB's post-show and head to Chinatown to load up on fireworks. On the way home, they would break into area golf courses to shoot all manner of explosives at each other in the dark. Their Jersey plates often gave them away before they made it out of the city, and they'd get a stern lecture before the officers would get back to more pressing matters. NYPD cops were no joke; unflappable and tough, they knew your deal without asking.

These cops—out here in the middle of nowhere—were not those cops, but they watched those cops on TV, so did their best to act like them. A fire was a huge event for them. The whole town would be talking for weeks, longer even. Jarek couldn't help but think they should be thanking him; if he wasn't there, they'd be mediating grocery store disputes, jumpstarting stranded cars, and shoveling up frozen roadkill.

Jarek had stumbled in with his hands cuffed behind his back, held upright by the two large officers whose arms were locked under his as they escorted him through the station door. A couple others looked at him as he passed the front desk, wondering what this kid with crazy hair and blood all over his face and shirt had gotten himself into.

Fluorescent lights buzzed overhead in a hallway that led to an empty room, where a plain wooden chair sat beside a simple wooden table. On top of the table was a complicated black box with wires that stuck out of it and disappeared below. On top of the box sat a microphone.

Jarek was placed, cuffs still on, in the chair. His head slumped towards his chest as bloody drool dripped from his lower lip, bright red against his white undershirt—all that remained after the fight, the cop, and being dragged into and out of a police car half conscious. He stared down at the red stain like an outside observer of events happening around him. He knew he was in trouble but couldn't remember why. A window separated Jarek's room from the hall, where three officers in short-sleeved dress shirts were engaged in an intense discussion he knew was about him.

The ache in the middle of Jarek's face was unbearable. As two of the officers walked away, the third walked in and looked at Jarek, shaking his head. Jarek couldn't tell if it was meant to say, "That sucks, I'm sorry this happened to you," or "You're in incredible trouble and should wish you weren't here." He got his answer soon enough.

The cop walked behind Jarek and around the table to the other side, tugging at the black cloth around Jarek's neck as he went. "What are you, a French painter?" he asked, blowing his breath between his teeth in a disdainful *pfft*. Jarek didn't respond or even look up. *Another tough lecture*, he thought. He'd had plenty, so he would weather the storm for now. Hopefully.

"Wake up, you little freak," the cop snarled.

Jarek's mind wandered back to his last interaction with the police—he and his friends running through the dark with backpacks full of roman candles and bottle rockets they had been shooting at each other—and smiled a little, eyes closed, remembering their escape. The cop noticed.

"I said wake UP!" the cop yelled, tossing the water from his foam cup into Jarek's eyes.

Jarek jumped and felt a throbbing ache return across the front of his face; his nose was either badly cut or broken, maybe both. He tried to bring a hand around to feel it but realized he was cuffed. The pain brought him back entirely, and the smell of hair tonic and moth balls told Jarek the cop was right in front of him. He remembered where he was and why, but there was something else gnawing at him. Something he saw in the museum. In the fog of everything that had just happened, he couldn't seem to remember what it was.

"Hey. Have you heard anything I've said?" the cop asked.

Jarek opened his eyes and nodded.

"You know that building is gone, right?" the cop asked. "Just a pile of smoky wood. Funny how the flick of a match can ruin your life forever, huh?" he smirked.

"Gone?" Jarek muttered. "No." It couldn't be real.

"So, one more time. I've told you the charges—three times actually—now this is the part where you repeat them into the microphone, so Uncle Sam knows *you* know why you're here. Got it? Your school is your legal guardian, so they have a couple of 'educators' on the way," the cop snorted. "So consider this a dry run. Name first. Say it again, nice and clear."

Jarek's thoughts were a blur, but slowly it came back to him. The fire. The dorm. The faces in the window. His room. Lucas.

He remembered falling backwards and dropping the torch. In trying to stop Morak, he had lit the fire himself, but it was an accident! Did everyone get out? Had he…killed people? He didn't know. What he did know was that he had tried to save Lucas, harder than he'd tried anything in his life, but Lucas would soon be gone…and it was his fault.

"Jesus Christ," he muttered to himself in confusion.

"Hey!" the cop barked at him from across the table, leaning in. "I've told you the charges. Snap out of it and spit them out!" he barked as Jarek winced at the escalating volume right in his face. "Name first, jerkoff."

Jarek closed his eyes. He couldn't think clearly. The dorm was gone, and his room with it. He could never go back. Lucas would die in a matter of hours. From the sound of it, others already had.

"Go ahead," the cop urged.

"My name is Jarek Dorrell. I'm…"

"Date. Again." the cop snapped.

"Today is February 5th, 1992. My name is Jarek Dorrell; I'm 17 years old. I'm under arrest… for arson and…"

He had a lump in his throat.

"…murder."

CHAPTER 58

"Looks like you made the paper."

McCracken turned from the front seat of Drummy's beat-up station wagon and tossed a newspaper into Jarek's lap.

"The paper?" Jarek asked. He looked down:

"*The Times Record*, February 6th, 1992. 'Boy Arrested in School Fire: Teenage boy arrested in connection with school dormitory fire in New Lebanon.'"

The tires spun in the gravel as Drummy pulled out. He'd waited all day for them to emerge and was eager to get the station behind them now that the sun had set.

"Great," Jarek said, his heart sinking a bit more, "the paper. God, this is crazy. So, what's left of the dorm?"

"Listen closely," McCracken said, slowly turning around in the dark. The headlights of passing cars showed the strain of recent events on his face as he looked Jarek in the eye and snapped, "What's left, Jarek, is smoking embers in a charred brick shell, dammit!"

Jarek raised his eyebrows in surprise as McCracken turned to face forward.

"Okay, everybody, okay," Drummy said, trying to ease the tension. "Big day. Let's just take a moment, and then we'll think about all this." He paused, then pressed on:

"Uh, Jarek, I hate to tell you, but your parents are a bit beside themselves. Worthing had to call them, of course. There's sort of a lot going on around here."

Jarek's heart sank. "Oh Christ, my parents," he said.

"Well," Drummy added, "the overdose call and the 'your son got arrested' call were the same call, so it kind of..."

"Sucks," Jarek said, adding with a sigh, "God, that sucks." He shook his head.

"Yeah," Drummy said with a nod, keeping his eyes on the road before changing the subject.

"So Jarek, the only reason we were able to get you out of there is minors can only be held for so long before being released. Everybody in this car knows you didn't start the fire—at least not on purpose—but you're the only one that's been charged. On the bright side; while there were a bunch of people in Brethren's who looked out the windows and saw you—standing there—watching the fire climb the side of the building looking guilty as sin." He turned to give Jarek a side-eye for getting himself in the situation, "A couple heard the commotion before and looked out. They saw two other students run off but couldn't identify them. In other words, you're not out of the woods, not even close, but at least for now you can leave the station."

Jarek was afraid to ask his next question. "Did anybody...?" He paused nervously before he could continue. "Did anybody get hurt? Did anybody...you know...not make it?"

McCracken heard the quiver in his voice and turned around, back to his regular self. "No," he said. "We weren't sure at first, but don't worry, everyone's fine, son."

Jarek breathed a deep sigh of relief and stayed quiet for a long time before breaking the silence himself.

"I think I got him," he said.

"Got who?" Drummy asked.

"Thaddeus," Jarek said dryly, "I think I got him."

"What? How's that Jarek?" McCracken asked, turning around.

"I took his ledger," Jarek said.

"You what?" Drummy replied.

"His ledger. I took it."

"Jarek!" Drummy proclaimed. "Outsmarting Thaddeus!? How?"

"Well, he beat the hell out of me, and I woke up alone in his office. I never saw him with the ledger, so I figured it had to be in there somewhere, and it was. He had it in a secret compartment under one of the drawers that fell out of his bookshelf when he threw me against it. Guess he's not so smart when he's angry."

"Jarek! Phenomenal work. Well done." McCracken said with sincerity.

Jarek added, "He killed Brother Armstrong. He did. I know he did. And if he hasn't killed anyone else, it's just because he hasn't had the chance." Jarek could still taste the blood in his mouth, and the sense of panic that had hit him in the police station returned. He shook his head, trying to clear it enough to remember what he needed to tell them.

Drummy was fixed on the news about the ledger, turning from the wheel: "Wait—what did you do with it?"

"Everything was mixed together. I was really out of it, but I had a feeling that I had to get to the Tannery no matter what. Like I was being pulled, I didn't know why. When I got there, I remembered that Abigail went in every morning to check the items heading to the store, so I put it on top. Then I woke up with Doc's needle sticking out of my arm."

"*Barely* woke up," McCracken corrected solemnly. "Let's see if we see anything different in the book when we get back."

"Oh, and Jarek," Drummy said with regret, "I'm afraid Worthing wants you in his office first thing tomorrow."

Jarek had no way of proving to Worthing that he didn't start the fire. He would see him tomorrow morning, and he would be expelled. He had lied over and over again. He'd stolen—and abused—medicine from the infirmary. And the fire? He was there, and that was enough, especially on top of everything else.

Jarek let it sink in. "Well, that's it then," he said. He had failed. Failed at school, failed himself, and failed his parents. Soon they would get another call—more bad news—this time about his expulsion. They would be devastated. Heartbroken. Tomorrow he'd say goodbye to Beth forever. He had failed at saving Lucas. The portal was gone. That was it. There was no way of going back.

They sat quietly for the last few minutes of the drive. Jarek didn't have the stomach to tell them the worst part: Abigail having the ledger wouldn't change anything in time. Lucas was still going to die. Thaddeus had won.

CHAPTER 59

The car rolled to a stop beside Wickersham. Jarek was to report to the infirmary, on the ground floor of the Dairy Barn, where Headmaster Worthing had demanded he stay while the other residents of his former dormitory had been scattered to different rooms across campus. All three got out and stood quietly for a moment. Drummy and McCracken leaned back against the car, and Jarek stood before them, mustering the courage to finally tell them what he knew: that all they had accomplished when they put their heads together—at least for Lucas—was nothing.

Jarek took a breath and lifted his eyes from the ground, speaking slowly.

"He kills himself. Lucas kills himself."

"Wait…what?" Drummy said, adding, "That can't be—how do you know?"

"It's in the book now. Sister Abigail wrote about it. It happens in…" he looked at his watch and spoke as someone resigned to accept something inevitable and terrible, "four hours and thirteen minutes."

"Oh my God." Drummy said, stunned and confused, "It can't be…does he?"

He looked Jarek in the eye, then at McCracken, scanning his face for any sign of hope that they might have any other options, something they could do. Anything. But he saw none. Grief and frustration came over Drummy's face as he realized they were out of options.

The page in the book, the final entry about Lucas, detailing the end of a terribly unfair and far too short life, would remain unchanged forever. "Oh my God," Drummy said again.

Jarek turned around and slowly walked towards the infirmary as they watched him; his head hung low, heavy with the burden of everything he'd taken on and all he'd risked. The sum of his failures and the death of his friend. Beyond him in the dark, grey smoke drifted through the glow of a solitary lamppost beside the blackened shell of what was once his dorm. After a few steps, he turned around and lifted his eyes towards them, saying, "Oh, one other thing…"

"What's that, Jarek?" Drummy asked, lifting his eyes toward him.

Jarek squeezed his eyes shut and shook his head violently back and forth. "God, I can't keep anything straight," he said. He looked up again as his voice cracked. "I saw Thaddeus's footprint in the museum last night. He's here."

"Wait, what? WHAT?!" McCracken's voice rang through the darkness "He can't be…it's not possible…why didn't you—" he stammered.

The weight of everything—the meaninglessness of all their efforts—crashed over Jarek in waves. He was defeated. He didn't care. "The Speckled Band," he mumbled at the ground. "He's here."

He turned again, and they stared at his back in shock and disbelief as he slowly walked away into the dark.

JAREK HAD A ROOM TO HIMSELF IN THE INFIRMARY BECAUSE WORTHing didn't want his primary suspect talking to anyone about the fire. Jarek was the only person present who had been identified, so he was still very much responsible.

He had been listening to the clock tick away, entirely unable to sleep and counting the minutes, wondering how close Lucas was to making his final decision.

"*Jarek!*" The urgent whisper of Drummy's voice called from outside his window, followed by the sharp *plink* of something hitting the glass. "*Psst!* Jarek!"

Quickly, Jarek opened the window to see his teacher standing under the cover of a nearby tree, gesturing to him.

"Worthing has someone at the front door," Drummy said. "Come on out the window." Jarek quickly shimmied out, hopping to the grass below to see McCracken standing next to Drummy.

"What's this?" Jarek asked.

"Come with us, and hurry," Drummy said. "No sign of Thaddeus, not yet, but let's not take chances."

They walked down the main road in the dark. "Where am I going?" Jarek asked.

"Well, there's something I didn't tell you," McCracken said. "When the Conscientia reach forward, as they did to you…well… your room is, or was, not the only one. So, to answer your question, Jarek: You're going into the past."

"Wait—there's another room like mine?" Jarek stopped in his tracks and stared at them. "Which one?"

McCracken was resolute. "Mine."

"Current time in the Village," Drummy looked at his watch, "is 11:20 am. We have one hour."

They looked around carefully—there was little chance that Thaddeus, wherever he was lurking, wouldn't see the three of them walking down the dark edge of the main road, even at night. He'd know Jarek in an instant.

They ascended the steps of a small house on the left. In Village times, it was a residence for some of the most esteemed elders. Now it was McCracken's, the mysterious gent who spent countless hours poring over dusty old documents, known to few for what he really was: the last of an ancient order of guardians who had protected this place for well over 200 years.

McCracken's bedroom had, at one point, been a place of worship and then accommodation for several very senior and devout elders. The ceiling was curved, just like in Jarek's room. Old etchings of Shaker faces hung on the otherwise blank walls. He was surprised to see the kind and familiar faces of Sister Abigail, Brother Armstrong, and several others. McCracken and Drummy quickly ushered Jarek to the one available bed. On the wall above him was a cross. On the far wall, mounted above a Shaker desk, was a hand-carved wooden relief of praying hands with the inscription "…and Hearts to God" just below.

Jarek tossed two small, white tablets in his mouth as he lay down. "Forgot I stuck a couple extra in this little pocket," he said with a smile, pointing to the small pocket on the hip of his jeans before quickly chewing up the pills.

"Uh, Jarek we need to talk," Drummy said with a shake of his head before looking back to McCracken.

"Jarek, listen to me," McCracken said. "If Thaddeus is here on campus, he clearly figured out how to get here even though—"

"Even though nobody…reached forward, or whatever, to get him here," Jarek interrupted.

"That's right," McCracken said. "There's a lot here I don't understand. But one thing I do know: Thaddeus now understands you're not a random orphan in the Village. He knows that the Elders called you back. He believes if he can stop you, he'll be stopping them. In this belief, he is, unfortunately, correct. So… listen to me, Jarek."

"I'm listening," Jarek said impatiently.

"Thaddeus sleeps above the seed store, at the top of the Ann Lee Building. That is on the complete opposite end of campus. You're going to wake up right here in this room. That means you've got quite a run ahead of you when you do. As you run through the

Village to find him, you'll be there looking for him, and he'll be here looking for you. That's when you are by far at your most vulnerable. I'll be here at the door. I'm not leaving you, but you'll have no way of knowing what's happening here, and we'll have no way of telling you. You're chasing each other through dimensions and dreams here, and I don't pretend to understand much of any of it, but what I do know—more than anything—is that you'd better run as if your life depends on it. Because…" he hesitated to sound too dramatic, "because it might. He knows you're here. He wants nothing more than to find you. And if he does? Well, son, we know what he's capable of."

Jarek looked blankly at him for a moment as this reality sunk in.

McCracken added, "Wake Thaddeus up and go find Lucas. You *have* to find Thaddeus first. If he finds *you* here first…well, it's all over."

"He'll kill you," Drummy added.

"Yes, thank you, Matt," McCracken gave him a look.

McCracken continued, "If he gets to you first, you'll never be able to save Lucas. Find Thaddeus in the Village, and you'll save both Lucas and yourself. And you'll get Thaddeus off campus in our time before he harms anyone here. Who knows what state he's in. We know what the past is like—pictures, stories—and it was still jarring for you to be there. He knows nothing of our time, and being *here* may make him more dangerous than ever. Find him, right away, and wake him up."

"Do whatever you have to do, Jarek," Drummy added.

Jarek paused for a minute, remembering the beating he got from Thaddeus the last time he saw him. The idea of going at him while he slept was deeply satisfying but terrifying. What would happen once he was awake?

Drummy and McCracken looked on in concern as the pills took effect.

"Okay, I get it," Jarek said groggily as his eyes began to close, resigned to face whatever was to come.

"Wait, what time is it?" he added nervously.

"In the Village, 11:58 am," Drummy said.

THE SAME SUDDEN CHILL CAME OVER JAREK THAT HE FELT BEFORE receiving gifts in the past. He closed his eyes and saw Brother Armstrong sitting at his desk as clearly as if Jarek himself was in the room. He could feel the tension in the air as Brother Armstrong's unswerving gaze betrayed the difficulty between himself and the figure fading into view from a far corner of the room bearing two cups of steaming tea. A familiar voice spoke: "Let's not let these matters too greatly affect our fellowship, Brother."

Brother Armstrong's skeptical glare faded slightly, grateful for the peace offering. "Thank you, Thaddeus," he said with a nod.

Jarek saw the edge of a small vial sticking out of Thaddeus's back pocket, just as Brother Armstrong lifted his cup to his mouth. Seconds later, the gentle Elder's eyes suddenly widened. He let out a cough and quickly brought his hands to his mouth. Thaddeus looked on with a smile and turned to walk out.

The vision stopped as quickly as it began. Jarek's eyes snapped open in shock.

"Christ, I've got twenty minutes. Will these stupid pills work?" As he said it, he immediately fell into a deep sleep.

CHAPTER 60

Drummy watched Jarek's chest rise and fall slowly and let out a sigh.

"Matt, let's not let our guard down. We don't know how long it will be until he comes back," McCracken said.

"*If* he comes back," Drummy responded, his hands nervously gripping each other.

"Yes. All we can do now is wait and hope. Our most immediate concern for the moment is Thaddeus. He's here somewhere. Let's not forget that everything he sees—cars, electricity, even our clothes—will be so alien and surreal to him he likely won't be able to process it normally. There's a natural stress reaction that occurs when people experience something shocking. They revert to the worst of their impulses as a defense. At these times, they are more volatile than ever, and Thaddeus was trouble enough before. Who knows where he is or how he hasn't found us?" He nodded to Jarek, sleeping soundly in the nearby bed. "But I don't doubt he's running out of places to look. I'm here with Jarek, but there's a killer among us in a campus full of kids. Find him, Matt, right now, and be careful. Look on your way to the museum, and get me the book right away. If any changes have occurred, I need to see them. Please hurry." Drummy looked at him quizzically, unsure of how that would help.

McCracken looked into the distance, then back at Drummy, adding, "Brother Armstrong's death was the greatest tragedy that ever struck the Conscientia. No one knew for sure what happened. Not until now. Matt, you are witnessing the final throes of a conflict that began over 125 years ago. One that I have the responsibility to...resolve."

Drummy paused at the gravity of his words, knowing that McCracken would stop at nothing to defeat Thaddeus however he could.

"I understand," Drummy nodded.

"No time to waste," McCracken added, rushing Drummy out the door.

Drummy ran out into the black night, unaware of the dark figure hidden amongst the nearby trees and the menacing face that watched him depart with a satisfied smirk.

CHAPTER 61

Jarek woke in the Village with a start.

He bolted out of the now pristine white structure—a stark contrast to its well-aged future self—and started up the road at a sprint. Most of the villagers were in the workshops or the field. He ran down the first stretch of road to the flat of the central Village, looking at the shallow but long hill before him as the bell tower began to chime. He didn't need to count; it only ever rang at noon. Except for today—unless he could stop the second toll that was coming in just a few minutes.

Thaddeus was looking for Jarek's sleeping body on campus. If he found him, he would kill him. And then Lucas would kill himself. Thaddeus would rule the Village, and Sister Abigail would be cast out to a cruel world, destitute and alone. He ran as hard as he could as the bell rang to twelve, each chime mocking his inability to go any faster.

THE FRONT DOOR OF MCCRACKEN'S DWELLING FACED THE MAIN staircase, which sat aside the main supporting wall to the left. The house had more than one entry but only one way upstairs—barring the fire escape, the ladder of which could only be deployed from the second floor. Jarek lay sound asleep upstairs as McCracken sat on the steps, not leaving anything to chance and listening carefully to the sounds of the night. Every whistle of wind in the windows startled him to attention. His eyes darted nervously to the front door each time an evergreen branch scratched the metal roof overhead.

McCracken knew of Thaddeus—what there was to know from the old books and documents. The line of Conscientia had paid close attention to anything they could learn about him. He effectively took over all matters of the Village after Brother Armstrong's death in 1866. There was no documented evidence of misdeeds, but in the Village's history, it had seemed to those who came after as a particularly unhappy time. McCracken now understood why. It was only a matter of time until this soulless criminal, this embodiment of evil, ran out of other places to look for Jarek and—finally—showed himself at McCracken's front door.

McCracken was stone-still, alert, deep in thought. Lucas, whoever he was and however he died, had been gone for well over a century. Jarek was very much alive. He was a kid. Thaddeus was a full-grown man, a sharpened criminal, and a strong one at that. Had he, Earl McCracken, let personal vengeance cloud his judgment? How was Jarek ever supposed to stop a man like Thaddeus? He wondered at the few possible outcomes and was immediately overwhelmed with guilt. He had likely sent Jarek to his death and would never forgive himself for it. He was angry at himself, at Thaddeus, at God.

He heard a click.

McCracken's eyes darted towards the latch on the front door. The arm was above the catch.

Someone was on the other side.

He waited a moment. The hinges let out a low creek.

The frozen, dry air outside sucked at the edges of the door, creating a whistling rush as it slowly started to swing open. McCracken stared in anxious anticipation, steeling himself for whatever might come as a cold wind reached his face, blowing the door open entirely.

Standing in the dim light and silhouetted by the blackness behind him, he saw a tall, dark figure, his face obscured by a black wide-brim hat as he slowly lifted his chin to the light. Thin lips slowly expanded into a cunning smile, which stood in stark contrast to his sunken eyes and his strong but skeletal jaw.

In his hand was a riding crop with a whip end and a blunt yet perfectly polished steel handle.

The stranger watched patiently as McCracken descended the steps without the slightest air of hesitation. He held in his hands a long wooden stick, curved like the handle of an axe.

The smile disappeared from the stranger's face. He spoke in a sly and deliberate tone: "You ever notice, Brother, how you only ever find something in the last place you would seek?"

"Perhaps you found more than what you'd hoped for," McCracken said. "I've been eager to make your acquaintance, Thaddeus."

He pushed his sleeves up as he descended the final steps, and Thaddeus's eyes widened in surprise. He saw the seal of the Conscientia, the Segno Sentinelle, emblazoned in pitch black against the pale skin of McCracken's sinewed arm as he gripped the handle.

"Oh, I promise I won't impose for long," Thaddeus said wryly, reaching for the steel crop at his side.

"Don't disappoint me…Brother." McCracken said as he tightened his grip and wound up to swing. "We've only just met…"

CHAPTER 62

The breakneck sprint across the entirety of campus had Jarek gasping for air. He ran past the Brethren's dwelling house that had been home to him and other Shaker men, starting up the hill as fast as he could, his eyes fixed on the white building far ahead on the left. The seed store downstairs would be closed for the lunch hour and upstairs would be Thaddeus, fast asleep. As he passed the main building and the small road to his right that entered the heart of the Village, he saw a solitary figure in the distance take note and start after him. One of Thaddeus's men.

Jarek saw the figure in the distance pick up speed, turning back to yell to another in the distance, who joined in the chase.

"Great," Jarek said under his breath. "Two." The second of his pursuers was maybe 200 yards away, the first 100 yards and—as Jarek's strength was fading—closing fast. Jarek knew he had to get to Thaddeus before they caught up with him. He raced up the hill, gasping for air, the first of Thaddeus's men right behind him as he entered the bottom door and bounded up the first flight of steps.

He sprang up the second flight. He heard the grunts of his pursuer getting closer. One more small flight of stairs to the topmost room where Thaddeus was sleeping. Jarek bounded up two steps at a time, but his topmost foot slipped from exhaustion at that very moment. As he quickly steadied himself to get up, he felt the vice grip of a mercilessly strong fist tighten around his ankle.

Jarek knew that Thaddeus was on campus, doing all he could to find him in Jarek's own time. He had to wake Thaddeus up immediately to get him back to the Village, to his own time, before he could do any harm. If he only knew the harm Thaddeus was already doing at that very moment, perhaps he would have fought harder.

McCRACKEN'S FIRST BLOW STRUCK THADDEUS IN THE RIBS. He grunted and looked up at McCracken, startled that matters had escalated so quickly. His face turned to a hardened resolve as all pretense quickly faded away, and the criminal, ready to fight for his life, emerged.

"Brother!" he said in mock surprise.

"Don't 'Brother' me now," McCracken responded. He wound up to unleash another left-handed swing, which Thaddeus expertly dodged. He was ready for McCracken's unwound form from the miss, so raised his right fist—wrapped tight around the end of his crop—and brought the steel end down hard on McCracken's lower back. McCracken let out a deep grunt as the air escaped his lungs. He buckled over but then uncoiled upward and swung the wooden handle, landing a blow on Thaddeus's cheekbone with a knock as loud and clean as if the well-finished handle had been struck against a log. Thaddeus reeled, and McCracken thought the fight was over.

He then made a grave mistake. The thought crossed McCracken's mind that the commotion might have woken Jarek, and he looked towards the top of the staircase. Thaddeus then knew exactly where he would find him. He moved with twice his previous ferocity, landing a backhanded upward swipe of the steel crop against the underside of McCracken's chin, a quick fist in the ribs, and—as McCracken crumbled against the steps—a merciless stomp with his heavy boots down onto McCracken's collar bone, which gave way with a snap. He howled and grabbed his shoulder as Thaddeus rushed past him, racing up the stairs and into the bedroom. He saw Jarek sound asleep and raised his crop, ready to bring it down onto Jarek's sleeping head with one devastating blow. He hesitated momentarily, unsure if his weapon was sure to end this matter once and for all, but quickly looked around the room and decided it would have to do.

The pause gave McCracken just enough time. He mustered every bit of strength in his bruised frame to charge through the door in the final instant. He may have had 15 years on Thaddeus, but the perfect hockey check he was revered for was still within him. The Conscientia's greatest enemy was before him. He couldn't let them down.

McCracken's hands were held wide on the axe handle as he barged through the open door, charging at Thaddeus and upending him with the shaft and his shoulders at the same moment the crop flashed downwards towards Jarek's head. With one final explosive push, McCracken uncoiled his crouched frame, sending them both out the fire escape door, where they landed beside each other on the cold metal slats and grappled for advantage.

Thaddeus moved quickly. With his crop still in his hand, he cracked the steel down onto McCracken's knee then climbed on top of him, sitting on his stomach and tossing the axe handle off the balcony. He pressed the riding crop firmly against McCracken's throat and pushed down with all his might as the older man fought, kicked, and struggled.

A sneer of satisfaction crossed Thaddeus's lips. He pressed the crop down harder, seeing McCracken's strength wane. McCracken struggled for his last breaths with despair in his eyes. He knew he was defeated, that this was the end, and that the order of the Conscientia—protectors of the Village for nearly 200 years—was about to die with him.

Jarek struggled to shake free of the grip Thaddeus's man had on his ankle. Breathless and exhausted from his run, he was caught—overpowered by a large enforcer he had no ability to contend with.

The reality of failure brought his mind to Lucas and Abigail. He thought of how close he was to Thaddeus, finally. The very thought put him into a rage. His vision narrowed, his hands tingled, and, with a strength not entirely his own, he grabbed the staircase railing. Jarek then looked back at the sinister and satisfied grin of the man gripping his ankle, wound up his other leg, and planted his boot directly in his face. The hand let go, the broken face contorted, and Jarek watched him fall backward down two steps and against the opposite wall, crumbling to the floor, out cold.

Jarek scrambled up the steps as fast as he could. He didn't know Thaddeus was choking the very last breaths out of McCracken at that very moment, but he knew he had to hurry. Grabbing a small side table just inside the door, he quickly lifted it high over his head with both hands, exclaimed loudly, "Brother Thaddeus…WAKE UP!" and swung the small wooden frame down, crashing it to pieces on Thaddeus's face and chest.

CHAPTER 63

Thaddeus vanished into thin air.

McCracken's weakening hands, which had pushed back in vain against the crop on his neck a moment before, now pushed at emptiness as his final grunt of protest sounded into the dark. He was alone, gasping for air as limbs of a nearby evergreen waved in the wind. The hinges of the fire escape door—which the two men had come crashing through moments before—creaked softly as it swayed. Aside from that, all was silent. McCracken sat up, rubbed his injured throat, and spit blood.

He had read in old Village documents that Thaddeus was "grand of stature." McCracken thought now of how little justice that description did to how powerful and ruthless he really was. But Thaddeus was now awake in the Village, and Jarek would soon be in a desperate struggle with him. After what McCracken had just experienced, he was sure of one thing: Jarek could never win. His heart sank as he looked back into the room at Jarek's sleeping form.

"On point, Jarek," he said quietly. "Find, focus, finish. On point, son. On point."

He then got on his knees, folded his hands, and there in the freezing wind—begging for the life of his young friend—he prayed.

IN THE VILLAGE, THADDEUS WOKE IMMEDIATELY TO THE PAIN OF THE wooden table crashing down upon him. Instinctively lifting his hands to protect his face, he opened his eyes and reeled for a moment. Jarek moved quickly, levelling a kick directly to Thaddeus's chin. The man sprung up to attack but felt the full impact of a second blow—Jarek's fist across his cheek—followed by the wooden shaft of one of the table legs brought down twice, hard, in solid cracks upon his head. The element of surprise gave Jarek the upper hand, and he had no intention of giving it up. He brought his arm back again, determined to strike hard, when the second of Thaddeus's men that had been giving chase came crashing through the door and right into Jarek's mid-section, sending him careening across the room, and cracking his head on the hard plaster wall. Stunned from the impact, Jarek felt Thaddeus's man spin him around, holding his elbows together behind his back with an immovable grip. Thaddeus then ceremoniously stepped before Jarek, parted his feet, lifted his fists, and struck Jarek again and again: the chin, the ribs, the stomach. The final blow buckled Jarek over with a grunt.

"Tie him up," Thaddeus said.

"Thaddeus!" a voice called from outside. "Thaddeus! Some commotion—I think you'd better see." Thaddeus glanced out the window to see Mr. Clarence Goodell waving him down and pointing toward the center of the Village.

Both of his men were now in the room. There was no need to stand on pretense anymore; Thaddeus knew who his enemies were. "Go find that bitch Abigail, wherever she is," Thaddeus barked at one of them "and bring her to me. She's got my ledger. Get it back, whatever it takes. I don't care if you have to beat it out of her."

His man nodded and turned to go.

"Whatever it takes," Thaddeus repeated.

"You," he said to the other man. "I don't have my ledger, so if somewhere in your small brain you can remember what Finch ordered, go to the barn and make sure it's together before he gets here or he won't pay, and I want that money."

He stammered, "Boss, it was a lot of things…"

"Then ASK HIM!" Thaddeus interrupted, stepping towards him like he was ready to strike as the man turned to run out.

At that moment, the chime of the bell sounded across the Village.

No, no, no! Jarek thought. *Lucas!*

Thaddeus looked towards the window at the sound of the bell, then looked at Jarek before he and his men left, leaving Jarek tied up and alone.

As soon as Thaddeus disappeared from the window, Mr. Goodell rushed into the room, taking in Jarek's bloody face, and untied him.

"It's Lucas!" Jarek said in a panic. Goodell didn't understand. Jarek frantically tossed the ropes off, talking to no one. "Lucas, God, no, no, no! I had eight more minutes, 12:23…" He mumbled repeatedly, "No, no, no…" as he ran out of the room, wincing from the blows he had received, and bounded down the steps as fast as his legs could carry him. Mr. Goodell tried to keep up, but by the time he got to the bottom of the first flight of stairs he heard the front door slam as Jarek ran out two stories below.

Jarek quickly stopped outside the door. He saw Thaddeus about 50 yards away and was glad the slamming door hadn't gotten his attention. Always one for keeping up appearances, Thaddeus strolled towards the center of the Village a little more slowly than usual to demonstrate that everything was just fine, despite his slightly bruised appearance and his urge to run towards the sound of the ringing bell, knowing it had something to do with the larger problem he was trying to manage.

Jarek watched Thaddeus's back closely as he quickly ran across the street, hiding in a row of maples. The peal of the bell moved him frantically forward as he darted from tree to tree, keeping a path parallel to the road yet unseen as he hurried beside Brethren's and along the evergreens towards Wickersham. It looked impossibly out of reach as Jarek gasped for air, pushing his legs as fast as they could carry him. The chime of the bell struck into his chest like an anvil.

Then Jarek felt a familiar chill. He heard Brother Armstrong's voice calling his name, *Jarek*, propelling him forward as fast as his legs could carry him. He listened to the sound of his own racing heart pounding in his ears. He heard Shaker voices rising to heaven in rhythmic chant. His eyes welled with tears as he heard the beep of Andrew's heart monitor keeping pace with his own, both in perfect double-time to the sound of the bell that rang out across the Village.

Jarek looked back and, seeing Thaddeus well up the hill and looking in the opposite direction, bolted the final distance towards the side door, rushing in and sprinting up the stairs. The bell continued to ring. He knew it had been too long. Lucas was dying.

CHAPTER 64

Jarek ascended the last flight to the top floor, breathless and exhausted. His mind raced and his heart broke when he realized the bell had stopped. He used his sleeve to wipe the blood off of his right eye so he could better see what he knew waited for him.

There was one entry in the book, the Book of the Mountain Kings, which he had read more than any other. Penned by Sister Abigail's hand, it was the account of Lucas's death, detailing what she had found in the bell tower. Jarek stifled a sob, knowing he had failed and that it was he himself who would see what she had seen: Lucas's shoes, still on his feet, swinging slowly back and forth as he hung, lifeless, from the belltower rope.

He quickly rounded the corner from the top step, turning down the hallway as a feeling of defeated dread hung on his soul like an anchor. He would make himself look at the horrible sight that awaited him. He deserved it.

He lifted his eyes and gasped sharply at what he saw. It couldn't be.

"Lu-" he stopped and stared in wide-eyed disbelief. Before him stood Lucas, reticent but alive, and sister Abigail.

"Lucas?" he shouted and ran forward to embrace his friend. "You're al—" a choke of emotion took the words from his breathless chest. "You're alive," he added quietly.

Jarek looked at Sister Abigail tearfully, overwhelmed with gratitude that she had succeeded where he had failed. She had known when Lucas would make the fateful decision to ascend the ladder into the bell tower. She knew because Jarek had told her. Maybe he did something right after all. She wore a knowing and satisfied smile and held a pitchfork upright in her hand.

"But…the bell…" Jarek said.

"Yes, that was me. I am sorry about that, my dear boy," Abigail said. "I needed you to hurry."

"I don't understand."

Far below, they heard the sound of heavy boots ascending the steps. It was Thaddeus. Coming to raise hell.

"Abigail," Jarek said quickly. "Thaddeus killed Brother Armstrong. I saw it."

She looked into his eyes for a moment and gave him a knowing nod. "Hurry!" she said.

A ladder used to access the bell tower hung in its resting place on a row of pegs high on the hallway wall. Abigail took it down and quickly set it beneath the wide circular opening in the ceiling, gesturing to the boys to climb up. Lucas went first, then Jarek. "Quickly now," she said. Jarek stepped up into the circular platform that formed the structure's base and, seeing she had not yet started up the steps, reached his hand down and said, "Abigail, come on."

She didn't move. "No, Jarek," she said.

Jarek was stunned. "What?" he said.

He braced himself on the platform, and seeing he meant to climb down, Abigail quickly moved the ladder away. He looked down at her upturned face, watching him consider the 10 feet between the bell tower platform and the floor far below.

"You stay right there," she said. "Jarek, many of us have been fighting this fight for a long time, and finally, we'll make it right. I'll make it right."

She was strong of mind and body, but they both knew she could never overpower Thaddeus. He couldn't let her face him alone, but she made sure he had no choice.

"No, Abigail, you can't—" but she interrupted his protest.

"I'm sorry we brought you into this mess, Jarek. I'll cause you no more harm." She looked to where Lucas was and called up to the platform, "Lucas?"

"Sister Abigail," he said quietly.

"You stay perfectly quiet up there," she said sternly. "Not a sound, no matter what happens."

"Yes, ma'am," he said, his voice trembling at the suggestion of an uncertain outcome.

Jarek started to speak, "Abigail—"

"Shh..." she said, turning her head down the hall as steps approaching the top of the stairs came to a halt.

She looked back up, and in her eyes, Jarek saw a flicker of doubt and sorrow as to how this would end. She smiled at him with deep affection.

"Jarek," she said. She then bowed her head, offered a small curtsy, and turned out of sight.

CHAPTER 65

Large windows at either end of the long hallway cast a dim light along the white plaster walls. Thaddeus rounded the corner at the top of the stairs and squinted into the glare at the opposite end. He saw the silhouette of a slight woman in a long dress and bonnet, her right arm thrusting forward and her back leg lifting as her frame unwound like the crack of a whip. He then saw a faint blur, heard a "*whish!*" and felt an explosion of pain piercing his right leg. He looked down to see a pitchfork with its tongs buried mercilessly deep into his right thigh.

Thaddeus let out a guttural scream and crumbled, clutching his leg and looking toward the quickly approaching form in a state of agony and confusion.

Abigail grabbed the wooden end of the pitchfork, staring into Thaddeus's contorted face. The look in her eye as she gazed down at him let him know the gravity of his position. The memory of all those he had treated so cruelly strengthened her tiny hands as she gripped the wooden handle. He stifled a scream, feeling each click and crunch of ripping cartilage as she twisted.

She drew the fork out, and he looked down in panic as his pant leg became immediately soaked with blood. His hands shook around the wound, trying to stop the bleeding as he gasped for air.

Abigail was expressionless. No gritted teeth, no angry glare, but as one resigned to finish a task that needed completing. She drew the handle back and aimed at his chest. Thaddeus kicked his feet against the floor to get away, though his back was already against the wall, pleading "No, no, no…" as he looked up at her with fear in his eyes.

Abigail then looked at him, tilted her head, and, to his surprise, gently put down the pitchfork.

"Brother Thaddeus," she said quietly, as she would to a child. "Do you remember the night one year ago when you refused to let me take that child into the Village? That frigid night. A beautiful innocent child, not three days in our care, whom some desperate mother left with us—having faith in us, as people of God—to provide some shelter to her baby?"

Thaddeus nodded slowly, understanding that, of all his cruel deeds—some against those much more powerful than even he—it was his callous indifference to the life of an infant that would finally be the end of him.

His pant leg was soaked in blood, and his skin was pale.

Unseen above, Jarek looked down in a trance at the terrible events unfolding before him, hoping Thaddeus got what he deserved, yet terribly afraid that he might not. Lucas kept his back against the wall of the bell tower enclosure, the very presence of Thaddeus seeming to terrify him. Jarek watched Thaddeus try to get up in vain while holding the wounds on his injured leg as Abigail spoke again.

"Do you know what it's like, Brother, to long for a child? The profound sense of duty and meaning that so many of us hope for, but some of us are so sadly deprived of? Do you know what it's like to have prayers that you gave up on so many years ago finally answered by a gift from God—beautiful, helpless, and innocent—and to have that gift turned out into the cold by…evil?" She looked at him. "Then trying with every desperate ounce of your soul to save him while he freezes to death in your arms? Well. Your heart breaks. It breaks in ways that will never heal.

"But," she smiled, "I forget myself. This talk of duty and meaning and broken hearts. And God. I don't expect you to understand such things. But do you know, Brother, the unbearable pain the human body experiences when the flesh is frozen solid?"

She reached up with her gloved hands and untied her bonnet. Grabbing the front edge between three fingers, she slowly pulled it back off her head.

"…or being filled with the devil's liquid in the vain hope you'll feel less of a blade…"

She turned slowly so Thaddeus could see.

"…as it takes off your precious ear?"

Thaddeus stifled his shock as he saw the tiny, mangled lump at the back of her cheek. All that remained of what was once her left ear.

Jarek's heart ached for the gentle woman he knew her to be and begrudged her none of her anger. This mystery, at least, made sense now. He steeled himself for what he thought was coming next as she tugged at her gloved fingertips, one by one, removing the right glove and then pausing.

She knew Thaddeus was helpless, and she had waited too long for this moment to hurry.

"Or can you imagine what it's like, Brother," she said, punctuating the last word with disdain, "to be helplessly tied to a bed while a surgeon grips your hand, like a tree stump, ignoring your pleas for mercy—*Stay still!'*—ignoring your screams, '*Stay still! Stay still!'*—the words you'll hear in your mind every day for years—as you feel the terrible vibrations through your entire body…"

She removed the left glove.

"…as he roughly saws through flesh and bone, cutting off the useless fingers that had frozen solid?"

Jarek watched in stunned silence. Thaddeus's mouth was open, and he stared in horror at the two mangled purple stumps where the outside fingers of her left hand once were.

Thaddeus scanned quickly down the hall for some way out. Jarek looked hard at Thaddeus as Abigail stepped out of sight momentarily. When she returned from a table several feet away, she held his ledger in her right hand; his eyes widened at seeing it.

"Oh, have you been looking for this? Well, I've kept it safe, don't worry," she smiled, adding in an assuring tone; "Now, I understand you might be concerned that I would provide this to authorities, as I believe there's enough here to put you away for the rest of your life." She tossed the book onto the floor, and it landed with a thump as she added, "But what would be the use, at this point…"

These last words made her intentions clear to Thaddeus; Jarek could tell by the look on his face. It was a look that turned to one of horror as she turned away and back once again. When Jarek looked towards Abigail, he quickly understood why.

CHAPTER 66

Jarek had seen Abigail's skill with a seed bag chisel many times. A metal handle on one end and a flat blade on the other, it was ideal for cutting open large sacks of seed to divide their contents into smaller portions. She now held one in her left hand, speaking slowly as she approached.

"'The time will come when God will draw the line between the righteous and the wicked, and the wicked cannot pass over it.' That's Mother Ann," Abigail said, "Have you heard of her, Thaddeus?" She looked him in the eye, adding quietly, "You should never have come here. You, *Brother*, are the wicked. *I* am the line. You will *not* pass over me…"

Thaddeus then managed to sit up, but in a flash, Abigail struck him in the neck with the heel of her boot, stepping onto his chest with one foot as the other stood firmly upon one of his hands.

"I don't believe in vengeance, Thaddeus. But justice, yes. Now…" she added slowly, "*stay still.*" She gripped the chisel and lifted her hand, ready to thrust the blade into his extended fingers.

Abigail was not herself. Her kind soul had been too damaged by Thaddeus already, and Jarek knew what was about to happen—even by her own hand—would only make it worse.

"Abigail, no!" he shouted from above. She quickly glared up as Thaddeus, having seen more than his share of bloody interactions and overplayed his distress, saw the moment he'd been waiting for. He swung out his good leg with all his might, kicking her behind the knees as she howled in pain and fell to the wooden floor, the chisel falling from her hand and sliding out of reach.

Jarek jumped from the bell tower platform to the floor below with a yell, crumbling onto his side and holding one of his legs. Thaddeus, now well aware of his presence, was energized by the opportunity to put an end to both of them at once.

Seeing Jarek was helpless, Thaddeus focused on Abigail, taking his riding crop firmly in his hand and lurching towards her as she tried to get up. He swung for her head with the steel end, missing the mark as she rolled onto her side, but striking her hard in the shoulder as she let out a gasp and tried to hurry to her feet.

The next swing struck her firmly above her mangled ear; she reeled, clawing in confusion at the worn wooden floor to pull herself away. Thaddeus watched with delight before grabbing her and flipping her onto her back. He placed the crop beside her on the floor and sat his full weight on her mid-section as she looked up at him, fighting in vain, entirely helpless under his weight and the strength of his hands. He didn't bother with the crop. She had been a thorn in his side; he wanted the satisfaction of something much more personal in putting her to an end.

He wrapped his hands around the base of her neck and squeezed with all his might, staring into her eyes, wide open and terrified. "Shh," he said, as her hands tried to pry his wrists from around her throat, adding, "Almost there. Stay still." Her small boots kicked against the floor as her wide-opened mouth fought for air. "Shhh, shhh, shhh," he whispered as she stared up at him. His mocking words steeled her resolve, but the fear of death overwhelmed her, and tears filled her eyes. Thaddeus looked back to see Jarek struggling to get to his feet in the background and, realizing he had time, turned his face back to Abigail.

Her hands trembled helplessly around his sinewed wrists. The satisfaction of his imminent final conquest roused his blood as the breath rushing through his gritted teeth sent droplets of spit spraying down onto her face. "Stay still," he said quietly with a comforting nod as his grip remained. "Stay still…"

Abigail's resistance ebbed. She had no strength left. He had won. His evil face would be the last thing she saw on earth, and the weight of this reality sunk in as she breathed her final breaths, overwhelmed with sorrow for all of those whom she loved and whom she had failed in the tragedy of her defeat. She let go of his wrists, and he smiled, the satisfaction of watching the life fade from her face taking all his ravenous attention.

Lucas looked down from his hiding spot above, terrified to see this woman—as much a mother to him as his own—in grave danger. He broke his promise and cried out, "Abigail!"

Grief overwhelmed her face, and she mouthed the words "No…No…" in a silent cry. Thaddeus turned his face upwards towards the bell tower. "Hello, Lucas!" he called out with a smile, delighted with how this had all come together.

As Thaddeus savored his victory, Jarek saw his opportunity. He charged into Thaddeus's side with a furious grunt, upending him from Abigail and into the wall. The air rushed into Abigail lungs as she gasped aloud and rolled onto her side, nearly unable to see the soles of Jarek's boots arcing against the floor as he struggled. But even Jarek's strength was no match for Thaddeus, who placed his right foot behind Jarek's left, pushing his upper body away as Jarek lost his balance and quickly stumbled backward. He kept his eyes on Thaddeus long enough to see him rush forward and raise his arm. The last thing Jarek saw was the riding crop flashing towards him before cracking him square in the temple.

Thaddeus smiled up at Lucas, who peered down from above. He quickly moved the ladder below the opening, holding firmly to his riding crop as he began his ascent, and Lucas's terrified face disappeared.

Jarek blinked his eyes open and gathered himself in time to see the anvil-shaped "T" on Thaddeus's boots vanish overhead as he heard Lucas scream. He quickly scrambled up the ladder with one foot and both hands, lifting himself through the opening in time to see the riding crop in Thaddeus's outstretched arm, ready to come crashing down onto Lucas as he crouched against the wall. Jarek quickly grabbed the crop, and Thaddeus responded by delivering a blow to Jarek's ribs, sending him to the floor, before turning back to Lucas. Abigail had just stepped up from the top rung of the ladder and ran forward to jump on Thaddeus from behind. He spun and pushed her away with a fist to the chest, but Jarek had risen to his feet and sprung towards him, grabbing the crop again from behind before it could strike his friend. Thaddeus quickly turned, looked Jarek in the eye and thrust his other arm into Jarek's stomach. Jarek's eyes opened wide. He gasped. They both froze for an instant as Thaddeus gave him a satisfied grin, relishing the moment just long enough to give Abigail the time she needed. Her hand reached discreetly along the waist of her dress.

She let out a furious scream and swung her arm towards his mid-section with all her might. He grunted. He froze. He looked down in shock to see two knitting needles plunged deep into his side. Abigail held on tight and pushed deeper as Thaddeus's head fell back. He let out a desperate howl, gasping for breath as his arms flailed and his fists swung wildly in the air. Lucas, behind Thaddeus on the platforms edge, grabbed the doubled loop of the belltower rope, and tossed it over Thaddeus's head from behind.

Thaddeus reeled backward, reaching his hand towards Abigail. She looked him in the eye as he tried to gain his balance, held her hand out in response, and then—with a slight curtsy—said, "Brother Thaddeus." She then planted her small hand in the middle of his chest and gave him a shove. Thaddeus stepped back to catch himself, but fear widened his eyes as his foot missed the platform. His body arched backward as he fell into the open space.

Thaddeus fell only a couple of feet before the rope stopped his descent, tightening quickly around his neck under the weight of his immense frame. His bloody fingers grasped at the tightening coil as his feet kicked in the open air. Overhead—the bell rang.

CHAPTER 67

For the first and last time in the Village's history—the belltower chimed three times during the day.

The customary chime at noon was followed by an unexpected one at 12:14 p.m. The third and final chime, at 12:23, was now for the consummate criminal who had terrorized the Village for so long, and whose body was floating rhythmically up and down against the weight of the immense bell that sounded across the Village.

Brothers and sisters throughout the Village looked up in confusion, unaware that they were hearing the sound of their liberation. Those first to arrive would look up to witness a pair of black boots, the best that money could buy, appearing and disappearing through the opening overhead, an anvil-shaped "T" emblazoned on the soles for all to see.

Jarek and Lucas stood quietly by. Abigail kneeled. "Heavenly Father," she said, "Thank you for your provision. Thank you for your justice. Thank you for deliv…"

CLANG!

Abigail jumped, stopping her prayer at the sound of metal hitting the floor below the bell tower. She turned towards Thaddeus's hanging form and quickly realized that something had fallen from his hands, now relaxed in death. Looking from the platform to the floor far below, she saw the fallen object come into focus: it was the seed chisel. At that moment, she heard a low groan from her left. She shot her eyes towards her friends, just in time to see Jarek collapse and fall to his back.

"Jarek!" Abigail shouted, rushing to his side. A large dark stain soaked the middle of his shirt and the top of his pants.

"No, no, oh dear God…" she said, pulling his shirt up, frantically looking for the source. She gasped and stifled a cry when she saw it. Thaddeus had driven the seed chisel straight into Jarek's abdomen, creating a wound that was wide, deep, and bleeding profusely. "Oh, Jarek, no." Her hands scrambled nervously for a handkerchief in her pocket.

Lucas fell to his knees beside Jarek, shock and panic on his face as he stared helplessly at his friend. Abigail tried to slow the bleeding as her shoulders started to shake with small sobs.

"Jarek, my dear boy. No," she said in refusal, uselessly wiping his bleeding stomach like a mother tidying up her child. "No, dear," she cried.

Jarek saw how bad it was, and, to his surprise, he wasn't scared. He reached to his mid-section, watching Abigail's grief-stricken and determined face as he placed his hands on hers to stop her efforts.

"Abigail," he said calmly.

"No," she said, pursing her lips and shaking her head, "No, Jarek." Her voice wavered as she refused his attempts, wiping the blood more quickly, though the bleeding had not slowed.

"Abigail," he said again.

He touched her hand and looked at her face. She stopped, and for a moment, she stared beyond his wounded body, her face void of expression, her teeming brain overwhelmed by this new grief. A moment later, her entire frame shook again with sobs.

Abigail turned her head away to collect herself before looking at Thaddeus—he who had taken so much from her. She then took a deep breath, clenched her fists, and leveled a scream at his lifeless body, so furious that it shook the walls. It echoed down the halls. It rang through the ages into the ears of every inhabitant of the old structure: living and dead, past, present, and future. Another strange sound in the air to fuel generations of stories about Shaker ghosts.

Abigail closed her eyes, steadied herself to face the brutal reality that was undeniably before her, and opened them slowly to face Jarek.

"Jarek, my dear boy," she said, her distress showing clearly as tears ran down her cheeks. She pushed his hair from his forehead with one hand, the other remaining on his stomach to slow the bleeding for whatever extra moments it might provide.

He looked up at her with admiration as she steadied her trembling lip, squinting her eyes in mock scrutiny and saying with affection, "*You*!"

Jarek smiled at the reference, remembering what she had said to him the first time they had met, when she was trying to decide what he was doing in the Village, and he was, too. This time, it was said not with the suspicion of a stranger but with the deepest affection her stalwart heart had to offer. It brought a smile to Jarek's face, conveying all he appreciated about this strong, persistent, and wonderful woman he was fortunate enough to call his friend.

Lucas's anguished face made his overwhelming grief clear, and, as Jarek saw it, he smiled at him, nodding towards Thaddeus. Lucas nodded back and forced a smile, the immense sense of relief he felt with every fiber of his being tempered by the imminent and unbearable loss of the one who had rescued him from the unimaginable cruelty he had experienced. The only brother he'd ever had.

They heard footsteps as villagers approached below, gasping at the blood on the floor, the red-stained seed chisel nearby, and Thaddeus's boots swinging from the belltower overhead.

"Abigail, I…" Jarek stammered weakly, trying to find the words to tell her what she and Lucas meant to him.

"I know, dear, I know. No time for that," she said, placing one hand on his shoulder. "Rather…" she said, leaning over to wrap her arms around him, giving him the firmest hug her body could muster. He felt a sob in her chest as she withdrew, and he turned to look at Lucas.

"Jarek," Lucas said with a cry, leaning down and putting his head against Jarek's chest, his body silently heaving with grief. At that moment, Jarek realized what it must have felt like for Andrew; hugging your kid brother, encouraging him, and then saying goodbye. He put his arms around Lucas and held him tight, the same way Andrew had hugged him at the end.

"Lucas, listen. You're gonna be just fine, you know? Your obliging place," Jarek said, looking at him with a smile. "You'll get there. I know it."

Lucas couldn't speak but nodded with a smile, wiping tears from his eyes as Jarek said, "Hey," and Lucas looked up; "I'll see you there."

Jarek was surprised to feel something come over him he hadn't felt in a long time. Not fear, not hopelessness, not the gaping void of a loss that had defined him. He was content.

The mystery that haunted the Conscientia for over 100 years had been solved. Brother Armstrong beckoned Jarek back for reasons he didn't understand, but stopping Thaddeus and saving Lucas had become the most significant undertaking of his life. As he now knew, it would also be the last.

CHAPTER 68

"So this is what it's like," Jarek whispered.

"What's that dear?" Abigail's bottom lip trembled with emotion as she leaned forward to hear more clearly.

"Death," he replied. "This is it." His eyes looked to hers for a moment, and he added, "It's not so bad…"

Abigail ran her hand over his head. "God bless you, Jarek," she said, wiping her tears. "Send us gifts."

He nodded his head and offered a weak smile.

They heard a gasp in Jarek's shallowing breath. Suddenly, his eyes widened at a point in the air beyond them.

The Conscientia had called him by name, and he had saved the Village, earning him, in his final moments, the most profound of their God-given gifts. Jarek's eyes brightened as a smile crossed his lips.

"Andrew…" he said. Jarek held his hand out into the air with what little strength he had left. Abigail turned to look, seeing the figure of a young boy before her, his own arm extended, holding Jarek's hand.

Jarek alone heard his brother's words and whispered to the air in response, "I will. I will." He then smiled and said, "My big brother. Greater than the greatest show on earth."

Abigail and Lucas knelt beside him and wept.

Jarek lay back on the floor, and his head slowly rested to one side.

His eyes closed.

They heard him exhale one final time. Then . . . silence.

He was gone.

CHAPTER 69

"Matt? Matt, did you hear that?"

Drummy had marveled at McCracken's ability to sit silent and stone still, keeping close watch over Jarek by the light of a small desktop lamp as the hours passed. Drummy himself fell asleep splayed out across an easy chair, hugging a pillow.

"Matt!" McCracken's voice startled him awake, and he jumped up.

"What—what is it?" He asked, sitting up quickly and looking towards Jarek.

"A cough or a grunt, something, I don't know." McCracken was worried.

Drummy jumped up in a hurry, leaning over Jarek with an ear turned towards him to listen.

"Is he breathing?" he listened. "Earl, he's not breathing. He's not breathing!"

McCracken stood up and listened closely. "Oh no, oh good Lord, no." He quickly looked Jarek over and sighed.

Jarek was still and silent.

McCracken pursed his lips, squeezing his eyes shut. "Oh, Jarek. Jarek, I'm sorry," he said, then turning to Drummy. "Matt, I'm sorry. I did this. Dear God, I'm so sorry."

"No," Drummy said flatly, his voice faltering as he shook his head in shock and refusal, then snapping at McCracken "*NO!*" He quickly turned towards the bed, leaning forward, his hands outstretched in growing panic as he shouted, "Jarek!"

Nothing.

"*Jarek*! JAREK!" he shouted again, grabbing Jarek's shoulder and giving it a firm shake.

Suddenly, Jarek shot bolt upright in bed sending Drummy and McCracken jumping backward as Jarek's eyes opened wide in surprise and he let out a yell: "*AHHH!* God, you scared the hell out of me!!"

His teachers, speechless at the tail end of a journey through panic, death, grief, and resurrection that had taken all of 30 seconds, stared at him in wide-eyed shock.

"What?!" he said with the confused impatience of someone shaken out of a deep sleep. "Jesus, will you stop looking at me like that?"

Drummy breathed a sigh of relief and looked at McCracken, who stood, mouth open, and spoke the only word he could muster: "Wow."

Jarek looked around, trying to figure out where he was, then got his bearings and shouted, "Wait!" He quickly rubbed his hands across his stomach, lifted his shirt, and exhaled. He was elated to find himself intact. "It's not true," he stammered, smiling. "It's not true." His relief gave way to exhaustion as he lay back and closed his eyes.

"What's not true, Jarek?" Drummy asked.

"When you die," he mumbled.

"When who dies?" Drummy was confused; Jarek was quickly nodding off.

"When you die," Jarek added, "you don't. You don't die."

And with that, he fell immediately back to sleep.

CHAPTER 70

Back in the Village, Abigail embraced Lucas, both sobbing and overwhelmed with grief. She led him to the ladder and prepared to explain all that had transpired to those gathering below.

Before they descended, Lucas, heartbroken and overwhelmed, turned to take one final look at his friend, lifeless on the floor. "Abigail," he whispered.

"I know, dear," she replied, looking towards the ladder.

"*Abigail,*" he said more insistently. She turned around to look, and she gasped.

"Oh, heavenly Father," she said, neither of them could believe their eyes.

"Lucas..." she said in a quivering voice. Where Jarek's battered body had been just moments before, lifeless and defeated, there was nothing. An empty floor. She knew what it meant.

"My dear boy!" she said to Lucas, pulling him close and smiling down at him. "He's alive. He's ALIVE!"

She lifted her hands over her head, closing her eyes and whispering, "Thank you, God, thank you." As her joy got the best of her, she began clapping her hands and chanting, "Thank you, God, thank you, God, thank you, God, Jarek, Jarek, Jarek" as she joyfully stomped her feet in a makeshift dance that had Lucas smiling from ear to ear.

He had gone back. He was alive.

CHAPTER 71

Jarek awoke to sunlight streaming through McCracken's window. For the past 10 hours, he had been finally, dreamlessly, soundly asleep. The beatings he had taken both in and out of his dreams had him feeling much worse for wear, but he was at least well-rested for a change. McCracken looked like he had been hit by a truck but was in good spirits.

"Son," he said with red eyes and a smile of relief. Jarek could tell he knew everything. Of course he did. It was history now, and he was the Conscientia.

Jarek looked at his watch. "Crap! I'm supposed to be at Worthing's office in 15 minutes." Whatever their own adventure had been, the fact was his former dorm was smoldering in embers on the other side of campus. It was a greater tragedy than the school had ever seen, and Jarek was right in the middle of it.

"Well, I guess this is the day I finally get kicked out," Jarek added, standing up, assembling himself, and heading for the door.

"Jarek," McCracken called out from across the room.

Jarek stopped and turned around, seeing that McCracken had the book in his hands, "The Book of the Mountain Kings" scribbled across the cover. "Jarek, what you've done here," he looked down at the book and then up again. "It's...." he widened his glassy eyes, "it's... astounding. Do you understand?"

He didn't know exactly what McCracken had read, but other matters were more pressing at the moment.

"Yeah, I think so…I guess we did it, huh?" he said, unable to say more. His head was spinning with questions about what it all meant, what came next, and what was about to happen in his meeting with Worthing.

"*You* did, Jarek. Thank you, son. Thank you."

"Okay, Mr. McCracken," Jarek said, squirming a bit under his gaze and adding, "I'll see you later," as he quickly walked out.

Jarek moved quickly through campus, a feeling of dread weighing upon him as he headed to Worthing's office. Where would he go? And what on earth was he going to tell his parents? He knew the look of deep disappointment he'd see on their faces. The very thought of it made his stomach sink.

He walked towards Wickersham, overcome for a moment by the idea that he was there mere hours before—though, in reality, it was over a century ago—involved in the fight of his life. A fight that ended with the death of Thaddeus. He tried to shake the thoughts off and focus on the fire, the police station, and his coming expulsion. God, would he ever get a break?

As he approached the entryway, his thoughts were too distracting for him to see the students gathered around watching him enter. Or Morak among them, glaring at him and saying something Jarek didn't at first hear as he passed him by.

Jarek turned his head and looked Morak in the eye.

"What?" Jarek said.

Morak repeated angrily but quietly so only Jarek could hear it, "I said, are you going to rat me out?"

Jarek looked at him blankly. Morak continued.

"Here's a pointer. Remember what your face looked like in the mirror this morning and realize this is when you say 'no.'" He moved closer to Jarek, leaning in and looking over Jarek's face, assessing the damage he had done. He smiled.

It was more than Jarek could take, after it all. He had more or less forgotten about Morak until this moment. But suddenly, every insult he had given him, every taunt, and every humiliation in front of Beth, of which there were more than a few, rushed at once back into his mind. He looked at Morak's face, and he saw Thaddeus. Younger and less experienced, but with the same ill will, evil intent, and string of cruelties that would someday lie in his wake. He pictured himself sinking his fist into Morak's face over and over again and dug as deep as he possibly could to restrain himself.

Jarek had just slayed a dragon in Thaddeus. He looked at Morak and saw something much less significant.

"No, David," Jarek said, shaking his head.

Morak's eyes widened in surprise at the very personal use of his first name.

Jarek added, "If I give you any thought at all, it will be out of pity."

Morak looked confused as Jarek added with a shrug, "Don't let the past scare you, man. Even you can learn something from it." He then turned away.

Jarek's accuracy as well as his indifference incensed Morak.

"What? What'd you say to me? What am I scared of POE?" He struggled against the grip of a couple of friends who held onto him. "Get back here and say it to my face!" he shouted as Jarek walked away.

Jarek saw Beth's face among the crowd. She gave him a resigned smile, glad for his restraint, as he walked directly to her, pulled her close, and surprised her with an unapologetic final kiss. He knew it wouldn't change her mind, and he didn't expect it to, but she kissed him back passionately before he quickly turned to walk away.

"Jarek, Jarek, wait." She pulled him close and whispered in his ear, "Jarek. The fire. The police are on their way."

His eyes widened in surprise. "For my meeting with Worthing. Crap," he said.

"First, I have something to show you." Beth quickly grabbed his hand and pulled him towards the parking lot behind the Dairy Barn, where her car was parked. "Hurry up!" she added.

CHAPTER 72

"Wait!" Jarek ran to the back of the Dairy Barn and down the steps into the infirmary as Beth followed.

He quickly gathered what was left of his things. "What about Worthing?" he asked.

"Forget Worthing," she said, nervously rubbing her car key between her fingers. "They're kicking you out anyway; he can wait."

Drummy then came rushing through the door, catching his breath. Jarek was relieved to see his face.

"Jarek," Drummy said. "I've been looking for you. Jesus, that was a bit much, no?" Jarek could tell he was referring to the death of Thaddeus, which meant he knew everything. They had a lot to discuss.

Beth was fond of Drummy as well, but there was no time. "Worthing has the police on their way," she told him. "We need to go right now."

Drummy looked blankly at Beth as Jarek brushed past her towards the door. Drummy stepped into his path to block his way.

"Hey, in case they cart you off in a hurry," he said, "one more thing." Drummy stepped in front of Jarek with a smile, and Jarek realized this was goodbye.

"Gosh. Shit." Jarek said, suddenly halted with emotion. Drummy was the one person who had believed in him, who lifted him up when he was at his lowest, and who inspired and challenged him. It hit him like a ton of bricks.

"Mr. Drummy, if it wasn't for you…" Jarek couldn't find the words.

"If it weren't for me, you'd have done it yourself," Drummy said with an assuring nod.

"No," Jarek said, "No way."

In an instant, Jarek had put his arms around him and squeezed him tight—his mentor and his guide.

"Thank you, Mr. Drummy," he said as he held on tight with glassy eyes. "You taught me more than you know."

Drummy widened his eyes as if taken aback by Jarek's emotion and smiled. "No, Jarek. Thank you. You know…you're going to do amazing things. You already have." Drummy added.

"You think so?" Jarek asked.

"I know so," he said. "Now get going."

Jarek headed for the door, turning around to look at Mr. Drummy one final time.

"Goodbye, Mr. Drummy," he said with a nod.

Drummy smiled at him. "Jarek, there's a world outside," he said. "I'll see you when you get back."

Jarek took it in, grabbed his duffle bag, and ran out.

CHAPTER 73

Jarek and Beth quickly ascended the steps and exited into the parking lot.

He took a deep breath and said solemnly, "I'm not coming back."

She was quiet for a moment as they hurried towards her car.

"Alphecca," she said.

He slowed down for a moment. "What?"

"Alphecca. Alphecca is my favorite star."

"What the…?"

"She's in love with Theseus. She tries to save his life…but fails.

"You always know what to say," he said sarcastically.

She added, "I, on the other hand, don't fail." She walked around to the passenger side door of the blue BMW 5 series her dad gave her for school and tossed the keys across the roof to Jarek. "Get in. We can do this—we really have to go."

"We?" he said.

He stared at her, his face expressionless, for another moment. She stared back and gave him a wink, adding, "Yeah, 'we.' Get in. You're driving."

They drove out along the small dirt road that led to the Tannery so they wouldn't be noticed. They could see much of the entire school community gathered in the distance to their right as they made a left onto the main road, speeding away under the canopy of trees, dust rising behind their vehicle as it vanished around the next bend.

"Jarek, I have something to tell you," Beth said. "McCracken made me swear on my life that I wouldn't forget."

She took out several sheets of copy paper covered in intermittent blocks of text in a hand that now looked very familiar to him.

"What is it?" he said eagerly, worried about another complication.

"Well, brace yourself," Beth said. She took a deep breath and began: "An account of the suicide of—"

"Wait, what?" Jarek looked towards her nervously. "It can't be."

"Shhh, Jarek. Let me read."

"Sorry," he said, looking back at the road.

Beth continued: "An account of the suicide of Brother Thaddeus."

"*What?!*" Jarek said, wide-eyed with surprise. "God, brilliant!"

She read him the entry, detailing the moments of discontentedness that its author had witnessed in Thaddeus as of late. Village life just didn't agree with him. It then described the discovery of his body hanging from the belltower, stating very clearly that he had proceeded there under his own volition and ended his life. Jarek listened in awe of the entry and with great affection for its author, one Sister Abigail Dorrance.

He thought of Abigail, in her dour wit, announcing to the village that Thaddeus had died by suicide, and then inserting the same account in the annals of history by creating this entry.

He remembered words she once said to him, "History, my dear, is written by the victors," and smiled from ear to ear. A moment later, the ache of another loss moved through his chest as he was reminded that he would never see her again.

Jarek and Beth fixed their eyes ahead as they sped down the main road in town. "Turn here!" she said, directing him to a sharp right, which he took in a skid.

"This looks familiar, somehow," he said.

CHAPTER 74

"There's one more," she said, as she flipped to the second paper in her hands. "An account of the departure of Lucas Dorrance from the Village."

Jarek didn't know Lucas had left the Village. He looked at Beth, stunned and eager to know more. But then his eyes widened as he looked out the window and blurted out, "Wait, what is this? I know this place…"

Beth clung to the door as Jarek propelled the car forward down a brush-covered driveway for a hundred yards before skidding to a halt in front of an abandoned old farmhouse.

"I was here," he said. "Jesus, I was here. 125 years ago."

"McCracken found some interesting things in the book after you returned," she said. "I brought you here to show you something." She smiled as he began to understand where they were.

"Is it…Mr. Goodell's?" he asked, adding, "Yes. Yes, this is it." He looked around wide-eyed at how different it was.

"The fields were full. The house was new and beautiful. I was here. This was his… he was my friend," he said, as a sad smile crossed his lips. "I helped him right here—right there," he said, pointing to the old barn. "His wife sat here," he nodded towards the porch as his voice trailed off in sadness. He looked at the trees penetrating open holes in the floor towards the overhang above.

Jarek had a realization at that moment, which, due to everything that had happened, hadn't yet occurred to him. He cast his eyes down as it set in. All those he had come to know so well in the past months were gone. In fact, they had been gone for over a century. He was overwhelmed by the feeling that everyone he knew had died all at once.

He stopped momentarily, gathered himself, and looked at the house again. The windows had been boarded up for so long that the boards were rotten and falling.

"Just the…" his eyes wandered across what was once a beautiful but quiet home, "…just the two of them. I wonder if it was always…you know…always theirs."

"Jarek, it was. It was always theirs. And…that's why we're here. It, um…" he saw the redness in her eyes as she continued slowly, "…it wasn't just the two of them."

He stared at her in disbelief. She pointed across the expanse behind the house, past the low brush that had overgrown a formerly lush field, to a tiny hill raised just enough to be seen across the tall weeds. On the hill were gravestones—at least a dozen of them.

"What? That's not possible. They didn't have children; they wanted them, but they couldn't.

"It's not possible…" he repeated and took off as fast as he could for the small hill in the distance. He ran through the brush and weeds, pushing through overgrown branches. She followed behind him as he tripped, stumbled before the frontmost stone, and looked up.

Mr. Clarence Goodell
Beloved Husband and Father
1826–1906

"What?" Jarek said, looking directly to the right at the stone beside it. That of Mrs. Goodell, Clarence's quiet and nurturing wife, who had spent much of her life heartbroken at never having the family she desired.

Sarah Goodell
Beloved Wife and Mother
1832—1910

"Mother?" Jarek said in disbelief, quickly scanning the other stones. "Mother of who?" Jarek's eyes moved quickly to the right at the others.

Margaret Croft Goodell
Beloved Wife and Mother
1861—1928

"I don't get it—wife of who?!" he said impatiently.

Before and behind this stone, there were more. The children of this beloved mother and their families.

He looked at the larger stone directly beside that of Margaret Croft Goodell. His mouth fell open as he caught his breath in disbelief:

Lucas Dorrance Goodell
1855—1926
Beloved Son, Husband, and Father

"What? Lucas?" Stunned, he looked back at Beth. "How is… how is it possible? And…" he stammered, "how did you know?"

"It's in the book," Beth said quietly.

"What is? They…" He couldn't think straight.

Beth spoke calmly. "Jarek, after you left, after everything happened, they adopted him. Lucas lived with Clarence and his wife. Jarek, this…this is his family."

"His fa…" Jarek's voice was choked with emotion. "His family?"

"Yes," she said, her eyes welling as she smiled at him. "This is his wife," she said, pointing to the stone of Margaret Goodell. "These are his children. His grandchildren."

Jarek imagined Lucas. He saw him finally finding the family he never had. Finding the peace that cruelly and unfairly eluded him for years.

Mrs. Goodell, sitting in her living room with Lucas as a young man nurturing him when he was sick. Mr. Goodell, at the beginning of a family meal on a summer evening, smiling, finally, at the loved ones that now surrounded his table, as his wife called their grandchildren in from playing in the fields, and they gathered around to pray.

And Lucas. Dear Lucas. Growing up until the house was his house, and the family was his family, and the farm was his farm. Folks coming around of a Sunday afternoon saying hello Lucas. Good morning, Lucas. And he would get the milk and put the plates on the table, and they would sit together as long as they wanted. Everyone would be very obliging, and they would look at him from across the table with deep appreciation in their eyes: "You're a good man, Lucas. Much obliged, Lucas. We love you, Lucas."

"He...he made it." Jarek said. A feeling of immense release and happiness took him over at the thought.

"Made it where?" Beth asked.

"His obliging place. It was just like this—this was it—God, it's perfect—he was here. His obliging place." Jarek said, his own eyes now welling with tears.

"One more thing," Beth said, "that Abigail wrote in the book years later."

Beth unfolded the final paper in her hands, took a deep breath, and read aloud.

> *I now have a family with my Brothers and Sisters on the mountain and another in the valley. Upon my frequent visits, Mr. Goodell and Sarah have provided for me a place of love and comfort such as I have never known. Watching Lucas grow into the strong and bright-eyed young man he was meant to be is the greatest joy I could*

> *imagine, yet he always finds ways to increase my happiness. His deep gratitude to the Goodells and me for the life we helped him find and the unconventional family we now compose has inclined him to honor all of us in a manner that will stand the test of time.*

Jarek stared eagerly at Beth as she continued.

> *The name of the Goodells and my own, that of humble Sister Dorrance, are to come together—to my great delight—to form a new surname for his children. It is with no small degree of surprise that I realize this name is not new to me but was borne many years ago by a dear friend whose time among us, though brief, has so greatly—and so happily—affected the outcome of our lives. I hope one day he might read the words that I write and know, surer than he has ever been in an uncertain world, that we are grateful, that he is loved, and that he has brought me more joy than I have ever known. As I begin my waning years, my happiness is complete. Lucas's children will bear the name 'Dorrell.'*

Jarek quickly looked up, blinking twice to clear his tears.

"Dorrell?" he said, shocked by what he was hearing, "*Dorrell?*"

He quickly scanned the other three stones. A boy born in 1884 and a girl born in 1886. Jarek's mouth fell open seeing the last one.

Elijah Dorrell
Devoted Husband and Father
1883—1924
Absent in the body, present with the Lord

"Beth, oh my God."

Beth smiled and recited, "In March of 1883..."

Jarek finished for her, "...*Elijah Dorrell came to be.* Beth," Jarek said, dumbfounded, "this is him. Elijah Dorrell. This is my..." he paused, "my great grandfather. This is him; I can't believe it. That means Lucas is..."

"Family." Beth smiled. "He's your great, great grandfather."

"I…maybe that's why Lucas…" Jarek choked up for a moment. "Why Lucas looked so much like Andrew."

"Yes," Beth said with a nod and a sad smile as Jarek wiped a tear from his cheek with one shaking hand. "And I suppose it's why Brother Armstrong came to you for help. You could never say no to helping someone like Lucas. Maybe Brother Armstrong knew that. And it seems he also knew you were the right person to ask because if someone didn't help Lucas, if someone didn't stop him from hurting himself…"

Jarek interrupted, "…then I never would have been born."

They sat quietly for several minutes, listening to two cardinals as they chirped and dipped in and out of the pine branches around them.

Beth broke the silence as they stared at the stones. "Look!" she said, pointing under Lucas's name.

Partially obscured by grass and earth from the settling of time, they saw the top of a row of letters at the base. Jarek knelt before the stone, quickly scraping leaves and frozen dirt away as it cleared into view.

Jarek saw the inscription, preceded by his own initials: "J.D."

He stared in disbelief. He saved Lucas, and Lucas lived a full life right here in this spot. Abigail had told Lucas, in due time, the truth about Jarek. Where—or when—he was from, and how he was called to the Village. Lucas thought Jarek might come to find him someday, and he had.

Jarek's heart was in his throat. The final words from the friend he loved so dearly and fought so hard to save were right before him.

He read the inscription in full. "J.D.—So much, so very much, obliged."

Jarek pursed his lips and held a fist to his mouth to steady himself.

"Dear God." He said in disbelief. "Thank you, Lucas," he mumbled. "I mean…thanks, Grandpa." Overwhelmed with fatigue, shock, and relief, Jarek sobbed as Beth stood quietly by with a hand on his shoulder.

CHAPTER 75

In an old Shaker Village in New Lebanon, NY, there stands a brick monument to Shaker ingenuity known as Wickersham. The very top of this building provides an ideal vantage point for viewing much of the community, as it did for Shaker elders and crew leaders hoping to see the day's progress in the fields. If one of those elders had been looking down towards the main road at that very moment in 1867, they would have seen a police wagon entering the community. Beside the police wagon was the horse-drawn cart of an undertaker, arriving to retrieve the body of a well-known leader of the community who, by all accounts, had hanged himself from the bell tower rope.

As the police wagon entered the Village, another was on its way out. A kind and very reasonable gentleman held the reigns of this very reasonable wagon, led by a very reasonable horse, and departing the Village for the last time. Though no one had reason to look too closely at the back of the wagon, if they had, they would have seen the barely visible feet of a young man sticking out from between several large sacks of grain, covered by a length of burlap carefully draped over them to deter the coming rain.

The horse clopped along, and the gentleman tugged the reigns without a care in the world. Occasionally, he turned his head back to the materials and spoke quietly: "You're doing fine, son," he said, as the boy did his best to keep still and remain unseen. "I'm proud of you, Lucas."

Lucas smiled ear to ear, eager for the new life he was escaping to. The one he had always wanted. And in the dark quiet of the creaking wagon, he thanked God for his deliverance as tears of joy rolled down his hidden cheeks.

As they passed the meeting house, rising above the rattle of the wagon wheels, they heard the sounds of the most exuberant singing they had ever heard. Because within that meeting house, should they have entered, they would have witnessed all the brothers and sisters of the community dancing with joy they had never before known. Tearful faces smiled at each other and to heaven as hands waved, feet stomped, and voices were lifted in praise and celebration for their new beginning.

(Song: "Simple Gifts")

'Tis the gift to be simple, 'tis the gift to be free,
(CLAP) (CLAP)
'Tis the gift to come down where we ought to be,
(STOMP) (STOMP)
And when we find ourselves in the place just right,
(CLAP/STOMP) (CLAP/STOMP)
'Twill be in the valley of love and delight.
(CLAP/STOMP) (CLAP/STOMP/STOMP)
When true simplicity is gained,
(CLAP) (CLAP)
To bow and to bend we shan't be ashamed,
(STOMP) (STOMP)
To turn, turn will be our delight,
(CLAP/STOMP) (CLAP/STOMP)
Till by turning, turning we come round right.
(CLAP/STOMP) (CLAP/STOMP/STOMP)

In the middle of this joyous celebration was a small woman, weary with toil and diligence and perseverance, humbly and tearfully accepting the admiration of all those present as she danced and sang and was lifted onto the shoulders of those who celebrated her; the one who delivered them from their oppressor. Sister Abigail, their new leader. She wept tears of joy and sadness, peering out the window for a moment at the passing cart with the boy she would have called her son, whom she held close and sent on his way, unnoticed in the commotion, to escape any suspicion surrounding recent events and flee to a better life.

And she danced and sang and danced and twirled her skirt and praised God with the most ecstatic adulation she had ever offered. She held her hands to the rafters as tears ran down her face. She placed them on her heart and thanked her brothers and sisters from the depths of her stalwart and humble soul. And they sang to her for fighting for what was right and good when they had all but succumbed. They showered her with gratitude, kissed her hands, and sang to her for her toil and her suffering and honesty as if their liberation and the new lives they had now been given were owed entirely to her. Because they were.

So began a new, joyous, and thriving chapter of Village life. It wouldn't last forever, but it would last for now, and that was enough. Sister Abigail would do right by them. They knew it, and they were grateful.

CHAPTER 76

Jarek and Beth slowly walked away from the gravestones, each deep in thought, moving deliberately through the waist-high grass back to the car. The engine was running as they both got in, shut the doors, and stared blankly into the distance, their minds spinning with every unbelievable chapter of this chaotic, difficult, and now concluded story.

"We should go back," she said.

Jarek kept his eyes forward.

"Beth," he said, "Andrew spoke to me."

"What, really? Last night?" she asked.

Jarek paused for a moment before looking towards her with glassy eyes.

"Yeah," he said, "I was, um. Well, he saw me dying."

"God," she said, overwhelmed at the thought of all of it. "What did he say?" she asked.

"He just looked at me for a minute and seemed, I don't know, so calm." Jarek said, "Then he whispered to me. He said, 'Jarek. Jarek, it's time to wake up.' I shook my head—because how could I? I mean…it was Andrew. Right there in front of me. Then he said, 'I'll see you soon, little brother,' and he smiled. He just… smiled like it was no big deal."

Jarek sniffled and continued.

"Then he said, 'Greater than the greatest show on earth.' I smiled, and he said, 'Jarek, for mom and dad…' then he shouted, 'Wake up!' And I woke up."

Beth held one hand to her mouth and put the other on his knee.

Jarek looked out the window and across the field. He let the gravity of all that had happened sink in, deep into his bones, his chest, his stomach.

The trials and the uncertainty he had been through. The uncertainty before him still. And her. There for him. Leaving with him. It was reckless of her and made him love how bold, brilliant, and unpredictable she was even more. He looked closely at her face and moved towards her.

"You know something?" he said.

"What's that?" she asked quietly, her eyes holding his as she gave his knee a squeeze.

He waited a moment, taking in the outline of her confident chin, the nape of her neck, and the tumble of deep brown hair swept over her opposite shoulder. He again breathed in the smell of her coconut shampoo and vanilla Chapstick. His mind raced with thoughts of the first time he saw her, their first kiss in the field under the stars, his late-night visits, and now—her risking everything—to be by his side.

"I love you," he said.

A heartfelt smile brightened her face, with her endearingly crooked lower lip catching his attention before his eyes returned to hers. She leaned forward and pressed her lips against his for a long time. His hand touched her cheek as she put her forehead to his, and they both looked out again across the land.

"I love you, too. But you already know that." She smiled.

He smiled back, "You always say the right thing." This time, he meant it.

Jarek imagined Mr. Goodell working the farm with Lucas by his side. He imagined Lucas's mother in the back of his parents' wagon as it left the Village, one hand over her mouth to stifle her sobs, the other reaching towards him imploringly as his father snapped the reigns, speeding away, and Lucas falling to his knees on the main road, shocked and broken, thinking there must be some mistake.

He thought of the unbearable cruelty Lucas had suffered by Thaddeus. The pain, the betrayal, and the loneliness that had become his life. The beatings and the uncertainty. Then he imagined him here, right in this spot, living his life until his final days, raising a family, working this land with his own hands, proud of where he was—of who he was—as he watched his children run in the fields, his wife smiling at him each day on the porch as they got older, "Thank you, Lucas. You're a good man, Lucas. I love you, Lucas."

He felt a sense of deep and abiding relief, of uncompromising joy, for his friend.

Of victory.

He turned his head towards the driver-side window, as a slight shudder of emotion moved his chest.

"Jarek, they'll be looking for us. We don't have much time." Beth reached down and squeezed the hand he had rested on his knee.

She saw pride in his eyes, welled with tears. He looked at her for a moment, then into the distance.

"Beth, you asked me a question once that I never answered. You asked me what my dad whispered when they dropped me off."

"Yes…" she said eagerly.

He took a deep breath.

"He said, 'Jarek, do something extraordinary. For all of us.' That's what he said. 'Jarek, do something extraordinary.'"

"Well," Beth said as tears welled in her eyes, "you just did."

They sat in silence for a long moment. Finally, he cleared his throat, "Let's go."

"Jarek," she asked, as he climbed in the driver's seat and she buckled in next to him. "Where do you want to go?"

"The vanishing point," he said.

He hit the gas.

CHAPTER 77

The car peaked and sagged around the swells and dips of Route 22. Jarek watched the road as they sat silently, all that had occurred heavy on his mind.

"Jarek," Beth said.

He wasn't ready to talk. To face reality. The landscape changed after a few more miles, letting them both know they were getting farther from the difficult reality they had to face.

She spoke again, "Jarek? We have to go back."

"Yeah?" he said quietly.

"I don't see we have many options here, ultimately." She added.

"Do we ever?" he looked at her.

"Well…maybe? Sometimes?" she smiled despite the sense of dread they both felt. "So…"

She waited for him to stop the car, turn around, and give some sign that they were on the same page.

"Jarek, we have to go back. For a million reasons. You know this."

"Yeah," he mumbled as he slowed the car and pulled into a gravel parking lot. Chalk writing on a slate beside a tree stump read, "Firewood $6."

"Are you okay?" She asked as he sat still. "You should be proud, you know."

"I am," he said, "but all of them—all of it—it's all gone."

Jarek shook his head in disbelief as he tried to comprehend it: all the villagers—their names and faces, their day-to-day lives—everything about them had vanished; buried beneath over a hundred years of shifting soil, resurfaced roads, and forgotten livelihoods. Part of a distant and forgotten past that no one alive, no matter how old, had experienced in real life. No one but him. The fire that consumed the dorm took moments to overwhelm the entire building. What Jarek was now perceiving—in fast forward—was the slow burn of decay, which was much more devastating. It erased everything in its path.

Twenty minutes later, they pulled onto campus and saw a crowd of students and faculty gathered around two police cars beside Wickersham. Jarek parked the car next to Neale house, directly across the street, and he and Beth got out to face the consequences, whatever they may be.

WORTHING HAD SEEN BETH'S CAR APPROACH AND EXITED THE SIDE OF Wickersham with conviction in his stride. Drummy, McCracken, and Em had been among the gathered crowd in front, so were several steps ahead of him. When McCracken—with conviction of his own—peeled off to intercept Worthing, Drummy and Em continued towards Beth and Jarek. Em greeted them both with a hug and spoke quickly.

"Hey. Two kids came forward and said they saw David and Billy trying to light the fire and that you were actually trying to stop them. Then they both admitted to it." She paused. "So, the cops aren't here for you, Jarek. Morak wanted out of here anyway, so mission accomplished. It's sad, really."

Beth let out a big sigh of relief as Jarek whispered "Oh, thank God."

"You're off the hook for the fire," Em added, "but that doesn't mean you're not still getting kicked," she said.

All four turned to see the discussion occurring across the street. Animated at first, Worthing soon stared at the ground, listening thoughtfully to whatever McCracken was saying. He then looked McCracken in the eye and, without another word, turned around and walked away. Jarek was astonished.

Jarek turned to Drummy. "Whaddya think he said?"

Drummy shrugged. "'Leave him alone, he's a good kid, we'll talk about it later.' Or something like that? Hopefully, he told him to shove it, but who knows."

Jarek leaned closer to Drummy and whispered, "Does Worthing know about McCracken? Who he is?"

"Yeah, he does, even if he pretends not to. Just him, though. And us," Drummy said quietly. He put his hand on Jarek's shoulder while watching McCracken with admiration as he approached.

McCracken greeted the group with a nod. "That's that," he said conclusively.

Drummy then turned to Jarek. "Jarek," he said, "come with us."

CHAPTER 78

Jarek firmly squeezed Beth's hand before letting go as the three of them—Jarek, Drummy, and McCracken— made their way silently towards the library. Jarek climbed the steps first and entered through the center door, confident that he had earned it, before following Drummy to McCracken's office in the back.

Drummy stepped through first. "Come in," he said, gesturing through the open door as McCracken stepped ahead of Jarek and directed him to a chair. Drummy peered out the door as McCracken sat across from Jarek, so close their knees were almost touching, in confidence. Whatever they were about to say, Jarek could tell they wanted to keep it quiet.

"Welcome back," McCracken said with a wry smile. "Glad you decided to return to us."

"Thanks," Jarek smiled, apprehensive as to what was next.

"Jarek," McCracken said gravely, "We've just concluded an incredible undertaking, as you know. In fact, I'm not sure we will ever entirely understand the gravity of what we've accomplished here."

"Yeah," Jarek nodded.

"...but it goes without saying that it is both remarkable and, of course, entirely between us."

"Of course, yes, of course," Jarek nodded.

"Matt and I have talked about this briefly. You saw something happening that was terribly wrong, you knew that only you could fix it, and you put every bit of yourself into making sure you made it right. Even putting yourself in danger to do it." He shook his head and exhaled to show he was impressed. "Well. We're proud of you, son."

Jarek was taken aback by the compliment and grateful. "Thank you, Mr. McCracken," he said, becoming more confident that something more was coming.

McCracken's tone was eager but measured as he continued. "Jarek, we think there may be… possibilities…here that we might explore. Do you understand?"

"Sure, I guess," Jarek said, uncertain what he meant.

McCracken looked to Drummy, then back. "The thing is, Jarek, we want to see if you can help with something else." He paused.

Jarek was intrigued. The three of them had been through a lot together. He trusted them.

"Oh?" he said.

"There's a bit of a…disagreement…around the same time period you are now so familiar with. We thought, in the right time and place, you might be able to…set some of it right."

Jarek thought for a moment. "Um, what kind of disagreement?" he asked, unsure of what he might be getting himself into.

McCracken looked at Jarek thoughtfully for a moment.

Seeing the door was open, Drummy got up, walked over, and peeked out one final time to make sure no one was around.

McCracken was solemn and still, looking Jarek right in the eye as he whispered…

"The Civil War…"

Drummy shut the door.

THE END.

SHAKER SONGS & MUSIC

Music and song are central to the spirit and community of the Shakers. Original Shaker hymns and dances appear throughout this novel, reflecting the importance of music in their worship, labor, and daily life.

The lyrics included in the story are drawn from historical Shaker sources and are presented in keeping with the traditions from which they originated.

Readers interested in hearing recordings of the Shaker songs referenced in this book may visit:

danielsholtauthor.com/shakersongs

(Or scan the QR code below.)

AFTERWORD

THERE IS INDEED A PLACE IN THE BERKSHIRES, TUCKED INTO THE SIDE of a mountain along the New York State line, called the Mount Lebanon Shaker Village.

The first Shakers gathered there, cleared the woods, and cut the roads to start their own utopia in that very spot starting in 1785. At their peak half a century later, they numbered as many as 600. Most of the buildings were built in the mid-1800s when the Village was bustling with hard work and the religious fervor of its many residents. Many are buried in the mass grave enshrouded by the nearby woods.

This book is based on extensive research into the lives of Shakers and their unusual beliefs, but historians will note I did take a few liberties:

-The Shakers did believe the dead could offer the living "Spirit Gifts" through dreams or visions. They also believed that some among them had the ability to see the spirts of the dead: *"I know the condition of souls who have left the body. Where I see one soul in the body, I see a thousand in the world of spirits"—Elder William Lee.* They also believed that their dancing was a way to minister to the departed. The belief that a spirit, living or dead, could pull someone physically through time is, however, fictional.

-While "The Book of Secrets" and a number of other texts which informed this story are real, the "Book of the Mountain Kings" and "Gifts from the Restless Dead" are fictional.

-The Shakers were indeed far ahead of their time in matters of equality. All presentations regarding the equality of women in Shaker communities are accurate, and the examples Sister Abigail provides to Jarek of upstanding African American community members were all real. It is difficult to overstate how remarkable their faith-driven belief in equality was given the time in which they lived.

-I've made some changes to Village geography for the purposes of this story, key among them is the presence of the building called Wickersham. Wickersham did not yet exist in the year 1866, as the Church Family Dwelling that previously stood in the same spot was not tragically destroyed by fire until January 30th, 1875.

-Shakers were passionate about their dance and music and wrote hundreds of original songs. The songs included in this story are original Shaker compositions.

-While any quotes attributed to individual Shakers through the course of this story are accurate, the Shaker characters themselves are fictional, especially that of Thaddeus. Sister Abigail is, in my opinion, a true embodiment of the humility, faithfulness, and diligence that the Shakers were known for.

-There is indeed a school within the remnants of the Mount Lebanon Shaker Village. It began in 1932 as The Lebanon School for Boys and, in 1939, took on the name it bears to this day: Darrow School.

- While every story needs an antagonist, the character of Headmaster Worthing is entirely fictional, and stands in stark contrast to the passion and dedication exemplified by every Darrow Head of School and faculty member I've had the pleasure of knowing.

-A campus dormitory was in fact destroyed by an act of student arson, but that incident occurred in the winter of 1963, nearly 30-years before the "current day" setting of this story in the early 90s.

-All the students and faculty depicted in the story are entirely fictional, with two exceptions: Mr. McCracken and Matthew Drummy. I took the liberty of naming Mr. McCracken after my grandfather, Earl, but his real name was Des. Des McCracken spent almost his entire life at Darrow, was a respected teacher and hockey coach, and was known for his ability to instruct players in flattening the opposition. Matt Drummy was held in very high esteem as an English teacher and dorm parent during the single year he taught at Darrow. Many alums from that time still consider him our favorite teacher. His passion was writing, and he was a Bob Dylan enthusiast like no other. Tragically his took his own life in 2006.

Darrow is a remarkable school, and I am fortunate to have spent formative years in such a beautiful and transformative place. Any success I've had in life is in part attributable to my time at Darrow including, to no small extent, the publication of this book.

To the entire Darrow family, I offer most sincere thanks from a grateful alumnus.

Sincerely,
Daniel S. Holt

ACKNOWLEDGMENTS

THIS BOOK COULD NOT HAVE BEEN COMPLETED WITHOUT THE SUPPORT OF many people who offered their time, expertise, and encouragement.

My deepest gratitude goes to Tiffany Brooks for her meticulous editing and unwavering belief in this story. I'm also grateful to Cassie Voll for her early insights, to Richard Godfrey for his help and support, and to my beta readers—Shelby Weston, Meagan Ledendecker, Justin Bakota, Tuck Barclay, Ronit Gerard, Sara Holt, Dara Wishingrad, and my wife Katherine—whose thoughtful feedback helped shape the final manuscript.

To my big and loving family—especially my wonderful mother, Jean; my wife, Katherine, and our children, Daniel and Hannah Grace; and my siblings, Allison and Jonathan, and his wife, Sara—thank you for your endless patience and encouragement throughout the long writing process.

I'm also deeply grateful to the many friends who believed in this book and encouraged me through its completion. You know who you are.

I promised my dad—Keith Norman Holt—the finest personn I'll ever meet, that I would finish this book as he was nearing the end of his life. I hope he's found his way to it.

Finally, I'm grateful to every reader who picks up this book and joins Jarek on his journey.

There's a world outside.

On point.

—Daniel S. Holt

ABOUT THE AUTHOR

Daniel S. Holt is a writer based in the Washington, DC area. He is an alumnus of Darrow School, located within the historic Mount Lebanon Shaker Village, the setting of *Ghost of the Mountain Kings.*

This is his first novel.

www.ingramcontent.com/pod-product-compliance
Lightning Source LLC
Chambersburg PA
CBHW020248030826
48979CB00030B/2652/J

* 9 7 9 8 9 8 7 3 5 6 7 3 9 *